THE MARK OF THE BEAR CLAN

DAVID ALLEN SCHLAEFER

Printed in the United States of America
Print ISBN: 978-1-953910-36-3
eBook ISBN: 978-1-953910-53-0

Library of Congress Control Number: 2021907022

Published by DartFrog Plus, the hybrid
publishing imprint of DartFrog Books.

Publisher Information:
DartFrog Books
4697 Main Street
Manchester, VT 05255

www.DartFrogBooks.com

Join the discussion of this book on Bookclubz. Bookclubz is an online management tool for book clubs, available now for Android and iOS and via Bookclubz.com.

For the little girl with dark hair

For the little girl with dark hair

Acknowledgements

I first became interested in Finland and its heroic tales as a child. I owe this interest to my parents, Dan and Jeanie, who collected an odd assortment of amazing books on all sorts of subjects. One such book was a *Reader's Digest* special on folklore of the world, which introduced me to Väinämöinen and the Kalevala. The other was part of a Time Life series on World War II and battles in Scandinavia. My interest whetted, I read everything about Finland I could get my hands on. Many years later, I jumped at the opportunity to serve in Finland as an American diplomat, fulfilling a lifelong dream and setting the stage for the Far Northern Land Saga.

My Finnish teachers, Anuliinna Santry and Anna-Mari Barrineau, provided inspiration and amazing instruction. I am particularly indebted to Anna-Mari, who helped me research ancient Finnish names and linguistic forms, as well as gave sound advice on many other issues. Her contributions to the story are everywhere, and are valued so very highly. The staff at the Gallen-Kallela Museum in Espoo, Finland, generously gave their time and patiently answered the strange American's many questions during my visits. I was also encouraged throughout the writing process by many friends, but Heikki Hämäläinen, Vera Stah, Marja Sevón, and Ulla Anttila stand out among them; I thank them profusely.

Throughout the lengthy process of editing and reediting, I would have likely abandoned my quest had it not been for the support and assistance of my editors: Rosanne Catalano, and Katelynn Watkins at DartFrog. They are amazing. Minna Koskinen, Richard Davos, and Jane Friedman likewise proved terrific sounding boards and beta readers. The gorgeous map of the Far Northern Land that accompanies this volume was created by Misty Beee, as was the map of Pohjola found in the third volume. The creative process that led to the final versions was one of the most rewarding experiences of my artistic career, and I encourage those interested in fantasy cartography and design to visit her website.

Finally, no author worth their salt can fail to acknowledge the support of their family, and I'm no exception. My incredible wife, Raluca, and my children helped me in so many ways, and I am grateful to all of them. Gaddison, Christian, Anastasia, Viktoria, Maria and Klara, I thank you all, with love.

Notes on Names and Language

The stories that appear in the Far Northern Land Saga are inspired by Finnish folklore, especially the famous work *Kalevala* by the great compiler of Finnish oral poetry, Elias Lönnrot. In addition to his expertise in medicine, ethnography, and many other fields, Lönnrot was a philologist and loved language. Having had the unique opportunity (for a foreigner, at least) to study Finnish full-time for an entire year and then live in Finland for almost half a decade, I naturally incorporated Finnish into my work when I set out to write the series. Beautiful in phonology and structure, it is not an easy language for non-native speakers to acquire, and I beg patience of readers who find themselves confronted by pages of unfamiliar words and letters with no mentor like Väinämöinen to guide them on the journey.

The chief peculiarity, at least to English speakers, is the extensive use of diacritics: the letters ä and ö. These letters represent distinct sounds, and their use is governed by the process of "vowel harmony." This, and the multisyllabic, compound structure that encourages long words with lots of double consonants, can be a challenge. But the recompense is that readers will catch a glimpse, however dim, of the sounds that Ulla, Egan, Väinämöinen, and the peoples of Iron Age Finland actually used and heard, and which they bequeathed down the centuries to their contemporary descendants. I believe this glimpse is worth the challenge.

By necessity, I have been inconsistent throughout my stories. For any violence done to the Finnish language, I can only offer sincere regret. Most words in the Far Northern Land Saga used to represent the speech of its inhabitants at the time the events occurred are contemporary Finnish. But I have "antiqued" some to better match the feel of the age in question. In a few instances, I have purposefully dropped diacritics, which Finns will quickly notice (*Etela* vice *Etelä*). Perversely, I have added them to one word. Most egregiously, in a few instances, I have used incorrect case: a cardinal sin. I can offer only apologies and the feeble justification that as Väinämöinen taught Ulla, balance in all things is ideal, and it was my intention to strike a balance between fidelity to the language and accessibility to non-native speakers. Undoubtedly, I sometimes failed, but I hope the sincerity of effort warrants forgiveness.

Finally, to assist the reader, I decided to spell out a few phonetic pronunciations of some of the chief characters and places, and a glossary of some key words here at the onset of the book. The proto-Finns who lived in the Far Northern Land at the time of this saga were divided into many clans and kinship groups. The chief groups each had their own totems, which often appeared in each clan's name or the name of its homeland. There are exceptions. The great kingdom of the south was *Etelamaa*, and its people were the *Etelalaiset*, which literally translates as "Southland" and "Southerners." However, their totem was the swan (*joutsen*) and they were colloquially called the Swan Folk by the other clans. Since these names can be confusing at first (and second and third, etc.) encounter, I've listed them below and encourage readers interested in such things to thumb back whenever necessary to this page in order to refresh their memory of who was what and lived where. The map will also offer assistance.

Proper Names

Väinämöinen—VĪ-na-MOY-nen

Lemminkäinen—LĔM-min-KĪ-nen

Löhi—LŌ-hee

Länsimaa—LĂN-si-maw

Ulla—OOL-la

Egan—Ā-gun

Kirsikka—KEER-sik-ka

Mielikki—MEE-e-LĬK-kee

Pohjola—PŌ-ho-YŌ-la

Homelands and Clans of the Far Northern Land

Karelia—Karelialaiset—(the Reindeer Folk)

High Länismaa—Karhulaiset—(the Bear Folk)

Deep Länsimaa—Hirvilaiset—(the Elk Folk)

Etelamaa—Etelalaiset—(the Swan Folk)

Tavastia—Tavastialaiset—(the Hare Folk)

Akkala—Kotkalaiset—(the Eagle Folk)

Susila—Susilaiset—(the Wolf Folk or Lost Clan)

Pohjola—Pohjolaiset—(the Northerners or Löhi's Folk)

Itälälset—(the Easterners)

Table of Contents

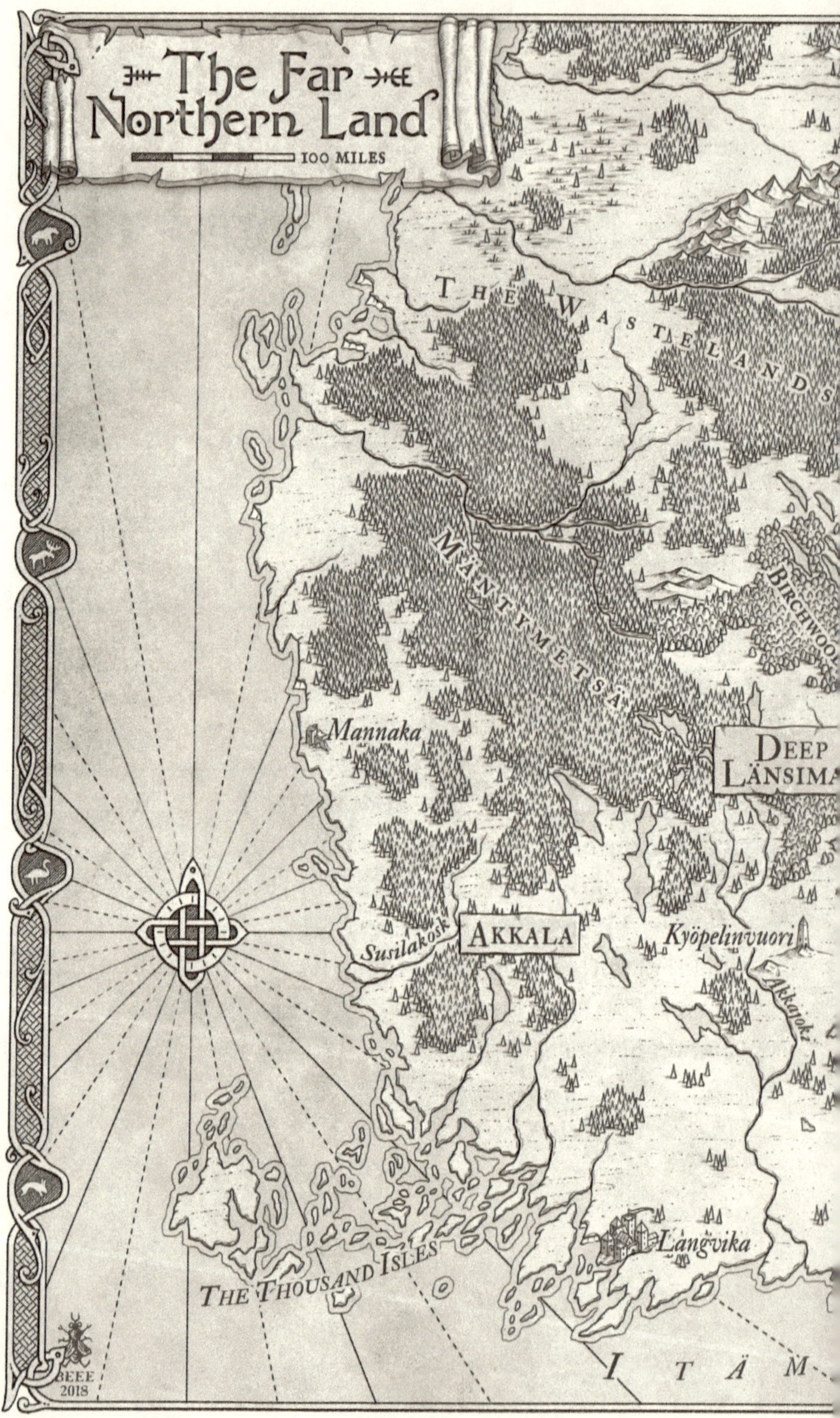

The Far Northern Land
100 MILES
THE WASTELANDS
MÄNTYMETSÄ
BIRCHWOOD
DEEP LÄNSIMA
Mannaka
AKKALA
Kyöpelinvuori
Susilakoski
Abkajoki
Långvika
THE THOUSAND ISLES
ITÄM
BEEE
2018

NORTH MARCHES
Grankulta
KARELIA
Gamla
LAKE SUURIJÄRVI
Metsäposti
Väinölä
ENCHANTED VALLEY
Valkeakosk
Jouksi
HIGH LÄNSIMAA
Keskimaa
BLUE LAKE
Sunesaare
Linnavuori
THE WALL OF THE GIANTS
LANISKITA
GREEN VALES
THE NECK
Kotanrannta
ETELAMAA
LAKE ETELAJÄRVI
Tapiola
Rajavesi
Hämejoukst
HAVASTIA
Stone City
E.rannta
Harmaaniemi
Sepällä
SEA

CHAPTER ONE

THE GIRL, THE OLD MAN, AND THE BEAR

The warm, early summer sun shone down on the green trees and blue waters. The south wind blew in measured, gentle gusts as the flickering aspen leaves shimmered and seemed to change color with each breath. The woods glowed with summer's blush of life. Summer in the Far Northern Land brought long days and short nights. Everything hurried to live, to grow, to bloom and thrive before the seasons turned again—for if the days were long, summer was not, and winter always waited just around the corner.

A little girl carefully picked her way through the scattered birch and pine trees. She swung a birch basket, looking from side to side as she gingerly stepped over mossy tufts and sudden holes filled with cold, dark water. At almost noon, the mosquitoes and biting flies were quiet, waiting for the cool evening to gather again and torment anyone brave enough to tramp across the wet forest floor.

The little girl, Ulla, had long, dark brown hair, unlike most of her fair-haired kinfolk. Green flecked her bright, golden-brown eyes, but her skin was pale and white. The people of her village, Grankulta, called her *Lumikki*, or *Snow White*. From her mother, Ulla inherited fair skin, the freckles that dotted her nose, and the green in her eyes. Even at the tender age of perhaps seven or eight, she seemed to have her mother's long, lithe limbs as well.

Her mother had given her these traits and her life, but little else. The green-eyed woman had given birth to twins, a boy and a girl, on a cold winter's night in the Far Northern Land. Afterward, exhausted from the difficult labor, she was racked with a fever that had passed through the district. The village women took the children from her so that they would not sicken, too, and so she died and her spirit fled far away.

Ulla's father sat beside his wife for hours, stroking her long, damp hair as if he could somehow call her back like a wizard or singer might—or so Ulla had been told. But he couldn't call her back, of course, and so he buried his wife next to the grave of their firstborn, took the babies, and moved to a small cottage—or *pirtti*—close by to Grankulta, where his wife's sister and others of her family lived.

The boy was named Janni, like his father, and the two children were nearly indistinguishable. Her brother shared Ulla's dark hair and hazel eyes, her long limbs, a ready smile, and a quick wit. Big Janni, as the villagers called the father to set him apart from his son, was a forester and hunter at heart, but a carpenter and cartwright by trade and necessity. He wasn't originally one of the Bear Folk, the clan that Grankulta's people and all those living in the neighboring villages and districts belonged to; he was born far away, in the deep forest of Karelia, and his father's family came from the Clan of the Reindeer. Big Janni was full of stories about the forest and the strange, wonderful things that lived there. At night, as the cold wind blew shrill outside the dark, smoky *pirtti*, the Karelian woodsman sat by the stone hearth with his children and told them what he had heard and seen and done when he himself was a child.

The *Karelialaiset*, the Reindeer Folk, dwelled apart from the other clans of the Far Northern Land. Less numerous than the other clans, they lived for the most part in scattered *pirttis* and tiny villages, building few towns of any size or permanence. Although they had given up herding reindeer long, long ago, their hearts retained the nomad's love of wandering, and they kept fewer possessions than other folk so that they in turn would not be possessed. Ulla remembered many of her father's stories, riddles, and old proverbs, even if she didn't always understand them.

What you shout out at the forest returns to you as an echo.

Be generous with your good fortune; the good give much of their little, while the bad give little of their plenty.

But more than admonishment or instructions, Ulla remembered her father's tales of the heroes that still lived among the Karelialaiset deep in the heart of the ancient forest. Singers and wizards, warriors and witches, elves and even stranger creatures made up the *Erilaiset*: people of the gods, children of twilight, the race of heroes that had once lived among all the clans, but had been driven to flee into the dark woods long ago.

Janni would peer at his children through the wisps of smoke that rose from the red coals while they huddled together under thick furs, giggling with excitement. Sometimes he sang and sometimes he chanted and sometimes he acted out the stories while the glowing embers made his round woodsman's face look strange and otherworldly. He scared them now and again with his stories of trolls and tall, dark elves. His sister-in-law scolded him for frightening them. But he was always quick to laugh and break the spell. Then he capered about to reassure them that everything was fine and that they were safe together in their small, smoky, cozy house.

Big Janni did more than sing the songs passed down from generation to generation among the Karelialaiset. As a boy, the woodsman had actually seen the Erilaiset. He told Ulla and Little Janni—and anyone else who would listen—many times about the strange and terrible things he remembered. When Janni was a boy of about ten years or so, there had been a terrible battle in the Karelian Forest.

The *Itäläiset*, the fierce, long-haired, warlike people of the east, had invaded Karelia. A great folk divided into many tribes and clans, the Itäläiset were tall, with light brown hair and long, sharp noses. Some of their tribes herded horses, and their warriors fought mounted on horseback and armed with deadly spears, lances and scimitars, the curved swords of the east. Generations ago, they had mounted huge invasions with thousands of warriors and tried to overrun all the Far Northern Land, for they held that the land had belonged to their forefathers years ago, and hated the "usurpers," as they called them. But when the terrible pestilence that killed so many in the Far Northern Land swept east, the Itäläiset, too, suffered greatly. Their numbers were diminished.

Still, ever and anon, the Itäläiset raided the borderlands, seeking slaves and whatever plunder they could find. As a child, Big Janni was once caught up in such a raid. Marauding bands of the Easterners forayed into the woods, pillaging and burning the cottages and villages as they passed. They killed many villagers and scattered hundreds more. Panicked, the lords of the Reindeer Folk did not know how to stop them.

Janni's family left their *pirtti* before the raiders arrived and fled deep into the forest with other refugees. They sheltered in a strong place, a camp surrounded by wooden walls and protected by ditches set with sharp stakes. The Itäläiset grew bolder, however. The different bands came together, pushing straight through the forest to the encampment, thinking to storm the strong place, kill the men, and capture hundreds of women and children to take back to their homes in the east as slaves. So thought the Itäläiset—but their plans took no account of the heroes.

Deep in the heart of the old forest, the Erilaiset, who had warred against the Easterners of old, were disturbed. They came forth from their hidden valley and marshaled the strength of the Karelians, leading the others to safe, hidden places. The Erilaiset made a trap for the marauding Easterners and, when the fierce warriors with curved swords reached the forest camp, ambushed them. Finally, they were driven away with great loss.

Janni's mother and sisters had hidden in a safe place, but the boy stayed with his father and the many other men who sprang the trap. Janni, too young to wield a sword or swing an axe, didn't fight, but he and some other boys drew and carried a great store of water to the encampment. They helped cut trees and lashed them together with rope and hemp to make barriers against the raiders' charge.

It was then that he had seen the tall Erilaiset man with a long beard and colored robes, accompanied by two smaller creatures that resembled dwarves without beards, but who had thick arms and legs. Strangest of all, he had glimpsed a tall, dark elf with long hair and a thin, cruel face.

Ulla and her brother loved this story most of all, and their father told it to them many times.

"*Isäni*," the little girl would say. "Father, tell us about the Erilaiset again! What did they look like? What did they wear? Did you really see the terrible elf?!"

Big Janni's story seemed to change a bit each time he told it; new details crept in while others disappeared. Ulla's uncle laughed while her aunt frowned, and both shook their heads, but Ulla and Little Janni never doubted their father's tale. They never doubted that, deep in the heart of the oldest forest in the Far Northern Land, strange and wonderful creatures still dwelt.

So, the little girl in the little village in the land of High Länsimaa, the land of the *Karhulaiset*, the Bear Folk, slowly grew. She played with her brother and cousins. She milked the cows and fed the sheep and, when she grew a little older, took bread and beer to the men in the fields, carrying the pails on a long, straight pole slung across her shoulders. Her aunt tried to teach her to bake flat loaves of rye—the farmer's staple in those lands—and the sweeter honey cakes filled with sour cream and butter, as well as to spin, mend, weave and wash as a woman should. The girl cared little for such woman's work, however, and was always slipping away outside whenever she could.

She often watched her father in his shed as he bent and fit the rough boards for the carts and sleds he made with his simple lathe. She watched as he shaped the great wooden wheels on which they rolled in the summer, and the runners on which they slid in the winter's snow. And Ulla travelled far with her father as he hunted.

Big Janni made his living as the cartwright for Grankulta and the other little villages and homesteads nearby, but his Karelian heart was that of a hunter and wanderer. He feared no wolf or rootless ghost wailing in the lonely wastes. He often took his children with him as he tramped through the woods and lakes hunting for squirrels and beavers, or otters and deer, or fished the blue waters.

Ulla and her brother learned to be very quiet and very still as their father bent his bow or set his traps. She liked to help pluck and dress the grouse they caught, and to eat bits of meat roasted on long sticks over an open fire. With her small, nimble hands, she even learned how to fletch arrows using stiff green and brown duck feathers wet with grease. Ulla looked forward to hunts with her father more than anything else in her little world, but it was on one such hunt that the great tragedy that changed and defined her life took place.

On a time, Janni grew restless. He couldn't sleep, and when he did, strange dreams disturbed him, dreams that he couldn't understand or explain. He decided to take his little boy and girl with him to the North Marches, many miles north and west of Grankulta on the border of the wild wastes beyond. It was very late winter, or very early spring—you could never be quite sure in the far north—and, although snow still covered the ground, the days were lengthening and the ice on the water was breaking up.

Big Janni thought to go to the Marches before the snows all melted; he hoped to find the big boar that came out early from their dens to snuffle in the muddy slush before other animals came back to life after the long, dark night. The boar would be lean without their summer's fat, but they were also hungry, bold, and less wary; a hunter using bow or spear could more easily take them. Or so Big Janni told himself. Perhaps his restlessness after the long northern winter also drove him on, making him impatient for summer's friendlier clime and journeys soon to come.

His family and friends urged him to wait, or to at least leave the children at home since he had never taken them so far afield. But he just laughed and repeated what his own people, the Reindeer Folk, had always said. *The timid know both fear and safety, but the bold know life's full worth.*

As a child in Karelia, he had travelled far with his own father and learned many things. He feared little, and Ulla and Little Janni were brave like their father. So the woodsman hitched a shaggy pony to a little sled and piled pelts, blankets, food, and then the children on top. They started off with his best dogs following, taking the winding road that led to the North Marches.

The journey took several days. The sun shone for the most part as they passed *pirttis* and small villages, then lonely homesteads where people called and waved to them or brought them dried meat or fish to eat and weak beer to drink when they halted to rest. Finally, they neared the Marches, and the homesteads and the road failed altogether. They slowly picked their way through the little lakes and thin woods that defined High Länsimaa's northern border and separated it from the wilderness beyond.

Big Janni searched for signs and listened intently for what seemed to the children like hours at a time, but there were no boar. That far north, there was not much open water yet, so the ducks and geese had only just begun to return. The children sat on the sled and quietly watched for game or played with the dogs among the snowy crofts and trickling streams that fed the lakes and mossy bogs. Except for some deer flitting among scattered stands of trees and patchwork white fields, the land seemed wide, silent and empty. Then the storm came.

It began with a threatening sky and big flakes of wet snow, but soon grew darker and colder—a rare, late winter cyclone that suddenly screamed down on the Marches. The wind blew in hurricane-like gusts, driving snow and ice before it and ripping limbs from trees. Boughs crashed down like an avalanche of white boulders ejected from invisible hillsides.

Big Janni put the children on the sled and, as well as he could, struck out for the road through the wild wind and wastes. When the pony fell and didn't rise again, he cut the little sled in two with his axe, buried his children under furs and pelts, and pulled it himself. Ulla remembered very little of this last journey with her father. She and Little Janni clung to each other, drifting in and out of an uneasy trance. She couldn't tell whether the voices on the wailing wind were real, or part of some dimly realized nightmare.

At last, Ulla's father stumbled on his feet and threw himself to the ground. He crawled on his knees to the broken sled and uncovered the children. The little girl never knew what he intended—to build a snow house to shelter them from the storm's fury, or to abandon the sled and set out on foot. Perhaps he had no plan at all and was simply exhausted, his wits scattered, his hope all but lost.

Ulla remembered standing beside the sled next to Little Janni: a clear memory of cold air and white snow, the woods almost glowing with their own luminescence. They had come to a halt at the end of a long defile beside a tiny lake covered in snow, with ice underneath. Ulla saw something in the corner of her eye, like a flickering candle wavering in the wind for a moment before it went out. One of the dogs barked. Perhaps Little Janni saw the candle, too, for the boy suddenly jumped the lake's low bank and ran out onto the ice and snow. A loud crack sounded that even the north wind couldn't hide. In the blink of Ulla's eyes, her brother was gone.

Her father loomed over her, all weariness forgotten, and seized Ulla, tossing her onto her back against the sled. For an instant, she saw his face: red and distorted, his beard white and frozen.

"Listen to me!" he shouted above the howling wind. "Stay here! Ulla, stay where you are!"

And then he jumped over the low bank after Little Janni and was lost in the smoky white whirls.

Ulla remembered nothing else. They found her about a mile from the road, half-frozen, walking across an icy field in her red Karelian boots. One of the dogs—Pilkka, her favorite—walked beside her.

When rumor of the terrible storm reached Grankulta and Janni still had not returned, Ulla's uncle and some of her father's friends set out on the northern road to find him. They also sent messages to the Wardens, who guarded and walked along the North Marches. In the end, two March Wardens found her. The little girl wouldn't speak.

After she was warmed and fed, and they saw that she was hale and wouldn't die, they sent her back to her folk. The Wardens never found a trace of Big Janni or his little son, not even when the snows melted and spring came. It was as if the earth and waters had swallowed them whole, or hidden them away where no mortal eyes could see them ever again.

The girl lived with her aunt and uncle then, for she was the last remaining link to her green-eyed mother who had married the Karelian forester from far away. Her aunt, her mother's only sister, loved her dearly. Though silent at first, Ulla ate and drank and clearly understood all that was said to her. Her aunt and uncle wondered if she would ever speak again, or if she had been struck dumb by the terror of the storm and whatever horror she had witnessed in the lonely wastes.

But Ulla was resilient; her stout heart beat strong, her hair and limbs grew longer, and her will, if only a child's will, was like adamant. After a while, she began speaking again, and laughed and romped about with the other children of the small village, as children will. The darkness lifted; the poor folk of the Far Northern Land, none of them strangers to death and loss, expected no less. Time, the world's great healer, passed, and life went on.

In many ways, hers was unchanged. She played with her cousins, helped her aunt with chores, tended animals, and picked berries in the summertime. She walked through the woods and looked up at the night sky. Her father and brother were gone, however, and didn't return. Perhaps because Little Janni had been such a part of her, she put all thoughts of him aside until his very memory faded from her heart. But it was not so with her father.

Ulla never spoke about him or about what she remembered—or didn't remember—from that fateful journey to the North Marches, and none pressed her. She knew that everyone thought Big Janni dead, though no grave or cairn marked the spot where he lay. Deep inside, however, Ulla fiercely clung to the belief that her father was still alive and would one day return to her. In what manner or from where, she didn't know, but the depth of her loyalty and love became a type of faith, and she drew secret strength from her unspoken thought.

One morning, more than two years later, Ulla carefully picked her way through the scattered trees, turning her head this way and that as she swung her basket by her side. It was too early yet for berries; the fat, plump blueberries came at high summer alongside black crowberries in the marshes. In late summer, red lingonberries would cover their little bushes on the forest floor for the poor folk of the villages to pack in barrels of cold water to last throughout the winter; cranberries ripened by the lakesides. It was even too early for strawberries, her favorite, to hide in their thickets and bushes, growing huge in the long days and summer sun.

That day, Ulla searched for something different: the season's first herbs, and especially the dark-capped mushrooms called *branni*, with their strange, spongelike appearance and distinctive smell. They could be poisonous if eaten raw, but were delicious when boiled and cooked. The villagers used them as strong medicine for any number of ills and even traded them at times to travelers from the south, who returned home to their towns to sell them. Ulla seldom came across any of the rare *branni* near the cottages or rye fields, but she sometimes found them farther out, especially in the forest where fire had burned some years ago. So she struck out deeper into the woods in the hopes of finding the first undiscovered cache of the summer, and her efforts were rewarded.

Ulla's basket was already half-full with *branni* when a flash of scarlet and gold caught her eye. She spied a patch of tiny green buds—strawberry buds—aglow in a beam of sunlight. Among the buds, one ripe, red berry, improbably and impossibly grown far too early, shone like a gift from the heavens. Ulla had never seen anything like it: a strawberry, two months too soon, ripe and ready, beckoning like a tiny star. The little girl with dark hair bent low and, brushing back an unruly lock that fell against her freckled nose, picked the berry and took a long, slow bite.

"Mmm," the girl said, savoring the strawberry's sweet flavor. She licked her lips and opened her mouth wide to finish off the red berry. Then, at just that moment, she saw the bear.

No more than ten feet away, looking straight into her flecked, hazel eyes, sat a small brown bear—a cub, more precisely, a ball of brown fur with a short snout and a tiny pink tongue nervously flicking its wet nose.

Ulla stopped short, the half-eaten strawberry slipping silently from her hand, and stared back. The two small creatures, the child and the cub, stood there like that with the warm, blooming forest all around, as if connected by a taut, invisible rope that pushed and pulled and bound them together in an uneasy equilibrium. The girl felt her heart speed up; it beat wildly against her tiny breast. She involuntarily drew in a deep breath, and then another. Ulla may have been a child, but she knew enough of the ways of the forest to understand the danger she faced. There was a bear cub in front of her, and she was alone in the midst of the woods.

Except she wasn't really alone, of course. The tiny bear's mother was surely near and ready to attack anything—even a dark-haired child—that came between her and her cub. Muscles tense, Ulla summoned all of her will and strength to overcome her paralyzing fear and break the spell that anchored her to the ground. She kept her eyes on the cub and, without turning, took one step back, then another. She felt the spongy turf give and sink a bit under her bare feet. She sucked in a sharp breath and made an instantaneous decision—turn and run, as fast as she could, even though she had been told many times never to run from a bear, large or small.

Ulla twisted round and slipped, catching herself with one hand and dropping the basket. The dark-capped *branni* spilled out onto the mossy ground. She straightened up, ready to sprint.

An earsplitting roar startled her and sent her sprawling again.

The mother bear loomed before her, just like her father had on that strange, sad day that seemed so long ago. And just as he had then, the huge brown bear, a creature of instinct beyond all human reason, raised its great paw and hurled the girl to one side like a stuffed rag doll.

Ulla landed on her back hard, knocking the wind out of her tiny chest. Her head swam as she gasped for breath. The bear loped toward her in two great strides. Hopeless, she tried to scramble to her feet and run. She hadn't taken more than a stumbling step when the animal lashed out at her with its claws, shredding her brown, homespun shift and tearing her flesh.

Searing pain overwhelmed her senses even as the great brown beast, roaring like a demon from the forest's depths, hit her again, its sharp claws raking her tender skin.

She crumpled to the ground, her head and shoulders halfway submerged in a shallow pool of cold, murky water. Ulla's eyes fluttered; her mind tried to slip away. Teetering on the verge of unconsciousness, she waited for the bear to finish the job and release her from the pain that enveloped her.

Even as her mind strayed into blackness, a booming voice, a man's voice, rang out over the mad ursine bellow. Crying out with authority, the voice challenged the animal's wrath.

The little girl managed to focus her eyes for a brief moment. Larger than life, the bear towered above her. It stood on its hind legs, raised to its full height with its front legs outstretched menacingly.

But the bear wasn't reaching out toward Ulla. Before it stood a man who was just as tall as it was, his own arms spread wide and bathed all about in an amber glow. In his hand he held a wooden staff blazing with fire. He shouted again at the bear, his great voice shattering the forest's calm.

Ulla's vision narrowed and flickered. She slid down into the dark.

***

After a long spell of forgetfulness, Ulla came out of a dark dream and walked again through the sparse woods, its colors changed or strangely muted. The trees and leaves seemed dun, grey, or a pale, dirty white against the sickly green sky. A mist hovered all about her, and it grew even denser in the distance. She walked slowly toward an unknown destination, where all light and color failed.

Something waited for her in the darkness ahead. It beckoned to her with unspoken words and shapeless sounds. Reluctantly, she walked forward to meet the mysterious, unseen caller. At that moment, another voice, a man's voice that she could actually hear with her own ears, called out from behind her.

"Ulla!"

She stopped and turned. Dim at first, but growing in strength as she moved toward it, the voice kept calling.

"Come back, Ulla! Come here, little one!"

And Ulla obeyed, only to slip back down into the dark, waiting dream.

Her sense of hearing returned first. She listened to a song in her dream, gradually becoming aware that she wasn't really dreaming at all, but lying very still on her stomach, with her eyes tightly shut. A man's voice, the same voice that had called to her in the pale forest, sounded beside her, chanting and humming in a strange, sonorous tone. Queer words and sounds mixed together, filling the little girl with a sense of peace and well-being. She felt she could lie there and listen to the voice forever.

> *Flesh be made whole,*
> *stop the red flood.*
> *Rents knit anew,*
> *staunch the bright blood.*
> *Dam the river,*
> *stem the tide.*
> *Choke the fall that karhu's knives have carved.*

As she listened, she slowly became more aware of her body, her senses sharpening little by little. She smelled the spongy moss beneath her nose. She felt a dull ache in her back; a soft breeze touched her skin from head to toe.

Finally, the voice stopped chanting. "Wake up now, little one."

Ulla opened her bright eyes and looked around. A man sat cross-legged next to her with his back against a tree. He wore great boots, which were either a dull yellow or gold, and that rose high on his calves. His grey eyes twinkled as he returned her ready stare.

"*Isäni*," said the little girl.

"No, I'm not your father!" said the man, chuckling.

Ulla saw at once that he spoke the truth. He had a long, curling white beard, so long that it almost touched his knees as he sat on the ground. His straight nose and high, sharp cheekbones were sunburnt and reddish-brown, contrasting with the pale skin on his long, bare forehead. His round, full mouth turned up in a smile.

"I'm not your father," he repeated. "Don't nail that charge to me, too! It's been many a year since I've walked in this land of little lakes and puny woods. Many a year!"

The man suddenly hung his head and sighed, then straightened back up, running a large hand through his long, grey-white hair. "There, now. It's passing. You've nearly worn me out, you know. At first, I wasn't sure I would be able to find you, or that you'd hear me or heed my call even if I did. You almost left this world, little one. You were badly hurt and you walked a long way alone through the invisible forest toward Tuone's home, the forest that mortals can't see. You heard the voices calling you, didn't you? But you're strong, little one! Aye, you're strong. There's a candle inside you, alright; burning very brightly, it is. I saw its light from afar and that's how I brought you back. Lucky for you that I came along just then, just when the bear did. As I said, it's been a long time since I've walked in these parts. Very strange chance, that—very strange indeed."

The man narrowed his eyes and looked hard at her.

"Ah, well. What's done is done. Karhulaiset—Bear Folk, my foot! If this is all your folk remember of bears and their ways—stumbling around blindly gathering *branni* when they're waking and hungry, then running from cubs like a scared deer—then you'd best choose another totem and a new name for your clan. Not that you see too many bears around here anymore, I suppose. You've cut down half the trees since last I was here, and burned the land. There are farms and fields on every patch of solid ground to be found. Still, '*Man is happiest when he plows the fields, cleans the soil, piles the rocks in heaps, and plants seeds that will grow into food for himself and his cattle.*' At least, that is what Akka taught me long ago."

The old man—for Ulla could see that he was old, even if he was quite unlike any other old man that she had ever seen—got on his knees and knelt closer to her. She noticed for the first time that his grey eyes were peculiar, the irises fluted and spiraling inward. The girl felt his hand on her back, touching the tender spot that still ached. A shiver ran through her from head to toe. She tried to sit up, but felt too weak. Her legs wouldn't quite obey her.

"Shh, easy now, little one," said the man in a gentler tone. "Not too quickly. Lie still a while longer, if you wish."

"Am I going to die?" Ulla asked.

"By the vaulted heavens, no, of course not! You're going to be fine, don't you worry! You are healed. You lost some blood. You'll feel that for a while—aye, you will. But I stopped the blood. I knit the flesh anew. I learned the song for that long, long ago, when the world was still young, and so was I! No, stopping the blood and mending the flesh was the easy part. Finding your spirit as it tried to flee—that's something different. But don't you worry; you are whole."

The girl tried to raise herself up on her arms again, this time succeeding. She sat upright and looked around. Her head swam woozily, her body felt stiff, and the pain in her back pulsed stronger, but she was alive and alert. She looked down at her tiny, pale body and realized that she was naked. A red mark, like a long, raised weal, ran down the inside of her right calf. She reached behind her back and searched for the pulsing spot; she felt raised weals there, too.

"You'll have scars there, I'm afraid," said the man as he stood up. "That can't be helped. Your wounds were bad, child. Very bad. And yet, a scar is a small price to pay for life." The old man stooped and rummaged in a large pack on the ground beside him, producing a woven yellow shirt. "Here, child, you can put this on. It will serve you as a dress. At least the sleeves are short!"

Ulla stood slowly, feeling warmth and strength returning to her limbs.

"Raise your arms," said that old man, but before he popped the shirt over her head, he caught her shoulder, turned her around, and looked at the scar on her back. He shook his head and finished dressing her. Then he grabbed a clay bottle wrapped in deerskin that sat next to the pack. "Come on, now; drink something for me."

The girl took a long draw on the bottle, then wiped a few stray drops of the cold water from her mouth, never taking her eyes off the man. Standing before him, she looked him up and down.

He was tall, taller than most of the men she knew from Grankulta or the district nearby. He wore a deep red tunic that hung down over the tops of his great boots, bordered about the hem and neck with fine gold thread, images of tiny reindeer, and coiled symbols that looked somewhat like stars. A long knife hung from his leather belt and, visible beneath his beard, a pendant fell from a thick gold chain around his neck. A tall, copper-shod staff leaned against a tree.

"Who are you?" the girl asked.

"Hmm. That's a fair question, and a good one," he answered, considering her most seriously. "I've spent most of my life trying to answer that question—and I have lived a very, very long time." The old man took a swig from the water bottle and wiped his beard. "We all think we know who we are. We think we know what we believe in and what we would do when put to the test. But the truth is that most men—if they even reflect upon their own lives at all—well, they see themselves in their minds' eyes as they *wish* to be, as they *ought* to be, for good or ill, and not how they truly are or how they appear in the eyes of other men. In so doing, they stay blind. '*The measure of a man is in deeds, not words.*' There's truth to that. But the seers say also, '*Truth (and beauty) is in the eye of the beholder.*'"

Ulla blinked. "Yes, sir. Thank you, sir," she said, not really sure how else to reply. "But—I'm sorry, sir—did you tell me who you are?"

The old man frowned. "Rather pert, aren't we? Not that I'd expect such a little one to understand sage lore, of course, at least not in these times. Very well. I'll tell you what you wish to know: my name, which is not exactly *who* I am, though maybe the opposite side of the same coin, as it were." He drew himself up to his full height and spread his arms out wide before him.

"Happy chance brought me this way today, child. Happy chance and good fortune for you! For behold! I am Väinämöinen! The greatest singer that this age of the world has ever known, and the last! Väinämöinen the Traveler, Väinämöinen the Wizard, Väinämöinen Erilainen! I have returned to mortal lands after my long slumber!"

The girl took a step back at the sound of the man's booming, thunderous voice and swallowed hard. His strange names meant nothing to her, however.

When she didn't react, the man spread his arms again with a sweeping gesture and bowed. "Väinämöinen, my child! It is indeed I, and none other!" Then he slumped and a sour expression spread across his sunburnt face. "Well, now. I presume you've heard of me, have you not? Your parents, your father, have they not told you tales of the mighty Väinämöinen?"

"No, sir," said Ulla. "At least I don't think so."

Väinämöinen sighed and shook his head. "The rising generation," he mumbled. "What's to be done? Well, whether your ears are stopped with clay that shuts out the old songs or not, and whether your folk are ignorant or forgetful, Väinämöinen is my name. Aye, it is. But enough now. There is time for instruction later, perhaps. Your folk are worried and we'd best be getting you home. They are calling for you, away yonder, though your ears can't hear them. And they were calling earlier, while you still wandered in the colorless woods on the borders of Tuonela. Your mother will be wanting you, that's for certain."

"Um, I don't think so. At least not my mother, sir. She died a long time ago—when I was born."

"Did she, little one? Well, I'm sorry, very sorry. May Ukko keep her safe in the heavens above! Let's get you back to your father, then."

"He's gone, too. He died in the ice—at least, that's what people say. I live with Aunt Päivikki and Uncle Reiko and Meria and Siria and the others."

Väinämöinen looked down at the girl. "Your father, too? Well now. Very strange, that is." And then, more to himself than to the little girl, he added, "Very unusual, indeed. I wonder; I do indeed wonder." The wind picked up a bit and rustled the tops of the tall trees while the old man stared. The little girl in the oversized yellow shirt shivered despite the warm sun.

He suddenly swept Ulla up off her feet, setting her down again by the pack and staff.

"Let's get you back to Aunt Päivikki and Uncle Reiko, then! But first, let me care for honey-paw, our fallen friend and unhappy foe."

Väinämöinen strode toward a dark mound a long stone's throw away. With a thrill, Ulla realized that it was the bear. It lay on one side, its head hidden beneath its mighty shoulders; even from a distance, Ulla could see that its fur was sticky with reddish-black blood. More blood stained the moss and grass nearby.

The old man knelt beside the fallen beast. There was no sign of the cub. Ulla watched him stroke the bear's fur and heard him softly singing in a low voice. The song's cant and cadence sounded like what he had sung over her as she had lain still and silent with closed eyes, somewhere between life and death. Väinämöinen bent low over the bear as he sang, his beard brushing the sticky fur. After a long while, he stood up and came back to Ulla, shouldered the pack, picked the girl up with one arm, and grasped the white-yellow staff with the other.

"There. I've done for *karhu* what I could and made amends as best I can.

Her spirit is welcome and free, and her little one can follow her into the starlight. There are some things that can't be helped, though none are at fault. It's part of the world's sadness."

Väinämöinen marched through the woods with Ulla in his arm as the low, lingering sun cast a net of rays and long shadows all about them. Ulla could scarcely believe what had happened, her mind racing from wild thought to wild thought as the big man tramped along and softly hummed. It had only been a few hours earlier—*hadn't it?*—that she was alone, on her own among the birches and firs, picking *branni* and tossing them into her basket.

A strange feeling crept over her, wrapping about her very being. Something was different; something had changed. The old man's humming made her drowsy, its power lulling her to sleep. Suddenly she roused and tugged on his beard; he cocked an eye toward her.

"I'm very sorry," she said with a cheerful smile. "But I was rude. I forgot to thank you for saving me! You saved my life, Väinämöinen."

The old man smiled, then he laughed out loud, and together, the two walked through the sparse stand of woods toward the wispy smoke that rose from the little village in the distance.

Chapter Two

The Mark of the Clan

Ulla's folk were indeed overjoyed at her return. Her aunt had feared the worst when Ulla disappeared from the long meadow where she was supposed to be minding the sheep and gathering spring herbs under the watchful eyes of the field hands. Tragedy had followed Ulla all her short life, and, if the little girl herself seemed remarkably unaffected save for a protective cloak of melancholy that wrapped about her at times, her aunt felt differently. The farmer's wife had sharply scolded the field hands, then sent them and the village's older children into the surrounding woods and paddocks to look for the girl.

They were still searching hours later when Väinämöinen appeared, stomping into the collection of *pirttis* and sheds that comprised the tiny village of Fallkulta, located about a mile from Grankulta and opposite the stand of woods into which Ulla had wandered. Ulla, who knew precisely where she was in spite of her ordeal and spinning head, tried to steer Väinämöinen in the right direction, but he had insisted on following the thin trails of smoke that rose from Fallkulta's hearths and fire pits.

Already irritated when they reached the village and confirmed his mistake, he grew downright surly after discovering that his horse, which he had left at the edge of the woods earlier that morning to graze, had wandered off and was nowhere to be found. His ill humor changed when he finally got Ulla to her home, however.

Virtually the entire village turned out, and the people were in awe of Väinämöinen. Ulla's uncle met the tall man and thanked him for bringing the girl back to them safely. Her aunt took her from the bard and, cradling her tightly, rushed inside their humble cottage. But neither Reiko nor the other folk of Grankulta knew what to say to the unexpected stranger in their midst, the stranger whose name and deeds were the stuff of legends.

Ulla may not have remembered the name of Väinämöinen just then (though her father had actually mentioned him quite often), but the adults did. Grankulta might have been only a small village in the rural north of High Länsimaa, but, if it was poor, it was not especially so, nor were its folk particularly mean or ignorant. Its farmers and maids knew many old songs and tales of Väinämöinen of the Erilaiset, the old man who had walked throughout the Far Northern Land since the world was young, singing songs and casting spells for good or ill.

But songs and tales were one thing, and the waking world was quite another. Having one of the ancient wizards among the villagers exceeded their experience and humble station. The men shuffled their boots in awkward silence, the women lowered their eyes while snatching quick glimpses of the stranger, and the children stared unashamedly—for they were children— gazing wide-eyed at the old man's yellow boots, long white beard, and staff.

Väinämöinen was pleased. He enjoyed their deference and reaction. He had received a colder welcome many times before, and appreciated the fact that he was not being chased back to the road with stones and arrows. But his mood soon mellowed and he tried to put the villagers at ease. He knew these folk—workers of the land, tillers of fields, spinners and weavers of cloth—and knew that, far more than idle lords in halls of stone or merchants weighing silver and counting long ships by the southern sea, these folk of the earth were the soul of the Far Northern Land, and its hope.

Reiko brought Väinämöinen into the house and gave him a seat beside the small spring fire. The old man told Ulla's family what had happened and how he had chanced upon the girl even as the bear attacked her. He warned them against disturbing the dead beast.

"Leave *karhu* be and do not take any meat from the carcass, or skin it, or take any tooth or claw as a charm. This was no hunt; the proud beast died in anger and without the right songs sung. Avoid the place where this thing happened for the next year, and definitely do not let this child go back! And when it is summer again, scatter any bones that you find and remove all memory of what was done. But if you find the skull, nail it high to a tree to help her spirit go free. And teach your children to be more wary when the world and its creatures are stirring!"

Ulla fell into a deep sleep not long afterward. She lay ill for several days, and woke for only short periods of time as she slipped in and out of a fever that made her cheeks red. Her aunt bathed her with cool water and brought fresh fennel, angelica, and feverstay to treat and comfort her.

Väinämöinen told the woman to not be afraid; Ulla's wounds were healing within, her body was recovering, and she was in no danger of dying. Yet Väinämöinen often sat at Ulla's side, sometimes humming or chanting in a low voice and stroking her damp, dark hair as she lay dreaming. He frequently checked the scars on her leg and back where the bear's black claws had struck. Reiko and Päivikki were too much in awe of the wizard to ask why he remained in the village and did not continue on whatever journey or quest had brought him to them in the first place. He was, after all, a healer, and the little girl was sick.

Now Grankulta's people were mainly fishermen and farmers, like most of the Bear Folk in those parts. They had built the village itself hard by a little lake—one of the hundreds, large and small, scattered across High Länsimaa. Pike, perch, and other fish filled the shallow, blue lakes. The villagers went out on the water in little birch boats and scared fish into their nets with long poles, then boiled the fish in a stew, dried them for eating later, or sometimes pickled them to keep during the long, dark months when food grew scarce and ice on the open water made fishing more difficult.

A long, narrow strip of land by the lakeshore was rich and fertile, unlike most of the land in the north. There, the villagers grew beans and peas and, every other year, yellow turnips. But rye was the staple throughout all those lands, and Grankulta's folk were no exception.

The Far Northern Land was blessed with many things—fish in the blue waters and game and fowl in the forests—but except for in the south, the land was poor. So, the people slashed and burned the woods, clearing the land to grow rye for their dark, unleavened bread or the porridge that they ate almost every night in their smoky *pirttis*.

The farmers would strip the bark from the tall pines, let them stand for several seasons, then return to cut the trees down, burn them, and beat the rich ash into the soil. When the fields were ready in early spring, they sowed the rye and then cut it at high summer with their hooked, iron *sirppis*. Finally, they carried it all from the fields in carts and sleds and into the sheds to dry. There, they threshed it with long, wooden flails, winnowing the chaff in the breezy air so that the women could grind it into meal.

After a season or two, they left a field fallow or let it grow into a meadow for their sheep and bony cows. Then, other trees would be felled and burned, clearing new fields so that open spaces slashed from the forests surrounded Grankulta and the other villages of the north. It was a life of labor and toil, and of risk as well; if it rained too soon or too late or in imperfect measure, there might be famine in the winter and fewer folk to face the coming spring. The people knew nothing else, however, and the dark times made their happier moments all the more precious.

Väinämöinen slept in a little cone-shaped structure called a *kota* behind the family's cottage and beside an old bathhouse where Reiko kept his spades, hoes and harrow. When the old man wasn't sitting with Ulla, he walked around the district, helping here and there as he could. Väinämöinen tended another sick child on a farm at the village's outskirts when the family besought his help, and the child quickly recovered. There was also an old blind woman in Fallkulta, who lay abed under thick blankets and coverlets, unable to move or to speak. Väinämöinen sat beside her for a long time, holding her hand, singing a slow tune over and over, and whispering words into the old woman's ear that her waiting family could not hear. She didn't rise from her bed, however, and, when Väinämöinen left the house, he silently shook his head at the old woman's grandson, the master of the humble home. The old wizard did not return.

Mostly, Väinämöinen played with Ulla's cousins and the other children who lived nearby. One afternoon he sat beneath an old rowan tree for several hours and spoke with a young man from Fallkulta, a bright-eyed lad with a fine, clear voice who often sang or chanted during the villagers' simple festivals and holidays. The young man only knew local songs—light, rustic tunes or snatches of the traditional songs of the Karhulaiset that the villagers still remembered. He knew nothing of the ancient songs and lays of the Seven Clans.

His family looked askance while the old man taught him new songs and tales. Midsummer's Day was approaching, so Väinämöinen taught him "The Summer Song," which was sung all throughout the great lands to the south, and the ancient "Lay of Sunsay," which told of the hero Lemminkäinen. But worried or no, the young man's folk did not dare to interfere or stop the old man from teaching what he would.

On the fifth day after the bear attack, Ulla woke early. Her mind was clear, all her pain was gone, and she was very hungry. Väinämöinen declared her well and told her to rise, but first he called for the girl's uncle and showed him the scars on her back. The long, thin weal on her leg had tightened some, but the raised, red scar looked much as he had expected it to. The scars on her back were different.

Even as Väinämöinen stayed the blood and channeled the earth's strength to mend the torn flesh, he had noticed the wound's strange shape. The bear's claws had rent four great, long tears in the middle of her left shoulder, and a fifth, shorter, tear below and to the side of them. Väinämöinen had seen many ragged wounds from claws and teeth—and he bore the scars to prove it—but never had he seen a wound or scar so like to the nails that caused it. The scars had changed even more as they healed. The raised tissue seemed transmuted, the cherry-colored troughs turned a dark brown, and the skin was smooth and without fault. The mark on Ulla's shoulder seemed the very image of a bear's paw, as dark against her pale skin as if it were painted upon her flesh.

As surprised by the strange mark as the old man had been, Ulla's uncle sent the child outside to play in the warm sun while it lasted. Väinämöinen sat on the little pallet where she had lain and questioned Reiko about the girl's life, especially about her father and the tragedy that occurred two years before upon the North Marches. When Reiko left for the fields, Väinämöinen sat alone in thought as the shadows lengthened. But the farmer's wife had listened outside the door as the two men conversed, and was displeased. She chastised her husband for telling the wizard about the girl's life and their family's misfortune.

Ulla was glad to be back in her element—outside, under the sun and sky, playing with her friends. The other children had kept quiet as best they could while she lay abed, but they were full of questions about the bear and what had happened in the woods. The little girl with dark hair liked being the center of attention, so she acted out the bear's assault, chasing her shrieking friends down the village's single dusty lane. Excited that Väinämöinen had stayed with them, Ulla tried to show off for him as he stood in his great yellow boots, smiling at the children as they played and ran about.

The next day, however, the old wizard announced that he was leaving. If the children felt sad to see him go, Ulla's aunt and uncle, as well as some of the other villagers, were of a different mind. They were grateful for Ulla's life, but not unhappy to see the mysterious Erilainen go and their lives return to normal. Väinämöinen planned to leave early, after the short summer night, so they stuffed his pack with dried fish and dark, round loaves of rye bread, then filled his bottles with clean water and home-brewed beer.

Even as they readied Väinämöinen's kit, another stranger rode into the village. The tall man, almost as tall as the old wizard, rode a large black horse and bore a long sword in a scabbard hanging from his horse's saddle. His great brown cloak—finely woven, if weather-stained—marked him as a March Warden, such as passed by on the North Road from time to time.

Dressed and equipped for a long journey, the Warden had heard rumor that the legendary Väinämöinen had reappeared in the tiny village, and had ridden to Grankulta to meet him.

That evening, it rained; the sky turned dark as ragged clouds hid the westering sun. The villagers took shelter in their homes, and the Warden joined Väinämöinen in Reiko and Päivikki's *pirtti*. Unlike other *pirttis*, theirs backed up to a gentle rise, so the corner-timbered house fashioned of cut, round logs had a natural loft of turf strengthened with rough wooden boards that reached out over the cottage's smoky, single room. The older children slept outside in *kotas* during spring and summer, but Ulla and her cousin Kaisa sometimes slept in the loft. After the adults put them to bed, thinking them almost asleep, they braided each other's hair and giggled. That night, when the rain grew harder, a new guest came inside the house. The two girls hid under their sheepskins and peered down.

Reiko and Päivikki stood next to the long table with benches and tree stumps at either end; little Onni, their baby boy, slept in a rush-filled crib. Another man stood nearby. Short and bald under his dripping hat, his ample girth strained at his leather belt. Ulla recognized him at once: Toikka Mäkkinen, the district's chief, whom she saw in Grankulta now and again. The tall March Warden, clad in the green and brown of his office, sat beside the hearth made of piled rocks and stones, warming his hands by the fire. Väinämöinen stood alone by the large wooden chest that Big Janni had built for his wife's sister. It held clay and wooden cups, a few knives and tin spoons, and her aunt's precious pieces of green glass from the south. Wearing a long, dull red cloak with its hood thrown back, Väinämöinen kept his hand on his great staff. His face looked very red and strange in the embers' glow; Ulla immediately thought of her father's face looming in the dark over a smoky fire, but this was not her father.

Reiko's round face also looked strange, unusually stern and hard. Her aunt's fists were clenched, though they hung at her side.

Kaisa poked Ulla in the ribs under their skins and whispered in her ear, "Lumikki, they are angry!"

"Look, Reiko," said Toikka while he wrung the water from his cap. "Let's be sensible here! The Lord Väinämöinen has made a very generous offer. He did you a great service, saving the girl's life. Indeed, he has done us all great services, and so we all have a stake in this matter. It is many years since our humble meadows and fields have been honored by one of the mighty among the Erilaiset. We must show him hospitality! After all, do not forget," Toikka bowed low to Väinämöinen, "he is a man of power, and do I not rightly say that he could take anything he desires?"

Reiko looked down at the earthen floor strewn with straw, but his voice was strong and proud when he finally spoke.

"Hospitality is one thing and that we have shown as best we can. But what he asks for is something else. And that I will not do."

"I do not threaten," said Väinämöinen in a steady voice. He ambled over to where the Warden sat and leaned on his staff against the hearth's low ledge. "I am not going to curse your fields and little farms. You need not be afraid on my account. And if, indeed, I could take what I wanted against your wishes, still I would not do so. That is not the way of any true man, mortal or no; it is certainly not *my* way. But come now! Listen to your lordling! His fears for his fields and sheep are misplaced, but his advice is not. Let the girl come with me!"

Ulla felt Kaisa dig into her side even harder. With a cold thrill, she realized that they were arguing about her.

"You have seen the mark on her back yourself," said Väinämöinen. "That is no normal scar. I am not yet sure what it portends, but it is clearly a sign: the Mark of the Karhulaiset, the very mark of your clan."

"Then all the more reason for her to stay with her folk!" Päivikki suddenly cried. She pulled on her husband's homespun shirt and, in a pleading voice, said, "Please, Reiko! Stop this right now—you must not let them do this!"

But the farmer pushed her away with a black, angry look.

"What brought me there in the woods at just that moment?" continued Väinämöinen. "Coincidence? Happy chance? It is many years, as I have said, since I last walked these lands; indeed, you were not yet born then. And I've been far to the north, beyond the Marches, on a pressing matter; I was return-ing southward to see your lord, Pekka, in Keskimaa. Aye, I have tarried here too long already. I left the road only to let my horse rest and graze, and to think for a while in the woods, where the air is fresh. And at just that moment I came upon the child! I wasn't sure at first, but I am now. It was no mere chance that brought me to her then, even if I do not yet understand the reason or design behind it."

"How can there be any doubt?" asked Toikka. "Whatever the design is, you clearly have claim to the girl. That much is sure."

"The Karhulaiset do not sell or trade our daughters," said Reiko angrily. "We are free men and women, and do not keep serfs or slaves."

"I don't want a slave!" cried Väinämöinen. "The girl will be free. But, I need a new maid to clean my halls and tend my home; my maid, my little Neito, has married and left, and my old housemistress is not getting any younger and needs the help. Let the girl come with me and she will be safe and have fine things! And perhaps one day she will be mistress of my household. Or, like Neito, she may marry and have her own family. I can make a fine match for her among the Karelialaiset, the Reindeer Folk, better than any that await her here. What are her prospects if she stays with you, free or no? A poor maiden with no parents and no dowry? An orphan in the wilds? Would you have her become an old spinster, a serving maid to our Toikka here? Or per-haps marry his goatherd? You have enough children to worry about as it is, whether they all live or no. Let her come with me!"

"No!" Päivikki shrieked. Ulla's heart thumped in her throat. "She is my sis-ter's child, my own flesh and blood. She is mine and mine alone. She stays!"

Väinämöinen brought his staff down hard on the hearth's grey stones. He suddenly looked up at the loft where the two girls peeked out from the heap of blankets. The old man gazed straight into Ulla's eyes—or so she thought. His expression was sterner and, as it grew darker outside, his long, flickering shadow crept further across the sodden floor and up the wall.

"So be it," said the mage. "I have tried to reason with you. I understand your love for the girl, if not your stubbornness or blindness to her best interest. I will honor your wishes. But you must consider, too, that I saved her life. I called her back from the darkness before she crossed the river and entered Tuone's kingdom. She is only a child and owes me nothing. But *you* are her family, and are answerable for her Life Debt."

The woman started, but Reiko held her back. In a sharp voice, he said, "Be silent!"

"Of course!" exclaimed Toikka. "The Life Debt! By the ancient law of the Seven Clans, she owes the Lord Väinämöinen for her life! How does it go again? The old song they taught us as children?

> *"When a man is saved from drowning,*
> *saved from death by fire's fierce flaming,*
> *taken from the Hand of Tuone,*
> *then the debt shall be forgiven.*
> *Only when hard gold is offered,*
> *silver fair must be delivered,*
> *then the debt shall be forgiven.*
> *When the gift comes from the living.*

"A great gift must be given, or a great debt of service must be paid. Come now, Reiko, what gift could you possible give to Väinämöinen to repay him?"

There were Seven Clans of mortal men in the Far Northern Land and, in the days of old, when they first came to the north and were befriended by the heroes, there had been Seven Laws to govern their affairs: the Laws of Honor, Blood and Home, of Soil, Toil and Chattel, and of Life—the Life Debt. The stuff of ancient legend was woven into old songs and tales, until the Seven Laws were hardly considered rules for men to live by, and were seldom invoked.

But the man who stood before them in the humble cottage was no ordinary mortal; he was an Erilainen and wizard, perhaps the mightiest the world had ever known.

The young farmer's face betrayed his confusion. Poor farmer though he was, he knew well the ancient law of the clans and the old verses that went with it. Saving another's life gave a man claim to a great reward or great service, and, if children were held unaccountable, their parents and kin were not.

The March Warden rose and spoke for the first time. "I wondered why you did not claim the Life Debt at once, Väinämöinen. You have certainly danced around it. It is a very old custom, if tales be true, and seldom mentioned in these days—more a relic of the ancient past than a law."

"Well and good," answered Väinämöinen. "A relic of the ancient past, you say? And so am I! More ancient than you can fathom. Be that as it may, it is still one of the Seven Laws, set down long ago by the *Vanhalaiset*, the Old Powers of this world whom men call gods, and who shaped the land and seas by their very thoughts. It is still revered in the Far Northern Land, but I do not invoke it! I only ask that you *consider* it ere I depart. The choice remains yours, and I make no claim."

The Warden laughed, then said, "You are right, Väinämöinen. There are Seven Lands and Seven Clans and Seven Laws to govern them and give men wisdom. But it was also the ancient custom, was it not, to ask no more from a man than he could afford? You ask much from these folk. No man, woman or child need go into bondage to repay the Life Debt. That was not the law."

"I do not seek slaves!" Väinämöinen said sharply. "And I grow tired of repeating it. Do you wish to instruct *me* in the law?"

There was a long silence until, at last, Väinämöinen sighed and leaned heavily on his staff.

"But come," he said gently. "Enough of this. I have asked what I have asked, and have given my reasons why. Choose now; let the child come with me, or no. But choose well and consider well what's best for her."

Päivikki opened her mouth to speak, but the farmer grabbed her wrist, looking hard into the woman's eyes. He turned to Väinämöinen, his shadow crossing the floor and blending with the wizard's, both wavering in time with the burning chips upon the glowing hearth.

"I will honor the Life Debt," he said at last. "What can I give you? We have little enough for a lord of the Erilaiset, but I will give what I can."

Väinämöinen gave a low laugh. "Little enough. I daresay. What have you to offer, Reiko? I don't need your sheep or a sack of rye flour from poor farmland that's too far north. There is only one thing you have of worth to me and you know what it is. Let the girl come with me. I will care for her as if she were my own, and no harm will come to her. Let her stay with me for a year and a day. For," he said, turning toward the Warden, "that, too, is a part of the ancient custom. And then she will choose freely whether to stay with Väinämöinen or return to her folk. And should she choose to return, I will bring her back to you. You have my word."

It was silent again, except for the pitter-patter of raindrops on the *pirtti's* angled roof. The farmer's struggle was plain to see even in the smoky murk, but he said nothing.

"Still another custom," the March Warden suddenly said, "may bring wisdom when matters are unclear. Disagreements over debt, any debt—even a Life Debt—were always brought to the head of the clan. You are on your way to Keskimaa to see Pekka, Lord of the Bear Folk, as he holds his court. Take the choice to him and let his judgment rule you both."

"Yes!" cried Toikka. "Surely that is the answer! Indeed, it is the law! And, as Lord Pekka's man in this district, I beseech you, Reiko, to submit this question to the court at Keskimaa. That is, uh—that is acceptable to you, Lord Väinämöinen?"

It was clear that Väinämöinen disliked the idea. The old man had looked askance at the Warden and furrowed his brow at the mention of Pekka and Keskimaa, but he sighed and shook his head.

"So be it. I am going to see Pekka the Fat. I will show him the mark and accept his judgment, for good or for ill. Perhaps that will be best in any case. If he allows the girl to come with me, it will be as I said; if she chooses to return after a year, I will bring her back next summer. You have the word of Väinämöinen of Karelia. What say you, Reiko of the Karhulaiset?"

Reiko looked at each of them and then finally turned to his wife, who pled with her eyes, but said nothing.

"Very well," he said at last. Päivikki sank to the ground.

"You must bring her and come with me," said Väinämöinen to the farmer. "Pekka must see the Mark of the Clan upon her shoulder to decide, but I won't stay long in Keskimaa. I plan to journey swiftly south afterward, so I cannot bring her back to you should Pekka rule in your favor. And if Pekka agrees with me, the girl must be ready to leave at once from Keskimaa."

Reiko, born in the northern parts of High Länsimaa, had lived there all his life. He was no traveler, and though Keskimaa, the City of the Karhulaiset, was in reality not so far from his home, to the farmer it seemed almost legendary, a shadowy name lost among the mists far to the south.

"I cannot do that," he said dully. "The season is short. It will be time to sow soon, very soon. One week maybe, if the rain stops—maybe two. The fields are not cleared. There is much to do and already we have few enough men. And even if my wife could be spared, it is no journey for a woman. You must take the child then, if you will."

"I will take the child with me," said the March Warden. "I am travelling with Väinämöinen to Keskimaa, for I, too, have news for Pekka, as he well knows. But my homeward road lies north, back to the Marches. I will speak for you, if you will, and fairly present your view to the lord of the Bear Folk; you do not wish the child to leave you! And if Pekka sees fit, I will bring her back to you when I ride north again. If not, if she goes with Väinämöinen, I will at least bring you tidings."

The woman sobbed, then abruptly rushed to the door and out into the downpour. The farmer hesitated, then, slower and more deliberately, went after her. But the little girl with dark hair in the high loft under the blankets lay awake for a long time, listening to her cousin's soft snores and the gentle music of the rain as she stared at the flickering shadows that played upon the ceiling.

Chapter Three

Keskimaa

Ulla rode before Väinämöinen on his flaxen horse, which ultimately had been found not far from where the wizard left it. They paused atop a high drumlin, bare and treeless, that looked down over the scattered woods and little lakes. Its forward peak sloped gently to the southwest, where the road lay at its foot. The March Warden, whose name was Ilkka, sat beside them on his tall black stallion. They could see the clustered *pirttis* and *kotas* of Fallkulta below and to the left, and could just guess where Grankulta lay beyond a line of tall fir trees. Smoke trails rose from village hearths into the cloudless blue sky, and ahead of them, where the winding road disappeared south behind green cover, more smoke hinted at homes and hearths beyond.

The farewell in Grankulta had been brief. Ulla dissolved into tears when her aunt told her that she would be going with Väinämöinen. She liked the old man, but her life was with her kinfolk and she had no desire to leave them. Päivikki did not cry, however. Woman of the Far North, she knew much of loss and of toil. She set her face like a mask, stoically preparing her sister's daughter to depart, packing the child's meager belongings, and ordering the other children about as if nothing were amiss.

So Ulla, dry-eyed but despondent in the end, had left the village. Her aunt and cousins had bid her goodbye in the dusty lane while the dogs ran about and the neighbors watched. Väinämöinen bowed low to the farmer's wife, speaking soft words to her that no one else heard; but Päivikki turned away, silent, and went inside the *pirtti* as they rode away. Her uncle, working in the fields, had said no goodbye, but watched the two horses dwindle into the distance from afar. Turning back to his work, he dug his spade bitterly into the muddy earth.

Väinämöinen and Ilkka rode down the drumlin's slope, taking the road to the south. The road—called the North Road by the Bear Folk—wound its crooked way through trees and round innumerable lakes and pools, but always found a true path on solid ground. At first, they passed through thickly wooded terrain much like the land near Ulla's home. The road sometimes ran straight beside long eskers of raised ground, always sloping and breaking to the southwest, and seemed sunken alongside the rise. Paths here and there led to small villages or farms; a few *pirttis* and homesteads fronted the road itself. They passed few people, however, only farmers and such on their business. Once they passed a caravan of five carts heading north, all filled with sacks, baskets and barrels.

After a few more days, they came to a larger village where the North Road joined a broad, well-travelled highway. Called the White Road because of the snow and ice that covered it during the winter, it ran for many miles beside Suurijärvi, the great lake of Länsimaa. The land changed as numerous rivers and streams emptied into the lake. Many *pirttis* were clustered together near the long, twisting shores of Suurijärvi, and a few small villages straddled the road.

The Bear Folk of Suurijärvi lived differently than Ulla's folk. They fished for pike, perch and roach, but used great nets and seines. They hunted not only in the forest, but also on the water; large seals lived in the lake, and their meat, skins, and precious oil were highly valued in the south. But the true wealth of the long lake came from the reddish-brown rocks mined from the slimy fens and bogs. The iron smelted from the rocks was strong and malleable. Each summer, long trains of wagons filled with ore left for the great southern kingdoms and for the smithies of Seppälä; carts filled with food, cloth, tools, and precious things returned north.

Ulla said little during the first part of their journey. She rode with Väinämöinen, bumping along in front of him in the horse's wooden saddle and watching the trees go by, all while keeping her sorrow and sadness to herself, as was her way. Väinämöinen spoke to her gently, singing songs and, like her father, telling her many tales. He told stories from the Karelian Forest and tales about the Erilaiset when the world was young, long before the Seven Clans set foot in the Far Northern Land. Little by little, the girl began questioning him, and by the time they reached the White Road, she could scarcely be contained. The March Warden said little, but winked and smiled when Ulla looked at him. He laughed sometimes at Väinämöinen's tales, which seemed to irritate the old man greatly.

Some of Väinämöinen's tales told of animals and the tricks they played on one another, and some told of lucky, clever young men who won the hands of beautiful princesses from faraway lands. But Ulla's favorite tales told of magic and mystical creatures. She especially liked one about a young girl not much older than herself who lived in Karelia with her nine brothers. As they rode, Ulla asked Väinämöinen to repeat it several times.

The girl in the tale grew up with nine older brothers, who eventually left home to live a ways off on their own prosperous farm. The girl missed her brothers terribly, and so, one day as she sat crying, her mother gathered her tears in a bowl and baked them into a round loaf of dark rye bread. Her mother told her to set the bread rolling like a wheel; if she followed it, it would lead her straight to her brothers' farm. The girl set out with her little dog and, just as her mother had taught her, said, "Roll, roll, round bread, roll." Sure enough, the round loaf took off straight through the woods.

Along the way, the girl met a wicked ogress, who pretended to be feeble and convinced the girl to help her by splashing cool water on her ugly face. As the girl did, the ogress quickly said, "My body to you, yours to me."

In a flash, the girl was trapped in the ogress's body, and the ogress—in the girl's own beautiful form—followed the rolling bread all the way to the nine brothers. Convinced that she was their sister, the brothers took her in and made her the mistress of their house. But the ogress put a spell on their real sister and left her in a poor village. The villagers set her to watching the shaggy goats because she was so wretched and ugly.

As chance or fortune would have it, the brothers came to that village on a time and heard the poor girl singing sadly in the fields about what had happened. They recognized her beautiful voice at once and questioned her until they discovered that she was indeed their only sister, for she knew things only their true sister might know. So, they took her home and tricked the ogress into splashing water on the girl's face to wash the soot from her eyes. "My body to you, yours to me!" cried the girl, and the spell was immediately reversed. The wicked ogress fled for her life, while the beautiful girl was reunited with her kin.

Ulla liked the story because it was about a girl and not a boy, and she liked the happy ending. She also wondered if it were true. If she herself baked a tear-bread, would it take her to her own father and brother?

"Väinämöinen," Ulla said one sunny evening as they sat among white birches while the horses nibbled mossy grass. "I was wrong when you found me in the woods and saved me from the bear—wrong about your name, I mean."

"What's that?" said the old man. "What do you mean, child?"

"There in the forest, where *karhu* was," she said. "I told you that I had never heard your name before. But I was wrong; my father spoke about you. I remember it now. He told me lots of stories about Karelia, though they're different from the ones you tell. But I remember now that he told me your name."

"Well, I'm glad to hear it," said Väinämöinen. "It's nice not to be forgotten, seeing as how your little lands and farms wouldn't even be here were it not for my songs!"

"Did you know my father?" asked Ulla. "I think he saw you one time in the forest."

"Saw me? And when could he have seen me?"

"When he was a boy in Karelia. He said there was a great battle with the Itäläiset, the men with curved swords. He said the Erilaiset came to fight them and he saw many strange creatures. He saw a tall elf in the woods, and a wizard with a long beard like yours." She paused for a moment. "Was it you? Do you remember him?"

Väinämöinen smiled.

"Hmm. Well, it could have been, I suppose. Aye, it could have been. There was indeed a battle in the forest then; more than twenty years ago now it was. The Reindeer Folk in the north were hard-pressed, but I was there, along with others, too. Not many Itäläiset came out of the forest to return to their own homes on the other side. I saw lots of people back then, my child, many boys and girls just like you. Come to think of it, I believe I do recall a handsome lad with bright eyes just like yours, but I can't be sure. Those were busy days!"

Ulla considered his words, blankly staring down at two small wooden figures in her hands: a boy and a girl, her brother and herself. Big Janni carved them the year before the storm on the Marches. He had painted them, but the colors were already fading. Päivikki had put them in a little soft beaver-skin bag along with her few other things.

"Tell me something else, Väinämöinen," she said. "How did you know *my* name?"

The old man took a long draw from a pot of weak beer they had been given in a village along the road, then handed it to the Warden. "More questions, eh? Now, how's that again?"

"My name," the girl said. "When I was walking through the forest without colors, I heard you calling my name: Ulla. But I had never met you before. How did you know my name?"

The old man grabbed the pot back from the Warden and smiled broadly.

"Listen to that, Ilkka! The child has a good head on her shoulders! So you've thought of that, have you?" Then his expression turned serious and he looked at Ulla with furrowed brows and a frown. "Well, that's difficult to explain, Ulla. Very difficult. Your name is a part of you: *who* you are, *what* you are. From the moment it's given to you as a child by your parents or kinfolk, it becomes a part of you. That gives your name meaning and power. If there were no *you*—if you didn't really exist—then your name would be empty, just a shade. Or perhaps not even that: just a sound, no different than the cry of an animal, without purpose or measure in the world of mortal men. Words have meaning, child. They are very important, but they can also be very dangerous. You can call a dark spirit to you if you speak its name carelessly. Beware!

"But you can also use names to your advantage. Everything has its proper name, or maybe many names in different tongues—the leaf here, the earth we sit on, or the sky above! Together, the two things—the leaf and its name—form a unity, a whole. Two sides of one coin, they are. But if you are a man of power—a singer, a mage—then you can use the names. You can weave the words. You can make the songs. You can see the leaf and say its name; you can learn its origin and from whence it came. Then you can be its master and shape it as you will, for good or ill. Leaves in the woods or great mountains in the north: it works the same for all. So I learned long years ago. And I know many songs!"

"Well, yes, sir," said the child. "I have heard you sing many songs, but what I wanted to know was how you knew *my* name, please."

The March Warden laughed. "Indeed, a good head on her shoulders, Väinämöinen! She puts the question to you twice!"

Väinämöinen tossed the empty pot to the ground and said crossly, "I was coming to that! It's not as if I expect an unlettered child from a rude village on the wrong side of the forest to understand me! And as for your name, I could *see* it. I can't put it any simpler than that. It is a part of you, as I said. One who knows how to seek such things can find them. As I told you when I found you in the woods—if you were listening—you have a bright light shining within you, child. I could see that candle from afar as you walked toward Tuone's river, and I could see your name flickering within it. And now, if you please, finish your bread and get out your blanket. The night is very short and I want an early start tomorrow. Good night!"

They rose early the next morning, as Väinämöinen wished, and continued down the White Road to the south. The villages there stood closer together, and there were more folk on the road. The people stared at Väinämöinen on his flaxen horse with his great yellow boots and red cloak, but they were not quite as awestruck as Ulla's folk had been. The peddlers and traders offered free bread and beer to Ilkka, for the Wardens were honored by all, but they haggled with Väinämöinen and tried to barter or sell to him what goods they had to offer.

The road turned away from the lake, still veering to the southwest and crossing many brooks and streams. The horses splashed through clear, cold water, or used flat-bottomed ferryboats to carry them across. Twice they forded rivers on broad earthen causeways that stretched far out into the water, then joined with bridges that led to the opposite shore; hissing white rapids boiled beneath the bridges, where the rushing water was channeled through a narrow way. One of the bridges was wooden, but the second was made of rock and sparkling stone, cool to the touch even when the sun shone down upon it.

As they journeyed down the White Road, a gradual, creeping realization slowly dawned upon the little girl. She had travelled much with her father, but always to the north. The scattered villages and farms they passed on their hunting trips looked like their own. With growing wonder, and not a little fear, Ulla saw just how small her home village was and how many people—beyond her imagining—really lived in the wide world. Everything was new to her, everything began to change, and she had started off down the path that she would follow to the end of her days.

At length, they came to a shallow ford of flat granite rocks over a swiftly running stream. On the other side, a broad track broke straight to the west while the White Road continued its journey south. They took the western road—hard-packed with red clay for horses—and began to ride faster, for Väinämöinen was impatient to reach Keskimaa. A new sense of urgency had come over him, and he said little as the two horses galloped into the sun. After two days of hard riding, they reached a thickly settled area and stopped for the evening at a large stone house with many shuttered windows. Ulla was amazed; she had never before seen a building made of stone, let alone

one so large, with two stories, several painted doors, and a large stable be-yond. She wondered if it was a castle for a king or a princess.

The building, of course, was no castle, but rather a small inn for travelers on the way to and from Keskimaa. After seeing to the horses, Väinämöinen put the girl to bed in a little room on the upper floor. The room and its contents amazed Ulla as much as the stone house itself. A strange frame of wood held feather-filled sacks in one corner, and a copper ewer fashioned into the shape of a bear sat upon a small painted table in another. The old man laughed when she pointed to the sacks. It was a bed, of course, a sim-ple traveler's bed, yet even that was beyond the girl's experience. Despite her soreness and aches from the long ride, the little girl was too excited to sleep. She sat for hours by the open window, running her hands over the wooden shutters; the simple curtains, blue and white with traced designs of flowers, seemed fairer than any cloth she had ever seen in her short life.

But if the modest inn amazed the girl from the Marches, the next day left her truly speechless. They started early again and, after only a few hours' ride, reached Keskimaa.

Keskimaa, the City of the Bear Folk, was not especially large; indeed, it was the smallest of all of the chief cities of the clans, no greater than many towns in the south. Built chiefly of wood—which was, after all, in plentiful supply—it stood at the end of a long, raised plain that had been stripped of trees. On its western side were many farms and fields, for the town sat next to a rare patch of fertile land. The townsfolk grew barley, rye, and many other things like turnips and cabbages. They also kept many animals.

A wooden wall had been built around the town, more to give some sem-blance of design or order than for protection. By order of the lord of High Länsimaa, no house or shed could be built on the plain within a horn's cry of the walls. Within the walls, traders and merchants, weavers and dyers, tanners and saddlers, blacksmiths and carpenters, all lived and worked in an irregular patchwork of streets and lanes filled with houses and shops. To Ulla, it was beyond her reckoning.

At length, they came to the town's main gate, which was not really a gate at all, but a wide break in the wooden wall where people, carts and animals came in and out. It was a clear, summer morning in the Far Northern Land, and the bright blue sky shone with the promise of a glorious day. Many folk lingered about the open gate. Beneath the wall, just beside the gateway, stood a small, green building with a high, arched roof. Green banners flew from its peak and from the tops of the wall, snapping in the summer breeze. The flags and banners bore a strange device: a white bear, its arms raised and threatening, facing a straight, white sword.

Several men stood nearby, each of them dressed much as Ilkka, save their raiment and cloaks were all green. They carried long, iron-tipped spears, and one of them had a sword hanging from his leather belt. Väinämöinen and Ilkka checked their horses before them and the old man raised his staff in greeting.

"Hail, men of the Karhulaiset!" he said so loudly that other passersby stopped and stared. "I bring you greetings from afar! It is many years since I have stood before the gates of Keskimaa, but today I return. Behold, I am Väinämöinen! I beg leave to enter the city on an urgent errand to your lord."

The men looked at each other in wonder, but their captain, the man with the sword, replied, "Hail, Väinämöinen! And welcome on your return from the Marches, Warden. But you need no leave to enter Keskimaa, unless you are trading or plan to make mischief. It is a free town; go about as you will."

Väinämöinen looked down on the guards from his high saddle, his face stern and serious, as if he expected something more, but they were silent.

Ilkka laughed and said, "Maybe things have changed since you came here last. I don't think such solemnity is necessary. These men are here to tax wagons on their way to market, not to deny you entry or announce even so famous a guest!"

Väinämöinen scowled. "Be that as it may," he said sourly, "I have not forgotten common courtesy, even if it fails in mortal lands. Let us go."

They left the guards, blinking and staring, and rode through the walls into the town. Ilkka brought his horse next to Väinämöinen and spoke in a more serious tone.

"I, too, have tarried overlong and have ill news for my captain. I ought to ride swiftly to the Warden House," he said. "But I guess that you wish to speak with Pekka straightaway and will go to him directly."

"Aye," answered Väinämöinen. "That I do, and that is where I go. I have news for him, as you well know, and there is the matter of the child to attend to."

"Then I will come with you, if I may. It may be that Pekka Verikiven should hear our news together."

"Very good," said Väinämöinen.

Many narrow side streets and lanes intersected the broad way they followed through the very heart of Keskimaa. Wooden houses—some with high, gabled roofs like the guardhouse beneath the town walls—lined the streets, one practically on top of the next. Along the town's main thoroughfare, however, Ulla saw shops and open stalls selling their wares, food or drink; she saw smithies and stables for horses, cattle, and other animals. In one open lot, men loaded rust-colored rocks onto great wagons. Ulla tried to guess what was in the shops and stalls, but mostly she watched the many different people, all new and strange to her, who lived in the City of the Karhulaiset.

The townsfolk stared at the old man with his long beard and colorful clothes, and at the little girl strapped down before him. Ulla saw children playing in the streets; small girls her own age wore colored kerchiefs over their hair. There were older girls, too, clad in long white smocks that nearly touched their bare feet on the dusty lane. They clasped their dark green tunics at the shoulder with pins fashioned in clever designs, and decorated their apron hems with green and yellow trim. The girls' hair was finely braided and they wore chains of copper and tin around their necks. Small figures, cunningly wrought, dangled from the chains: birds, beasts, spindly frogs, and the occasional tiny elk or bear.

The town girls pointed and laughed at the girl from the countryside in her dun, homespun shirt and the single, rude braid hanging down her back. But when Väinämöinen's dark glance fell upon them, they quickly turned away.

The broad thoroughfare of Keskimaa eventually opened into a wide, open place where traders and merchants did business and animals were sold. On the other side of the square, against the town's southern wall, there was a great building. In front, a wooden palisade enclosed a dusty courtyard sheltered by a few large alder trees, which were rare finds so far to the north. The bright green and yellow, rectangular building beyond was low on its eastern side, but the highest in the city—standing at three stories and topped by a gabled roof—on its western end. Many doors and windows stared out at irregular intervals. So Ulla first saw the Hall of the Karhulaiset, where the lord of High Länsimaa and his council held court and did business.

Väinämöinen and Ilkka hitched their horses outside the palisade and, after brief words with the guards at the open entrance, passed inside with Ulla in tow. Through the hall's central door, they came into a large room where many men stood about or sat at various tables, weighing coins and unwrought silver and gold on little scales. Colored tapestries, furs, and antlers of deer and elk decorated the walls between long, narrow windows that spilled yellow sunlight onto the wood-slatted floor. Ulla looked closely at the finely woven tapestries. The images and scenes on each unique tapestry together seemed to tell a story about a figure dressed in red and a great bear hunt.

At the front of the room, beside a round table with many chairs and surrounded by a group of men, stood a well-dressed figure with a long, drooping mustache and a huge belly somewhat held in check by a great, golden belt: Pekka Verikiven, the Lord of High Länsimaa.

The rulers of the Karhulaiset, the Bear Folk, did not govern by heredity, so Pekka Verikiven was no king or prince; the lord of High Länsimaa was chosen every seven years by a council of notables from the chief districts of the land. But the taxes, tariffs and wealth of High Länsimaa flowed through their hands, and they grew very rich.

The Verikiven family, a clan unto itself, had been powerful in that part of the Far Northern Land for generations. They owned much good land in Keskimaa, and bought and sold many beasts, but most of their wealth came from the bloodrock mined in the bogs near Suurijärvi and the other great lakes in the region. Pekka the Fat, as he was universally known, had twice been elected lord of the clan. Shrewd in business and trade, he had many interests. The Verikivens had many rivals, however, and the politics of High Länsimaa were no easy affair.

Väinämöinen and Ilkka strode to the front of the hall with Ulla trailing along behind. Ilkka placed his right hand over his breast in the Warden's salute, but Väinämöinen bowed very low and, with a flourish, brought his staff down with a loud crack on the wooden floor, startling Pekka and his retainers.

"Hail, Pekka Verikiven," Väinämöinen cried. "Chief of the Karhulaiset and Free Lord of High Länsimaa! It is with joy that I return at long last to your fair hall and to the city of your folk. It is I, Väinämöinen, Singer of the North! In hour of need, I return!"

Pekka bowed as best he could and returned Ilkka's salute, but his face expressed surprise and wonder.

"Hail, Väinämöinen," he managed at last. "It has indeed been a long time since you were last seen or heard of. So long that many men doubted if you or your kin still walked the earth or would ever return to our lands again. I admit that I count myself among them, and never expected to see you again—here or anyplace else. But in any case, welcome to Keskimaa. Or, perhaps I should say welcome back. And good Warden, I know your face, but forgive me if I don't recall your name."

"No pardon is needed, my lord," said Ilkka. "I thank you for your gracious words. I am Ilkka, son of Jurma, born far to the west, among the northern vales of Deep Länsimaa. But now I am the chief of the Fourth Company of the North Marches, sent south to our captain here in Keskimaa. And I fear I have ill news for you, for him, and for others."

"Well," said Pekka. "That sounds bad indeed. And we've already had much bad news this summer. There is less rock than usual so far this year, and even if prices are up, an empty wagon earns nothing. But bad news is best heard up front and without delay. So tell me, what has happened?"

"If it pleases you," said Väinämöinen, "I will tell my tale first, for the two are entwined. But I have the greater knowledge of these things, and greater urgency."

Pekka laughed. "I don't doubt it! I was only a child when I last saw you, Väinämöinen, but I don't recall patience being one of your many virtues."

"I remember you, too," answered Väinämöinen. "A likely lad of about ten years, I'd say, right here in this very hall when your father was lord and master. He was a great man, your father. And you have followed in his footsteps and grown great as well, in many ways."

Pekka looked sideways at the old man, but said, "My father taught me many things. And I remember his lessons about you well, Väinämöinen, child though I was at the time. You were not always among his favorite counselors, even if you weren't exactly an outlaw among the Bear Folk, as the case may be among some other clans. What is your tale, then? Why have you returned to us from your wanderings?"

Väinämöinen hesitated for a moment, looking keenly at Pekka, then laid his staff on the round table. He drew himself up to his full height—he *was* very tall—and stood before them, a shaft of sunlight from a narrow window falling directly upon him. Bathed in golden light, the old man looked strange and otherworldly. A gentle glow suffused his figure: red cloak, yellow boots, long white beard, and all.

He glanced quickly at Ulla—so far, the child had stood quietly beside them and no one seemed to have noticed her—and declaimed in a sonorous voice, "Hearken to my tale, men of the Karhulaiset! I will speak a word to you, a word of warning. There are Seven Lands and Seven Clans, and many strange things under the moon and sun. But not all things remain the same forever. Behold! The world is changing. I can feel it in the earth. The Vanhalaiset sing a song for those who know how to listen. A power stirs again in the farthest north, a power that has slept for many lives of men, and a power none thought would return again to trouble the unhappy world.

"Listen to me! Löhi is awake again! The Mistress of the North is alive and awake; she marshals her strength and builds her power. In the dark land of Pohjola, in her dim halls in dreary Sariola, the lamps are lit, hammers crash unceasingly, and great toil is done among the din. The Witch of the North gathers all evil things to her, awakening those who also slept and filling them again with hatred for all men and women in the Far Northern Land. She bides her time while her power grows, but doubt me not! She intends to take back all that once was hers and to destroy all the clans, each in turn. It is her last chance, and she will show no mercy."

"The Witch of the North!" cried Pekka. "Löhi? These are the tidings that you have returned with? By the North Star! Väinämöinen, you come back after decades, out of legends, bringing tales of legends with you. The Witch of the North has been dead and gone for five hundred years, if ever there was such a spirit. What is Löhi now but a name men curse during winter's chill, or a story told by the fireside to scare little children? Löhi!"

"It is no fireside tale, Pekka Verikiven," said Väinämöinen. "Do you doubt your own history? Your own past? Do not the fair tapestries that bedeck your hall tell the story of Lieto the Founder, the first lord the Bear Folk, whom I taught to hunt so long ago?"

Väinämöinen pointed to one of the hanging tapestries. Ulla saw that, next to the red figure under a tree, a tall man with a curling white beard and yellow cap stood, holding a staff.

"We know our history," said one of the men who stood by Pekka. "And all men know the name of Löhi, though, in truth, it seems a name out of the ancient past. But history also tells us that the hero Lemminkäinen killed Löhi in the Great Battle long ago. What makes you think that she has returned from the dead to trouble us again?"

"Did you not hear me?" Väinämöinen asked. "Do you not remember who I am? I sing many songs and I listen to many songs, too. The world is changing. I can feel it in my very bones. And Löhi has not returned from the dead! Only mortals believed she was dead, truly dead, for mortals need explanations that they can see and touch and measure for things they cannot really understand. If it is beyond the measure of their sight or their minds, then to them it does not exist. My knowledge is deeper and of a different sort.

"Löhi is of the Erilaiset, the greatest ever among us. Her cold fire cannot so easily be vanquished. No blade, though enchanted, could send her forever to her long home. Long she has slept, aye, a very long time. And I admit that I, too, thought she slept as the Vanhalaiset do, and would never again take shape in the waking world. But I was wrong. She came into my dreams and I have seen her."

"So you dreamt about her?" asked Pekka. "And you feel her in your bones? And thereby you know she lives and plots our ruin?"

"Not through dreams alone. I have been in the north, Pekka, far beyond the Marches. Not to Pohjola, surely, for though I can see many things from afar, even I will not dare travel that road alone. But I saw more than enough to confirm my fears: evil things waking, walking abroad, and gathering in the cold, barren places. Riders of the Itäläiset hasten to and from Pohjola, again in league with the one they once called queen."

"If I may speak, my lord?" Ilkka suddenly said. "For it may be that my news fits best now. The Lord Väinämöinen may indeed have the greater knowledge of these deep matters—I am only a simple Warden from the Marches—but I, too, have news of evil things and deeds in the wild.

"I know nothing of the Witch of the North, and cannot speak to such affairs. But strange things have happened on our borders since last year. We began seeing fell shapes in the forest during the winter. Large shapes, larger than any bear, slip in and out of dark shadows, then disappear into mounds or pools if pursued. Two of the cabins that we use for shelter were ransacked and burned. Some of my companions caught a better glimpse of these things than I, and have put a name to them; they are trolls."

"Trolls!" cried Pekka. "Now you, too, Ilkka, weave legends into waking life. Trolls still lurk, some say, in the deep forest in Karelia, or perhaps in Akkala or the wild wastes far beyond the Seven Lands of mortal men. But on the borders of Länsimaa? That I have never heard!"

"And not only trolls," said Ilkka. "We have seen other shapes—smaller, but gathered together—spying on men and filling the forest with eerie cries and wails. But the worst news I have is the most recent. Nigh on two months ago, we found a small settlement near Vähäjoki burned and ravaged. A family lived there, wandering folk of the Karhulaiset who had made a small clearing and built a *pirtti*. They were dead—adults, children, all cruelly hewn. It was no attack by bear or wolves. We sent several Wardens up the river and across the border to follow what seemed to be a trail, or maybe several trails. They found nothing. But one of them, Lippo Idänkylä—of the Karhulaiset, your own clan—failed to return. We searched long for him, but found no sign. It is with this ill news that I was sent back from the north."

Pekka's round face grew more serious as he said, "Your news is ill indeed. I will speak with the captain of the Wardens of High Länsimaa. It may be that we should double the watch until the truth of these strange things is discovered."

"Is that all that you would do?" Väinämöinen asked. "Do not mistake my words. What Ilkka has reported is only the beginning. You may have some time left—a season or two, perhaps three—ere Löhi strikes in earnest. She is only probing now, testing your defenses and spying on your lands. But fire and murder on the North Marches are the least of your problems. When she comes, she will come with war, Pekka, with bright swords and long spears, with armies and legions in her train. You must prepare for that day, prepare for what you have not faced in many lives of men: war.

"Do not send all your iron to the smiths in Seppälä, but forge blades again in Länsimaa. Arm your folk and take counsel with the other clans, both near and far—with your near kin in Deep Länsimaa, and in Etelamaa, and fair Tavastia, and all throughout the Far Northern Land. Only through the strength of all the united Seven Clans was the Witch defeated long ago.

Your numbers have recovered from battle, plague and pestilence, but your lands are divided, and therein lies her hope."

"It's been a very long time since we've been threatened with war," said Pekka. "And who could threaten us now? The Bear Folk are grown to a great people. The Itäläiset are far away in their homes to the east and make no raids on our land. And what armies are there in the frozen wastes of the north to attack us? They say the reindeer herders still follow their ski trails far away, and maybe the dwarves in their distant mountains still mine for gold. But what is that to us?"

"There are many things in the frozen north of which you know not," said Väinämöinen. "The Easterners are not as far away as you think, and there are other men from other lands that Löhi can marshal. Things outside of mortal ken still linger in the world: fell things, spirits, and even Erilaiset, who, like Löhi, long for the world of old. And she is gathering the strength of the *Hiisia* of the north, and they are multiplying."

The men laughed at this and Pekka put his hands on his round belly as he chuckled.

"Väinämöinen, my friend!" he said. "Now you go too far! Hiisia? Little goblins that creep about homes and barns at *Kekri*-time to steal food and make mischief? Next you'll tell us that there's a sea serpent in Suurijärvi waiting to swallow us up!"

The look on Väinämöinen's face changed; he narrowed his eyes and frowned. One of the gathered men took a step back as he glared at them.

"I cannot account for the failure of mortal wisdom," he said slowly. "Nor for what has been forgotten or strangely changed into idle tales of fairies and firesides. But if the Hiisia of the north come for you, Pekka Verikiven, I assure you, you will not laugh."

It was Pekka's turn to frown. He hooked his thumbs in his golden belt and looked up at the old man.

"Thank you for your counsel and words of warning," he said coldly. "We shall speak with the Wardens. If there are trolls to be hunted on the Marches, or thieves and raiders, whatever they be, we will attend to it. If you have no other news for me, Väinämöinen, then I bid you farewell. May you have a fair stay in our town and be sped on your homeward way."

Väinämöinen stood silent. The golden light about him dimmed somewhat, but his grey eyes shone beneath his thick, white brows. Very slowly, he took his staff from the round table and turned to the little girl who still stood quietly to one side.

"Come, child," said the wizard. "Now is the time."

Ulla came forward. She felt the eyes of the assembled men turn toward her and her heart started to race. Väinämöinen held her gaze, however. A measure of calm and a feeling of peace swept over her. The old man spoke no word, but Ulla heard his instruction as surely as if he had whispered into her ear. She lifted her long braid and pulled her shirt down at the shoulder. Dark against her pale skin, the mark of the bear stood out for all to see.

"Consider one more thing," said Väinämöinen. "Here is a child of your folk, only eight years old. She lives with her mother's kin in a village in the north of your land, for her own mother and father are dead. Look well, men of the Karhulaiset! See the sign with your own eyes. It is the mark of your clan."

The men crowded around the girl. Pekka reached out his pudgy hand and touched her shoulder, tracing the mark's outline with his fingers.

"What is her name?" he asked. The little girl looked at him over her shoulder.

"My name is Ulla," she said clearly.

Pekka turned to Väinämöinen. "She was born with this mark?"

"No. And that is even stranger. I had just returned from the north, where I was searching for signs, as I have said. As I made my way down the North Road bound for Keskimaa, I turned aside to graze my horse. Wandering in a little wood, I came upon the child just as she was attacked by a brown bear in fear for her cub. I slew the bear, for I had no choice. But the girl was gravely hurt and had already started down the path to Tuone's dark river. I found her and called her back; I stopped the blood and healed the torn flesh. She lived. But where red scars should be, this sign then appeared: the mark of her clan!

"I did not put it there and I did not foresee it. It is a strange thing. But did chance bring me there, Pekka? Is it chance that this sign appears even as Löhi herself returns? I do not understand it; I make no claim to do so. But old words and prophecies come into my mind now and trouble me. Consider this mark well as you make your counsel. And I would take the child with me, if I might, to consult with my kin among the Erilaiset and seek the wisdom of she who knows these things best. This benefits us all, the girl not the least."

"That brings us to another matter," said Ilkka. "For the girl's family is not here and I promised to speak for them. Väinämöinen asked that they let the girl go with him to his home in the forest, but they did not wish to lose her. Still, Väinämöinen saved her life, of that there is no question. And he spoke of the Life Debt. The girl's family would honor the debt, but are poor farmers and have nothing to give. So all agreed to seek your judgment on whether the girl should go with Väinämöinen or return to her kin when I go back north."

"I did not invoke the Life Debt," said Väinämöinen. "But truly, I asked that it be considered. And I named my wish. Let the child come with me for a year and a day, then she will choose. Should she wish to return to her folk, I will take her. You have seen the sign upon her shoulder. I deem it best that the girl should come with me."

The lord of the Bear Folk again looked closely at the brown mark on the little girl's white shoulder. Then he straightened his spine and cleared his throat.

"I know the ancient laws, but never in all my years have I seen or heard this old custom invoked or put in practice, much less with a child. The Karhulaiset are a free people and we do not keep serfs or slaves, nor do we sell our daughters into servitude—especially to an old vagabond of the wilds who still clings to long-forgotten beliefs and peddles legends from the past. Return the child to her folk where she belongs. But, if Väinämöinen still needs recompense, give him a golden crown—no, five golden crowns from the town's coffers. Then I will hold this matter to be closed."

A great tension filled the air as Pekka spoke, and even Ulla, only a child, could feel it as if it were a tangible thing and could be touched. She had never expected Pekka to return her to her aunt and uncle. She had already accepted that her path lay with the old wizard. Her surprise at Pekka's words would have to wait, however. She knew Väinämöinen well enough by then to expect his quick temper and waited to see what he would do or say; indeed, Ilkka and the other men waited, too, fearing some terrible turn.

But Väinämöinen gave no sign. At last, he brought his staff down hard on the slatted floor and then, slowly, bowed very low.

"So be it," he said. "You may keep your gold, lord of the Karhulaiset. I have my own. Or, better still, give it to the child, for her family shares not in your good fortune."

Without another word, the old man turned and strode swiftly from the hall.

Ilkka exchanged a few brief words with Pekka and one of the other men, then took his leave. But as he took Ulla by the hand and made to go, Pekka caught her shoulder and gave her a strange look through his clear blue eyes, though he said nothing.

They found Väinämöinen in the dusty courtyard, leaning heavily on his copper-shod staff and staring blankly at the palisade and beyond. Ilkka stopped and stood before him.

"Your news was ill received," said the March Warden. "I feared as much. They are a young people here and place more stock in the present and the future than in shadows or warnings from the past. But I go now to see my captain. Are you coming with me? Perhaps your warnings will fare better there."

Väinämöinen stirred as if shaking off some deep reverie and answered the Warden, "No. At least, not yet. There are others I wish to speak with first, before Pekka's report reaches their ears."

The old man suddenly stooped and, squatting with his red cloak spread out about him, gazed right into the little girl's hazel eyes. He stroked a lock of her dark hair away from her face with a big brown hand.

"Listen to me, child," he said. "Your lord has spoken and, beyond your aunt's hope, you will return to her. Be a good girl; honor your family and your elders. But if any ill chance should befall you, or evil beset you, remember that you are strong. You are filled with light. You have walked through the wood with no colors and returned. Never give up, child! When all seems lost, when darkness and despair surround your heart, never stop fighting! You always have the power to choose your course for good or ill, don't ever forget that. I may visit you again soon—aye, I may indeed, and perhaps I will take all your kin with me to a better place. Go now in peace, and don't forget old Väinämöinen!"

The old man laid his hand on the little girl's head. He closed his eyes and whispered soft sounds that only she heard and understood. Then, popping up like a spring, he ran through the palisade's gateway, leapt onto his flaxen horse, and clattered off down the busy main street of Keskimaa.

Chapter Four

The Prince
of the Stone City

Egan lay in his bed under blankets and covers as the early morning slipped away. Across from him were two long, narrow windows with the shutters pulled back. As the sun rose and morning passed, the light reached out from the windows and stretched across the floor like long yellow fingers, then began its retreat. When the yellow fingers withdrew to the room's center, Egan saw that he had only a little time left and tried to savor every moment. When the light touched upon the white wood of his table, the boy knew he had to rise or face his teacher's wrath—and possibly his father's, too—for again being late to his lessons. Still, he hesitated, and only when Orvo, the old butler who was also Egan's manservant, rapped on his door did he stir and get out of bed.

"Come on now," said Orvo, shaking his head at the sandy-haired boy with bright blue eyes after Egan opened the chamber's door. "The way you crave sleep, you would think it was deep winter and not high summer—and just after Midsummer's Day at that. You know Master Tervo is not going to be happy."

"I'll only be a minute," said Egan as he splashed cold water on his face from a silver bowl on the breakfront. "And I wasn't sleeping, thank you. I was thinking. One needs a brain for that, Orvo, so I excuse you for not un-derstanding me."

The white-haired old man just shook his head again and sighed. "Your brain is only as good as what goes into it," he replied, "and a man's quality is measured by what comes out of his mouth. *'Tell a man by his words, an ox by his horns.'*"

Egan quickly threw on a simple white shirt with blue embroidery around the collar and darted out of his room with Orvo trailing behind. He hurried down the cold, stony corridor and, rounding a corner, passed his parents' large chamber—the bedroom of the king and queen of Etelamaa— on the right. One of the big, round doors was open, and Egan caught a quick glimpse of his little sister—all of seven years old—bouncing on a divan while a maid tried to quiet her down. But he didn't stop, either to lend a hand or join in the fun. He was late and pushing his luck with both his teacher and his father. He bounded down the irregular stairway laid out with thick rugs to prevent spills on the slippery stone, and left Orvo behind as he hurried to the chamber where Master Tervo waited.

Corridors and short stairways twisted this way and that in the old part of the castle, built centuries earlier of hard stone and granite when Etelamaa was founded. The city had since given its name to the kingdom that grew until it stretched for many miles along the southern shores of the Far Northern Land, and on the banks of the vast Lake Etelajärvi. The castle, now part of the Keep, was built on an island in the middle of the narrows that led to the shallow bay beyond. A broad stone bridge with rocky piles sunk deep into the water connected the Keep to the main part of the City of Etelamaa—or the Stone City, as men called it, for, although most of its buildings were built of wood, the heart of the city, its oldest part, was fash-ioned in stone like the Keep.

Etelamaa had become a great city with many people, second in size only to Langvika in far-off Akkala, where trading ships from different lands made port. The Stone City boasted many beautiful buildings and fine houses, far more comfortable than the ancient, brooding castle where Egan and his family usually lived. But the Keep had been the home of Etelamaa's royal family for hundreds of years, so the House of Joutsen, Egan's house, and the House of Vipunen before it, and the still older royal houses of the *Etelalaiset*, the Swan Folk, had lived there since time immemorial.

Egan, the prince presumptive and heir to his father's throne, was fourteen years old; he would take up his full princedom in two years. Short for his age, he was barely taller than his brother Eglano, who was only eleven. What he lacked in size or stature, he made up for with a nimble mind—if a bit too precocious for his parents and masters—and an indomitable spirit. Not the fastest child nor the strongest, he showed no natural excellence in sports or the arts of war—in which all of the royal house were trained—unless it pertained to agility. Egan was disciplined, however, training hard and practicing any task over and over until he mastered it and became a match for others born with more skill but less determination.

Egan's sharp mind set him apart. Unlike the Bear Folk, or the Elk Folk of Deep Länsimaa, the Swan Folk were a lettered people, and Egan had learned to read and write at a very young age. He understood what he was taught and quickly grasped subtle thoughts and theories. His masters were pleased that he questioned what they put before him, and was unafraid to argue his point if he saw things differently. There, his precociousness gave him trouble, though, for Egan knew well just how clever he was and sometimes argued with his masters not out of conviction, but simply to annoy them or to test his own logic against theirs.

The young prince excelled at politics, rhetoric and administration. Each year he learned more of the complexities of ruling a great kingdom with many thousands of subjects, all with different interests and different needs. Egan's favorite subject was history, however. The boy learned by rote all of the history of Etelamaa and the Clan of the Swan, and as much as he could of the histories of the other great clans of the Far Northern Land. He studied old battles and, with his masters, reenacted them, taking one side, then the other, all while pondering the moves and decisions made by the captains and generals. In fact, to become a mighty warrior and captain like his grandfather had been was his heart's deepest desire.

Of all the histories and old legends, Egan loved best the tales of the Erilaiset and the magical races and creatures that had lived alongside men when the world was young, but were since banished or had withdrawn into the deep forest. The stories of how some of the Erilaiset had betrayed the folk of the clans troubled him, as did tales of how others had been driven forth unjustly, although they had not joined with the Witch who sought to destroy the lands of men in days gone by. His interest in the tales displeased his masters, who considered the time of the Erilaiset long since passed. Egan would one day rule the greatest kingdom of men—at least in his masters' eyes—in the Far Northern Land, and they turned his attention to its ordering and prosperity rather than to legends lost in the mists of time.

For some time, Egan's chief instructor had been Master Tervo, a stern man with thin lips, a narrow nose, pale blue eyes that were almost grey, and a smooth, bald head. Tervo waited for him in the stony chamber that served as their classroom, a windowless room that was always cold, even at the height of summer. The boy came bounding in ready with excuses, some of them rather stale. Tervo sighed and took a seat opposite Egan at the small, round table that, besides their two stools, was the room's only furnishing.

"Now that you have wasted half the morning, let us begin," Tervo greeted him. "Our lesson will be short enough in any case. Your uncle is arriving today from Kotanrannta and your father wishes you be there to greet him. And perhaps another visitor will arrive today, one who will greatly interest you. But first, did you study the list of taxes on the fields of Poronlinna Province, their types, and their distribution?"

Though often late to his lessons, Egan seldom came unprepared; when he did, he could usually dissemble, although doing so was more difficult with Master Tervo than with his other masters. Today, he knew the list Tervo asked for.

"There are seventeen products grown in the fields of Poronlinna," said Egan. "Twelve of these do not leave Etelamaa and are assessed only in their local districts. Three go north and are subject to the border tax. The other two may go abroad by sea and the royal tax may also be levied, and, depending on where they go, an assize to the Shipwrights Guild. The first of these seventeen are yellow turnips, the second is green chard, the third is—"

"Enough!" said a smiling Tervo. "Very good. Irresponsible you may be, but at least you know how to cover your tracks when you have strayed from the trail. But we will discuss Poronlinna later, when we have more time. Today, I want to discuss something that will be of more use when—*or if*—the visitor I referred to arrives. And well you know his name, I daresay, for I speak of Väinämöinen of the Erilaiset."

"Väinämöinen!" exclaimed Egan. "Väinämöinen the Singer! Coming here?"

"So it seems," replied Tervo. "I heard of it this morning from your father while you yet lay abed. There have been messages from Tomio, where a great wagon train of bloodrock for the Smiths Guild arrived from High Länsimaa. The drivers said that Väinämöinen had reappeared in the north and was seen in Keskimaa. And just yesterday, a messenger returned from Valkeakosk in Deep Länsimaa with the same news. Väinämöinen was seen in that land, too, where he met with Teemu, High Lord of the Elk Folk, near our very borders. And he was travelling south; some say he is already in Etelamaa and even now making for our city."

Egan could scarcely believe his ears. He had never seen one of the Erilaiset before, although once, near the northern shores of Lake Etelajärvi, he had glimpsed strange shapes in the trees. Now, the greatest of the singers of old was coming to the Stone City.

"Why is he coming here, Master Tervo? What has he been doing in the other lands?"

"I do not know," answered Tervo. "Yet perhaps you will find out after he arrives—if, indeed, he comes. But tell me, Prince Egan, who is Väinämöinen?

And what are the chief tales spun about him? That is your lesson for today, should you, in fact, chance to meet the singer."

Then Egan told his master all he knew about the bard, repeating many stories and legends that he had learned by heart. He told how Väinämöinen, the eternal singer, had come into the world long ago. Some said he had been born to one of the Vanhalaiset, maybe even Ilmatar, the Mistress of the Winds; others held that he was born of a spirit of the deep waters. And the boy reported how the old man—for he was already old by then—had ordered the world, how he had tamed the forests and calmed the waters and brought forth living, green things when all the north was still covered in snow and ice. Then Egan spoke of how Väinämöinen and others of the Erilaiset, the children of the gods, had met the first men and women who came to the southern shores of the Far Northern Land, shivering in their rude huts by the shores of the Itämeri Sea.

The Erilaiset had taken pity on the poor and ignorant folk—refugees from other lands, where they were enslaved and beset with foes—and named them the *Kaamoslaiset*, the Folk of the Darkness, for they found them during the long winter night. They had taught the men many things—how to till the soil and make it rich, how to husband the reindeer and elk of the north, and how to build trusty boats and great ships to fish or protect their lands from foes. And they taught the men to mine the ore of the rocky hills and swamps and to use bronze and iron to make beautiful, useful things.

Moreover, Väinämöinen marshaled the different groups and families into what would become the great clans; he taught their leaders songs of power, and they became the founders of the Seven Clans of the Far Northern Land. Väinämöinen and other wizards among the Erilaiset taught some of these mortals many ancient mysteries: how to channel the Old Powers of the natural world, the Vanhalaiset that men called gods, and how to sing and cast spells of different types. The mortals who learned these things became powerful, forming orders and schools among all the Seven Clans. These bards and shamans increased the number and prosperity of their folk in the harsh lands of the north.

"Well said," replied Tervo when Egan had finished. "You have spent many hours poring over the old tales and legends. Perhaps your labor may soon be rewarded, though none would have foreseen it. But who knows which of the old legends are true? Who can say what really happened in the depths of time, when the world was still young and the clans first came to the Far Northern Land?"

Egan was irritated by his master's tone, though he hid it well. His teachers frequently scolded him for reading the old tales and neglecting his lessons. Egan wanted the legends to be true so badly that sometimes he dreamed about them. Somehow, someway, he believed that his life would be connected to the heroes. Could this be the moment that he had been waiting for?

"And tell me, Prince Egan, how was it that the Erilaiset, who the tales say once dwelt amongst us, came to be expelled from mortal lands or else fled of their own accord into whatever dark places they now inhabit, save for some few of which we know?"

Egan knew the answer.

"It was the Witch of the North," said Egan. "She hated the men and women who had come to the Far Northern Land to live in freedom. She was the queen of the Erilaiset and turned their hearts against us in her attempt to destroy the Seven Clans and drive us from our homes. She sent snow and ice to freeze us, dark spirits to afflict us, and pestilence to kill us. She made war upon the Seven Lands, and many of the Erilaiset fought against us or bewitched us with their black magic. And so began the Witch's War."

"Indeed," said Master Tervo. "So it began. And so it continued for many years, until all the lands were well nigh ruined. But in the end, the Kaamoslaiset came together. There are Seven Lands and Seven Clans; together they finally defeated the Witch and destroyed her evil host. The hero Lemminkäinen threw her down and, despite her great magic, cut off her head with his sword of silver steel, perishing in the deed. All the lands were cleansed of the foul brood of the Witch and, in time, made whole. Only the *Susilaiset*, the Wolf Folk, were nearly all destroyed. The survivors joined other folk, so while they are still reckoned among the Seven, they are known as the Lost Clan and their old land is now empty.

"And in Etelamaa at that time, a king was set to rule over the folk. Then men turned away from the magic that the Erilaiset had taught, believing it to be unnatural to us, although useful at times. Mortal wizards who had worshipped the Witch were hunted down and slain; singers were shunned in many places. Men trusted only one another and their own powers of thought, rather than the dark mysteries of the magic of the Erilaiset."

"But not all of the Erilaiset turned against us," Egan said a little defensively. "So it is written and so many tales say. The heroes remained true. Väinämöinen fought alongside Lemminkäinen against the Witch. And many others—singers and wizards and even elves—helped the people of the clans in their struggle, yet they, too, were driven forth."

The bald man sighed. He looked kindly at Egan, but shook his head disapprovingly. They had debated this many times before. "Indeed. And I did not say all that was done was just. Many things happen in the world that are wrong. Yet they still come to pass, do they not? At the time, the people of the Far Northern Land were afraid of the Erilaiset; they could no longer trust them. And listen to me, Egan— they are still perilous to mortal men, be they good or evil.

"But you err, my prince. Not all of the Erilaiset were driven out of the Seven Lands. In Akkala, where the war was most terrible, and where many mortal wizards turned against their own folk, the Erilaiset were banished; to this day, such is the law in that land. And in Tavastia, too, they were exiled long ago. But it was not so in Etelamaa or the other lands. We turned away from the old faith of deceitful magic, but we did not hunt down one singer or creature of mystical race or turn them out by force. The twilight was upon them and they left mortal lands for whatever homes they preferred in the forest depths, where the trees grow as wild as they. Only the Karelialaiset still live by the Old Ways and they are a strange, scattered folk, all but sundered from the other clans."

Tervo rose, pointing to a map on the wall, a map of the southeast showing the chief villages and towns of Etelamaa, the great lake of Etelajärvi, and, marked in green with the shapes and figures of many trees therein, the Karelian Forest.

"There is the home of the Karelialaiset, the Reindeer Folk—save for some few that live in the northeast of Etelamaa, near the forest eaves, and have given up their wandering. And there, too, is the home of Väinämöinen, Lord of the Erilaiset. If the others of his folk forsook our lands to haunt the dark forest paths long ago, it was not so with the Great Singer. Ever he remained involved in the affairs of men until at last it seemed that he, too, was gone. As you know, he has not been seen in Etelamaa since your grandfather's time, during the Kultasaare Wars, when evil and strife stalked our land and the House of Joutsen came to the throne.

"If you were not so tardy, we might now discuss the wars and all of Väinämöinen's dealings with Etelamaa that are recorded or remembered. But there is no time and, in any case, that happened long ago. Who can say what business might bring Väinämöinen to us today? Go now to your father, Prince Egan; the midmorning bells will soon ring. And next time be prepared to finish your report about Poronlinna and its taxes!"

Egan bowed, taking his leave of Master Tervo. He liked his master, who was stern and often aloof, but still fair and even kind at times—usually when Egan least expected it. He couldn't concentrate on anything but Väinämöinen, however. Väinämöinen! If Väinämöinen truly came to the Stone City, he would at last have a chance to see one of the old singers, a living legend, and perhaps his questions would finally be answered.

The young prince came to a newer part of the castle: still old, but not as rough or as cold. In the great Hall of the Swan, appointed with many fine things and painted brightly in the pale blue and white of the Etelalaiset, he found his father holding court.

As part of his lessons, Egan often observed his father at work. Soon after Egan took his own place in the hall, his uncle—Alder of Kotanrannta, Grand

Duke of Etelamaa—arrived. Alder had brought his son, Aldon, with him, whom Egan found annoying and tried to avoid as much as possible. To add to Egan's disappointment, his father said little about Väinämöinen, save that the wizard had been seen in the north and *might* be journeying to the city. Egan sat impatiently while his father and Alder discussed various matters and his cousin needled him about some prank they had played last winter, until finally the king—clearly irritated with Egan's impatience—signaled that he might leave.

After observing morning court, Egan spent most of the afternoon slinking around the Keep and dodging Aldon as best he could. From time to time, he walked out onto the high wall that overlooked the stone bridge to check for any sign of the old wizard, but saw only the usual press of merchants and guards, messengers and servants, children and animals that made up the street life of the Stone City. In the late afternoon, he reported to his fencing master and sparred with the long sword, which was heavier than what he usually worked with. His master had introduced it into their sessions as he grew older and more accomplished. In the evening, he sought his mother, finding her where he expected to: atop the tower, looking out over the parapet at the sparkling waters of the bay. A strong breeze from the south blew about her, snapping the blue and white banners of the Swan that flew from the tower's heights and fanning her long flaxen hair, streaked lightly with grey, around her face.

The young prince paused for a moment at the top of the stone steps to watch her. Vendla, Queen of the Swan Folk, was a slender, slight woman with pallid skin, who had been born into a great and ancient house of her people. Egan thought her the most beautiful woman in the world. His love for her ran strong and deep, as deep as the cold, dark pools in the north of their land, wherein precious pearls, pink and pale, could be found. The queen sensed his presence and turned, motioning for him to join her where she stood with his sister Marjatta. She smiled as he came to her side and silently slipped his hand into hers. Boy of fourteen though he was, he felt suddenly and completely overwhelmed by his love for her, the love of a child for his mother.

Together they stood high atop the tower and gazed down on the bay. The evening sun hung low in the west, a red orb spilling its fiery image onto the glassy water and casting long shadows that slowly advanced across the gleaming surface. Fishing boats returned with their catch, ready for the morning's markets. Their bright, colorful sails dotted the waves like multi-hued birds taking wing. Across the bay, in a rocky cove beside the wharfs, they saw a bevy of swans, the totem and namesake of the Etelalaiset. They appeared tiny in the distance, white spots against the sea's blue shimmer, but Egan's young eyes could still make out their long, graceful necks. As they looked out over the gleaming bay with the friendly sun warming them in the summer breeze, Egan felt transformed. A feeling of utter peace grew inside him until, in that moment, he could imagine no darkness, no blight, no ill of man or nature that might threaten his world or the love he felt.

Later that night, he took his leave of Orvo, who had brought a basin of fresh water to his chamber and a small bronze bowl of bitter sea buckthorn berries. He ate the berries while absentmindedly leafing through a small sheaf of old poems that his grandmother, who had died only two years before, gave him. Egan kept his windows unshuttered at night, delighting in the smell of the sea's tang on the evening air. Although he had actually done very little that day, the boy soon grew drowsy as he lay on his bed. He closed his eyes without dimming the oil lamps on the table. He fell asleep like that, still dressed and above the blankets, with vague and tattered thoughts meandering from Väinämölnen to the sun on the waters of the bay.

When Egan finally dreamed, it was not of the old wizard or of his mother the queen and her sparkling eyes. His dreams turned dark, filled with fire and a great burning, then a terrible storm of cold, white ice that chilled him to the bone. He tossed and turned in his troubled sleep, until at last he awoke in a cold sweat with a racing heart. The cool night air flowed over him, but still he didn't move, staring at the cold stone walls as the hours slowly passed.

CHAPTER FIVE

THE BLACK PHANTOM

Väinämöinen stood on a high, bare ridge and gazed down on the gentle plain far below. The tumbled slope, steep in some places but level in others, fell many hundreds of feet until it abruptly flattened out. There were great boulders here and there, but few trees even though it faced south and basked in the warm sun during the summer.

The ridge on which Väinämöinen stood ran east-west as far as the eye could see in either direction before finally winding its way southwest like a vast snake, cutting the Far Northern Land in half. It stretched for hundreds of miles across the land's breadth and separated the gentle farmlands and fertile fields of Etelamaa and Tavastia from the thicker forests and thin soils of the lands to the north.

The men of the Far Northern Land had named it the Wall of the Giants. Their legends and songs told that it had been built by a race of giants long ago to keep the evil things of the forest out of the south. The songs also told that mortals had given the giants' chieftain and his ten vassals necklaces of gold, set with rubies and amber, to reward them for their great service.

Väinämöinen knew the true story, however. Never were there any giants so great or so numerous to have done such a deed—not even when the world was young, and not even for a river of gold or a boat filled with diamonds. The long ridge that divided the lands had another name among the Erilaiset—Löhi's Fence—for it marked the line where, in the days of her dominion, her mountains of ice and rock had stood, ere they fell and retreated when she withdrew to the furthest north.

Väinämöinen saddled up, spurred his horse, and began the long descent down the Wall's slope, sometimes riding along lesser shelves for a ways until he found a suitable path with gentle grade for his sure-footed beast. He had reached Etelamaa the day before and was heading south toward the Stone City, where the king of the Swan Folk lived.

The old singer felt weary and depressed; his return to mortal lands had been disappointing so far. Although the March Wardens heeded his warnings and sent new strength to the northern borders, they were still few. He had no better luck with the other lords of the Bear Folk than he had with Pekka Verikiven and, when he had tried to see Pekka a second time, the fat lord of the Karhulaiset had refused him. So, he left Keskimaa on Midsummer's Day and journeyed southwest toward Deep Länsimaa, the land of the *Hirvilaiset*, the Folk of the Elk.

He thought to make for Valkeakosk, the capital of the Hirvilaiset that had been built beside a swift river with white rapids, but news reached him that Teemu, High Lord of Deep Länsimaa, was hunting in the south. Väinämöinen had changed course to meet him and his folk nigh to the borders of Etelamaa on Siinisaare, an island in the middle of a fair lake, beside which many people dwelt.

Teemu and his retinue were much more in awe of Väinämöinen than Pekka Verikiven had been. To his satisfaction, they treated the old singer with a courtesy bordering on reverence, so great was his legend in their minds. The sudden appearance of the wizard with his strange tale was beyond their reckoning, and they quickly grew wary and afraid.

Teemu was a young man, and if the Elk Folk were a more settled clan than the Bear Folk, they were also scattered across Deep Länsimaa in many districts, each with their own lord. And, like their lord, they were a young folk who remembered less of the ancient songs and their own beginnings than did the Karhulaiset. To them, the name of Löhi was but a dim echo of things long past. They did not understand Väinämöinen's warning, but they grasped his earnestness. Teemu promised to speak with the Wardens of Valkeakosk and to send word to his scattered vassals and chieftains, but little else. So Väinämöinen had left him and, turning south again, headed for Etelamaa.

Väinämöinen reached the Wall's foot and soon struck a hard road to the southeast. He rode swiftly across the flat plain broken by the fences, ditches, and low, raised shelves that bounded the well-ordered fields and farms of the Etelalaiset, the Folk of the Swan. The plain held many farms, both large and small, as well as numerous villages, for the Swan Folk were a great clan with a rich and fertile land. The villages were not, for the most part, like the rude, rustic hamlets scattered across High and Deep Länsimaa. The Swan Folk grew many crops and had no want of food, and they raised herds of cattle and horses besides.

Their ships, and those of the Shipwrights Guild, sailed to faraway ports and traded for many things. Their great smiths, who also dwelt near the sea, made objects both useful and beautiful. In their villages lived not only farmers, but craftsmen, too: leatherworkers, weavers, tinsmiths, candlers, brewers and ropers, to name but a few.

In each village and town, the women and young maidens wore distinct dresses: finely woven and white, or else pale blue or cobalt, with sleeves, aprons and hems decorated in colors unique to their homes, and all clasped at their shoulders with broaches or pins. They wrapped chains of tin, bronze and silver around their necks and covered their hair with veils or bands. The women wove many symbols and fair designs therein, especially images of the White Swan of Etelamaa.

Väinämöinen avoided the villages as best he could and rode quickly toward the Stone City. Although people often stared or called out to him, he spoke with few and chose to ride on, sleeping under the open sky. Nearly two months had gone by since he had left the north and passed over the Marches back into the lands of the Seven Clans. As the days slipped by, he grew ever more anxious. The old man knew that, of all the Seven Clans, the Swan Folk were the most likely to heed his words and perhaps stir the others to action so they would not be wholly unprepared for what he feared must surely come. Väinämöinen had had many dealings with the Etelalaiset in the past, but that was long ago. A generation of men had come and gone since he last travelled south. He did not know their king or his nature, and had no idea what to expect.

After several days, the mage came to a dense stand of forest, thicker and larger than elsewhere in the kingdom, where many trees had been felled. He left the road as the sun began its slow descent to the horizon, where it would linger for hours. Even from a distance, he could see the tall southern pines and firs that grew on the crest of a rise of a small hill in the middle of the woods. The woods were called the Totkametsa, after the town of Totka that lay near to the east, but the rise was called the *Verimäki*, the blood hill, and nearby townsfolk shunned it. Few remembered why it was named so; they only knew it as the haunt of ghosts and other fell things.

Väinämöinen knew the tale, however. He had once lived not far from the Totkametsa, and had fought alongside the lords of the House of Vipunen years ago when its crown was contested and war raged across the fields of Etelamaa. In that evil time, a group of prisoners—simple men at arms who had thrown down their spears in surrender and sought only to return to their villages and farms—had been driven into the thick woods by their captors. There, on the blood hill, they were murdered, several dozens all told. The silent earth still held their bones within its vault.

But Väinämöinen feared no ghost of mortal men. Tired, he sought the shelter of the green-leaved forest to rest and to think. He also wished to send forth his spirit far away and speak to others of the Erilaiset in order to see what was happening north of the Marches. The Totkametsa may have been unwholesome, and the Verimäki grim, but there was power in the earth there, where echoes of the cries of anguished souls might still be heard by those who knew how to listen. Väinämöinen could draw on that power.

He let his horse roam free a ways and set off on foot for the deepest part of the forest. There were many old trees around him and a certain feeling in the ancient place, not unlike that of his home in Karelia. There were other, darker airs, too, and Väinämöinen knew that neither mortal nor hero would ever live in these woods again. He had walked for about two hours when he suddenly came upon the steep, tree-covered rise: the Verimäki. The old man stomped to the top of the little hill in his yellow boots and stood amidst its tall trees as the dim light of the fading day filtered through. In the very middle of the hill's highest point was a great bare mound. Many stones lay scattered about its top or tumbled at its foot—the remains of a wall that once ringed the mound. It was the very site of the terrible slaughter, where its victims had been buried and left to sleep uneasily as the long years passed and the world grew old.

The old man sat down, ate some hard rye bread, and washed his face and hands in a little babbling stream. Then he gathered kindling and, with a single word, sparked a small, red fire that crackled and smoked on the hilltop. He drew a pouch from his belt, scattered some reddish powder from inside it on the fire, and sat cross-legged before it, his staff across his knees. Väinämöinen began to sing in a low voice, melodious at first and then more rhythmic, until he was almost chanting the words in the ancient tongue of the Erilaiset.

Now Väinämöinen had no drum to help induce the trance like a mortal shaman, but he needed none; his song was strong and his power great. He could send his spirit where he would. He did not intend to make a true frontwalker or *etiäinen*. To do so would actually send his spirit and soul away, leaving his body behind. It was very dangerous for any lone wizard, mortal or Erilainen. An *etiäinen* might not readily return if it journeyed far; it could be delayed or even trapped by another mage or spirit. The wizard's physical body, helpless while its spirit was away, could be harmed or slain by ill chance or design. That night, the old man sought only to reach out with his farseeing mind and *sight* to discover what was happening in the north and in his own land of Karelia, in the heart of the forest. Väinämöinen's *sight* was strong, the strongest among all the wizards and magic-users of the north, save for Löhi herself.

The fire burned lower. Väinämöinen stared at the unknowable pattern of the shifting, glowing embers. His eyes remained open as he sang, but the fire soon faded from his vision. It all went dark, and his mind fled like a bird into the sky above. He turned his thought north and stretched his *sight* beyond the little woods in which he sat. At first, he saw nothing but pale sky and dim stars. Then, as if he were a hunting falcon soaring high in the air, he caught glimpses of things that seemed far below. He saw the lines and boundaries of fields and meadows, and little roads connecting and crossing through little towns. Great towers of rock and stone loomed up, immovable by mortal hands: the Wall of the Giants.

His thought passed over the Wall and toward the lands beyond. He saw flashes of lakes, streams and pools, and the innumerable trees that covered the Far Northern Land. The old wizard pushed harder and suddenly a broad, flat plain appeared. In the distance, he saw a walled city with many wooden houses and a press of carts and wagons going in and out: Keskimaa. For a brief moment, he caught a glimpse of a tiny figure, far away, walking alone through a field of high grass beside a running stream. Then he moved on and pressed even further past the North Marches to discover what was happening in the Wastes, where he had last seen the servants of Löhi.

As Väinämöinen looked north, however, black clouds crept in and obscured his vision. The clouds rolled as if he were caught in a great storm. Try as he might, the singer's *sight* could not pierce the darkness: a solid, impenetrable mass that hid the Marches and all that lay beyond. His mind turned toward Karelia and the Erilaiset, for he also wished to see his home and perhaps find a friend to converse with in shared dream, as wizards may sometimes do. But even as he turned east, the way was blocked. The darkness followed him, boiling like the sea amidst a great tempest. He could not see the deep forest or the Enchanted Valley where lay his home, and the effort exhausted him.

Suddenly, Väinämöinen felt an urgent warning, as if a bell's shattering peal had sounded directly beside him. His mind fled from the black cloud and raced back across the miles to Etelamaa. The trance broken, Väinämöinen pulled free of the vision and was again aware of himself sitting by the fire atop the Verimäki.

It was dark by then, true night, for though it seemed to his waking mind that little time had passed, it was not so. Such was the way of farseeing, and he knew it well. The fire had burned down; only a few glowing embers remained. The shock of the broken trance made him jerk upright and then fall back, catching himself with one arm. At that moment, the old man realized two things; his staff was gone, and he was not alone.

Väinämöinen lay on his back, propped up by an elbow, staring up at a tall black figure, featureless but still threatening, that loomed over him. Darker than the shadowed forest night, blacker than the night sky above, it wavered slightly as if moved by the breeze, but made no sound or sign. The phantom was taller than any bear or troll, perhaps fifteen feet high. Whether it had followed his thought back across the miles to find him there, or had lurked nearby to ambush him, its unseen stare bored into him.

Two long, dark arms slowly reached out toward him. Väinämöinen feared no ghost or shade and knew a dozen songs that would chase away any restless or unclean spirit. But this was no wight come to haunt the bloodsoaked earth of Verimäki, or a spirit of the dead from Tuonela unveiled. The mage could feel its power, strong and pulsing, a tremendous sorcery within it bent upon harming him. If it was an *etiäinen*, it was like no *etiäinen* that he had ever encountered.

The old wizard gathered his wits and opened his mouth to speak a word of ward and protection, but the sound died on his lips. Before he could speak, a voice came from the phantom: a toneless voice, neither low nor shrill, that broke the forest's silence. And the phantom spoke a single word.

"Väinämöinen."

At once, the singer was struck dumb. So great was the power behind the voice that, mighty wizard though he was, it bound him. The phantom raised a shadowy arm and began a slow gesture, a spell or an invocation. Väinämöinen felt its strength wrap around him, enveloping him in a darkness from which there might be no escape. Väinämöinen had been caught before and had always gotten free, but seldom had he faced a power such as this. He could not speak and knew that he must act quickly, before the phantom's spell took him wholly in its grip. He glanced around frantically for his missing staff, then scrambled to his feet, backing away from the shadowy figure waving in the wind until he stood with his back against a broad elm tree.

Väinämöinen's heart beat hard within his breast. He grasped the golden talisman that hung around his neck, closed his eyes, and drew on his entire being to break the spell that bound his tongue. Still, no word or incantation came from his lips, but a scream tore from his lungs and pierced the night— as terrible and wild as that of a cornered animal. An unearthly greenish sheen illuminated the hilltop as Väinämöinen's fear and wrath blazed high. The phantom stopped the incantation and seemed to grow even larger, rising almost to the height of the treetops. For a moment, Väinämöinen thought to turn and flee, to escape in any way he could, though he knew flight might prove disastrous.

Just then, even as he prepared to spring, cherry and saffron suffused the greenish glow. The short summer night passed. Away in the east, where the sky grew lighter, the sun's fiery crown crossed the plane and pierced the forest's gloom with shafts of light.

The dark phantom turned to the east. It did not flee the coming dawn like some wailing ghost of men, but Väinämöinen could still feel its hesitation. The old man took heart. He made one last attempt and put forth all his might. Finally, he felt the bonds fall from his voice and wizardry.

"*Oi Ukko Ylijumala!*" he cried in a great voice. "*Suojaa tietäjää tuholta, vapauta vainon väeltää!*"

The words he spoke in the old tongue of the Erilaiset were words of ward and warning. Väinämöinen felt them cover him like a cloak as he stepped forward, heading straight toward the phantom and whatever onslaught came next. The menacing shape turned back to him. For several moments they faced each other, silent, as the light on the Verimäki slowly grew.

Then the old man realized that the specter before him was fading, its strength withdrawing. He watched its black outline as it faded from sight against the still dark sky overhead, until nothing was left. Even as the phantom disappeared and melted into the branches and boughs, he heard a sound that chilled him to the bone: laughter, faint and far-off, dimly perceived even by the sharp ears of the Erilaiset.

Väinämöinen sank to his knees, utterly spent. He closed his eyes and stayed like that for a long time, breathing slowly while the daylight grew around him and the birdsong filled the air with music. At last he arose, and, after drinking again from the babbling brook, gathered his scattered things and made to leave the hilltop.

But still, he did not find his staff.

***

The old singer came upon his horse where he had left her, near the eaves of the Totkametsa. He felt relieved; he had feared she, too, might be gone. Tired as he was, he mounted and set off at once for the southerly road that led to the Stone City.

He was shaken by the encounter with the phantom, but as he rode along, the fear and shock wore off, and was replaced with bewilderment. What was the nature of the strange thing on the hilltop? How could it have so much power and strength? Was it lying in wait for him, or had it followed him from far away? It knew his name and seemed to wield great power over him, but he had been surprised and acted like a fool, setting no charms of ward or protection. The gentle lands of fair Etelamaa were safe—or so he'd thought. There were many evil things in the world, and many dangers for a man of power. The world was changing. He could not be so careless next time.

Väinämöinen was even more anxious to see the king and deliver his warning, for he deemed he had been wrong and that there might be less time than he'd hoped to prepare for Löhi's assault. He rode swiftly, and, after several days, came to a hard, paved road. It was the Kingsway, which led directly to the Stone City. The Kingsway passed through several small towns, some boasting fountains and stone houses of cunning masonry surrounded by high walls and towers.

Word of his coming passed before him, and after he reached Kotanrannta—the great duchy of the Swan Folk in the heart of Etelamaa—it became impossible to avoid crowds of people eager for a glimpse of the famous singer. The streets and lanes filled with a great press of men and women calling his name. At any other time, Väinämöinen would have been greatly pleased indeed. He rode in haste now, however, waving to the people and gently calling on them to make way as he pushed on. At last, he neared the shores of the Itämeri Sea and the Stone City.

It was evening as Väinämöinen came to the city. In the distance, he could see the shimmering water and hear the cry of gulls as they followed the fishing boats back to the bay. Six riders approached him from the city, all of them mounted on fair white horses and wearing the finely wrought mail and blue tunics of the knights of the Etelalaiset; they bore the token of the Swan. They checked their horses before him and the foremost rider bowed his head and saluted.

"Hail, Lord Väinämöinen of the Erilaiset," he said. "My name is Vilho Linnalainen of the Keep's Guard. We heard rumor of your coming and are bidden by our lord, the king, to welcome you to Etelamaa and to escort you with honor into the city and the Keep, where the king awaits—if that, indeed, is your purpose."

Väinämöinen bowed his head. "Hail, Vilho Linnalainen," he said, thoroughly approving of the man's formality. "I thank you and your lord for your fair words of welcome. It is a happy hour for me that I return at last to the Southland, great Etelamaa, Land of the Swan. I thank you, too, for your escort, but the honor is all mine. I ask but one thing; let us ride swiftly, for the hour is already late and the day is fading. I would speak with the king today if it is at all possible. And to speak the truth, both I and my horse are very tired; we are ready to reach our journey's end."

"Then let us ride swiftly!" said Vilho. "We expected you earlier and the hour is indeed late. Follow us now to the City of Etelamaa!"

They pressed on then, down the paved highway toward the city. The road ran for a ways beside the northern end of the bay, looking out at the southeastern end of the island on which the Keep was built. Many ships, large and small, anchored there. Men were working on the wharfs and loading fish onto wagons and carts while seabirds wheeled about overhead. As the road bent round the eastern end, which the city folk called the Deep Bay, it skirted berths where great ships of war or trade docked or were built. A many-oared war galley of the Shipwrights Guild lay there now, dark and silent.

So they came to the city's first gate, wide and tall amidst a great grey wall, and passed within. The horses clattered down the streets past fair courts and buildings, through the second gate and the city square, where people had gathered to call Väinämöinen's name. Finally, they crossed the stone bridge into the Keep of the king of Etelamaa.

Men waited for the mage inside the Keep; some took his horse to be stabled and others led Väinämöinen into the castle. There, inside the great painted hall, waited Nigan, King of the Swan Folk.

Väinämöinen felt a rush of memory and emotion as he walked across the colored flagstones beneath the white, vaulted ceiling. He had walked into this hall so many times in his long life to consult with and counsel the lords of the Etelalaiset—but that was long ago. Now there were few in the kingdom that, save perhaps as children or young folk, he had ever seen with his own eyes.

Nigan stood at the top of the hall below a raised dais that bore a great throne of black, carven wood. His queen, Vendla, stood beside him and there, too, were the princes of Etelamaa: a sandy-haired boy with shining eyes, and another with chestnut-colored hair. A thin man with a bald head and a short, pointed white beard stood next to the king. Väinämöinen read the wonder and surprise in their eyes as he approached and realized how he must appear to them—a wild Erilainen out of the Wastes with his great boots caked in mud, his clothes and cloak rent and torn, and his long beard matted and tattered after his long journey. At the moment, however, he felt far too tired to care overmuch.

Väinämöinen stopped several feet from the king and bowed; he keenly felt the absence of his staff.

"Hail, Nigan, King of the Etelalaiset!" he said in as impressive a voice as he could muster. "I thank you for your most gracious welcome. Long has it been since I walked in fair Southland, and long have I missed its white shores. It is an honor to stand before you and to meet you at last. Well did I know your father, and many were the dangers we shared. I am at your service, my lord."

The king of Etelamaa bowed low, then straightened and considered the old man. Nigan, dressed in a simple tunic of pale blue with a darker cloak clasped at the neck, wore only a thin filet with a single amber stone in place of a crown. His dark hair, flecked with grey, was cut short and his face was strong, its features only slightly masked by a thin beard. Väinämöinen smiled; in Nigan's face he saw many he had known long ago, reflected as if in a distant mirror.

"Welcome, Lord Väinämöinen," said the king. "It has indeed been many years since you last graced our kingdom, yet I know that of old, you were once as familiar with these halls as I am. Let me then say, welcome back. Your service to my House is not forgotten, no matter how many years have passed. It is an honor for us all." Nigan turned toward the others, who also bowed. "May I present my queen, Vendla, and my sons, Egan and Eglano. And this is Toiva Merikainen, my chief advisor. We have awaited your coming for many days, for we heard news that you were in Etelamaa and journeying south. But you were expected earlier, and as the day waned, we retired, thinking that you had turned aside for the night. I fear this is a poor welcome, but there are others who also hope to greet you. And so they shall—in the morning. I can see that you are weary and that your journey has been a long one. Please take some refreshment ere you retire; food and drink await you if you desire it, and quarters have been prepared."

At a sign from the king, a footman came forward with a silver platter bearing brown bread, wine, and water. Väinämöinen took the water and drank deeply.

"I thank you for your hospitality," he said. "As the wise tell us, '*Give bread to the hungry, beer to the thirsty, and a place beside the fire for the weary guest.*' And I won't deny that I am weary. Still, I would rest easier if I could speak with you, my lord, before turning to bed. Lovely as fair Southland is, I come not for rest or pleasure, but rather with a message and words of warning."

Nigan's face grew serious before he said, "I thought as much. I doubt not that you are in earnest, and yet perhaps that is all the more reason to wait till morning. I would have all my counselors with me to hear your message, especially my brother Alder, who is now in the city. But there is no time to call them now; any summons must wait for dawn."

"Then I shall be brief," said Väinämöinen. "But I would still beg your indulgence. I have words enough for all your counselors tomorrow and, indeed, for any others who will hear me. May we not speak?"

"Very well," answered the king. "If you do not wish to rest now, let us speak."

"The queen and your sons may wish to retire," said Väinämöinen. "It is a grim tale that I bear, and perhaps not for all ears—at least, not yet."

The king looked doubtfully at his wife, but she had already turned to take Eglano's hand.

"I shall take my leave now," said the pale woman. "But I look forward to hearing your tale in the morn."

The old singer bowed as she left the hall, dragging her younger son after her despite his muffled protests. Nigan, however, put his hand on Egan's shoulder and, much to the young prince's relief, indicated that he should stay.

"Now we are alone," said Nigan. "Egan will remain with us, for he will soon come into his full princehood. In any case, I doubt he could bear it otherwise. So tell us, Lord Väinämöinen, what is the grim tale that you bring to trouble our counsels in Etelamaa?"

"It is grim to be sure, grim and deadly serious. Your kingdom is threatened, my lord—you and all your folk and, indeed, all of the Seven Clans of the Far Northern Land. Your enemy of old has returned and plots to finish what she began more than five hundred years ago. Listen to me, king of the Etelalaiset, for I come to give you this warning! Löhi is awake!"

They looked at the wizard with wonder, troubled by more than just his warning. The Swan Folk did not speak Löhi's name, and it had long been taboo among them to do so.

"Erilainen you may be, Väinämöinen," said Toiva. "Yet we are not. Would you bring down ill fortune on the Etelalaiset by uttering that name in the Hall of the Swan?"

Väinämöinen laughed grimly.

"Darkness may find your doorstep come nightfall without ever being named," he said. "But it's true that I forgot your custom. You need not fear Löhi's name. You will not summon her or her ill will by speaking her name, even were you singers and men of power. She is too strong for that. Whatever you call her, these ill tidings are the same. She has awoken after her centuries-long slumber, and her dim halls in dreary Sariola, the Witch's Keep, are lit again. The world is changing. You will all soon be at risk."

"How do you know this?" asked Nigan. "Wizard you may be, Väinämöinen, but the songs and legends tell us that the Witch of the North died long ago, slain by Lemminkäinen, the greatest of us all. Some say she lives on as a spirit of menace during winter or times of pestilence. But awake? In the flesh, you mean? How can that be?"

Then Väinämöinen told his tale. As with Pekka the Fat in Keskimaa and Teemu in Deep Länismaa, he told of his unrest and his journey north beyond the Marches, and of what he had seen: scouts of the Itäläiset and unclean things and other signs of Löhi's stirring. He also told the king of Ilkka's report of murder on the Marches, and the seeming return of trolls from distant woods. The old man said nothing about the black phantom in the Totkametsa and the trial of his strength, however. He feared saying too much too soon, and doubted they would believe that such an evil was already within their midst.

His tale was new to the king, and Nigan found the March Warden's report especially troubling. There was a Warden House in the city, and many men of the Swan Folk served on the Marches, but no news like this had yet reached Etelamaa. He comforted himself that, even if it were true, the North Marches were far away and Etelamaa was very strong. Even if Väinämöinen had really seen these things, it did not mean that the Witch had returned or that the kingdom was threatened.

"Your news is evil indeed, Lord Väinämöinen," the king said at last. "If true, it is possibly the worst that has come to Etelamaa in all of my time. Tomorrow I will call my council and you shall repeat your tale. Then we will consider how these things may affect the Swan Folk."

"Very good," said the old man. "May you consider well. And, if I may be bold, I will offer my counsel as I offered it to your forefathers, for I fear the storm is closer than I had hoped, my lord. I am ill at ease and without rest, and my disquiet has grown throughout the summer. I deem you must act soon or it will be too late."

"We shall see," answered Nigan. "But at least tonight you may rest at ease. My men will show you to your quarters."

Väinämöinen took his leave of the king, and Egan watched the tall old man in his travel-stained clothes leave the blue and white hall. The boy, fascinated by the singer and his story, had scarcely been able to contain himself. Only a quick, stern glance from his father, who sensed his excitement, had kept him from breaking in with questions. As the king and Toiva withdrew to discuss the mage's tidings, Nigan bid his son good night. Egan knew he wouldn't be able to sleep. His heart and mind raced with visions of Väinämöinen the Singer and the tale of Löhi.

***

Egan went to his chamber and pretended to prepare for bed. As soon as Orvo left, however, he slipped out and crept about the castle's lower chambers in hopes of coming upon Väinämöinen. Egan knew the old castle better than anyone, and he knew how to keep out of sight. Sure enough, he soon found the wizard alone in a small room off the main kitchen. The old man had just pushed back a large plate that appeared mostly empty. He poured the dregs from a jug of beer, which also seemed mostly empty, into a great mug, upon which the Swan Crest of Etelamaa was impressed.

Egan's father had not instructed him to avoid the old man or stay away, though the boy knew that neither his father nor his masters would be pleased if he spoke with Väinämöinen alone—at least, not until they knew more about the singer and the strange errand that had brought him back to Etelamaa. He felt guilty as he approached the old wizard, as if eyes were watching him while he committed a crime, but he was too excited to pass up the chance to talk to the legend who had so unexpectedly come among them.

The wizard looked different than when he first arrived. Väinämöinen had washed away the stains from his journey, and his long white beard was neatly brushed and forked in two. He wore a fresh tunic of pale blue with a glittering golden chain around his neck. Egan, polished son of the king of Etelamaa though he was, felt self-conscious standing before him and awkwardly bowed. Väinämöinen raised his mug in salute and nodded. He spoke first, trying to put the boy, who was clearly uncomfortable, at ease as best he could.

"Good evening, my young man. What can I do for you? I'd ask you to pull up a chair and have a mug with me if there were any beer left, or if you were older. But it's nice—aye, it is—to have a jug full of cold southern beer. Clean and strong! Northern barley's too poor, and home brew's too weak up there. It takes a southerner to grow good hops and make strong drink!"

Egan noticed that the old man's face was red and that he seemed in much better spirits than earlier. After a moment's hesitation, the boy plunged in.

"Excuse me, Lord Väinämöinen. I hope I'm not disturbing you. I was passing this way and thought I might have a word with you, if your lordship permits."

"By all means," said Väinämöinen, approving of the prince's formality as thoroughly as he had Vilho's. "A fair spoken word should not be denied, especially when the speaker is a prince. I am at your service. What can I do for you?"

There were a thousand questions that Egan wished to put to Väinämöinen—questions about the Erilaiset, the world's origins, the magic that the great singers had mastered, or the history of the Far Northern Land and the many wars that had swept across it. Try as he might, however, Egan could not put a single one into words.

He stood on one leg while the old man watched him until he finally blurted out, "I have read and heard quite a lot about you, Väinämöinen. Studied, I mean. I have studied many things about you and your deeds."

"I'm glad to hear it," said the wizard. "Then knowledge and learning have not wholly disappeared from mortal lands, nor is all lore forgotten."

"Oh no," said the prince. "Not in Etelamaa, at least."

"And what tales have you studied, Egan? What do they teach now in the Stone City?"

"Many things," answered Egan. "Tales about the world's beginning, about the coming of men and women into the Far Northern Land, and the origins of the Seven Clans. I have heard songs about your battle with Joukahainen, how you caught the great pike in Lake Etelajärvi, and how you stole the Sampo from the Witch's halls after she had taken it from Tapiola, the White City of Tavastia. And I have read about the Great War, and how all the lands were laid waste by the Witch of the North. And you were there! Hundreds, even thousands of years ago, before the Kaamoslaiset ever came to this land!"

Väinämöinen, well pleased, stood up and bowed low to the boy. "I am at your service, my prince. I can see you have a question in you, or perhaps many. Go ahead; don't be shy. Ask away!"

"Well," said Egan, more comfortable now and growing bolder. "Is it true what you said earlier about Lo—about the Witch, the queen of the Erilaiset? Are you sure that she has really returned?"

"You may speak her name if you wish to, Egan. You heard what I said earlier. You won't summon her that easily—not Löhi. It's strange that here in Etelamaa, and perhaps still in Tavastia, too, men won't speak Löhi's name, and yet the Swan Folk and all the other clans speak that which used to be taboo—the right names of your totems—without fear or hesitation. The contradictions of youth! But yes, my young friend, I am afraid it is so. I am sure, quite sure. Löhi is awake again. She has returned."

"But the Erilaiset, the heroes, befriended men of old. They helped us—*you* helped us—and taught us many things: how to live in this land, the very center of the world. Why does Lo—why does Löhi hate us? Why did your queen betray us?"

Väinämöinen sat back down and considered the boy's earnest face. "First of all, let's get one thing straight; Löhi is no queen, or at least no queen of the Erilaiset! It is true that some Erilaiset served her, but so did other folk, even mortal men; many Erilaiset tried to stop her, which men do not now remember. I know. I was one of them. But she came to call herself a queen in order to frighten mortals and to drive a wedge between them and the Erilaiset. In that she succeeded, though she herself was thrown down and her armies destroyed. The queen of the Erilaiset indeed! I think not. We are free and none have any claim over us! But Löhi is strong, Egan, strong and powerful. Indeed she is. She is the strongest of any of us, and always has been."

"Stronger than you, Väinämöinen?"

"Aye, lad. Stronger even than old Väinämöinen. She has become more like the Vanhalaiset now, who mortal men call gods—like Ilmatar, the Lady of the Skies, and Akka, Mistress of Earth, or old Tapio, Lord of the Forests, and Ahti, Master of Waters. The Vanhalaiset came into this world ages ago, long before Väinämöinen and the Erilaiset. They were sent by Ukko the

Creator to shape this world and mold it, prepare it for the things that were to follow. The oldest songs of the Erilaiset tell about how they walked the earth or flew through the skies in forms both fair and terrible. Ahti gathered the waters and made the great seas and rivers; Akka raised her hand and up rose tall mountains from the shapeless earth. Yet this was long before the time of the Erilaiset.

"But as the ages passed, the Vanhalaiset came to walk in forms less and less like those of mortal race. Their power and being encompassed all the world and passed into the very elements themselves. Tapio sleeps within the heart of each tree in the forest. The power of Ahti runs through every stream and brook and rolls the waves of the deep sea. Theirs is the power that the singers drew from, and which makes possible our spells and charms." Väinämöinen drained the dregs from his mug and sighed.

"Not so with Löhi," he said. "She may dominate others or teach them fell things, but no true singer or wizard draws their strength from her essence or being. Her magic is black and false. Great as she became—beyond the measure of mortals or Erilaiset—still she fell short of that mark. Like to the Vanhalaiset she became in some ways, but she will never be one of them."

"But in what ways is she like the Vanhalaiset?" asked Egan. "They are everywhere, all around us, are they not?"

"Yes," said Väinämöinen. "And such was Löhi's ambition. I knew her long ages ago, Egan, back when I was young, and the green of the grass and the blue of the sky were new and unstained. She was very beautiful then. Her hair was long and dark, and her skin white as alabaster. Mighty among the Erilaiset she was, even then. Far and wide she roamed over the world, and often I roamed with her. We were always looking for new things and trying to discover their names. And we made and sang many songs!" Väinämöinen sighed deeply and shook his head.

"You know, Egan, it was so long ago that now, when I tell the tale, it's as if I'm talking about someone else or remembering a song that I was taught. But it was me! These things I saw with my own eyes and did with my own hands, even if they are now lost and confused in the murky and sad realm of memory.

"But as for Löhi—well, as I said, she roamed far and wide. And she learned to take on many new forms, too. I have never been much of a shape-shifter, although a dear friend of mine is one of the best. It's a dangerous thing to do, even for the greatest mages. The longer you stay in different forms, the more difficult it is to come back; you may forget who you are and perhaps never return. Not so with Löhi! She took many shapes and had no fear. Sometimes we saw her soaring high in the sky like a great eagle, then like a silver seabird, fleet of wing. She bounded through the woods as a great white hart and swam with the creatures of the sea. Less wholesome forms she took as well, but I don't care to remember those.

"Slowly, she became estranged from most of us—or, at least from me and my friends, and our closest folk. Always she had best loved the cold climes of the farthest north, until at last she seldom left them to come among us. When she did, I didn't care for the company she kept: trolls and dark Hiisia, elves that shunned the sun and walked only in the deepest forests, and other unfriendly things. She was enamored of the cold winds and frozen ice, and of winter's dark power, so she made her abode in the north. Only, it wasn't called Pohjola then, but Talvimaa, which is *Winterland* in your tongue. And something happened then, Egan, that we do not understand. Even today, I don't understand. Somehow, in some way, Löhi changed.

"We are all vessels, Egan, filled with light or clear water perhaps, shining in the world's dark uncertainty. How much of that radiance shines forth depends upon our choices and what we do with our lives. Mortal or Erilaiset, we are great or strong in spirit according to this measure. But none can shine brighter or grow more powerful than their native strength allows. Vessels are finite and circumscribed. They hold only so much. Can you understand that, Egan?"

"I think so," said the boy. "You mean that there are bounds to our strength or to how strong we may become. But some people may never come near those bounds, nor ever reach their potential."

Väinämöinen smiled. "So it is for all living things, or so we thought. Not so with Löhi! Alone among mortals and Erilaiset, she somehow broke the natural bounds that encompass us all through the sheer strength and force of her will. She realized her potential and thirsted for more, and somehow became greater still! She was changed. And the world changed with her.

"Her power and being spread far and wide. In some ways, it seemed she'd mingled the elements of the Vanhalaiset together. She commanded the cold winds of Ilmatar and twisted the frozen waters of Ahti into strange and wondrous shapes. I walked through her ice castles then: white towers with frozen spires that reached higher into the sky than any mountain in the world. No tree grew in Tapio's snow-covered forests, save those under her dominion, and the very earth was frozen and mixed with frosts. She raised great mountains of ice and rock, and like the Vanhalaiset, her being passed into them. Nearly all the Far Northern Land was covered with snow. Only here, along the coasts, was the land free from Löhi's frost.

"No more did Löhi walk the earth in visible form, but we heard her voice in the north wind, calling to us! We felt her touch in the walls of ice. We saw her face in the flurries of snow. She called to us to worship her, or to join our power to hers. I tried to talk to her at times, walking through the white forests as the wind blew. I don't know if she heard me, or if she *could* hear me by then. I think she sought no less than to cover all the world with ice and snow, and to bring all things under her dominion. But that she could not do. She was no Vanhalainen, only a pale imitation. Great as she was, she could not be in all places at once. She could not stop the seasons or rule the tides, stars and sun. Mistress of Winter, she could be no more: such was her appointed place. But what did Löhi care? Her cold hand stretched over all the north, and all things in the Far Northern Land—birds, beasts and Erilaiset—lived according to her rhythms."

Väinämöinen suddenly stopped and stared down at the empty mug. Egan was fascinated by his tale. No one in Etelamaa—at least no one he had ever heard—knew the old man's story and the history of the earliest days. He waited for the wizard to continue, but Väinämöinen seemed tired, or perhaps lost in a reverie, and fell silent.

At last, Egan, eager to hear more, broke the silence.

"But what happened next, Lord Väinämöinen? How did you win back the Far Northern Land? And you haven't yet told me why Löhi hates the clans."

The old man looked up at the boy with a sad and weary, but still patient expression on his face.

"Win back the land? We didn't. It was no power of the Erilaiset that broke Löhi's grip. I know many things and can guess many others, but I don't know everything. How can I explain it? The world changed, even as Löhi had changed it, or as I feel it to be changing now. Perhaps Löhi lost herself and slept too deeply, or perhaps the Vanhalaiset were finally roused and pushed her power back. Perhaps it was something else. It began slowly, very slowly, but then it quickened!" Väinämöinen became animated again as he continued.

"The summers grew warmer and suddenly lengthened. Ice on the lakes broke up early. The sea didn't freeze during winter. Löhi's great mountains retreated and fell apart, leaving their rocks and boulders scattered far and wide. Then was the springtime of the Erilaiset! Löhi's reach withdrew even to the bounds of old Talvimaa, and wide lands that were lost to us were again green and covered in trees. Many new things we found then: spirits of the forests and waters made flesh, newcomers to the Erilaiset, and, for the last time, many children were born to us. I sang many songs as the land bloomed, and still Löhi showed no sign.

"Then, even as her power waned and the world was renewed, mortals came to us: the fathers of your longfathers, fleeing from enemies in the south who had all but destroyed them. That tale I think you know, or at least part of it."

"Of course," said Egan. "The Erilaiset helped the people in their time of need and taught us how to live in the Far Northern Land."

"If only more of your folk remembered it," said Väinämöinen. "So it was. Such was the part appointed us. Mortals may be short-lived, but ever they increase and multiply, while folk of other races fade. And so, mortal men—the Kaamoslaiset, as we named them—thrived and spread throughout the lands, and the great clans were founded, and finally even the great kingdoms. All seemed well in the Far Northern Land, even if mortals warred against each other or against the fathers of the Itäläiset. But it was not so. Löhi was awake at last!

"Who knows the hour when at last she became aware of what had happened—that she was again fenced in a small land and her dominion diminished? I don't know, but I think she watched for a long time and what she saw, Egan, was *you*: mortals, newcomers that she had not known before, coming to the north, cutting down its trees, taming its wild fields, building villages and towns, and spreading throughout the land—her land, if you will. And she hated you and blamed you for her fading.

"And then, Egan, she surprised us yet again. Löhi, Mistress of Winter, the most fell spirit of the dark born on the north wind's wings—after an age, she again took form and walked the earth wrapped in flesh. She came to me then, and made an offer that I rejected. Strange she looked, her face smooth and expressionless like a mask, as if she had forgotten what a real woman looked like during her long sleep. Strange she looked and strange it was to see her again in flesh incarnate after so very long. I believe she thought that if she could but drive out the Seven Clans and destroy the usurpers of her domain, she could again reclaim her own. Perhaps she was right. There are songs and prophecies among my kin that speak of such things.

"But you know, or should know, what followed next. She made herself into a great magician and gathered to her all evil things; the Hiisia of the north became her servants, and others besides, even mortals of different races with whom she made league. She gained new powers and could send her *etiäin-en* before her, even to enter into dreams and so make the dreamers do her bidding. Then Talvimaa became Pohjola—Northland—and she became its queen, the Witch of the North. She warred with the clans and nearly all the Far Northern Land was laid waste ere she was defeated."

"And now she has returned again, Lord Väinämöinen?" Egan asked.

"Yes, Egan," the old man said. "She has returned."

If at first Egan was speechless out of awe for the old wizard, by then there were easily a thousand questions on the tip of his tongue. The story of Löhi filled him with wonder, as well as a dimly felt fear or foreboding. He was too excited to dwell on fear, however.

"Lord Väinämöinen," he said. "What abou—"

"More questions?" Väinämöinen interrupted. "I thought the tale of Löhi, that I have not told in full to any mortal in many a year, would be enough for you to chew on for one night!"

"I do appreciate my lord's generosity and patience," said the boy, instinctively falling back into the language of court that he knew so well. "But if I may be so bold as to ask one more question before my lord retires..."

"Oh, very well," said Väinämöinen. "A fair tongue, well-practiced I should think, should not be denied."

"Thank you, my lord. I only wish to ask you this. I understand better now, if not perfectly, why the Witch hates men and women. But, my lord, what about *you*? I think I can guess the offer the Witch made to you, and though I knew few tales about *her*, there are many tales about *you* that are remembered among the Swan Folk. Löhi chose to be our enemy, but you chose to be our friend. You aided my grandfather during our time of troubles. Even now, you return again to warn us, to help us. Why?"

"We all have choices, Egan. All of us, mortals and heroes alike. And yet, if a man or woman grows in stature and wisdom, our true choices become fewer. Therein lies the paradox and the real test of our being. We have choices because we are free and are not like animals—creatures of instinct—or like elements of nature, wild and unthinking. We have minds and souls, and know within us right and wrong in good measure. Lord of Etelamaa or slave in Akkala, we choose what we do and what mark we make in the world. But someone who carefully considers their deeds and their effects—in time, they choose little. They have the strength of their convictions and so finally they do not do what they *choose*, but rather what they *must*. It's a difficult thing—aye, a difficult thing." Väinämöinen smiled. "And that should answer your question, young prince, about my deeds, at any rate. Not that I'm answerable to you, a half-sized truant of a prince, if tales be true." The old man laughed, a rich, infectious laugh, and Egan found himself laughing, too.

"I like you, Väinämöinen," he said with a child's certainty and sincerity, and the old man smiled still more broadly.

"I like you, too, Prince Egan," he said. "In fact, I like you so much that I'll tell you a secret—there's an old man not far from this place looking for you, and, from the sound of it, he'll be here any minute."

"Orvo!" said Egan. "He would be looking for me now."

"Then you should go quickly if you do not wish him to find you."

Egan ran to the door, but turned and called back to Väinämöinen.

"I'll see you again tomorrow, won't I?"

"Indeed you will, if you are with your father. For I have much to discuss with him still."

Väinämöinen watched the boy disappear, then stared blankly at the door for a few moments before shaking his head. "Aye, they are indeed alike," he said to himself in a low voice. "Very alike. Bright shines the candle within them."

The old man had been given a small room in the castle's newer halls. He lay on his back on a soft bed filled with goose down and closed his eyes. Seldom had Väinämöinen felt so tired, and the thought crossed his mind that, Erilainen though he was, he was growing very ancient; perhaps the change of the world that he felt in his bones would be the last he would see. The long weeks spent on the southward journey had made him weary, and the encounter in the woods with the dark spirit deepened his tiredness. He wished only to drift off into a deep slumber of forgetfulness and lay aside his many cares for a night.

But the sleep of a wizard was not like the sleep of other men, and strange dreams and visions often came unbidden to trouble them. For, as the wise said, *What happens today was dreamed of last night.* Väinämöinen's mind wandered down the path of rest and repose, but in the end, he found neither. Even as the young prince of Etelamaa's, his dreams were quickly filled with fire and burning.

Väinämöinen was no mortal boy, however. His mind was subtle and his eyes saw far. He understood what he saw, and he put forth his power, and his spirit flew out into the dark night. He watched the flames consume the little world of men, and heard the screams of mortals as they fled in terror; he saw the curved swords stained with blood. He finally pierced the darkness that strove to block his sight and so passed through, even to High Länsimaa and the Marches. When at last he found what he had sought, he was afraid.

When Egan awoke the next morning, he dressed quickly and ran to the Hall of the Swan, where his father waited for Väinämöinen—or so he thought. He found many people there talking excitedly, but not the singer. The guards atop the Keep's high wall and at the stone bridge reported that the old man had ridden off in the early morn while others yet slept, and as the sun's red orb rose, casting an orange glow upon the Far Northern Land, he had galloped through the streets like a gale and struck the Kingsway to the north. So passed Väinämöinen from the Stone City, and rumor of his strange coming and going spread throughout the kingdom.

But soon there were other tidings to consider, which made men forget the ancient singer and his short, mysterious visit.

Chapter Six

Flight

Päivikki was standing in Grankulta's dusty lane throwing scraps to the dogs and trying to keep order among the village's young children when Ilkka and half a dozen Wardens appeared, bringing the little girl with dark hair back to her home. Ulla's return was as welcome as it was unexpected. Nearly a month had passed since Väinämöinen had taken the little girl with him on the road to the south, and neither Päivikki nor Reiko thought to ever see her again.

There had been much commotion and excitement among the children when the men rode up on their tall horses. The villagers had begged the Wardens to stay the night and celebrate Ulla's return with them, but the men accepted only a quick meal, some dark rye bread and smoked fish for their packs, and hay for their horses before starting off again for the Marches.

As for Ulla, while she was happy to be with her family again in the little village in the north of High Länsimaa, she was sad to see Ilkka and the Wardens ride away. She had grown used to travel and speedy journeys in the weeks since the bear attack, and she enjoyed the Wardens' company, their rough but kind manners, and the feel and smell of their great horses. There was something else as well, a difference about the girl that she herself could perceive, even if she lacked the words to express it.

She had experienced things that were previously unimaginable to her; she understood now that a wide and wonderful world existed beyond the narrow confines of Grankulta. From the iron mines of Suurijärvi to the peaked roofs and painted gables of Keskimaa, she had seen many things and so was changed. Moreover, the little girl knew there was no one in Grankulta, and no one in the other little villages nearby—not Päivikki, nor Reiko, nor anyone she had ever known—who could say as much or truly understand what she had seen, what she wished to tell them. If there had been a thin veil between her and other folk before, woven by her losses and the sadness thereof, it was thickened now and made closer. Still, she was glad to be home, and this *was* her home; a maid-child of a poor village in the Far Northern Land she was, and remained.

Päivikki used most of the family's precious honey to bake several round, sweet cakes to celebrate Ulla's homecoming, and her uncle slaughtered a fat sheep and boiled the meat in a great copper kettle. The girl was excited because she had gifts for her folk. The Wardens had bought copper rings in Keskimaa for her cousins, as well as a fine tin chain with several thin hoops of dark bronze and a spiral clasp for her aunt. Väinämöinen himself had given Ilkka silver to buy a short, bone-handled knife made of bloodrock for Ulla's uncle. Made winterfast by smiths in the south, it easily cut through the thickest hide or toughest sinew, and would never become brittle in the bitter cold of the long northern winter.

So the homecoming was celebrated, and the little girl's aunt held her close, and all seemed right with the world. But the toil and work of humble folk on the northern borders waited for none; soon the rhythms of life in Grankulta returned and the remarkable events of that peculiar summer receded.

It was late summer, and the Bear Folk had to harvest the rye that grew in their fields and gather it to be threshed, winnowed and ground for bread, or mixed with peas and beans for porridge, or else fermented into *sahti*, the home-brewed beer of the north. Afterward, when fall came, the fields would need to be spread with manure for the coming year. Markets would be strung along the North Road, where the villagers could barter what little they had to offer: birchsap and honey, or pelts of red squirrels, foxes, beavers, and sable or the black grouse, alive or dead, whose feathers were prized in the south.

In exchange, they might obtain useful things of bronze or iron, bolts of finespun wool from southern sheep and hemp for cloth, or swine and other animals. Sacks of turnips, and pickled greens and cabbages that grew in better soil were always in demand. The pelt of the bear that had attacked Ulla might fetch a heavy price: a pony or a small milk cow, or barrels of dried apples to last throughout the winter. But the villagers remembered Väinämöinen's words, and even if some were tempted to seek it out, none did so.

On a bright, late summer day, the little girl with dark hair stood in the dusty lane, looking back toward the cone-shaped *kotas* and the other sheds and outbuildings scattered behind the village's little cottages. The yellow sun was hot, and a warm breeze blew from the south. The wind fanned the trees so the leaves seemed to flicker and change colors, from green to yellow and back to green again. It seemed then to Ulla that she had never seen the colors around her so sharply or clearly before; she felt a strange sense of excitement and tension, a feeling which had been growing within her ever since she had awoken with the Mark of the Clan upon her shoulder.

Down the street, the brown and tan of her family's *pirtii* stood out against a background of brilliant green. A ditch ran the length of the road on one side, filled with shiny black mud with silver trails; the blue, cloudless sky was luminous. The day was so bright that the little girl almost felt she couldn't contain herself, and for some reason was compelled to commit every detail to memory.

She was standing with her cousins Meria—who was older than her—and Siria, and several other children, looking out over a fallow field where the sheep grazed, a field that stretched to a distant tree line. Most of the adults and older children were working in the fields beyond the trees, cutting and stacking the ripened rye, although Päivikki and some other women were baking bread in the *pätsi*, the piled-stone oven that stood among the *kotas*. The children watched a hazy cloud of black smoke rising from somewhere behind the tree line. It broke and drifted on the wind, staining the blue sky beyond. The previous evening, just before sunset, the folk of Grankulta had seen a great black smoke far to the north. It was too early to be burning stubble in cut fields or clearing new land, and some thought there was a fire in the distant forest. It was far away, though, and of no concern to them; this time, the black smoke seemed much nearer.

Several dogs—the long-haired, shaggy, black and grey hounds of the Karhulaiset with blue eyes and wolf-like muzzles—ran about the children, nipping at their knees and begging for scraps. Meria spoke sharply to them, pushing away one that leapt up on her. The fair-haired girl held a baby boy in her arms: Onni, Päivikki's youngest child, who was born the previous summer. She narrowed her eyes and peered at the funnel of smoke above the green.

At that moment, two figures emerged from the trees and ran across the sheep's field, past the animal pen—not toward the children, but toward the cluster of cottages down the lane. Even from a distance, Ulla could make out who they were: Kaiho, a young man who lived with his wife and baby in a nearby *pirtti*, and an older man named Siuoko. They seemed to be running wildly, as fast as they could, stumbling now and again as they came on. Handing the baby to Ulla, Meria cupped her hands around her mouth and called to them, but they didn't hear her, or else paid her no attention. The dogs took off down the street to meet the men, and the children came bounding after them.

By the time the children arrived, Päivikki and several women had come round from the big stone oven behind the cottages. The old man, Siuoko, dropped to the ground and gasped for breath, but Kaiho spoke frantically in a wheezing voice, his eyes darting wildly about him.

"Take the children and run!" he shouted. "Go now, and don't wait for anything! There are men everywhere, men on horses, riders of the Itäläiset! They're already in Fallkulta, burning and killing as they come; go into the woods, hide now, and stay hidden! Run!"

The women shouted frantic questions back at him about their husbands and children in the fields, but Kaiho, his face red and sweating, seemed unable to understand them and implored them to run all the more urgently. He turned toward his own *pirtti*, where his wife, having heard the commotion, waited in the doorway. But Päivikki grabbed his shoulders and turned him around.

"Where is Reiko?" she asked sternly, as if speaking to an unruly or impertinent child. "Reiko and Kaisa—tell me where they are."

The young man paused a moment and caught his breath. "I don't know," he said, shaking his head. "I don't know. Just take the children and go. Go now!"

Confusion was all about, and Ulla didn't understand what was happening. Some of the women and children began crying, so she began crying, too, though she wasn't sure why. Her aunt snatched little Onni from her arms and pushed the three girls—Ulla, Siria and Meria—into their *pirtti*. The sobbing girls shouted at Päivikki, trying to make sense of things as the farmer's wife rushed about and the baby wailed. Päivikki understood the young man's words of warning well enough; moments earlier she had been a simple woman of the north, baking bread and managing the ceaseless toil that was the lot of the women of the Karhulaiset, but in an instant, that world had changed and nothing again might ever be the same. Only one thought ran through her mind, one overwhelming priority. *The children must survive.*

Päivikki quickly put shoes on the girls' bare feet, grabbing whatever was closest: birch-bark shoes for Meria and, for Ulla, her red winter boots from Karelia. She tied leather straps with small pouches around their waists and shoved pieces of hard rye bread inside. Setting Onni down, she gathered the girls to her and knelt before them, brushing the hair from their faces and hugging them each in turn. Ulla could see tears welling in her aunt's eyes, but her face and voice betrayed nothing.

"Listen to me, all of you," she said sternly. "Go now and don't look back. Run as fast as you can into the woods past the stony brook. Run across the road and as far into the deep forest as you can! Hide there and stay there until we come for you; do you understand? Hide there and stay! Meria, take care of them and do what I say! I will find your father and the others, and we'll come for you later. But run as fast as you can now and don't come out, no matter what you see or hear, until it's safe!"

"*Äidini*," said Meria through her tears. "Mother, no!"

But Päivikki pulled the girls out of the smoky cottage and into the lane. Villagers and animals were running about everywhere, but one group of women and children was loosely gathered beside a *kota*. A thin woman, Hebla, called to them as the crowd began to move down the road.

"Päivikki!" she cried. "Come quickly! Come with us!"

Päivikki pushed the girls into the crowd, tearing herself loose from Meria, who still clung to her mother's arm.

"Meria! Ulla, Siria, run! Go on now, run! Follow Hebla and the others, and stay in the woods until I come for you! Go!"

So Ulla found herself scampering off with the gaggle of woman and children down Grankulta's dusty lane. Black smoke was rising now from the direction of Fallkulta and the little girl could hear cries, shouts, and a rumor of distant commotion. Where the lane ended, they took to the gentle rise behind the cottages and ran across a small meadow, through the shallow brook, and into the forest beyond. Ulla looked back toward her *pirtti* and saw her aunt, clutching little Onni and racing across the sheep's field toward the tree line. Then Meria was beside her, yelling at Ulla to keep running, and she turned and sprinted with the others into the little wood.

The women and children moved quickly through the sparse wood. Meria was some ways in front, but frequently turned and called back to the younger girls to keep up. As confused as she was, Ulla still understood somewhat more than the other children about what was happening and why they were running wildly through the forest. She had heard what Kaiho said about the Itäläiset and remembered her father's stories and Väinämöinen's tale. That had been long ago and in faraway Karelia, however. How could the Easterners be here in Grankulta, and what could they possibly want?

Ulla could run swiftly, and kept her eyes on Meria's long brown skirt and tried to stay close to her. The group spread out as they moved through the woods, but Ulla caught a glimpse of Siria to her right, running with a boy from their village, while Pilkka and several other dogs trailed excitedly behind.

There were more figures to her left, shouting as they half-ran, half-stumbled through the trees. Ulla realized they were not from Grankulta, but strangers, perhaps from Fallkulta or elsewhere, coming from further south. The groups mingled and soon became a mass of people moving more or less together through the woods. Much shouting and cries came from behind them and, even through the trees, the frightened villagers could see smoke in the sky, rising close by and from the direction in which Grankulta lay.

If Ulla had considered it, she might have realized she was near the place where the bear attacked her and where she first met Väinämöinen, but she was growing weary and concentrated all her fading energy on pumping her legs and following Meria. For a moment, there was a young man directly beside her; he was probably from Fallkulta since she didn't recognize him. He carried a small boy, perhaps two years old, who smiled and laughed as he bounced on his father's shoulder, reckoning nothing of fear or flight on the mad romp through the woods.

Then the trees failed, and she saw Meria motioning and calling, "Lumikki, Siria!"

She crashed out of the forest onto the North Road, which, in one direction, led to the Marches and, in the other, carved a path toward Suurijärvi and finally the heart of High Länsimaa.

Ulla stood in the road, breathless and panting, while more villagers charged out of the trees, but an older woman from Grankulta gave a cry and pointed north. On the road ahead, perhaps a hundred yards away, sat two riders on great brown horses. The little girl's sharp eyes could see their black garb, festooned with flashes of red, and their long hair. One of the men stood in his stirrups, his face turned up and head cocked to one side as if he were staring at a bird high in the sky or listening intently to distant sounds. The other sat beside him, a long, curved sword in his right hand. The swordsman suddenly noticed the Karhulaiset spilling into the road and called out in the Easterners' harsh tongue. He spurred his horse on, straight toward the gathering crowd, his companion following close behind, and the Bear Folk screamed in terror and plunged into the thicker forest on the North Road's far side in headlong, panicked flight.

Ulla ran madly through the dense trees, stumbling and scrambling as she went. There were dreadful screams and cries all about her, and a great din of yelling from the road behind. She caught glimpses of people everywhere running wildly, but couldn't find Meria or recognize anyone in the confusion. She began screaming for her father in her fright and didn't stop. Then it seemed to the little girl that she suddenly heard Väinämöinen's voice, as if he were whispering in her ear, faint yet clear, the words he had spoken at their parting.

"Never give up, child! Even when all seems lost, never stop fighting!"

Ulla closed her eyes for a moment, shutting out the surrounding chaos; she clenched her tiny fists. When she opened her eyes again, her mind was made up.

It was difficult to find a clear path through the woods. The trees, stripped of bark by the farmers to be cut and burned the next season, grew close together with many fallen trunks and branches blocking the way; there were slippery stones and puddles scattered across the marshy forest floor. Ulla had often hunted with her father in deep woods, but they had usually gone west, so she was a relative stranger to the thick woods east of Grankulta. She had no real idea where she was or where to run. Fire, danger, and terrible riders lay behind her, so she ran as fast as she could to escape them and, as she dodged a fallen birch that blocked her path, crashed straight into an Itäläinen who suddenly loomed before her.

The man was tall, taller than Big Janni or Reiko and most of the men in the district around Grankulta. His curling brown hair hung loose to his shoulders and, though he was almost beardless, he had long, drooping mustachios. Sweat and grime streaked his pale face. He wore a vest of hard black leather and sleeves, or vambraces, which were also made of leather and etched with red markings. Ulla could see flashes of the crimson shirt he wore beneath. The Itäläinen grabbed her before she could react and laughed, holding her close to his chest in a vise-like grip.

Ulla struggled like mad and kicked her legs, but the man paid no heed as he laughed and spoke in his strange tongue. He held the girl tightly against his chest with his left arm while he worked a rope around her flailing legs with the other. She abruptly noticed someone on the forest floor off to one side, a young woman, her homespun dress torn and rent, her feet and legs tightly bound, struggling to raise herself on her more loosely tied arms. Ulla could feel the cords looping and tightening about her legs and realized the Easterner was tying her up as a man would tie a goat or calf. If she didn't do something, *anything*, in the next few seconds, she would be caught, a captive of the Itäläiset, a slave to be sent back to their distant lands.

The man's bare left hand was close to Ulla's face as he held her tight, though his right hand, his rein hand, was gloved. One of the girl's arms was pinned beneath her, but the other was free, and with a strength she had never known before, Ulla grabbed the man's bare hand and wrenched it to her mouth, biting as hard as she could with her small, sharp teeth into the fleshy spot between his finger and thumb. She jerked her head violently like an animal fighting for scraps and felt the flesh tear; the salty taste of blood filled her mouth. The Easterner screamed and cursed in his own tongue, but although Ulla slipped down to his waist, he didn't drop her. The girl kicked and thrashed about, feeling the cords loosen and slide from her knees.

Suddenly the world was spinning; trees, leaves and earth whirled before her eyes. The Itäläinen turned the girl upside down and, holding her by the legs, began to bind her again. He shook her and spoke sharply as he reached for his rope, blood dripping onto her face from his wounded hand. Just then there was a loud barking and snarling and, even as the Easterner made ready the knot, Pilkka was there, leaping at him with open jaws. The man fell back with a muffled grunt. Ulla dropped to the forest floor, scrambled to her feet, and ran as fast as she could.

By chance or deep design, the little girl ran further into the woods and away from the road, dimly aware of other villagers running in the same direction. Her heart raced as she sprinted through the trees with the Itäläinen close behind. She could hear his curses and raspy breath, and expected to feel his grip on her shoulders at any moment.

She allowed herself one quick backwards glance and saw the man charging toward her from some ten paces behind. His red face was angry and distorted, and he no longer held any rope in his hand, but a long knife bent on killing and vengeance. Pilkka was nowhere to be seen. Gasping for breath, Ulla raced through the forest and instinctively began to jump from side to side and turn sharply. The little girl and her friends often played chase in the woods, leaping from stone to stone, or dodging trees at the last moment and quickly slipping past. She ran now as if playing such a game, turning this way and that, bounding over mossy holes and deftly sliding past trees. The Easterner's curses grew fainter as he fell behind the sure-footed little girl, struggling to cut sharply on the spongy turf in his great riding boots. Suddenly, he tripped on a slimy rock and sprawled on his face while Ulla ran on.

The girl turned again and saw the man some ways behind her, bent over with his hands on his knees as he tried to catch his breath, eyes glaring in her direction. He straightened, scowling, but then unexpectedly smiled at her, shaking his head. Then, to Ulla's surprise, the man turned and moved back through the woods toward the road, where the other "catchers" of the Itäläiset stood in a line among the trees, waiting for those of the Bear Folk whom they most desired as slaves.

Ulla was like a wild thing. Her senses heightened, she became a creature of instinct. Cries still echoed all around her and people stumbled through the trees, so the girl ran, too, pushing ever deeper into the unknown woods. As the long day passed, the cries became scattered and more remote. Ulla fell in with a small group of refugees who walked rather than running: a boy her own age, several older women, and a young man, perhaps sixteen or seventeen years old, with a red weal flecked with blood across his check. But they were not from Grankulta, and said little to her. The young man seemed more familiar with the woods than the others and, when now and again the women wished to stop and wait, he would sharply urge them on.

"Keep going!" he said. "Can't you hear the cries behind us? The Easterners are still there, and they're coming through the woods. If you sit here, you will die; don't you understand? Keep going!"

And so the little group struggled on as the sun disappeared from the sky above, the shadows lengthened, and the forest slowly grew dark.

As dusk settled over the woods, they came out of the trees into a wide, round clearing like a shallow bowl filled with tall grass and round, black boulders. There were many folk already there, perhaps two dozen, and others continually straggled out of the woods in ones and twos. Exhausted as they were, the people could go no further and, despite the danger, stopped their panicked flight.

Ulla was exhausted, too, and fell to the ground beside some other children. For a while, she lay still. She didn't sleep, however; she was slowly coming back to herself. At length, she stood up and wandered around the clearing, looking for someone she knew. She found a boy from Grankulta—Auvo—and recognized an older girl and her grandmother, but there was no sign of Meria or Siria, or of her aunt, or of anyone else she knew. Whether they were still in the woods, or with another group of Karhulaiset, or captives or victims of the Itäläiset, none could say.

Ulla sat on the ground near the boy from Grankulta and ate some of the bread in her pouch. Many of the Bear Folk were weeping, but others sat very still, staring blankly at the earth with their heads hung low. The girl felt a ball of stuffed rags beneath the dark rye bread in her little pouch and drew it out. There, wrapped in a piece of fine green cloth from Keskimaa, were the two small wooden figures—the girl and her brother—that were her only real possessions in the world. Her aunt had put them in her pouch during those last few frantic moments in the *pirtti*. She looked at them, their paint shining faintly in the darkling woods. The little girl began to cry then, alone as she was, with all that she knew or cared for having been ripped away again. Soon she was sobbing inconsolably, calling out to her father to save her and take her to another place safe from harm. But he was not there.

***

More Karhulaiset came into the clearing during the night as Ulla slept. Most came from the north, from villages distant from Grankulta. Among them were men with axes and knives, some with wounds and bloodied clothes. Not all of the villagers had fled without a fight. One man arrived with his old mother and several children; they had been walking for three days since their village straddling the North Road had been sacked and burned by the Easterners.

Some said that they should stay where they were, for the shallow, grassy bowl seemed a place of relative safety; others thought to wait for dawn and then make their way back to their homes, if possible. When dawn came, however, the wind carried new cries and harsh voices from all around them. An orange glow to the west made it look as if the nearby woods were on fire. They took flight then, scatterlings of northern villages and farms, pushing on south and east to escape the death that lay behind them.

The woods east of the clearing were thinner, and the Bear Folk moved through them quicker. A woman who was somewhat older than Päivikki had brought water to Ulla during the night, so the little girl stayed near her and a small group of children. From time to time, the woman stopped and said a few kind words to her, making sure that Ulla and the other nearby children were alright and that they kept up. They came to a small river that had been forded with slippery stones, and a man suddenly scooped up Ulla and another girl in his brawny arms and carried them through the waist-deep water. The mass of people continued through the forest for the better part of the day, until the trees thinned, then finally stopped at the foot of a gently sloped esker, upon which ran a path.

The path was not as broad as the North Road, but still wide enough for a wagon or cart, and seemed well used. A wide, cleared space stretched from the tree line to the esker's raised top; on the far side, the woods again grew thicker. The villagers hesitated as they came to the tree line, fearful of what lurked on the road or beyond, but saw no sign of any rider and heard no whinnies or hoofbeats. Slowly, they crept from the woods and climbed up to the path. Some pointed south, saying they should take to this new road to speed along their flight, but before any debate began, they heard what they had all feared.

Harsh cries and a horn's call shattered the late summer air. Horsemen suddenly appeared to the north, many more than before, and they charged down the road toward the gathered crowd.

"Run, child, run!" the woman screamed to Ulla. She raced across the cart path toward the trees beyond, but the little girl stood still, staring northward as if transfixed by the tragedy unfolding before her eyes.

The villagers fled this way and that, some running back down the esker's western slope while others plunged into the eastern woods. A few ran past Ulla, fleeing straight down the road in their terror.

Many Itäläiset left the path and swept their horses in front of the panicked people, cutting several down with their curved iron blades and spilling red blood upon the earth. Ulla watched as others chased folk down like trappers, throwing hemp nets over them so that they fell to the ground, hopelessly ensnared. A single Easterner on a tall brown horse sat astride the road, still and calm, with a bent bow ready to shoot at any threat that might arise. He turned his dark gaze on the little girl and, either for sport or because of an evil will, drew back the bow and pointed an arrow at her. She looked straight into his eyes for a moment, but then, as if a spell had suddenly been lifted, she ran, tearing across the road in headlong flight and into the woods on the far side. Behind her, the screams and cries of the scattered Bear Folk echoed through the trees.

So Ulla again found herself moving through the woods, further and further away from the only home she had ever known. She couldn't find the woman who had spoken kind words to her, or Auvo, or anyone else that she recognized, but there were still villagers in the woods, fleeing as best they could from the Itäläiset. The girl followed them through the thick trees and around the little lakes and rushing streams. When darkness fell, she stopped, exhausted, beside a green pond where a few other folk rested. She was asleep almost as soon as she closed her eyes.

She woke before dawn to find a thick mist all about her. Strange figures moved among the trees like flickering ghosts or spirits. Ulla started, fearing they were Itäläiset, but quickly saw that they were not. The dim figures in the misty woods were even as she: poor farm folk in homespun clothing, weary and worn from their ordeal. The girl stirred and followed the ghosts eastward, away from the fear that still loomed behind her.

After several hours, the woods failed abruptly and Ulla came out of the trees onto a low, grassy rim that sloped sharply down to yet another road—this one as broad as the North Road—that bordered a long blue lake and ran southeast into the distance. There were many Bear Folk strung along the road; others sat in the grass and reeds beside the lake. The people could go no further. The eastern way was blocked, the lake was wide and deep, and there were many other streams and marshes beyond. The refugees had come all the way to the lands just above Suurijärvi, and there were few paths through those parts. They could only take the road, stay in the wood, or make their way back toward their homes. Some of the folk debated about what to do, but despite the danger and their fear of the horsemen, they finally began to move southeast down the road, first in small groups and then in a long, straggling chain—men, women and children of the north. The little girl with dark hair, from the village that was no more, went with them.

So began the great flight of the Karhulaiset that afterward was woven into many songs of loss and woe. For three generations, the Folk of the Bear had spread throughout the northern reaches of High Länsimaa, building farms and villages where none had been before, and in the space of several days, it was all swept away. The red fire of the Easterners brought an end to the world they had built. For this was no small affray at the borders, but a great raid by hundreds of warriors such as had not been made in many long years. All across the north of High Länsimaa, large bands of Easterners roamed, sacking and burning the villages until the black smoke rose high into the sky, and the forest itself seemed on fire.

And there were other raiders who gathered the slaves they most desired, bound them, and drove them toward their faraway homes or to the great slave markets in the east, where they could be sold for rich reward. They took few men of any age unless they were very young, for the Itäläiset said that men who had been free made poor and dangerous slaves who would turn against their masters and seek vengeance for all they had lost. But boys who knew not what it was to live as a free man would more easily accept their lot. Above all, however, the Itäläiset sought young women and girls, for they would make them servants in their halls and homes or else forcibly take them as their wives or concubines. And healthy children with long lives before them and strength, always fetched the greatest price.

For ten days, Ulla walked that road with the great mass of refugees. Smoke from burning villages was always in the northern and western skies: sometimes distant, sometimes lingering in the blue heavens like a cloud of doom, and sometimes close. The people hurried then, expecting to see the Easterners charge down the road at any moment. As they moved south, more people joined the crowd from all directions, until it swelled to several hundreds spread out along the road. Some of the newcomers brought animals with them—goats and fowl or hungry dogs that loyally followed the masters, reckoning nothing of the swords of the Itäläiset or the disaster of which they, too, were a part. Ulla trudged along, too much in shock to even try to understand what was happening.

One day, as Ulla walked among the press of people, she noticed that another small girl, perhaps a year older than she, walked beside her. The girl was plump, with copper hair and pale skin dotted with freckles from her head to her toes. Her tattered, homespun shirt was even humbler than Ulla's, but she clutched a sack in her hand as if there were treasure inside. Ulla realized that this plump girl was watching her and turned to her with a scowl, but the red-haired little girl smiled, a thing so incongruous amidst that scene of death and despair that Ulla was taken aback and almost smiled herself. She did not speak to the freckled girl, however. She had not spoken since the first night in the clearing, when she called to her father who was not there. Since then, she had returned the words of those who spoke to her, in the woods or on the road, with silence.

The refugees stopped now and again to rest or drink water from clean pools or streams, and when Ulla sat down beside a clump of broken pine stumps to rest her aching legs, the plump girl sat down next to her. She ran her hands through her long curly hair and sighed.

"I don't know if I can keep going much longer," said the girl. "I feel so tired that I can barely walk. I'm from Bassböle, and I've walked, or run, every step of the way. Where are your mother and father? Are they here?"

Ulla studied the strange girl, but said nothing. She thought her very stupid, for if Ulla's parents were indeed among the crowd, she wouldn't be sitting alone. But the red-haired girl was undeterred.

"My name is Kirsikka," she said. "You know what that means, right? Cherry. You probably think they named me that because of my hair, don't you? But you're wrong! My mother said that when I was born, my face was bright red and it stayed that way for a long time, even though the rest of me was white. So she named me Kirsikka. What's your name?"

Ulla looked away.

"So you don't like to talk? It doesn't matter. I heard those men over there talking: the ones with the little cart. They said that they know where we are going. There is a big city in the south, where the lord of the Karhulaiset lives in a great castle made of stone. He has hundreds of warriors with spears and long swords, and when we get there, he'll send them north to kill the Easterners and save our families." Kirsikka sighed again. "I wish we would get there soon."

Heedless of Ulla's silence, Kirsikka kept talking; indeed, the girl seemed capable of producing a never-ending torrent of words, and Ulla began listening in spite of herself. Kirsikka described her village, which Ulla had never heard of. It was a tiny hamlet, smaller even than Grankulta, nestled beside a clear blue lake. Kirsikka had been washing clothes with a few other girls in a rocky, swift-running stream when the Easterners attacked, setting fire to the houses and chasing the villagers into the woods. Almost captured, she had fled down the road in terror. She had seen riders several times on the road, and twice had narrowly escaped their nets, until at last she came upon the crowd of refugees. There were two young women from her village among the crowd, but no others; she had no idea what had become of her parents, her grandmother, and her five brothers and sisters.

Kirsikka groaned and rubbed her freckled legs. Ulla looked at her. The red-haired girl's shoeless feet were torn and bloody. She suddenly reached inside her sack and said, "Oh well. I'm starving to death and can't walk much farther. Now is as good a time as any other. Besides, soon we should be coming to the great city where our warriors are waiting."

Kirsikka pulled out a large hunk of reddish-brown bread, a blood-bread such as the northern villagers made, and tore it in half with some difficulty. She handed half to Ulla, and when she didn't take it, tossed it onto her lap.

"You can have it, really. That's the last there is. I had two loaves and some cheese when we went down to the stream. But this is all that's left."

Ulla had long since eaten the rye that Päivikki packed, but she didn't touch the stale bread at first. It was hard and dry, but Kirsikka still tried to eat some, sucking on the hard crust until it was soft enough to tear off a bite. Relenting at last, Ulla did the same, savoring the blood-flavored bread as if it were the sweetest honey cake she had ever tasted. Halfway through the modest meal, for the first time in several days, Ulla spoke.

"My name is Ulla," she said. "I'm from Grankulta, but I don't know anybody here; I don't know where my family is. They're all gone."

"Ulla?!" exclaimed the red-haired girl. "That's a funny name! I've never heard of *anybody* named Ulla before. But that's alright. I've never met anyone else named Kirsikka, either!"

From that point, the two little girls were friends. Since each was alone with no one to care for her, they walked together, sometimes hand in hand, as the Karhulaiset continued to move to the south and to the east and sought to stay ahead of the Easterners. Ulla told her new friend a little about her aunt and uncle, and life in Grankulta, which was not very different than Kirsikka's after all. She even told her about the journey to the North Marches, when her father and Little Janni had disappeared. She said nothing about the bear, Väinämöinen, or her amazing visit to Keskimaa, however. She didn't think the red-haired girl would believe her, as fantastic as it all sounded. She also didn't have the heart to ruin Kirsikka's hope about the lord of the Bear Folk. Keskimaa was indeed huge—at least to Ulla's mind—and there were more than enough men there to fight off the Easterners. But Ulla had enough wits about her to realize that lost though they might have been, they were nowhere near Keskimaa, which required a journey of many days on horseback, even if one went down good roads. They could plod along for months in the marshes before they ever found it. Her only hope was that someone, *anyone*, would rescue them.

The land began to change as the birches and spruce gave way to firs and pines. The road was true, but it bent this way and that, meandering around lakes and skirting bogs that could be seen—and smelled—even from a distance. Ulla didn't know it, but she was in the lands east of Suurijärvi, between the great lake and the edges of the Karelian Forest. There were fewer villages and fewer people there because the earth was poor and grew little, although bloodrock was mined from the marshy bogs.

Ulla and Kirsikka huddled together for warmth during the short, cool night. Soft underbrush pillowed their heads. The forest's calm lulled them to sleep despite their hunger, while stars twinkled through the canopy.

The next morning, the girls woke early. The bright sun reappeared after its brief rest, cheerfully sparkling just the same. Green leaves flashed golden yellow as sunlight glistened off the dew. A gentle westerly wind stirred the treetops while birdsong filled the air. On such a fine late summer morning, the girls might normally have been eager to start the day off with a gambol through the fragrant, pine-scented forest. But that life seemed a million years and a million miles away, and the desperateness of their situation quickly descended like a dark cloud rolling down from the hills.

Kirsikka stretched her pale, speckled arms high above her head and groaned. "I don't know how much longer I can take this. I don't think I've ever been so hungry in my life. I've been dreaming of my granny since this started, dreaming of her every time I closed my eyes. Oh, how I hope she's alright! But just now, just before you woke me, I was dreaming about food. What I would not give for a pot of pea mash right now, bubbling and hot straight from the kettle."

Ulla sighed. "Don't talk about it. It's better not to. My father told me that when you're hurt, it's better not to talk about it or look at it. Pretend that everything is fine. You can forget the pain that way."

"You'll starve to death all the same," said Kirsikka, practically. "At least the pain reminds you to try to do something about it. What about your granny? Do you think she escaped from the riders?"

Ulla hesitated. Kirsikka's easygoing, open manner seemed so strange. Ulla felt that she already knew more about Kirsikka and her kin than she did about most of the people in her own village, but she herself was much more guarded.

"My father...my father came from the deep forest, far away to the east. All his family is there. But I had a grandmother once, from my mother's kin. I remember seeing her a few times, and she lived not so far away with some others. I don't really know them. Anyway, I think she died when I was very small. It was a long time ago."

"A long time! You make it sound like you're an old woman already yourself. What about your brothers and sisters, or your cousins that you said you lived with?"

But Ulla was closed again, the veil drawn tightly around her. She fell silent, stretching beside her friend and narrowing her eyes as she peered east toward the slowly rising sun. Several people around them were stirring, ambling here and there with dull expressions and weary eyes. She noticed an older man carrying a birch bucket before he disappeared through a gap in the tree line.

"Water," she said.

"What?" asked Kirsikka.

"Water. He's going for water. So is that other woman there, the one with the torn apron. There's a pool or stream nearby. Come on, Kirsikka." Ulla looked down at her dirty arms and legs, scratched and streaked with blood, sweat and grime. "Come on. It's not so cold this morning. Let's go with them and bathe in the water. We can drink away the pain, maybe, and at least clean this filth off. Come with me. Look, some people are still sleeping. If we hurry, we won't be left behind."

The two little girls took off at a brisk pace through the gap and into the green, blossoming wood. They followed the man at a distance. The marshy ground sank beneath their feet, squishing softly as they padded along. Any pool nearby would be boggy and unclean. At first, they wondered if their errand would turn out to be useless, but soon heard the telltale sound of rushing water filtering through the birdcalls and rustling boughs. After a short jaunt, the forest opened up to a steep depression that trailed down to a broad sward beside a narrow, swift-moving stream. Many people were already gathered beside the water. Across the stream, trees stretched down almost to the shore.

Ulla and Kirsikka walked a ways upstream and stopped at a low spot in the bank, where eddying waters had fashioned a semicircular pool. Kirsikka gingerly bathed her painful feet in the cold water while Ulla washed the dirt from her arms. The clear, clean water gurgled over dark stones, speeding away to feed the marshlands below. Kirsikka lay back and looked up at the unmarked sky. She worked her hands through her copper-red hair and sighed.

"If only we could sit here all day," she said. "Sit and wait until we were rescued, and then taken to a village somewhere with all types of good things to eat."

"You are talking about food again," answered Ulla. "Drink, Kirsikka. It's fresh and not too icy. We need to get back soon."

But Ulla herself felt like she could sit on the riverbank all day. She had been awake less than an hour and was already feeling sleepy, if sleepy was the right word. Exhausted. Weary. These were perhaps closer to the mark.

The endless flight from danger into danger sapped her will, strong as it was. She sighed and, cupping her hands, began to drink from the stream.

The cold water coursed through her. Splashing it on her face and neck, Ulla felt a jolt like a lightning bolt reinvigorating her tired soul. She stooped and splashed some more on her skin. Slowly raising her head and peering across the river, the water streamed down her face. She blinked. Facing almost due east, the climbing sun dazzled her eyes. When her vision cleared, she saw them.

Directly across the river, on the opposite shore, stood two men. No more than a long stone's throw away, they silently stared back at her. The taller of the two was clearly an Itäläinen. Arms crossed, face impassive, his crimson shirt gleamed dully in the sunlight. But the second man seemed exceedingly strange. Shorter than his companion and clad all in black, his face was somehow distorted—long and angular. His jet-black hair fell almost to his waist, and was braided in intricate fashion. The strange man suddenly smiled at her, a thin, cruel smile from an overlarge mouth that made Ulla recoil.

Before she could react, cries broke out, both nearby and in the distance, where the mass of refugees still waited on the road. Kirsikka shot up at once.

"Run, Kirsikka, run!" screamed Ulla. "The horse riders are here! Run!"

Ulla had just enough wits about her to pull her boots back on before the girls scrambled up the low bank and onto the greensward. They immediately saw the reason for the panicked cries. Several mounted Easterners had emerged from the trees and were riding hard toward the frightened people, blowing horns. They raced toward the wood, and two horsemen swept past them. Targeting the old man with the basket as he fled, the first rider brought his scimitar down across his back. The man screamed and fell to the ground. The second Easterner trampled him beneath his horse's hooves.

The girls had almost reached the wood when more horsemen emerged from the tree line before them. They stopped and turned back, running this way and that amidst the pandemonium of screaming refugees and galloping horses.

"Run to the river, Ulla!" Kirsikka yelled above the uproar. "It's our only chance! Cross to the other side and into the trees!"

Slipping on the dewy grass, they made a beeline straight for the low bank. It was too late, however. Ulla looked back just in time to see two riders approaching with a net stretched between them. Before she could cry out, the Itäläiset cast the corded hemp net upon them. They stumbled to the ground and flailed about in their panic, hopelessly entangling themselves. Ulla tried to rise, but toppled over at once. Kirsikka lay prostrate on her stomach, sobbing. They were trapped.

Ulla clutched her friend's hand and watched the chaos unfolding around them as if in a dream. The Easterners chased down more villagers, capturing some and killing others. Some people simply cast themselves to the wet grass and awaited their fate. A few escaped into the trees. The cries slowly subsided, replaced by moans and muffled sobs as the Itäläiset turned to the business of binding their captives.

Ulla lay back and stared at the sun, now hazy and uncertain as if it, too, were caught in a snare. An Easterner loomed over them and fastened leather straps to small hooks in the netting. Mounting his horse, he began to haul the girls up the bank. Kirsikka screamed in terror, fearing they would be dragged to their deaths, but the horse sauntered slowly through the wet grass. Ulla shut her eyes tight, burying her face as best she could into Kirsikka's hair. The girls clutched one another as they slid across the bumpy ground.

Then the world turned upside down. Something heavy was tossed upon them and they tumbled about as they were lifted, drug, then lifted again, and all the while, Ulla kept her eyes shut and listened to the pell-mell rhythm of her pounding heart. Finally, everything was still.

A voice spoke sternly above them in the Easterners' alien tongue. They opened their eyes as an Itäläinen clad in red and black expertly unraveled the heavy, coarse net, untangling their twisted arms and legs in the process. The two girls spilled out onto the dusty ground.

"*Stewatz,*" said the man dispassionately, digging at them with his black leather boot.

They stumbled to their feet. Blinking in the suddenly bright sunlight, the little girl with dark hair saw that she was back on the road—or, at least it looked to be the same one she'd been on before. What had happened to most of the other refugees was unclear.

A small group of frightened Karhulaiset stood unsteadily to one side. Several horsemen sat watching them while other Easterners rolled their nets and packed away bits of gear. Further down the road, a much larger band of riders clustered together. She recognized the strange man with the cruel face. He appeared to be giving orders to the others.

Fifteen captives stood there, most of them young women or girls except for two boys, both young and strong and on the cusp of full manhood. Ulla and Kirsikka were the youngest of the lot. The Easterners separated the prisoners into three lines and lashed them together so they could walk, but not escape. The red and black-clad men put iron collars on some of the women, but the two little girls were too small for them, so the men used rope instead. The girls found themselves at the end of the last line.

Ulla watched the Easterners closely. Their long brown hair, strange mustachios, and leather gear looked much the same, and she had difficulty telling them apart. One man stood out, however. His hair was yellow and braided, and his skin very sunburnt. The yellow-haired man tied the rope around her neck, speaking sharply in his strange language. As he fastened the knot, her tattered, homespun dress slipped, exposing her shoulder.

"*Chira...chirajilika,*" he mumbled, stepping back. The Clan Mark stood out in the morning sun, black against the little girl's pale skin.

Coming forward, the Easterner traced its outlines with his gloved hand. Ulla jerked away at his touch and pulled the dress back up over her shoulder. The man glared, but she gazed back defiantly. Narrowing his eyes, the blond-haired Itäläinen called to a companion. Seizing Ulla roughly by the shoulders, he pulled down her dress and showed the mark to another rider while Ulla struggled fiercely.

After the men released her, Kirsikka tried to comfort her sobbing friend. The two Easterners seemed to quarrel about something until the yellow-haired man spat on the ground and walked away, muttering to himself.

"What was it, Ulla?" asked Kirsikka. "What's on your back that he was angry about? Are you alright?"

But at that moment, the band of two dozen or more horsemen spurred their mounts with a shout and went galloping down the road. Sweeping past the captives, they rushed by in a cloud of dust and pounding hooves while the terrified prisoners shrank together. Several of the nearby Itäläiset mounted their horses and set off to join their kinsmen, leaving only five men behind with the villagers. One man rode a bony horse that seemed to have gone lame, but the others were on foot, the yellow-haired man among them. The horseman yelled something in his harsh tongue and they set off in the opposite direction—not southeast, to follow the riders, but north, to where more Easterners waited and where the long journey back to their homeland with the captives and spoils would begin.

The Itäläiset set a steady pace, but not one too swift for the half-starved prisoners, who shuffled along as best they could. At the end of her line, Ulla found it impossible to talk with Kirsikka. She watched her friend's red hair bob up and down and fought to contain her own rising panic. The little girl wondered where the Easterners were taking them. Väinämöinen had told her that the horsemen wanted slaves, and she tried to imagine what her life would be like among them—one of toil, labor and drudgery, no doubt, and of sorrow and anguish, too. She made up her mind then and there that she would try to escape at the first opportunity, no matter the cost. But after a while, she grew so tired that her thoughts became foggy, and numbness replaced despair.

The Easterners said little, slogging along beside their captives in silence. One man mocked some of the older girls whose garments were torn and who tried to cover themselves in their shame, but for the most part they seemed as weary as their prisoners. Ever and anon, the yellow-haired man would fall back in line and glare at Ulla with his clear blue eyes. She avoided his gaze, but grew terrified of him. He was clearly startled by her scar, but why? Was it only the surprise of seeing so rare a mark against her pale skin, or had he somehow heard about her or been searching for her?

Twice the Easterners stopped for short rests as the day wore on. They gave food to the prisoners—dried grouse and round, salty wheat cakes with an oily taste that Ulla disliked, though she gobbled it down just the same. Several of the women threw up, Kirsikka included, and the men laughed, but the captives did not refuse the food when offered again. Their enemies drove them on until the red sun began to wester and the warm air suddenly cooled while shadows crept across the dusty road. They had seen no one during the whole day's march, no one except for two horsemen riding swiftly to the south with drawn scimitars, passing them without a word and vanishing into the distance. No Karhulaisen refugees reappeared.

At last they came to a clearing beside a grey pool where two large *pirttis* stood among many *kotas* and outbuildings. It was a farm, but there was no telling what had become of its former inhabitants. The Itäläiset apparently used it as a gathering place. Several dozen horses stamped about a makeshift pen. Another group of captives sat despondently beside a well, guarded by a few Easterners with clubs. Others moved about here and there. The two little girls were cut loose from their unfortunate companions and drug to a small *kota*, where they were pushed roughly to the ground.

Kirsikka stared blankly at Ulla with eyes that clearly stung from crying. "What are we going to do? I thought I was going to die, but this is even worse. The warriors will never find us now, and we'll be taken who knows where."

"There's nothing we can do," Ulla replied dully. "Not yet, at least. But there must be some way that we can get away from here, some way to escape. I cannot walk all the way to Eastland. I don't want to leave the Far Northern Land."

"Who knows what they're going to do to us? Maybe they'll kill us after all."

"No," replied Ulla. "That's not what they want. They want slaves, thralls. They won't kill us, not unless we run."

"Not unless we run. How *can* we run, tied together like this? But I hope they give us more food. It tastes terrible, but I could still eat it all day, I'm so hungry."

Ulla noticed the yellow-haired man walking toward them with several others. He gestured excitedly as he spoke with a tall Easterner who seemed to be a captain of some sort: older, grey-haired, clad in a black leather hauberk with a lynx-like creature embossed in gold.

Kirsikka poked Ulla with her elbow and whispered, "They are coming."

Stopping some ten paces away, the grey-haired leader nodded and motioned to one of his companions. The man walked over to them and crouched as he smiled, looking them up and down. He appeared different than the other Itäläiset: bald, round-faced, and almost clean-shaven, and strange blue marks seemed to be painted on his face and arms. Neither Ulla nor Kirsikka had ever seen tattoos before and had no idea what to make of them. To their surprise, the painted man suddenly spoke in their own tongue.

"Karhulaiset, yes, Karhulaiset. Like all the others here, but still just a little different, yes? So where are you from, little one? What is your name?"

He spoke directly to Ulla and with a shock, she at once recognized her father's accent, the strange, almost melodious inflection that she had never heard any other person use before. Indeed, the tattooed man was Karelian, a slave taken by the Easterners long ago and who served them now during their great raid as an interpreter.

"Too shy to talk, are we? That's alright. You'll get used to things soon enough. Cheer up, you're still alive, no matter what's happened to your folk. Things could be worse, and maybe they will be if you don't tell them what they want to know. Now, what is your name, Karhulainen?"

Somehow, inexplicably, Ulla knew not to trust the man. She remembered Väinämöinen's lesson about names and how he said such knowledge could be a dangerous thing among those who wished you harm. She remained silent, staring straight back at the Karelian while Kirsikka hid her face in her hands.

"You're a brave one, alright. A bad wife you'll make, but maybe a good overseer, if you keep that pride in check. Come now, Karhulainen, tell me your name; and tell me something else, too. Tell me about this mark on your back they're so interested in and how you came by it?"

A thrill ran down Ulla's spine. He knew about the Clan Mark!

"A bear claw, they say it is: the very totem of your clan. How'd you come by it, Blackhead? You've got some scars on your leg there. Is this mark a scar, too? Come now, tell me how you got it."

Anger suddenly welled up in Ulla's heart and she defiantly blurted out, "If it looks like a bear claw, then I guess a bear put it there, didn't it?"

The painted man was taken aback for a moment, then laughed heartily. He stood up, shaking his head. "So be it, little fearless one. But remember what I told you. Keep that pride in check or you'll come to a bad end no matter your spirit. It looks like you won't be for the markets after all; it seems they want you for Sariola. Maybe you'll do better there, but then again, maybe not. But be ready to leave early, and say goodbye to your little friend here. I don't think you'll see one another again."

The Karelian walked back to his companions. The men stared at Ulla and talked; the leader seemed to grow angry with the yellow-haired Easterner, or so she thought. But they soon walked away, leaving the girl alone. Not long afterward, the girls were fed, their feet lashed together, and then they were carried to a small *kota* to pass the short summer night.

Alone in the *kota*, with the red glare of a nearby campfire flickering through the opening, the girls huddled together. Their shock at the Karelian's warning that they would be separated and that Ulla would be taken away by herself had worn off, but Kirsikka was inconsolable. Her dry, stinging eyes could barely open.

"I can't believe I just found you and now I'll be alone again already. What is it about your scar that makes them angry? Do you think they will let me come with you?"

"You don't want to come with me," answered Ulla. "I don't know where they want to take me, but I think it's even worse than where they come from—worse than Eastland."

"What does that matter? Everyone's gone: my family, my friends. You're the only one I know now. You're all I have."

"Don't worry, Kirsikka. I'll come back for you, I promise."

"How can you come back? You can't get away from them."

"They can't keep me tied up all the time. I have to walk, I need my legs at least. I don't know how I'll do it, but I swear I'll get away somehow and come back for you. I'll find you on the North Road or wherever you are, and together we'll escape back into the woods. And besides, there are other people out there looking for us. And there's Väinämöinen. I'll find him somehow and he'll rescue us. I've got to find Väinämöinen."

"Who's that? And how can he rescue us, alone and lost in all this wide country surrounded by enemies?"

"He can find us, Kirsikka. If anyone can find us, it's Väinämöinen."

But despite her brave front, the little girl felt only despair; she doubted whether she could really get away from the Itäläiset or if Väinämöinen could find her, even if he knew to look for her. Kirsikka fell silent. The two little girls lay still, hand in hand in the dark *kota* as the minutes passed. The red-haired girl's breathing grew soft. Ulla wavered on the edge of a dream. A shadow passed across her mind and she opened her eyes. The shadow was real. Against the fire's red glare, she saw the yellow-haired Easterner.

The big man held a long, bone-handled knife in his hand. He approached the girls and loomed over them. Ulla had no idea why the man hated her so, but anger was clearly written across his face, evident even in the dim light. He laid a trembling hand upon her leg.

"*Chirajilika,*" he hissed in his own strange tongue. *You're coming with me.*

Ulla shrank from his touch. Kirsikka awoke and stifled a shout.

"*Bamolchyet!*" he ordered. *Silence!*

The Easterner fumbled with something made of iron, something that rung faintly in the cool dark. He grasped her shoulder and began to wrap the collar around her neck. She struggled, and the blond man slapped her. Stunned, Ulla shot upright. Over his shoulder, she saw another shadow, another figure slipping inside the *kota*, but this one was no Easterner. Draped in a long cloak, the figure raised a sword.

The yellow-haired man must have seen the shadow reflected in Ulla's eyes, because he flinched. Spinning around, he threw up his knife hand just in time to block the swordsman's blow. The blade cut through his fingers; the knife fell to the ground. The man snarled and tried to regain his footing, but the next blow was swift. The swordsman ran him straight through. He fell on top of the terrified girls, face up. A thin rivulet of blood spilled from his mouth.

"Hurry now," said the man, laying his sword aside and taking up the dead Easterner's knife. "We've got to cut your bonds and get you out of here. Do as I say and—" He stopped short. A look of wonder spread across his face. "Ulla! By the Seven Clans, it's Ulla! Oh, child, how did you come to be here?"

"They came to Grankulta, Ilkka. I ran. And then they caught me."

Heaving the dead man's carcass away, Ilkka quickly embraced the dark-haired little girl and then began cutting their bonds while he instructed them in a low whisper.

"Tales will have to wait, though I wouldn't have thought to find you here for all the world. Old Väinämöinen must have been right about you after all. Listen to me now! I am here with more Wardens and we're trying to rescue as many of you as we can. We need to get away before the Itäläiset are roused. Come with me and be silent! But when I tell you to run, run with all the strength you have into yonder woods where the moon sails high, and don't look back!"

Even as they stepped out of the *kota*, shouts erupted throughout the camp. One of the *pirttis* was on fire and the picketed horses brayed in panic. The Easterners raised the alarm. Several Karhulaiset ran past, making for the woods. A riderless horse almost struck them as it dashed madly across the field. A Warden shouted to Ilkka above the din.

Ilkka pulled the girls after him to the well. Moonlight bathed the farm in an eerie yellow glow. Fighting broke out between the Itäläiset and the would-be rescuers while the Karhulaisen women screamed in terror.

"Run, Ulla!" shouted Ilkka. "Run into the wood and keep going until you're far away from this place. Follow the rising sun!"

Kirsikka, scared and confused, was all too ready to follow his instructions, but Ulla held back. Having found Ilkka beyond all hope, she was not going to leave him. The Warden understood her hesitation at once and bent down to look into her hazel eyes.

"Go, Ulla. Do what you aunt wishes, what Väinämöinen wishes, what *your father* would have wished. Take your friend and flee! You must escape. I'll find you again, don't worry, but go now!"

The little girl reluctantly pulled away, but then, having made up her mind, took Kirsikka's hand and sprinted toward the tree line behind the farm. Dodging horses and people alike, they reached its cover swiftly. She looked back and caught a final glimpse of what she thought was Ilkka fighting sword to sword with an Easterner, scimitar against straight blade silhouetted in the moonshine. Then they ran into the woods and kept running until their breath was ragged, their heads spun, and their aching legs could pump no more.

The short night was swiftly passing. Already a faint glimmer above the treetops signaled dawn's approach. The forest was cool, green and silent; they were totally alone.

Ulla answered Kirsikka's questions about Ilkka as best she could while they rested. They both feared the Itäläiset might appear at any moment.

"We should keep moving, Ulla. If they catch us again, we'll be cooked. No one is going to rescue us a second time, not in these parts."

"But Ilkaa may come after us. If we go any further, the Wardens may miss us."

"Maybe the Easterners will, too, which is what we want. Besides, there's no food here, no clean water. That Warden, your friend, said to go east. Let's do what he said! That's what he wanted."

After a while, Ulla consented, and the girls began walking again. As children of the forest, they knew from the sky's shifting color where the sun was, whether they could see it or not, and followed it as best they could. Tall pines towered over them and the resin-scented air moved gently across the forest floor. Squirrels scampered about. Cuckoos sang overhead, flitting from branch to branch as if to guard the girls' progression. Never an enemy did they see or hear the whole morning; their fear gradually subsided as they trudged along. They grew tired, and Ulla was just about to suggest they stop and sleep a while in the soft bracken when they unexpectedly stepped out of the trees and onto a hard-packed road—another of the many that ran across that part of High Länsimaa, which were made by the miners who worked the swamps for bloodrock.

The girls were taken aback. Stretched out along the road, as far as they could see in either direction, was another line of refugees heading south. The sullen people glanced at the two little waifs, but said nothing. Just like that, they were back to where they started, alone among strangers as the flight of the Karhulaiset ran throughout all the north of Deep Länsimaa. With a sigh, and not knowing what else to do, they swung into line and rejoined the exodus, hoping that they wouldn't be caught by the riders this time.

Toward the evening of the fifth day on the road, they came to a crossroads; a well-worn cart path running due east-west crossed their way. By chance, a small group of people on two great wagons arrived just then, fleeing east from the riders behind. The wagons, pulled by old cows, were like those Janni had built with large, high wheels and deep beds. They left the path and pulled onto the road amidst the crowd, near to where the little girls stumbled along.

Soon, an argument broke out among those close by. Men shouted and children cried. Suddenly, a large man with blond hair first seized Ulla, then Kirsikka, and lifted them into the foremost wagon. Other men tossed out various things—clothes and tools, bundles of hastily gathered belongings—and loaded as many people into the wagons as they would bear. The carts' original owners cursed in vain and begrudgingly made room for their new companions. As many of the children, the old, and the sick and exhausted as possible were crowded together in the wagons. They moved along slowly after that, with the rest of the refugees plodding on foot.

The two little girls huddled together in the wagon's deep bed. Although it had probably saved her—she could not have walked much further and would soon have dropped from exhaustion—Ulla disliked being in the crowded wagon. The old woman sitting next to her seemed to be dying. Her face was grey, the thin skin stretched taut like leather drawn tightly over a skull, and the little girl tried not to look at her. And day and night, a young woman heavy with child moaned in agony while an older woman tried to comfort her. Just once the young woman met Ulla's gaze and stared straight into her eyes, but Ulla saw that her eyes were green and quickly looked away.

Even Kirsikka said little and, for the most part, Ulla slept uneasily or stared blankly at the passing land as the wagon slowly bumped along. Only once did they pass a village of any size that lay directly on the road. It was deserted, save for a few fowl left behind scrabbling in the dust, which were quickly caught by the starving wanderers. However, they passed lonely homesteads and farms here and there along the way, some of them burned and looted. Ulla saw black bodies on the ground beside one ravaged *pirtti*.

The people were afraid then, for it was clear that the Itäläiset were before them as well as behind. It seemed to some that they were heading into a trap; but there was nowhere in that land of pools and bogs to find safety or to get food, and so they pressed on.

As the days passed on that bitter road, Ulla grew famished. The Bear Folk of the Marches had fled their scattered northern villages with scant warning and no time to prepare, running in terror from the Easterners with little but the clothes on their backs. Water was plentiful in that land of streams and lakes, but food was scarce. Some folk shared what they had with Ulla—chiefly bread or dried fish—but when that was spent, there was nothing else. They slaughtered the few animals among them, but there were hundreds of mouths to feed, and little enough for any one.

Ulla had known hunger before, while hunting in the woods with her father or during winter's dearth, but she had never imagined a pain such as this. Her body cried out and raged in its misery as if it had turned against her, warring on her mind and soul. Her hunger seemed a thing apart from her body, a palpable presence with a terrible life of its own. When at times the wagons stopped, Ulla and Kirsikka scrounged in the spongy turf like animals, looking for anything—wild berries, mushrooms, or sunflowers—to momentarily ease their plight, but there was precious little to be found.

Just when Ulla thought she would go mad, the pain subsided, as surely as if she had plunged a burned hand into an icy stream. She awoke around midnight and looked up at the hundreds of bright stars above, twinkling like snowflakes against a black winter sky. She felt no hunger, no burning; indeed, were a feast laid before her, she felt she would leave it sitting there and pass it by. She cried then, though no tears came to her dry, stinging eyes. But she took Kirsikka's hand and held it close, drifting back into a merciful forgetfulness, if only for a while.

At some point, the dark-haired little girl realized the crowd of refugees was thinning. Small groups or singletons had come and gone throughout the exodus, but Ulla saw the line of scatterlings was growing noticeably shorter. Each time the villagers stopped, some few did not continue and others dropped out along the way.

Riding in the wagon, disinterestedly watching the trees pass by, Ulla's glance chanced upon an old woman and a boy, perhaps ten or eleven years old, sitting on the side of the road. Their clothes were in tatters and a short crutch lay beside the child, who was lame. They sat still as stone while the crowd silently passed them, as if they were already dead. Only their eyes moved and flickered with life. They watched the little girl as the wagon drove by, but made no sound and gave no sign, yet their eyes bespoke a silent reproach, perhaps mingled with quiet resignation or despair.

On the tenth day after the Karhulaiset had taken to the road, the sky darkened and a late summer storm broke across the fens that girded High Länsimaa. A bright red glow lit the western horizon beneath a lip of black canopy. Rain poured down on the refugees, further adding to their misery while they struggled along. As evening fell and thunder rumbled in the distance, they came to another crossroads. The road they were on continued southeast, but a wide, hard-packed way that was clearly much travelled cut off due north and disappeared into distant woods.

After a short rest, the girls loaded up and prepared to set off. The cow pulling the wagon would not rise, however, and presently turned on its side, breathing hard, as rain beat down upon it. So Ulla spilled out of the wagon with the others and, to her surprise, found that the second wagon, which had been following a ways back, was nowhere to be seen. She had no idea what had happened to it or to those who rode within.

Ulla and Kirsikka spent the night sheltering beneath the wagon. The next morning, the remnants of the Karhulaiset slowly moved on. The rain had stopped, but the road was wet and slippery, and in places shallow pools stretched across it. The girls stumbled forward through the mire. They were very young, but understood well enough that to stop and give up, as some had done, was to give up everything; they would die. So, Ulla tramped along with the dwindling crowd toward an uncertain end.

There were few dwellings to be found as they pushed deeper into the noisome marsh, save some empty *majas* and cabins used by the men who mined the peat bogs for iron and who had made the road. Ulla became aware of a mist rising before her face like a fine veil; her sight grew blurry at times, and when she blinked, her eyes lost their focus. Without knowing why, she kicked off her worn, ragged boots—the boots her father brought her from Karelia—and left them on the road, a red patch amidst the black mud. If Kirsikka even noticed, she said nothing.

The late afternoon sun became hot as the road suddenly narrowed to little more than a seldom-used cart path. It plunged through a defile like a green tunnel, bordered on each side by tall fir and pine trees growing on solid ground. The defile ran for about a mile before ending abruptly to open out into a wide, semicircular plain that led down to a rushing river. The great river was larger than any Ulla had ever seen or imagined, larger than any she had crossed on the way to Keskimaa. The tree line on its far bank could barely be descried, yet the grey water flowed swiftly as it hissed and boiled around rocks and black boulders. This was the Jouksi, the great river of the Far Northern Land that marked the bounds between

High Länsimaa and the eaves of the Karelian Forest. It ran for miles until at last it emptied into Lake Etelajärvi, far to the south.

There was no way across that broad river without a boat, and even then the passage would be perilous. To the south was a grassy swamp, where rivulets flowed into impassable marshland filled with reeds and flowering cattails; to the north, the trees marched almost to the riverbank, where only a small opening remained. The villagers walked some ways on the plain and then, as if in answer to an unseen call or signal, they stopped. Utterly exhausted, they could go no further. Indeed, there was nowhere left to go save back to the road from whence they came. Singly, then in twos and threes, they sat down in the tall grass, past caring that they were exposed to unfriendly eyes and too spent to heed any danger.

The villagers had scarcely reached the Jouksi when a sudden horn blast broke the peaceful summer's buzz—a sound they had not heard since the very day they took to the road. Some people stood up and pointed north. There, in the gap between the river and the trees, was a single horseman: a small black figure in the distance. He raised his horn and blew a second blast; two more figures appeared beside him. The horsemen galloped toward the frightened refugees, and soon enough, all could see that they were clothed in the black and red of the Itäläiset.

Then many of the Bear Folk began to wail and cry, for, despite all their suffering, they were trapped at the last, caught between the Itäläiset and the river. There was nowhere to flee to even if they'd had the strength, so they sat and waited for what was to come. The riders stopped about fifty yards from the huddled refugees and sounded the horn a third time. There came an answering call in the distance. The horsemen made no sign, but sat still, some ways apart from one another, and watched the villagers.

Even with her stinging eyes and failing eyesight, Ulla could see their faces: dirty, streaked with sweat, weary. The raid had not been easy on the raiders, but they were intent on their prey at hand and on rounding up the last of the fleeing Karhulaiset while they were still within their reach. The

Easterners had taken many slaves, and the roads and paths to the north were filled with long lines of fettered Karhulaiset and wagons piled with plunder. They were ready to return to their homes in the east.

Two men suddenly broke free from the huddled folk and ran toward the horsemen. They had short hunting bows of the kind often used in High Länsimaa, and, in their desperation, sought to kill or drive off their tormenters. Coming within bowshot, they loosed their arrows at the Easterners, who turned their steeds toward the bowmen to narrow their profiles. The arrows went far wide of their targets. With a cry, one of the horsemen spurred his mount and charged the bowmen. Sweeping out his curved sword, he cut down one of the men as they fled in terror, staining the grass with bright red blood. The Itäläinen ignored the second man, however, and wheeled his horse around to gallop back to his two silent companions.

"Look!" Kirsikka cried in a hoarse voice. She stood up and pointed to the opening of the defile behind them.

A large wagon pulled by horses had appeared, with great wheels like to the type that Big Janni had fashioned. Four Itäläiset stood in the wagon behind the driver amidst a mass of rope and chains, and seven more horsemen trailed behind. But the little girl with dark hair turned away from them and looked to the tiny gap between the river and the woods, where the first rider had appeared.

Ulla descried a glimmer in the distance, a bright golden light that flickered like the sunset on troubled water. Then a horn sounded from the same direction, like unto the calls of the Itäläiset, but different in pitch and quality. A black-garbed horseman appeared by the river and galloped swiftly toward them with several others close behind.

The Easterners guarding them turned round; two rose in their stirrups, peering intently to the north. The horn call sounded again. Ulla could make out the red-stamped leather of the Itäläisen riders as they charged ahead. But suddenly there was a flash, far brighter than they'd seen before. It blinded the Karhulaiset and Itäläiset alike, as if a star had descended in their midst.

When the gleam faded and they could see again, there were not merely a few riders bearing down upon them, but some three dozen or more, all spread out in two lines and dressed in different colors—some in green and brown mounted on great black horses, and others in myriad of colors on smaller mounts. Foremost, on a great grey horse, rode a tall man with a long white beard, brandishing a long, straight sword in his raised hand. *Väinämöinen!*

The Easterners yelled to one another. Two of the guards unsheathed their swords and galloped toward the oncoming crowd. The seven riders escorting the wagon did likewise, riding to meet the newcomers head on. The Bear Folk, all weariness and starvation cast aside, leapt to their feet and cried out to their would-be rescuers, but the single horseman still on guard turned toward them and, brandishing his sword, angrily cried out in his harsh tongue.

"*Stòite tam, dge stòite! Ne dvìgaites!*"

The horsemen soon converged on the open river plain. Ulla saw Väinämöinen raise his hand, and yet another brilliant flash lit the daytime sky. When the villagers blinked and shook off the light, there was no sign of the Easterners save for a single rider galloping madly to the north and several riderless horses running free across the plain. With a cry of anger or perhaps disbelief, their guard spurred his horse toward the defile. In the distance, the wagon turned, careening crazily, and did the same. One man had apparently fallen off and chased after the cart, desperately trying to catch up to his companions before he was run down. Some two dozen of the rescuers peeled off and gave chase to the fleeing raiders, but the others, led by Väinämöinen, went swiftly to the miserable folk.

The scatterlings of the Karhulaiset, still more than five score all told, crowded around the horsemen and cried for joy as they called out to Väinämöinen, for they had guessed who he was. He rode among them, touching their hands and heads and speaking soothing words of comfort, for he was saddened by their ragged countenance and grasped their evil plight. Ulla saw that several of the riders were March Wardens, dressed in their customary green and brown. She recognized Ilkka among them. The other men were dressed in many bright colors, chiefly red and blue, and wore vests with intricate designs. Their brown hair was wavy and unkempt, and they had long beards, for they were Karelialaiset, the Reindeer Folk and Ulla's father's clan, though she had never seen any Karelian save him.

"Listen to me, Folk of the Bear," Väinämöinen suddenly cried in a great voice. "Happy indeed is the hour and, beyond hope, you are found and freed from the swords of the east! But you are not yet safe, not here. The Itäläiset may return, and if they do, it will be in greater numbers. I know you are tired, but you must follow me now back north, away from the banks of the Jouksi. It is not far, and there you will find food and sustenance with your cousins from Karelia; many men are there and you will be safe. Let any who cannot walk come forth, and we will do what we can!"

The rescuers organized the ragged tatterdemalions and lifted onto their horses some who were too weak to continue. Väinämöinen sat atop his grey horse while people crowded around him. Suddenly his glance fell upon Ulla, standing a ways off with Kirsikka and watching the old wizard with her hazel-green eyes. Väinämöinen leapt down from his horse and went to her with sadness in his eyes, but with a gentle smile on his face.

"Well, well," he said. "So you are here after all, little one. I was going to go look for you; Ilkka told me that he had found you a captive of the Easterners but had set you free. Not that we had much hope, of course. But here you are after all! Are your folk with you?"

"No," said Ulla. "I don't know where they are. I was following Meria, but I lost her…lost them all. They are all gone."

"Well, now," said Väinämöinen. "I see. I am very sorry. But we can talk of that later. You are coming with me now!"

The old man reached out as if to pick her up, but Ulla took a step back.

"No, Väinämöinen," she said. "I am *not* coming with you. Not unless Kirsikka comes, too. She's my friend. We stay together."

Väinämöinen looked at the freckled, red-haired girl in her tattered shirt. The girl's eyes were wide with amazement, and her face flushed pink.

"So be it," Väinämöinen said gravely. "You shall stay together. But you will *both* come with me."

He lifted the two girls atop the grey horse, then mounted up himself. The remnant of the Bear Folk at last moved away from the banks of the swift-flowing Jouksi. None knew where they were in all that wide land, or precisely where the old wizard was taking them, but at least they could leave the terror of the Easterners behind for a time.

CHAPTER SEVEN

THE ENCHANTED VALLEY

The Bear Folk encamped beside a great bend of the Jouksi. More refugees joined them in the days after their rescue, for there had been other groups lost amidst the marshlands. Ilkka and the Wardens freed a long line of people who had been bound and chained, then driven north to the slave markets by the raiders. One of the newcomers was a woman from Fallkulta, but she was frightened and exhausted. She had no news for Ulla, nor any idea of what had happened to her own family. There was no one at all from Bassböle.

Many people from the Reindeer Clan came from the forest to succor the starving refugees, and Väinämöinen labored to heal those who were hurt, to save those who could be saved. A strong force of the Karelialaiset, travelling mainly on foot but armed with axes and bows, pushed on into the marshes to join a company of Wardens that arrived from Etelamaa. The Easterners they encountered fled, however. They were scattered into many bands, not gathered together to fight a battle, and quickly withdrew from that part of High Länsimaa.

None knew what the situation was in the north, along the Marches.

With the strength of youth, Ulla and Kirsikka quickly recovered. At first, they ate small amounts of fish and were allowed no milk or cheese, but after several days, their hunger returned. Then they ate ravenously, devouring all the food the Reindeer Folk brought to them. Ulla saw little enough of Väinämöinen, though he paid special attention to the little girls when he could. The old man was busy, and once disappeared for several days on an errand he would not discuss. As he tended her, however, he told the girl enough of how he had come to their rescue to satisfy her curiosity.

When Väinämöinen had seen the Itäläiset with his wizard's eye, sacking the north and pillaging the villages of High Länsimaa, he had left the Stone City at once. He had ridden with all haste to the north, so swiftly that his flaxen horse would have died but for the singer's magic. The old man had thought to come to Keskimaa first and help marshal the strength of the Bear Folk, but word reached him that, although the borders were well nigh overrun, many people had escaped into the empty lands north of Suurijärvi while being pursued by the Easterners.

He rode then to the forest eaves and urged the Reindeer Folk who lived there to gather strength and go quickly to the aid of their cousins. The mage himself found as many riders as he could, for there were few horses among the Karelialaiset, and sped toward the marshlands and peat bogs. There they found Ilkka and a remnant of the Wardens who had harried and fought the raiders all the way from the North Marches to the Jouksi; together, they drove off the Easterners and so found Ulla's band of refugees, and others besides.

Ulla and Kirsikka stayed in the camp of the Bear Folk for some three weeks, sleeping in an improvised tent of reindeer and elk skins that rose like a funnel with an open top for a chimney. The wandering Karelialaiset lived in such makeshift dwellings, even as their ancestors had long ago when mortals first came to the Far Northern Land. They could not stay there long, however. The wind came from the north and the chill of autumn was in the air; ducks and geese flew overhead, seeking warmer climes. It would soon be winter. Yellow and brown birch leaves and red aspen leaves fluttered to the ground in the gusts. The Reindeer Folk brought many things to the refugees, but could not do so all winter long. Väinämöinen made plans with the Wardens and the leaders of the Karelialaiset and, at last, riders arrived from Keskimaa with news.

The Bear Folk had finally gathered an army and moved up the North Road toward the Marches, but the Easterners had fled or else were already gone, having despoiled the northern villages and taken many Karhulaiset for slaves. Some of the refugees who camped beside the Jouksi wished to return to their homes in the north. Most, however, made ready to go with a guard of Wardens to shelters that were being prepared, at Pekka Verikiven's orders, near Keskimaa and along the Suurijärvi. The remainder—too ill or despondent to return again to High Länsimaa—would go to Karelia and join themselves to the Clan of the Reindeer.

At first, Ulla was afraid that Väinämöinen would send her back to High Länsimaa. She had looked desperately for her aunt, uncle and cousins during the long flight from the Itäläiset, but was terrified to return to Grankulta. Just as she cherished the thought that her father was still alive and would one day return to her, she harbored hope that the rest of her family had escaped the swords and nets of the eastern marauders. If she went back, her hope would be put to the test, for, if they could not be found—or were slain— she would know the terrible truth.

A man and woman among those returning to the north said they knew where Grankulta lay and offered to take Ulla with them to search for her folk. The little girl's fears were baseless, however. Väinämöinen had no intention of letting her go a second time. As for Kirsikka, she said there was no reason for her to return to High Länsimaa ever again; she believed her family was gone, and had no hope whatsoever of learning otherwise.

So they broke camp and found four wagons to carry the refugees who wished to go to Karelia. Väinämöinen and several Karelian horsemen went with them, as did Ilkka and six other Wardens. The Wardens escorted them only as far as the passage over the Jouksi, however. Ilkka had orders to accompany the refugees who planned to return to High Länsimaa, and would then ride to Keskimaa, where many lords and captains were gathering to take counsel.

The wagons set off on a chilly morning and rumbled due north beside the river. The girls bounced along in the wagon, much to Ulla's disappointment;

she had hoped to ride on one of the big horses with Väinämöinen or Ilkka. This was no panicked flight, however, and there was plenty of food and frequent stops. The girls also had new attire, for the Karelialaiset had cast aside their tattered rags and given them new clothes to wear. Ulla wore a bright blue, woven shirt, a yellow skirt traced with clever designs, and another pair of short, red boots, not unlike her old pair, which was lost forever. Kirsikka wore a bright green dress and soft, yellow boots strapped high to her knees; both girls had fresh kerchiefs of many rich colors atop their braided hair. Ulla's father had often worn brightly colored Karelian clothes, as had Ulla herself when she was younger. Kirsikka had never seen such colors, however; the plain-woven clothes were finer than anything she had ever known, and the soft boots beyond her experience. Despite her grief, the freckle-faced girl beamed from her seat in the wagon.

They travelled very slowly to avoid disturbing the ill and the wounded. The passage across the Jouksi was not far, though. As the late afternoon sun struggled to peep out from behind ragged clouds on their journey's second day, they came to a place where the banks were firm and the river narrowed out. A single wharf on the western shore stuck out into the slow current alongside some wooden piles. A small boat had been drawn up to the rocky shelf at the water's edge. On the eastern bank were many buildings and two large, flat-bottomed ferryboats that looked big enough to hold several wagons laden with people, animals or goods. As one of the ferryboats was slowly drawn toward them, Ilkka and the Wardens bade them farewell.

"So, Väinämöinen," said Ilkka. "Our long journey together comes to an end. I return now to Keskimaa with such as are left of my company, and who can say what the future may bring? But I suspect that we shall see each other again, and maybe soon."

"Perhaps you are right," said Väinämöinen. "There will be need for me soon enough in Keskimaa. I was wrong when I spoke with Pekka, and I greatly rue it now. The storm was much closer than I realized, and so many lives are now lost or ruined that might have been saved. But such is the way of things. At least my foresight's failure proves all the more to Pekka that Löhi is indeed moving and her plans—long prepared, I deem—are finally ripe."

"I'm not so sure of that," answered Ilkka. "Not that I doubt your words. Sadly, I am all too ready to believe them. But whether Pekka will see in a great raid of the Itäläiset the threat of which you warned, I do not know. Easterners seeking slaves and booty are one thing; witches from the ancient past are quite another."

Väinämöinen frowned. "If he still doesn't believe me, he's a bigger fool than I was. But we shall see what comes to pass. I go now to Karelia, to my old home Väinölä, deep in the forest, to consult my kin. Much has happened since I left and we have many things to consider—the child not the least among them."

Ilkka turned to Ulla and smiled. "Farewell again, Ulla of the Karhulaiset! Not for the last time, I think. At least, I hope not. Had we not found you by happy chance, I was prepared to ride through a host of Easterners back to the North Marches to look for you. And still I shall look for your family while you go with Väinämöinen. Do not give up all hope yet. Who knows what to-morrow may bring? Goodbye!"

Ulla looked down and said nothing as Ilkka and the other Wardens turned their horses and started south again. She was glad she was not riding with them to the Marches, but, just as when Ilkka returned her to Grankulta only weeks before, she was sad to see her friend leave.

The long, flat-bottomed ferry arrived at the near shore and Väinämöinen led the Karhulaiset onto it, signaling to the ferrymen on the far bank to draw the boat across. The little girl watched the water rush by, clear and transparent near the shallow banks, but deep blue in the Jouksi's middle. The wide river flowed south into the distance as far as the eye could see, and many of the Bear Folk were awed to find a water so great, familiar as they were with the little rivers and streams of their homes in High Länsimaa. They were soon across and, after a meal with the ferrymen, the wagons struck a road that led east toward the Karelian Forest.

The wagons drove slowly down the road as the days grew shorter and the wind colder. The land changed as they passed through the eaves and neared the forest proper. There were thick stands of many different types of trees all around them: birches and alders, larches and ashes, and, of course, tall spruce and firs. At first, the land rose and fell in long, gentle waves, but soon it was scattered about with many small hills, short with mild slopes and topped by bushes or rings of trees. The boggy marshland west of the Jouksi gave way on the river's eastern side to folds and ridges that suddenly rose from hollows to heights among the woods. Winding like a snake, their road looped and twined round the little hills as the north wind blew red and gold leaves all about them, for fall had come to the Far Northern Land.

They passed a few villages nestled among the hills; they were no more than collections of several cottages, smaller even than Grankulta or most of the villages of the north. But one day the road climbed up a taller hill, bare on top, and they looked down upon a small town. Many buildings and cabins spread along a lane that branched from the road.

The cabins, unlike the corner-timbered *pirttis* of the villages of High Länsimaa or the wooden plank houses of Keskimaa, were made of logs. Like pillars hewn from great trees, the logs were stacked to different heights like the cone-shaped *kotas* of the Bear Folk, but much larger. There were other buildings, too: long, low homes with grey smoke rising from central hearths, and taller sheds in which animals, goods, or many men could be gathered. Such was the fashion of the cabins of the Karelialaiset, for the Reindeer Folk were woodsmen and used the forest for nearly all of their needs.

The villagers stared down in wonder, but not at the cabins and sheds of the Karelialaiset. Beyond the town, the road disappeared into a great wall of thick, dark trees that stretched as far as they could see to the north or south and beyond the horizon before them in the east. The Bear Folk were forest-dwellers, too, but the forests of High Länsimaa were sparse, and the trees mostly thin birches, firs and pines. Never had they seen a sight like the Karelian Forest, the great wood of the Far Northern Land, with its soaring trees of many kinds pressed against each other, stretching for hundreds of miles like a many-colored canopy of leaves laid out by the hands of giants. The Karelian horsemen gave a shout, but Väinämöinen raised his hand and cried out in a great voice.

"*Katsokaa! Lopultakin, Minun Kotimaa!* Behold the forest, where the Folk of the Reindeer live free, and where deep within the Erilaiset yet dwell, and where my home is!" He turned to Ulla, who was riding in the foremost wagon, and winked at her, a broad smile spreading across his ruddy face. "Now, little one, you'll see some real trees! Not the puny sticks you live among in your northern homes." With another joyful cry, he spurred his horse toward the downward path, and they descended to the town.

For the most part, the Reindeer Folk lived in the forest itself, or else in villages farther to the south among the eaves that bordered Etelamaa and the banks of Lake Etelajärvi. In that part of Karelia, the town they came to—Metsäposti, or Forest Town—was their chief settlement. Long ago, a river had emptied from the forest into the small valley below the bare hilltop, and though the land was now dry, sediments had made the earth uncommonly rich with thick, brown soil. Men grew rye and barley in well-tilled fields, and the folk of Metsäposti kept many animals, especially sheep, small herds of cattle, and even reindeer.

There was a long cabin where they brewed *sahti* all year round, and another with many ovens where black rings of rye were baked to feed not only the townsfolk, but all of the Karelialaiset that lived in the forest nearby, too. Dyers worked in yet another building, for the Reindeer Folk knew how to use many things found only in the forest to make the rich colors and deep hues that did not fade and were famous throughout all the Seven Lands. Other secrets of that trade they learned from the Erilaiset, but Metsäposti was chiefly a trading post: all year round for the Karelialaiset, and in spring and summer for merchants from High Länsimaa and Etelamaa. Long sheds, open on one side, stood mainly empty, but in the summer they would be filled with people and goods, or with animals for sale or barter. Then, folk came out of the forest or from many miles away to do business, filling the little town with their carts and *majas.*

The scatterlings from the Marches were put in three new houses that had been made just for them: two big Karelian *kotas* and an even larger cabin where many people might dwell. But Ulla and Kirsikka were put up in a sturdy cabin with Väinämöinen, for they would be going with him. Ulla noticed that the Karelialaiset seemed to know the old wizard well. They treated him with respect, but not fear, for unlike the other clans, there was no estrangement between the Reindeer Folk and the Erilaiset; they still shared the forest, as they had for centuries.

The people of Metsäposti were anxious, for many men from the district were still away, across the Jouksi, and news was scarce. Osmo, the Master of Metsäposti and lord of the surrounding land, greeted Väinämöinen and sought his counsel about what was happening in High Länsimaa. The old man reassured him that the Itäläiset were scattered and withdrawn, and that the Karelialaiset who had gone furthest into High Länsimaa would soon return; in their absence, the women and children had worked hard to harvest the rye, barley and oats. But he warned Osmo that the danger was not past and that the life they had long known was over.

"You must be wary now," he said. "For the Easterners may come back, or other things less wholesome, seeking your ruin. The world is changing, and Löhi has come again. Nothing will be as it was before. Keep watchmen with swift horses or sleds several days out, even to the banks of the Jouksi. And be prepared to abandon your cabins quickly and flee to hidden places in the forest. The Karelialaiset are not a greedy folk, and possessions have less hold on you than they do other clans, but it is still hard to abandon the homes where you have lived long in safety. Do not tarry! If warning comes, go at once and leave all that is not needed behind! And look to the Erilaiset to help you in your time of need, for if it is in our strength, we will do so, and not forget you!"

They stayed several days among the Karelialaiset in Metsäposti. The town was filled with children, and Ulla and Kirsikka, despite their ordeal, soon found themselves laughing and playing as if they were back in their own villages with friends they had known all their lives; for children are children, and in all lands share the same innocence and joy. But it is only when they are grown, and corrupted by the world, that its stain shows upon them and they grow apart.

The children dressed in the bright colors of the forest, just as their parents did. Some of the boys wore necklaces of small, colored stones, polished and smooth, or else strung with small spiral bones from the fish of nearby streams. But the girls in their long skirts and fur-lined boots wore chains of bronze about their waists, and many rings on their fingers. The weave of their dresses was less fine than those found in Keskimaa or the Stone City, perhaps, but the designs and patterns were more intricate and varied: reindeer, elk, bears, hawks, and many symbols of wards, protection and increase decorated them.

The Reindeer Folk delighted in taking care of the two little girls, especially Ulla. When they learned that her father had been born among them, although Janni's home was far from Metsäposti and none there had ever known him, they considered her a part of their clan. Ulla felt at home with the Karelialaiset. Their accents and laughter, and the songs and stories they told at night by the fires reminded her of her father. She did not wish to stay there anymore than she wished to return to Grankulta, however. The little girl felt restless, waiting for something unknown and mysterious, but inevitable nonetheless, to happen.

One night, she crept from her cabin and saw Väinämöinen sitting by a roaring fire with another old man—a shaman from among the Reindeer Clan—and a younger man beating a drum made of taut reindeer skin and painted with many symbols. Väinämöinen and the shaman chanted, their voices' rhythmic cadence and the drum's steady beat almost putting the little girl herself into a trance. Later that night, her dreams were troubled, and the feeling of restlessness only grew sharper.

A few days later, a large party of men, mostly on foot, came down the road from the Jouksi. They were the last of the folk from Metsäposti and the surrounding district to return from the pursuit of the Itäläiset in High Länsimaa. There was much rejoicing among their families that they were safe and home at last. Väinämöinen spoke with them for several hours to glean the latest news from the north. The Itäläiset were gone, and the Bear Folk had returned to some places near the Marches, or else sought refuge near Keskimaa.

A few of the men were wounded, so the old wizard tended to their hurts. Two were beyond his care, for the Karelialaiset had burned their bodies after they fell to the swords of the Easterners. They brought back the ashes and bones to bury among the trees. The mortal shaman took the bones and went with women from the men's families into the deeper woods, for such was the custom among the Reindeer Clan. Then Väinämöinen sighed and told Ulla and Kirsikka that it was time for them to journey on, before the snow came, to his home at Väinölä, deep in the Karelian Forest.

On a dark, misty morning, so foggy that Ulla could barely see five paces in front of her, they left Metsäposti. Väinämöinen put the girls before him on his horse, and, taking leave of Osmo and a few others, struck out on the eastward road. Ulla was glad to be moving again, and although Kirsikka would have preferred to stay and live among the people of Metsäposti, she was excited to ride with Väinämöinen on the great mare. The red-haired girl had seen a full-size horse a few times in her life, but had never been on one until the day of their rescue from the Itäläiset, when she was too exhausted and starving to enjoy it. The horse clopped off down the road, and the cold autumn mists swallowed up the town of the Reindeer Folk as they left it behind.

They were well outfitted for their journey, for their hosts had given them sacks filled with black bread, dry fish, and smoked grouse that would keep for many days, as well as the sourmilk cheese only made in the neighboring district. They had also given the girls new clothes to guard against the onset of winter: thick, hooded cloaks dyed a rich blue and lined with reindeer fur on the inside, coats made from many pelts stitched together, and gloves for their hands. But Väinämöinen still wore his red cloak and yellow boots, worn and stained from his long journey, but of better weave than anything that mortal hands could make.

Their passage into the forest, called the Green Gate by the Reindeer Folk, was not far. Before the short day's sun began its descent, they reached the tree line. There were a few cabins in open fields near the road, but as the mists cleared, they saw that the road disappeared into the forest through an opening that had been cut to resemble a great arch. The road was wide enough for large carts or herds of animals to pass through, and the trees had been cut on either side for some ways so that light streamed in and one could see well in any direction. For all that, the forest was still far denser and thicker than any woods the girls had ever seen or imagined; they immediately felt a sense of closeness as they passed under the canopy.

Not far within, Väinämöinen checked the horse next to a great tree that had been shorn of its limbs and branches and that stood like a tall, straight pole in the middle of the road. It was wide and thick, adorned with intricate designs and strange symbols. At its top was carved the image of the head and antlers of a great reindeer, its mouth open as if it were crying out in anger as it defended its herd, but its blank eyes stared blindly down the road.

Väinämöinen jumped off the horse and set the girls down beside him. He closed his eyes and touched the carven pole, running his hand over its grooved surface. The old man then turned to the two girls then as they stared up at the great wooden head.

"Behold, children!" he said. "And do not be afraid! This is the totem of the Karelialaiset, and it guards the forest where they live free. All of the clans once had such totems and they stood in many places across the Far Northern Land — even among the Folk of the Bear in the land where you both were born. But they are gone now save for this one here in the Karelian Forest, unless it may be that some still stand in Tavastia or Akkala. There is great power in them."

Kirsikka took off her gloves and touched the totem, rubbing the dark wood up and down with her freckled hand. "It's smooth," she said matter-of-factly. "Cold and smooth."

But when Ulla did the same, she immediately felt a thrill run down her spine. She could sense the power Väinämöinen spoke of in her very bones, and her skin tingled even as it had in the woods when the old man used his magic to heal her torn body. She quickly drew her hand back, but noticed Väinämöinen's eyes were on her. When she met his gaze, she saw the strange look on his face—intent and deliberate—as he watched her. The wizard said nothing, however, and she was glad when the old man lifted them back onto the horse and continued down the road, leaving the totem behind to guard the silent forest.

They journeyed down the forest road for several days. There were cabins and *kotas* here and there in cleared fields, where folk had felled many trees. Once, they passed a collection of tents where a wandering band of Karelialaiset had made their home for a season before they'd move on again in the spring. The people they met were friendly and offered to shelter them for the night, but, despite the cold, Väinämöinen preferred to sleep outside among the trees. He built a small fire each night, sparking it with a spoken word and quick gesture to Kirsikka's lasting amazement. The old man spoke much to the red-haired girl and explained to her in simple words what Ulla had already learned about the return of the Witch of the North. Kirsikka nodded in her good-natured way and sometimes asked questions, but such matters were far beyond her; the simple folk of her rude village had forgotten what little they had ever known about the wider world. Kirsikka had only vaguely heard, so she thought, of the Erilaiset.

More than the old wizard's stories, Kirsikka and Ulla were fascinated by the trees of the Karelian Forest. Most of the trees were the ubiquitous firs, pines and spruce that covered the Far Northern Land. The girls were all too familiar with those, although they grew much taller here than they did along the Marches in High Länsimaa. Many trees were new to them, however: twisted junipers with wild branches entwined about one another and solitary maples that had just lost their red and orange leaves. There were ashes and beech trees with smooth, ruddy bark, and a few rowans bearing red winter berries. The tallest and most wonderful were the stands of oaks and elms, thick in the middle and with many long branches, standing proud and soaring high into the sky. Neither girl had ever imagined trees so large and beautiful. The old man smiled when he caught them staring, wide-eyed, at the woods.

The road was, for the most part, straight and level, although at times they could see the ground along its sides rolling upward toward crests or hills. It was crossed by many brooks and shallow streams, and set with stones for travellers. At one point they came to a great wooden bridge that spanned a wider river. There were many lesser roads and paths branching off from the main way, and Väinämöinen would stop and tell the girls the strange names of the places to which they led. All along the road a wide swath, which sometimes stretched for twenty yards on each side, had been cleared of trees so that the way was open to the wind and fresh air, and could be lit by sun, moon and stars. The trees came near to the road at other points, however, and, where they did, the girls felt the closeness return.

Perhaps a week had passed when they came one afternoon to a strange path that cut from the road and led away south. A single white stone, some four feet tall, stood beside it, smooth and with no markings or lines that they could see. The path was narrow and the trees marched down very close to its borders, but it seemed clear of leaves and fallen trunks. Väinämöinen dismounted, set the girls down, and then untied their packs and remaining food sacks.

"Well, little ones," he said. "Here it is at last. Almost a year has passed since I last stood by the White Stone. This is the path to Taikalaakso—the Enchanted Valley, you might call it—where the Erilaiset of the forest yet dwell. It is still a ways off; aye, it is. We have to tramp along for a ways yet. But before the moon in the sky waxes full, we shall at last reach my home in Väinölä."

"But what are you doing with all our things?" asked Kirsikka. "Are we going to leave them here?"

"No," replied Väinämöinen. "We're going to carry them ourselves, or at least some of them."

"But what about our horse?" Kirsikka asked. "Why can't he carry them?"

"First of all," said the old man, "He's a *she*, as I've told you before. And secondly, *she* can't carry our packs because *she's* not coming with us. The way is too narrow and there is no proper place for a horse in the deep forest. We will go on foot from now on until we reach the Valley."

"But what about the horse?" exclaimed Ulla. "You can't just leave him here!"

"I am not going to leave him—er, her here," said Väinämöinen with a frown. "I'm not abandoning her, if that's what you're worried about. There are friends of mine nearby, Karelialaiset who dwell not far from this place. They will welcome such a beast and treat her well. And perhaps we will see her again if we come back this way. We've journeyed far together, and she deserves her rest."

Väinämöinen stroked the animal's neck and whispered in its ear. The flaxen mare immediately lifted its head and tensed its back. With a slap to its rump, the old man cried, "*Menkää!*" The beast took off at a gallop back down the road, toward the forest gate.

"There," he said. "We are on our own now, which is not such a bad thing. We have some walking to do, but I'll try to remember that your short, skinny legs can't keep up with mine. Let's go!"

So they left the road and started down the narrow way that bent to the south. The trees came very close to the path, and at times it felt like they were walking through a living tunnel of leaf and wood. The path was always clear, as if it were constantly tended and swept, but they saw no more Karelialaiset. The forest was silent except for the rustling of animals and birds among the bracken and, one night, the wailing of wolves in the distance. It was very dim and stuffy, for they seldom felt the cold wind on their faces. If the girls looked up during the day, they could see the pale sky through a maze of limbs and branches, but at night, it was black, and without the red fire that Väinämöinen kindled when they camped, they would have been blind in the dark.

They had seen few animals on the main forest road except for squirrels, for the Reindeer Folk were great hunters, and animals that lived near them were shy and wary. Now they saw many creatures of the forest scampering across the path before them or staring at them at night with shining eyes as they sat by the fire. Hares were particularly common: large, brown hares that raced about the woods. Brightly colored birds with red and purple feathers—like the black grouse in High Länsimaa, but smaller—called to them from above, as did cuckoos and pheasants, and other kinds of birds that neither Ulla nor Kirsikka had seen before. They also saw deer, smaller than that of the Marches, with light brown coats and white ears. As children of the woods, both Ulla and Kirsikka had been raised to be wary of wolves, so their plaintive cries were unsettling at first, but Väinämöinen smiled when he heard them. The girls knew that as long as he was with them, they had nothing to fear.

One night, they were sitting in a clearing near the path beside their small, bright fire when Väinämöinen vanished into the trees and reappeared a while later with three brown hares. Their bread had been gone for several days, so the only food left to them was dried fish. The old man doled out several of those to the girls, then Ulla helped him dress the hares. They toasted small bits of meat on long sticks, like Big Janni had done when she was small. Before he skinned the hares, the mage laid them side by side and softly chanted over them in a voice like to the one he'd used when he knelt beside the bear in the woods near Grankulta.

"It's important to thank *jänis*," he said. "Remember that. They died to give us life, and for a hare as much as for a man, that is no small thing. But such is the way of things for beasts, mortals and Erilaiset."

Ulla watched the old man as he sat back, wrapped in his cloak, and ate the hot pieces of meat. Despite his long, white beard and aged face, he again reminded her of her father as the red light flickered about him in the dark.

"Väinämöinen," the little girl said suddenly. "What am I to do when we reach your home?"

"What's that?" said the old man. "Well, I'm not sure what will happen myself. We shall have to wait and see; the one who knows such things best will be there to meet us. Perhaps we shall not stay long in Väinölä."

"But am I to be your maid?" asked Ulla.

"My maid! A poor house one so small would keep!" laughed Väinämöinen. "Whatever gave you that idea?"

"You did. Don't you remember? You told my aunt and uncle that your maid was old and could no longer keep your house and that you needed me to help her."

The old man sat up and moved closer to the fire. "Oh, that. Well, she's old, that's true enough, and she certainly can't keep house; but no, I don't need you as a servant, little one. I have gotten by on my own for some time now."

"But doesn't she need my help?"

"Not exactly. She is a bit beyond your help—yours or mine, for that matter. She's dead."

"Dead!" Ulla exclaimed. "But what happened to her? Did the Itäläiset go to your home and kill her?"

"No, of course not! No Easterner would set foot in the Valley and come out of it alive. No, old Lempia died peacefully enough. Let's see, it was three hundred thirty-seven...no, three hundred thirty-eight years ago. Seems like yesterday!"

"Three hundred years ago!" cried the little girl. "But you told my uncle that she was old and couldn't mind your house anymore, so you needed my help!"

"So I did. You've a good memory for a child."

"But that wasn't true! You lied to us."

"Well, now," said the old man. "I wouldn't go that far. Alive or dead, she's certainly old, isn't she? Besides, there was something more important at stake. I wanted to bring you with me and there was a foresight upon me. Men must do what men must do at such times. And if you *had* come with me, perhaps much pain would have been avoided. And I found you again, didn't I? Don't think there's no design in that, even if you can't see the pattern yourself."

Ulla screwed up her face and looked at him hard. "You lied to us. That's wrong."

"It's very wrong," said Kirsikka, rousing herself from drowsiness and throwing back her fur-lined hood while her breath smoked in the chill air. "My father told me that it is always wrong to tell a lie, no matter what. He beat us if we lied to him. And he told me a story about a bad boy who was always telling his people that wolves were coming to catch their goats, all because he liked to frighten them and see them run. But one day, wolves really did come and, when the boy ran to tell his family, they didn't believe him. So all the goats were killed and the family had no meat or milk for the winter."

"Thank you for the lesson," Väinämöinen said sharply. "But I don't need the instruction of ignorant children from poor villages too far to the north. Spare me your wisdom since you can't understand mine. And you—" He stood up and pointed to Ulla. "You would do well to keep your thoughts to yourself if you can't show more gratitude.

"Let *me* tell *you* a story. One day, a brown bear was walking through the woods with a pheasant in his mouth, and he met a fox. The fox danced about and tried to get the bear to drop the bird, but honey-paw just walked on. Then the clever fox cocked his head and said, 'Well, you're a stupid one, aren't you! I'll bet you don't even know from which direction the wind blows when the noon sun is in your eyes, but the wind blows on your back.' 'Oh yes I do,' said honey-paw. 'It blows from the north!' But when he opened his mouth to speak, he dropped the pheasant. In a flash, the fox had it and was gone. And what's the lesson? Know when to keep your mouth shut! Now finish the meat, for at least *it* hasn't been eaten by wolves, has it? And we're going to go faster from now on, so your puny little legs need the strength."

Despite Väinämöinen's warning, they didn't seem to walk any faster the next day, although the girls gradually became aware that they never felt quite as tired as they expected to. They possessed a stamina they had never felt before.

The forest about them began to change. The narrow path remained the same, but the woods thinned out and the trees became more varied. The firs and pines failed, while stands of tall oaks loomed in the distance. Faded blooms and shrubs filled the brakes along the path. It also grew colder, for it was now almost winter. They came across little ponds and small, shallow pools with thin crusts of ice on top of them each morning. The land began to slope downward, and the travellers slowly descended a great shelf that leveled off here and there before gently plunging down again.

Late one afternoon, they came to the edge of a steep crest. The path tumbled down sharply and disappeared into the gloom below. Ulla thought that she could hear the telltale tinkling of water, as if many drops were being sprinkled over a wide pool. Tiny snowflakes began to fall: winter's first reluctant flurries. Väinämöinen suddenly swept the girls up, and, holding one in each arm, bounded down the sloping path with a shout until they came to a small, level lawn of short grass and tiny red flowers. He set the girls down and stood with his hands on his hips as they looked about in wonder.

"Here we are at last!" he said.

Before them a black river wound like a dark ribbon through the woods. The river was not wide, but its banks were steep and plunged straight down. The current moved slowly, and the water appeared dark and deep; ducks paddled softly near the shore. A bridge of white stone, no more than thirty feet in length, gracefully arched over the water and met the path again on the other side. The bridge's sides were fluted with what seemed to be the shapes of vessels or urns. It gave off a pale luminescence amongst the dark woods, faintly shining in the gloom as snowflakes fell around it and vanished into the water. If it were made of stone, the girls could see no lines or seams, nor blocks nor markings of any kind. It was white and smooth, as if carved out of a single great slab of pure marble, though Ulla could not imagine how the stone got there or how such a thing might be fashioned.

"This river is the Mustajouki," said Väinämöinen. "And it marks the border of the land of the Erilaiset. And the bridge is called the *Ankkaportti*, the gateway to the Enchanted Valley. I am glad to be home, little ones."

Väinämöinen walked onto the bridge, and the girls followed him. He stopped at its midpoint and looked out at the snow falling lightly on the black water. Ulla and Kirsikka turned to the opposite side. Standing on the fluted bridge with their hands on the rail, they could just see over the top. They peered down at the dark current flowing slowly beneath the bridge, a few leaves troubling its smooth surface. Ulla was mesmerized by the falling snowflakes and the river's faint sound, but suddenly realized that, only a few feet away in the murk below, something was rising out of the water—a figure of some sort, but whether of a man or something else, she couldn't tell.

The shadowy figure rose higher until Ulla could make out its head and two long arms at its sides, as if a man or woman was standing in waist-deep water in the middle of the river. She could not make out its features, however. It seemed to be the same dark color as the river from which it rose, and looked smooth and glassy in the dim, misty light. It had no mouth, no nose, no ears. Indeed, as Ulla peered at it, it seemed completely featureless except for the slightest hint of light that vaguely suggested two eyes.

Ulla opened her mouth to call to Väinämöinen, but to her horror, no sound came out. Her voice was frozen and when she tried to move she found that her limbs and body wouldn't obey. She felt a tingling throughout her whole body and sensed an unseen power or force all around her, binding her, keeping her still and unmoving. Her heart raced, but at just that moment, Kirsikka cried out, "Väinämöinen! Väinämöinen, look!"

Even before Kirsikka's words died, Väinämöinen stood between the girls, looking at the shape in the river. He laid a hand on each of their heads and at once Ulla felt the terrible force diminish, releasing her tongue and body.

"Väinämöinen, what is it?!" she cried.

But Väinämöinen laughed and called out to the mysterious figure. "Well, *Näkki*, what news is there from the Mustajouki? I am back from my long journey and come again to my homeland. What have you to say to me?"

The dark shape was silent, swaying slightly from side to side in the current.

Väinämöinen frowned.

"So now, is there no news that the waters flowing into the forest from many lands have brought with them? I am Väinämöinen! Loose your tongue and speak to me!"

But still the dark shape remained silent.

"Very well," said the old man, and Ulla heard the displeasure in his voice. "I will repay your rudeness with the same coin. In any case, what could Näkkiä tell me that I don't already know, or won't learn soon enough? But listen to me! These mortal children are with me and under my protection. They will not be about alone, but just the same, leave them be! If you don't, I'll sing up a storm the likes of which you've never seen and I'll suck you and all your folk up into the clouds, spreading your spirit in a million raindrops all across the Far Northern Land. It will take an age for you to ever come together again and the world will be changed by then, and your time over. Do you understand me? Now go back to your watery home!"

The dark shape swayed for a moment, raising an arm in a strange gesture, but then it slowly sank back into the black water until it disappeared, save for its eyes; they were still visible, glistening in the shadows below. Väinämöinen shook his head and pulled the girls down from the rail.

"What was that?" the girls said together as they crossed over the white bridge and came down onto the path on the other side.

"That was a Näkki," said the old man. "Didn't your parents warn you about them? He was one of the *Vedenkansa*: the water folk. Näkkiä live in rivers and lakes all across the Far Northern Land—at least, they used to. There are still many here and there, I suppose. They especially like to live beneath bridges or by fords, and if mortals aren't careful, they'll put their spell on you and take you with them down to their dark homes among the reeds. They prefer foolish children, but any mortal will do if they have a mind for it."

"Will they drown you?" asked Kirsikka.

"Perhaps. That can certainly happen. But there are other things they can do down there that are even less pleasant, and that little ones like you don't need to know about. Let them be! But no harm will come to you as long as you're with me. The Näkkiä of Ankkaportti are the guardians of the Enchanted Valley. Nothing can cross the Mustajouki without their knowing it. And if you've paid attention, you know where we are now, for we're across the bridge and are in the land of the Erilaiset! We'll soon reach my home in Väinölä!"

"Is it far?" asked Ulla.

"I said we'll be there soon, didn't I? No, not far. An hour or two, perhaps. We shall be under the stars in Väinölä tonight!"

Ulla looked back and glimpsed the bridge shining softly behind them. She fancied she saw several figures in the river beneath, swaying this way and that in the swirling snow, but it was dark. The bridge and the swaying figures were soon lost in the distance.

They followed the path down into the river valley, keeping the Mustajouki, bending and curving, always within sight—or sound—to their right. From the Ankkaportti, the path grew broader and was paved with flat stones, black and smooth like glass or fresh ice. The forest was much less dense, with stands of trees separated by patches of short grass and bramble. Here and there, larger trees of different sorts, chiefly larches and willows, rose right beside the path or stretched their branches out over the river. The snowflakes continued to fall for a while, but gradually tapered off as the sky cleared above them.

Bright starlight suddenly lit the darkling forest. Väinämöinen sped up, and when he saw the girls stumbling to keep up with him, stopped, scooped them up again, and strode on down the path, singing to himself as they walked in the cold night air.

Ulla and Kirsikka were bouncing along on Väinämöinen's shoulders when they suddenly heard a peal of laughter break the nighttime silence. There was a stand of oaks right beside the path, and the laughter seemed to come from the trees. The old wizard stopped and looked up as the laughter rang out again.

"Well, well, if it isn't old Väinämöinen," said a voice. It was the voice of a young woman, and seemed to come from the tallest tree. "So you've come back after all. We were beginning to wonder."

Ulla looked up and saw two women sitting on the oak's lower limbs. Despite the cold, they were clothed in delicate dresses of green and brown, and their light brown hair curled about their shoulders, save for a few thin braids. Their legs dangled down, their feet shod in small leather shoes lined with white fur. Even in the dark, Ulla could see the women were not mortals, but Erilaiset. Their pale faces were long and thin, and their bright eyes were slightly too large for mortal kind. Ulla could see leaf-shaped ears peeping out of the long curly hair of the woman on the lower limb. The women smiled as they looked down at the old man and the two little girls.

"Yes, I'm back," said Väinämöinen. "And if I tarried, I had good reason."

"No doubt," said one of the women. "And we can see the reasons! You've gone looking for a mortal wife again! I suppose you've learned from your past mistakes, though. When the first one runs off, you can marry her little friend. You might need more than two, however!"

"They are a little young, though, aren't they?" said her companion. "Still, I suppose a mortal child may be better for you after all. They're too stupid to think much on their own, and you can catch them easier, before they drown themselves! Just make sure the Näkkiä don't get them if they wander off!"

"You might have found some that aren't as ugly as these two," said the first woman. "But I guess an old man can't be choosy, can he?"

The women began laughing again, and the sound seemed to fill the forest. Väinämöinen cleared his throat. He had a tight, thin-lipped smile on his face, but leveled the women in the trees with a dark gaze.

"If I *were* looking for a wife, why not look among mortals? Do you think I'd look among the scraps of the forest? But I'm glad to see that all is well in the Valley, and just as I left it. The stars shine brightly, the trees grow tall, and their low-hanging fruit have the same weak hearts and weak magic."

"Is that the best you can do?" laughed the first woman. "I suppose you're tired after your long journey—unless you've really been drinking in the cabins of the Karelialaiset for the past year. But don't underestimate our magic until you've felt a taste of it!"

"Good, good," said Väinämöinen. "I'm glad you're feeling so strong! Perhaps we can put that strength to good use soon. Because I haven't been drinking with the Karelialaiset—more's the pity—but burning their dead and riding through their wasted lands, where I found these children. But when Löhi reaches out her cold hand to the Taikalaakso, I'm sure your magic will protect you! After all, you know what she did to your aunties in times gone by, don't you? If you've forgotten, just go ask those who still live!"

The second woman laughed again, but the smile disappeared from her friend's face and, with a spiteful scowl, she looked away from the wizard as if it were suddenly painful to meet his eye. But Väinämöinen turned, hitched Ulla and Kirsikka up higher on his shoulders, and continued down the paved path.

"Foolish *Metsäneitoa*," he muttered. "I didn't pass through mud, blood, and eastern steel for a whole year to listen to their silliness the day I return. But then again, those two are only about two hundred years old, and the young have some right to be stupid."

"But who are they, Väinämöinen?" asked Ulla. "Are they Erilaiset?"

"Of course. There aren't any Kaamoslaiset in the Enchanted Valley, not normally—except for you two just now, that is. They're Metsäneitoa: tree maidens. Sylphs, your folk called them in days gone by. Harmless enough, I suppose. They'll grow up soon."

The woods opened up even more now and a cold wind blew down upon them from the north. Lesser paths began to branch off from the main way, leading toward stands of trees or disappearing behind small, brushy hills. The Mustajouki took a bend to the south, but the path turned northeast and they soon lost sight of the river's dark line, and no longer heard the tinkling water. There were lights up ahead in the gloaming, and here and there the sound of voices or laughter. At last, they came to a narrow lane that turned sharply north, away from the stone path. Two rowan trees marked its entrance. Väinämöinen set the girls down so that they could all walk side by side as they took to this northward lane.

About a mile down the lane, the old man and the two little girls came to a large round clearing bordered by a babbling brook, which ran over a rocky bed. They splashed through its shallow water and stood in an opening in the trees, looking out at a well-tended meadow. A sweet forest smell was in the cool night air, richer than the wood smell of the forests of the Marches. Väinämöinen put his hands on the girls' heads and smiled.

"We're here," he said. "This is Väinölä, my home."

Ulla and Kirsikka stared in wide-eyed wonder at the sight before them. The clearing was surrounded by huge rowan trees, larger than any the girls had yet seen, their branches still green and groaning with red and golden berries. There were lights, chiefly blue and white, hanging among the branches like great lamps, but the girls could not see how they were fashioned. In the center of the brightly lit circle was an outcropping of stone, and amidst all, a bubbling pool from which issued the brook they had crossed.

On the clearing's far side grew a mighty oak so tall it seemed on a scale not that existed for mortal men or the waking world, but rather for a dreamscape in a land of giants. The Oak of Väinölä, mighty *Isotammi*, was indeed the tallest tree in the Far Northern Land. Two hundred feet into the sky it rose, with innumerable limbs and branches, and it was so wide that it seemed almost a small cottage or house. Indeed, a doorway in its trunk opened to the clearing, and a yellow light shone out from the living tree, for Väinämöinen's home was within.

As the singer led them into the circle, Ulla saw that there were many people gathered about, who came forward to greet them, singing words of welcome and return, and crying, "Väinämöinen! Väinämöinen!" Some of the folk looked almost like mortal men and women, save for a certain light that shone in their eyes even in the dark; others were more obviously Erilaiset, with long, thin faces, or else statures half that of the folk of the Seven Clans, though they were not children. And, like the Reindeer Folk, the Erilaiset of Väinölä dressed in many bright colors, with capes or coats of warm fur wrapped about them.

Väinämöinen, laughing and clearly pleased, strode across the clearing to the mighty oak, embracing many friends along the way. The Erilaiset smiled at the two little girls with him, and brought them wooden cups filled with a sweet, milky drink, as was their custom.

As they approached the great tree, Ulla noticed two figures standing next to it: a man and a woman. The man was so like to Väinämöinen that he could have been the old wizard's brother. His beard was long and white, his face round with high cheekbones. He was wrapped in a great green cape with many fine and clever symbols stitched into it, and wore a tall green hat. Even the high leather boots strapped round his thighs were cut like Väinämöinen's, though they were dark brown rather than yellow; he leaned on a copper-shod staff.

But the woman was very different. She stood tall and erect, her fair face neither young nor old; Ulla at once thought her the most beautiful woman she had ever seen. Her dark brown hair, rich and full, cascaded in many curls about her shoulders. Her lips were cherry red, and her large, green eyes shone with an inner light. She wore a long, green dress that fell like velvet, and a silver belt, fashioned like so many forest leaves, hung low about her kirtle. But her white feet were bare on the cold turf.

"Well, Väinämöinen," said the man. "It has been a year and a day since we parted at the Ankkaportti, when you left the Valley. Many tidings have flowed down the Mustajouki to us since then. It has been hard to keep track of you! But I daresay you have tidings enough for us as well."

"Indeed, indeed," said Väinämöinen. "But you disappoint me, Turi. I looked for you to greet me at the Ankkaportti, if not even earlier. After all, *'Food and fire are the traveler's want, but a friend's welcome best of all.'*"

"Don't be so hasty!" said Turi. "When the cold beer, new mead, and hot meat on the spit that await you within are found wanting, then you can complain! But welcome back now to Väinölä. Take your rest ere we talk of what we must."

"Aye, I must rest before we swap tales. I'm not as young as I was a thousand years ago, and my bones are tired through and through. And these little ones are at the end of their endurance."

Väinämöinen embraced his friend and they laughed, but the tall woman stepped forward toward the girls, the barest hint of a strange, thin smile on her face.

She reached out her long hand with slim, clever fingers adorned with silver rings and stroked Kirsikka's curly red hair. Kirsikka blushed and turned away, but the woman spoke in a clear, even voice, "Welcome to the Enchanted Valley, little Cherry." She turned to Ulla and bent low, peering at the dark-haired girl closely and carefully. Looking back at Väinämöinen, she asked, "Is this the child?"

"This is the one," answered Väinämöinen.

She stared intently at Ulla. The little girl suddenly felt the power in this beautiful woman, and a tremendous compulsion to meet her gaze, to stare back into her bright green eyes. This was not like the Näkki's spell, which bound her body so that she could not move or speak; Ulla knew that she could look away at any time, but had neither the will nor desire to do so. The woman's lips did not move, and the thin smile stayed on her face, but Ulla heard a voice within her very mind speaking words that no one else could hear.

"Hello, little daughter. Long have I awaited your coming."

She straightened then, touched Ulla's cheek, and said aloud, "Welcome, Ulla of the Karhulaiset. You are under our protection here in the Forest. Have no fear; let your mind and soul be at ease while you are with us, for I am Mielikki, daughter of the Vanhalaiset, and all this place is beneath my power."

Väinämöinen came up to the girls and again laid his hands on their heads. The stamina and strength that had sustained them beyond the measure of even full-grown men was suddenly gone, as if a great tension were released. The girls were at once exhausted, even more so than after their flight from the Itäläiset. Ulla's eyes fluttered and she swayed on her feet.

"Your charges are tired, Väinämöinen," said Mielikki. "Go now and take your well-earned rest! Your folk have seen that your house is prepared."

"Well and good," said Väinämöinen. "Though I may test Turi's promises before I sleep, at least about the beer." The old man smiled at the little girls. "Come, my children."

Taking them each by the hand, he led them through the oaken doorway where the yellow light spilled all about, enveloping them in a soft, radiant glow.

Chapter Eight

The Shadow of Loveâtar

A dark shadow of uncertainty hung over the Stone City of Etelamaa. The bright summer's promise of plentiful harvests and uninterrupted peace had given way to a winter of doubt and despair.

First had come Väinämöinen's return after many long years. Rumor of his strange disappearance from the city and wild ride back to the north had spread throughout the land. Then came news of the raid of the Itäläiset, striking out of the wastes beyond the Marches. Such a thing had not happened in many long lives of men. Nigan the King sent a company of soldiers to the border with High Länsimaa to help the Karhulaiset if they could, and to protect the Etelalaiset who lived in the Vales between Lake Etelajärvi and the forest, but the raiders did not go that way.

Soon, even worse tidings reached the Stone City. Several ships of the Swan Folk were attacked by raiders in the Itämeri Sea, including a great, many-oared trading vessel filled with spices and precious things from the south. Some said the raiders flew the flags of the *Tavastialaiset*, the Hare Folk, but Tavastia sent denials and word that its own ships had been assailed as well. Then, men landed in several longboats, attacking a small port town on the coast where fishing boats were built. The strange men burned the shipworks and sacked the port while the townsfolk fled in terror, then put out to sea again before help arrived. No living man in Etelamaa could remember so brazen an attack by raiders from the south.

By now, many in the city had heard of Väinämöinen's warning about the Witch whose name was not spoken in Etelamaa, and though few believed such tales, they still feared that evil times were returning to the Far Northern Land.

While winter deepened, Egan's life continued much as before. The young prince went about his lessons and trained with his masters and, at times, played with his brother and sister, or with old Orvo when there was no one else. Though his days appeared normal, Egan was distracted and, for the first time, truly displeased his masters. He could not put Väinämöinen out of his mind and thought constantly about the old singer's tale. He eagerly sought out whatever information could be found in the city about the Erilaiset, and often neglected his studies. His masters scolded him, but Egan was convinced that the old man's words were true, and that the ill tidings that came to the city from all quarters were proof of Löhi's return and evidence of some grand design in the making.

If Egan's studies suffered, other lessons did not. More than ever before, he threw himself into his training, practicing swordsmanship and archery for long hours and increasing his skills. When news arrived of the raid on the coast, Egan planned what he would have done, had he been there, leading a charge of Etelalaisen soldiers against the raiders and rescuing the townsfolk. The boy grew more restless than ever; he simply could not wait to grow up and wear the sword, shield and armour of a warrior for real.

Snow came early that year, and a harsh winter wind blew strong out of the north. Vendla the Queen took ill, and for some weeks stayed mostly in bed or in her chambers. Egan waited on his mother and helped care for his little sister. He often sat at his mother's bedside, and together they looked out at the bay as snow fell on the cold water. The queen's illness passed, but a sadness lingered about her that had not been there before. Her dreams were troubled, and she would awake in the middle of the night with a vague sense of foreboding and disquiet; sometimes Egan had these same dreams and felt this same unrest.

So the early winter passed, and time drew on to Midwinter's Day—the shortest day of the year, when the pale sun was above the horizon only a few hours before sinking again. This was a great holiday all across the Far Northern Land, for so the Kaamoslaiset sought to lighten the long winter's darkness, and the new year was reckoned to begin with the coming of the next full moon. All the clans celebrated the day, though by different names; in Akkala they celebrated the Long Night, and the Hare Folk in Tavastia made the Feast of *Talvijää,* or winter's ice, but the Swan Folk celebrated Sunwelcome, for they looked forward to winter's end and the spring that would come after.

The Swan Folk spent the day of Sunwelcome among family. They gathered in their homes with their nearest kin, and others that lived far away joined them, if chance allowed. The people prepared a great feast according to their measure. Women used the last of the summer's honey to bake sweet cakes and breads; they slaughtered sheep, swine, and ate white fish and herring that had been pickled so as to keep through the long winter months. The king's cook might make gingerbread or blood sausages, or fish pies baked in dark rye. In the city, throughout the day and night, the people burned candles in their windows. Some went to graveyards, where their kin were buried or entombed, and lit candles there as well, in memory of their loved ones. The candles burned throughout the night, like hundreds of tiny tongues of flame dancing in the darkness.

The Royal House of the Etelalaiset traditionally invited prominent men of the city to feast with the king and queen in the Keep at Sunwelcome, and so Nigan sent word to several wealthy merchants and traders to join him, along with the Captain of the Wardens of Etelamaa, the Shipmaster, and some noblemen from the coasts. The Hall of the Swan was arrayed with many fine and beautiful things, and the long tables heavily burdened with food and drink for the visitors. Egan was surprised because, for the first time, he was seated at the main table with his parents and their chief guests. His cousin Aldon glared at him from across the hall, where children were gathered, and where Egan himself had sat for the celebration in the past. The young prince would come of age in the new year, however, and Nigan thought it time to prepare him for the role he would one day play by introducing him to the men he would both work with and lead.

Egan spoke courteously, but mostly listened to the others as he ate the sweet breads filled with summer berries brought in barrels from the north. The king's feast was a time for merriment, but there was less mirth than usual this year, for all were concerned about the ill news. The lords from the southern coast were especially worried; they had argued against Nigan's decision to send more soldiers to the northern borders. Vendla seemed worried as well; she said little to the ladies at table, and her pale face with its fine features was troubled.

When the feast ended, Nigan bid his guests good night and retired with his brother Alder and his counselors to a private chamber. Egan felt restless and decided to go out onto the walls by the tower where he could look down over the bay. He wrapped a thick, hooded cloak around himself and had just started to steal up the irregular stone steps when Orvo caught him.

"It is rather late and rather cold to be going outside," said the old servant. "Take off your cloak and come back! Your mother is still awake in her room."

"Nonsense," replied Egan. "I want to watch the lights. If you're so concerned, why don't you grab your cloak and join me?"

"I'm too old to be tempting fate and looking for colds by standing on the roof in the freezing wind. You'll catch your death up there tonight! Come back down, my prince, and I'll fetch you hot cider from the kitchens."

"No, Orvo," said the boy. "I'm going up. Good Sunwelcome to you; now leave me alone!"

"Your mother will be very displeased," said Orvo. "When she finds out what you're doing, there will be consequences."

"She wouldn't find out anything if it wasn't for you," said Egan. "But I'm not a child anymore and your threats are growing as old as you are. Now good night to you and goodbye!"

Egan bounded up the steps as Orvo's protests faded behind him, coming out through a small turret door onto the flat courtyard atop the Keep. It was cold—very cold—and even with his warm garments, Egan felt the bitter chill. The boy carefully walked across the icy stone courtyard to the low parapet that overlooked the bay. He glanced up at the old tower and saw the watchman, silhouetted against the yellow light of a guttering torch, standing in its window. Below him was the icy bay. Winter had come early to Etelamaa, freezing the bay over several weeks ago. Egan saw beached ships and boats resting on wooden beams, protected from the ice that could crush smaller vessels. All about the city, he saw the flicker of candlelight and torchlight, twinkling in the snowy dark. Egan enjoyed its beauty, which seemed reflected by the twinkling stars in the clear sky above.

The waxing moon hung low, spilling its light across the bay. Wisps of clouds drifted across its surface as the wind picked up. Egan pulled his cloak tighter around him. Turning to go inside, he saw something strange in the northern sky; a dark spot had appeared among the stars.

No ragged cloud or patch of distant snowfall, the shadow crept across the moon, slowly growing larger. Like a great bird it seemed, with vast wings outstretched. Blacker than the night sky, it raced toward the city and bore down on the Keep. Without warning, the wind blew from the north like a gale. Egan staggered backwards as the flags and pennants snapped. The watchman cried out; the boy saw him point to the menacing shape.

Speeding across the bay, as huge as a dragon in flight, the black shadow swept over the Keep, passing just above the tower and battlements. Overcome with sudden sickness, Egan crouched down as the wind blew about him. He fell to his hands and knees, retching. A piercing cry rang out over the city, a ghastly wail of pain and misery that filled his heart with horror and despair.

The wind died down as suddenly as it began, and as his sickness passed, the boy stumbled to his feet. The watchman was gone. Egan heard voices and shouts here and there in the dark—guards atop the Keep or folk about on the streets below. He ran to the turret door, almost slipping on the ice, then sprang down the steps and raced through the passage to his parents' chamber.

Many people were already there. The queen had been sitting at a window with her younger children, watching the twinkling lights. Marjatta was crying while one of her nursemaids tried to comfort her. Orvo and several other servants stood about, and one of the guards, dressed in full regalia for the feast, had come to check on the royal family.

"Did you see it?! Did you see it?!" cried Egan.

"Where were you?" Vendla asked sharply.

Egan glanced down at his frost-dusted cloak; he had obviously just been outside. He looked at Orvo, who shook his grey head.

"I was up on the wall," Egan replied. "Forgive me, Mother, but a dark shadow passed over the city! And a great wind and a terrible cry. Did you see it?"

"We saw it," said the queen, shaking her head disapprovingly. "It was like a black cloud, blacker than night. It seemed to come straight toward us, and then it was gone. Many lights in the city below were put out by the wind!"

"But what do you think it was?" asked Egan.

"Perhaps it was indeed only a cloud," said Orvo, "blown toward the city by a storm out of the north."

"It was no cloud," said the guard. "Or at least no storm cloud of *this* world. To me, it was like a great shadow with wings, or else a black beast trailing the remnants of a tattered cloak. And I, too, heard a cry, and so came here to see that nothing was amiss."

"Whatever it was, it is an ill omen," said Vendla, taking Marjatta into her lap and stroking the little girl's fair hair. "There has been much news of late, and all of it bad. And now this thing happens, even at Sunwelcome! Go and tell the king that I request his presence. Whatever his counsels, he will want to know of this immediately."

Word had already been sent to Nigan, and he soon arrived. As he'd been meeting with his counselors in one of the Keep's inner chambers at the time, he had neither seen the shadow nor heard the eerie wail, but many others had. The king had no doubt that *something* strange had happened. Nigan stationed more guards along the walls, while the whole royal household watched through the night to see if the shadow would return. But nothing else happened; the shadow was not seen again. And so the longest night of the year passed, giving way to a cold and uncertain dawn.

Many Swan Folk in the Stone City or along the bay's northern shore had seen the shadow as they returned to their homes from celebrations. Rumor of the omen—for many, like Vendla, deemed it as such—spread throughout the city. The next days passed uneventfully, however.

Egan turned his hand to many tasks in those days. As he grew older, his father looked to him to perform the duties of a full prince. For example, every year, in anticipation of the new year, the Swan Folk made a great wreath of living fir and red winter berries to place atop a tall marble column in the Great Square. The likeness of a swan graced the column, hearkening back to the clan's ancient totem that had once stood there, though few now made the connection. This year, Nigan sent the young prince to preside over the wreath ceremony, and the gathered folk cheered him as he mounted a scaffold and helped hang the wreath.

The prince was also busy packing. The king's household would leave the city shortly after the new year and stay in Kotanrannta for several weeks. Kotanrannta meant Aldon, and Egan was never enthusiastic about weeks spent with his irksome cousin. Kotanrannta also meant getting away from the city to hunt in the snowy woods and ski on frozen lakes; those things made Aldon endurable, if no less irksome. Egan packed his favorite things, especially the charts and maps he loved to pore over for hours, then helped his mother direct the packing for many others.

On the first day of the new year, Nigan gathered his counselors together in the Hall of the Swan. They had several issues to discuss before he left the city, especially the complaints of the lords of the coastlands, who, by then had returned to their homes. Several great Houses of the Etelalaiset had warred against the House of Joutsen and the rightful king in Egan's grandfather's time, especially those whose wealth was based on traffic upon the Itämeri Sea. Those days of war and strife, though long past, were not forgotten—at least not in the coastal fiefs. This year, the king's decision to send soldiers to the borders of High Länsimaa, when, in normal times, they would be home for harvest and winter, displeased the lords of the coast. They would rather their own defenses be strengthened, though more raids by boat seemed unlikely while the sea was frozen.

The king asked Egan to attend and invited several other guests: Alder the Grand Duke, Toiva Merikainen, and Juvari, the Marshall of the Army of Etelamaa among them. Egan knew these men well and saw most of them regularly, but he noticed they greeted him differently now that his father was treating him as a full prince and heir to the throne. Toiva, in particular, seemed to watch Egan closely as he greeted the king's other counselors. They had just begun to discuss the lords' complaints and the dispatch of soldiers to the north, when Kultimo, the king's chamberlain, came rushing into the hall, accompanied by a man dressed in white with red stripes sewn to his sleeves.

"Forgive me, Your Majesty," Kultimo said breathlessly. "But I have urgent news! I have been much about the city and I fear a terrible thing is happening!"

"There is no news but ill news these days," sighed Nigan. "Speak, Kultimo. What is this terrible thing you fear?"

"Well, there is—there is a sickness, my lord."

"What kind of sickness?" asked the king.

Kultimo looked at his companion, a somewhat disheveled young man with a stubbly ginger beard. "It is best left to him to describe," he said with a nod to the young man. "This is Sankki, a man from the Sick Wards. Tell the king what you have seen."

"Well," the young man said nervously. "It is an honor to meet you, my lord. As the Lord Chamberlain said, my name is Sankki and I'm one of the Healers in the Sick Wards of the city. Aarva, the Master Healer, has left the city to visit his family near to Etelajärvi, so I am in charge of the Wards until his return."

"Then be welcome in this hall," said Nigan. "And be at ease, Sankki; tell us what seems to be amiss."

"Well, my lord," replied Sankki with more confidence. "It began some five days ago. People began carrying their kin into the Sick Wards with a strange illness. There are always some folk in the Wards, of course, those ill or hurt in some mishap. But this was different. There were but few at first, yet they all showed the same signs: burning with a fire that feverstay would not relieve, and pale, as if the blood were drained from their faces. And many could not speak or lost their speech soon after coming to us."

"How many suffer from this affliction?" asked Nigan.

"Not many at first," said Sankki. "Although we heard reports of folk still in their homes afflicted likewise. But yesterday and today, more have been brought in—many more. There are now cases from all the seven districts of the city. Young and old, man and woman: we can see no pattern as yet."

"But the king asked how many are sick," said Toiva. "What is the number of folk so afflicted?"

"I do not know for sure, my lord. At first, perhaps a dozen among the city's three Sick Wards. Since yesterday, perhaps two score."

"Two score!" said Nigan. "So many! What is the course of this sickness? Have any died?"

The young man glanced nervously at Kultimo and cleared his throat.

"They have *all* died, my lord."

"All of them!" exclaimed several of the men together.

"Yes," said Sankki. "Or at least, all who first came to us. There are none still alive that have been with us longer than three days. We have tried many things, but cannot save them. They have all died."

There was a long silence; then the king sank into a chair, shaking his head. "But what is the nature of this thing?" he asked.

"We do not know, my lord," Sankki said in a somber tone. "Perhaps Aarva, were he here, would have some idea. But it would seem to be Plague."

"Plague!" exclaimed Toiva. "But Plague is a disease of summer! How can this be? It's not possible."

"Who can say?" said Sankki. "But it is not the Pox. It is not the Red Fingers. There is no rash, nor marks on the skin. There are records of a pestilence long ago—during the time of the Witch—that was called the Winter Plague. Perhaps it is the same."

"During the Witch's time!" Kultimo said suddenly. "Yes! There is still more, my lord. Tell him!"

Sankki seemed reluctant to say more, but the king nodded for him to continue.

"My lord, some of those in the Wards who could speak told a strange tale before they fell silent and died. They said that they saw a strange figure, like a wizened old crone, and they were terrified. Shortly after that, they became ill. It would...it would seem to be only a feverish rant, my lord. But others have reported this across all the city's districts. And some say this began the very night of Sunwelcome, when many people saw a shadow flying over the city and heard the terrible keening that followed. I do not know about such things, my lord, but people...people are already beginning to talk. And the nurses that work in the Wards, at least, have put a name to this strange ghost: Lovêatar, the Mistress of Disease."

Shocked by Sankki's strange tale, none of the men said a word, but all knew the name Lovêatar and somewhat of the legends surrounding that dreadful spirit, whether they believed them or no.

Prince Egan had long studied the old legends and tales, and so he knew more than any of them. He put his hand on the king's shoulder and said, "Father, what are we going to do?"

Nigan stood up and faced Sankki. "Very well. It is clear that we must act, whatever the truth of these rumors. What is your counsel, Healer?"

"Aarva is the Master Healer, lord," said Sankki. "And there are others with greater knowledge than mine who are also away from the city."

"But it is *you* who are in charge now," answered the king. "And we cannot wait for Aarva's return. It is up to you to guide our counsels, for we are not sage in these matters. Now, tell me. What do you recommend?"

Sankki looked from face to face, and finally back at Nigan. "My lord, my counsel is that you should declare this a Plague and publish the news in all parts of the city. Then there are measures we can take to stop or slow its spread; there are homes with more than one soul afflicted, and it would seem this illness communicates from one to another. At the least, we may keep it within the city and spare the countryside."

"There will be panic if a Plague is declared," said Toiva. "People will flee the city and all commerce will stop, and it is already the deep of winter. How do you know this illness will not burn itself out as so many have done before?"

"I cannot say what will happen, my lord. But if we do not take measures now, I believe it will worsen. And as for panic, many already speak of it. The rumor will spread throughout the city soon enough, my lord, whether it is declared or not."

Nigan turned to Toiva and his other counselors, but they bowed their heads and awaited his decision; only the king might decide such a thing. At last, he made up his mind and spoke in a clear voice.

"We will wait one day. I want a report brought to me tomorrow morning of what has happened and how many new cases have come into the Wards. But if it is clear that this thing is not abating, I shall declare a Plague; the Healers will have authority to order things as they see fit."

Kultimo and Sankki bowed and took their leave, while the king's counselors spoke in hushed tones. The issues that had seemed so weighty only moments before were now an afterthought. Nigan went and sat on the Black Throne, beckoning Juvari and Toiva to his side.

"Have a messenger made ready for a long and uncertain ride," he said, putting his hand atop his son's sandy hair. "I want news of what has happened taken to Väinämöinen—wherever he may be found."

***

The king waited anxiously for the report from the Sick Wards the next morning, though with little hope.

Word came that people continued to arrive at the Wards with the strange and deadly sickness. The king declared a Plague and marshaled the city's guard to help with the necessary measures. No traffic was allowed in or out of the gates without special permission. The houses of those afflicted were marked with the *mustaristi*, the Plague Sign. And that sign was a black cross painted on the door to warn passersby. Those within were confined until the illness ran its course. The dead were taken to a graveyard beneath the old city's walls and buried quickly, without ceremony. There was no question of the royal family going to Kotanrannta, for if the king left the city, all order might break down into panic. Nigan indeed considered sending his wife and children out in secret, but Vendla would not agree, nor would Egan leave his father.

Even as Toiva had feared, all business in the Stone City ceased. The Etelalaiset shut themselves in their homes and came out as little as possible to avoid meeting those with the Plague. Others sought to flee, despite the Guard and the freezing cold. Yet, terrible as the sickness was, a greater fear filled the hearts of the Swan Folk with horror.

As Sankki had told the king, rumor spread of a ghastly apparition, seen by many folk in all the districts of the city. Some saw a shadow in the flickering candlelight within their homes, moving slowly across the wall toward rooms where children slept; afterward, someone would fall ill. Others saw a dark, crooked figure that crept about the dim, snowy streets. Wrapped in long, black rags, it had the wizened visage of an old hag beneath its tattered hood, its wrinkled face mottled and splotched. The crone wailed and cackled in a high-pitched, broken voice, and a terrible stench hung about her. Still others saw a different aspect, a tall young woman with flowing hair, beautiful save for a deathly white face utterly without expression. Her right hand remained hidden under her long black robe, but her left hand held a whip with nine tails.

Then a whisper grew. A name was heard on the tongues of all the Swan Folk, even sober-minded men of commerce who doubted that the Erilaiset existed, or that there ever was a Witch in the north: the name of Lovêatar.

For in their legends, the folk of the Far Northern Land still remembered that the evil spirit Lovêatar was the Mistress of Disease. The daughter of Tuone, the Lord of the Dead, she sent forth her dreadful contagions from his dismal realm into the world of living men to afflict them and bring them misery, for she herself was so afflicted, and pain and misery was all that she knew. And she was blind. Her spirit was bound to Tuonela save for times of great sickness, when a pale shadow, not even a true *etiänen*, might trouble the waking world. But all that changed when she met Löhi.

Löhi, bold and fearless, had visited Tuonela and explored its shadowy bounds of old. She learned many useful things there. She seduced dark spirits of the dead and returned them to the world of the living, where they might serve her. Nor did she fear being trapped in Tuonela herself, for she was strong and cunning. On a time, she met Lovêatar, and together they made terrible plans. And the Witch discovered—or else created—a portal through which Lovêatar might enter the living world with her help.

Then Lovêatar was glad, for she desired this and had been denied it by her father. She entered into league with Löhi, pledging to serve her and honor her as one of the Vanhalaiset, which pleased Löhi greatly. Lovêatar's awful spirit was made incarnate and she came into the Far Northern Land, spreading pain and sickness throughout the Seven Clans. But when Lemminkäinen threw down Löhi and the Witch vanished from mortal lands, Lovêatar was herself banished to Tuonela.

Few in Etelamaa knew all this tale, but the folk of the Stone City remembered enough to have little doubt that Lovêatar walked among them, and that the Witch of the North—Löhi—had finally returned. Väinämöinen's tale had been true!

As the weeks went by, the number of dead mounted until several hundreds had perished. The Plague struck down folk from all walks of life. Rich and poor, man and woman, parent and child—none were safe from the lashes of Lovêatar's whip.

Word came at last that even the Healer, Sankki, had succumbed to the sickness. And it was said that as Sankki sat at his desk tallying victims, he felt a presence at his shoulder and turned to find the hag, smiling, standing beside him. Then he opened his ledger, made a final tally mark, and closed it again; and before the day was out, he, too, was dead.

During all this time, Egan stayed inside the Keep on his father's orders. As chance would have it, none of the royal family or their household fell sick. The young prince spent most of his days with his brother and sister, playing games or instructing them since their masters were not permitted within. But Egan often sat alone in his room, staring out the narrow windows at the cold, lifeless city below. At last, reports came that the Plague was letting up, at least in some parts of the city. Fewer victims came into the Wards, and some of the afflicted survived the illness, though they were very weak afterward. One day, Tervo was allowed to return and Egan spent the entire morning with him, but it did not ease the prince's restlessness.

Egan had not been outside the Keep for several weeks, except to take cold walks along the walls or around the snowy courtyard. Now, despite his father's admonition, he decided to sneak out and walk the streets. Egan knew the guards at the bridge gate well and had little trouble getting past them. Bundled against the bitter cold, he marveled at how easy it was to leave the Keep and wondered why he had waited so long to do so. Egan wanted to walk the silent streets, but, more than that, he secretly hoped to see the specter of Lovêatar, or at least hear her baleful cry. He was no fool and knew that many who saw the evil spirit had sickened and died. But he was young, and, with the confidence of youth, he felt that *he* was different and that no harm could come to him no matter the risk. Egan also believed that Väinämöinen would soon come to their aid, and he wished to be able to tell the wizard that he had seen the hag himself.

In the silent, empty streets of the City of Etelamaa, snow and ice were piled high in places, for the lanes had not yet been cleared. Egan saw some few people hurriedly going about their business, but most still kept within their homes. He walked without aim or purpose, then turned down a lane that led to the Great Square. His eyes chanced on something in the snow.

Sticking out from a drift were the legs and booted feet of a man or woman who had fallen there—a victim of the Plague, forgotten by all, left alone on the silent street. Of all the horrors of that terrible winter, something about this solitary, sad image filled his heart with searing pain that such a thing could happen in the very streets of Etelamaa! He felt a sudden sense of urgency and, forgetting the square, hurried back through the icy streets to the Keep.

Egan had slipped easily out of the Keep unnoticed, but found several people waiting for him when he returned. Tervo stood in his chambers, attended by one of his father's servants, and, of course, Orvo awaited him, but Egan found it quite strange to see Toiva Merikinen there as well. He expected to face their wrath for having disobeyed his father, but he saw that their faces were serious, not angry. The boy, shrewd as he was, grasped the significance at once.

"Who is it?" he asked.

"Your father," said Toiva. "It is time for you to go to him; do not tarry, Prince Egan."

Egan walked with the men through the Keep and up the steps toward his parents' chamber, his heart beating faster with every step. He realized then why Tervo had come into the Keep that morning: to distract him and keep him busy. For Nigan the King had fallen ill during the night, and the children had been kept from him until the course of his illness was known. There could now be little doubt. The king burned with fever and rapidly weakened; he was already abed, unable to move or speak.

All eyes fell on Egan when he entered the room. The queen beckoned him to his father's side. Vendla sat by the bed where her husband lay, her face calm and stoic, but Egan could see her red eyes and knew that she had been crying. Alder stood beside his brother, having arrived in the city some days before. Several of the king's counselors were gathered to one side with a few of the household's maids and servants behind them, for though it was dangerous, none would abandon the king in his hour of need.

Nigan lay on his back beneath warm covers. His beard had been shorn, which Egan thought strange. His face was deathly white and his skin taut, as if he had aged many years in the course of just one day, but his eyes flickered with life when his son sat beside him.

Egan took his father's hand and stroked it, sitting quietly beside him for some time. It took all the strength he could muster to keep from crying inconsolably, but tears still found their way down his cheeks. Prince or no, he was yet a boy and he loved his father dearly. At last, the queen signaled that he should go and he started to rise. Nigan suddenly stirred and raised his hand, grasping his son's arm with surprising strength. He looked into Egan's eyes and held his gaze, but no words came from his bloodless lips.

Egan turned to his mother and fell into her arms, sobbing like the child he was. Vendla held her son close to her, then took him from the chamber to another room, where Marjatta and Eglano waited with their nursemaid, Paiju. The boys stayed with Paiju, but after a while, Vendla returned to her vigil beside her husband. Egan played distractedly with his sister, trying to focus on anything to relieve the panic and pain that welled up inside him. Strange thoughts entered his mind.

Only a day before, he had shot arrows atop the walls while his father watched. Only two days before, he had gone with him to the stable. Only three days before...

It was only a short while, perhaps an hour, before Tervo appeared in the doorway. The dour teacher made an unlikely messenger, but he spoke gently to Egan, his face kindly and sad. And so it was that Nigan, King of Etelamaa, died of the Winter Plague, his spirit fleeing far away to Tuone's realm, such as should not have happened yet for many long years.

The king's body was taken from the chamber and laid out in an alcove within the castle, then covered by a fine pall since his face reflected his last agony. The nobles and counselors did not publish the ill news in the city, however; they gathered those within the Keep and swore them to silence. Many urgent decisions needed to be made: first and foremost, whether or not to open the city. The Plague was lessening, but clearly had not yet passed, and food was in short supply.

The strange rumors of what was happening in the city had already created great uncertainty elsewhere throughout the kingdom. The king's counselors feared what might happen if the Swan Folk learned that Nigan had perished in the Plague, or if their enemies, whom they now perceived to be all around them, were emboldened by the news. But many guards and servants came and went from the Keep, despite the Plague, and the king's death could not be kept secret long.

While the counselors debated, a distraught Vendla remained in a small, cold chamber in the old castle with her children. Egan sat by the hearthlike *takka*, feeding the fire with seasoned hardwood. He had little energy and little appetite, refusing the food that servants brought to them. His favorite dog, Tuli—a shaggy, black bearhound—lay its head in his lap, and the boy stroked its long fur while the fire crackled and smoked. The children slept that night in the same chamber while the queen, afraid they might sicken, too, watched them closely. But no shadow darkened their doorway and they slept soundly, save for Egan who only pretended to sleep as he stared at the burning embers until his mind finally drifted away.

The next day, the prince was restless again. He slipped away from his exhausted, sleeping mother, wrapped himself in a great bearskin coat, and went out onto the walls. The sky was cloudless and the day bright and sunny as Egan took in the clean, fresh air. A company of soldiers, royal guards in full regalia with long, shining spears, was mustered on the bridge before the Keep, and Egan listened to the officers barking orders. After a while, he went inside, shucked off his coat and snow-covered boots, and wandered about aimlessly. As he walked toward the Great Hall, not far from where he had found Väinämöinen the past summer, he neared a large, square room that was known as the map chamber because it held a long oaken table, upon which maps and other parchments were often laid out. Egan heard voices inside and stopped just outside the entrance to listen.

He heard many men arguing about something, and recognized the voices of his uncle Alder, Juvari, and Toiva Merikinen, as well as another of his father's counselors, Sinio. As Egan listened, the young prince realized with a cold shock that they were discussing *him*.

"I grow weary of repeating myself," said Alder. "Egan is the prince presumptive and the heir to Nigan's throne. He is the rightful king of Etelamaa. I will not take the crown."

"I have heard you," said a voice that Egan did not recognize. "But have *you* heard *me*? You haven't answered our concerns. He is only a boy and not yet a full prince of the kingdom. There is already trouble with the Houses of the Coast. All is amiss in the city, and it seems we are beset with enemies—north, south, and terror within. There are some among us who will not accept him, not at such a time."

"Lord Meripäivä is right, Your Grace," said Sinio. "You know the history of the Kultasaare Wars. A child of the House of Vipunen was made king then and much ruin came of it. The Houses of the Coast remember it well; old Verro is still alive, and might have been king long ago had things gone otherwise. His grandson, Kallas, is very rich and very bold. It is a risk to put the boy on the Black Throne—and not only because of Kallas. Many hard choices and many problems lie before us, maybe even war. The prince is a fine boy and perhaps his time may come, but I think that time is not yet at hand."

Strange as it might seem, Egan had not even considered such matters, or the fact that he was, of course, the heir to the throne. Wholly consumed with grief for his father's death and concern for his mother, he had not even paused to consider what it meant for him. He pressed himself hard against the wall in the cold, stony corridor as the men went back and forth in their debate.

"If you will not take the crown," said Meripäivä, "then at least declare yourself regent and rule in the boy's name until he is older."

"That might be well," said Alder. "But if what you say about the lords of the coast is true, then would they not also use a regency to claim that I had usurped the throne, and so put forward one of their own?"

"That is a danger," said Sinio. "Too great a danger, I think. No, if you will act, you must do so outright and take the crown as your brother's heir, not your nephew's regent. Do not forget the lessons of the past; let us remember to take the position of Tavastia into our counsels. Can we trust the king of the Hare Folk when he denies any part in the piracy that afflicts us? Can we trust him to not take advantage of an uncertain time should a child again be made heir? Consider these things well, Your Grace, ere you make your weighty decision."

"And whatever you do," said Toiva, "It must be done soon. Rumors will soon spread throughout the city, if they haven't already. The king's death cannot be concealed much longer."

"It was my brother's wish that Egan be his heir," replied Alder. "As his brother, I would honor his wish because I loved him. As his subject, I would obey his wish because he was king."

"Consistency in all things may be admirable," said Sinio. "But the exception may prove the rule, and can sometimes be the wiser choice."

"Do right and wrong change as the sun sets?" answered Alder. "Or should we strive for good and eschew evil only when we feel strong enough to do so? As I have already said—"

Just then, the door from the Great Hall was flung open and old Orvo came into the passage. Egan, startled, jumped away from the wall and stood facing him in the corridor, in plain view of the men gathered inside the map chamber.

"Egan, my lad!" cried Orvo. "What are you doing here? I was just coming up to see you."

There was no sound for several seconds. Trapped as he was, Egan almost turned and fled from the astonished old man. Then Alder appeared in the map chamber's open door. The grim-faced duke looked down at his nephew.

"Well and good," said Alder. "Come, Egan."

The boy walked into the map chamber with a fluttering heart. He was painfully aware of how he must appear to these stern men—disheveled, with his hair uncombed, his feet bare on the cold stone, and clad in the same tunic he had worn since the day his father died. Indeed, given his height, he looked more like an eleven- or twelve-year-old street urchin than the fifteen-year-old prince of Etelamaa. He tried to keep his head up, and, despite his blushing cheeks, looked the gathered men in the eyes.

Juvari sat at the long table and several other men stood about: Sinio, Toiva, Kultimo the Chamberlain, and the Captain of the Wardens of Etelamaa. There were several other royal counselors, and, to one side, a richly dressed man whom Egan guessed must be the nobleman Lord Meripäivä. He was tall and thin, with a dark complexion and long, black hair, drooping mustachios, and a short, pinched beard. Egan felt their piercing eyes on him like a thousand spears.

"You heard our debate," his uncle said. "Or at least enough of it."

Egan nodded.

"Then I put the choice to you, hard as it may be. You are your father's eldest son and chosen heir, and though none foresaw that this time would come so soon, so it has. By the ancient laws and customs of the Etelalaiset, you are the rightful head of the clan, and heir to the throne. Will you take this burden upon you?"

Egan's face burned and his limbs shook. Everything and nothing raced through his mind. His whole life—his whole existence—came down to this moment. He saw the cold look in the eyes of the king's men, but didn't waver. Instead, he thought of his father. With a surety that comes only to children, he knew in that moment what his father's eyes had tried to tell him as he lay dying.

Egan's voice trembled, but was proud nonetheless. "I will take the burden," he said. "I am the heir of Nigan, Lord of the Etelalaiset, and I will be king in my turn."

Alder reached out and touched the boy on the shoulder, then turned to the others.

"So be it," he said, deeply moved. "Egan has my fealty and my allegiance. Decide now, men of the Swan Folk! If you will not support the rightful king, then declare yourselves now and do not betray him later like the rebels of old!"

There was a moment's silence while all stood still, but only a moment's.

Juvari rose from the table, drew his sword, and knelt in front of Egan. "You have my fealty, my king, and that of all the Guard of Etelamaa."

Then one by one, the others bowed or knelt before him; finally, at the last, Meripäivä slowly bowed, his dark face somber.

So it was that on the third day after Nigan's passing, in the Great Square of the City of Etelamaa, Egan was crowned king. Many folk gathered in the snowy dusk. The Company of the Guard of the City was arrayed there in serried ranks, as were the Wardens, and the Mariners of the Shipwrights Guild. Alder brought the Amber Crown from the Keep. That crown was ringed in precious amber from the southern shores of the Itämeri Sea, rich brown in color and wonderful in clarity. But the crown bore, in its center, a stone of shining, pale blue amber, both beautiful and rare.

As was the custom among the Swan Folk, the widowed queen took the Amber Crown and, with the Chamberlain, placed it on the prince's head. And so Nigan's son was proclaimed Egan II, King of Etelamaa and Chief of the Clan of the Swan. The city was opened, and messengers were sent to publish the news throughout the land.

But still there was Plague in the city, and ever and anon the cries of Lovêatar echoed throughout its streets.

Chapter Nine

Mielikki's Prophecy

Kirsikka was very hungry when she awoke. She lay in bed, only half-awake, and only barely remembering where she was and what had happened. She stretched, aware of soft covers piled on top of her and a feather pillow beneath her head. Finally, the red-haired girl sat up and saw Ulla beside her, still asleep, her dark hair splayed about. Kirsikka got out of bed, her bare feet slapping the cold, hard floor, and crept from the small, dark bedroom into a large, round chamber. She stood there blinking in the bright yellow light of two great lamps suspended on unseen filaments from the high ceiling. The girl's eyes lit on a winding staircase across the room, and at last she remembered how she came to be there.

Väinämöinen had led the girls into the gigantic oak and down a spiral staircase, past three landings, until finally they came to the round room. In her exhaustion, Kirsikka had spared no thought for anything but getting to sleep, but now she walked slowly about in amazement.

Although it was obviously underground, it was impossible to tell if the chamber was fashioned out of a cave or tunnel, or from the living tree itself. The flue of a large, stone-piled hearth disappeared into the roof above. Several round doors led to smaller chambers like the bedroom the girls had slept in. Colorful tapestries and soft pelts adorned the walls; beautiful works of glass and finely wrought silver and gold crafted into cunning shapes decorated the room. A strange musical instrument with ten strings hung above the hearth, alongside several drums marked with queer symbols and designs. Amidst all these wondrous things, however, Kirsikka only had eyes for what she saw spread out on a long wooden table.

She had never seen such bread: light and fair-colored loaves unlike the dark rye of the Marches. Beside the bread stood a large silver pitcher filled with cold sour milk, the curds still floating on top. Wooden bowls held red and yellow winter berries and pale, white butter; sweet dried apples were piled upon a plate. But most amazing to the little girl of the north was a great bowl of golden honey, more than she had ever seen before or even imagined. The little red-haired girl—who had been plump in Bassböle, but was now almost as thin as Ulla—dipped a finger into the bowl and savored the rich, sweet taste. Kirsikka pulled up a high-backed chair and broke her fast.

She was finishing off her second loaf when Ulla finally appeared. "Look, Lumikki!" she cried. "It's a feast! But you'd better hurry, or else I'm going to eat it all myself—at least all the honey!"

The girls were still sitting at the table and marveling at the wondrous things in the strange house deep within Isotammi when Turi came down the stairs.

"Aha! You're awake now! And it looks like you had no trouble at all finding breakfast—most resourceful. How are you, little ones?"

"Very good, sir. Thank you, sir," said the girls together.

"And I take it everything is to your liking?"

"Yes, sir," answered Kirsikka, wiping her mouth on her sleeve. "It is all very good. We were very hungry."

"Good!" said Turi. "I'm glad to hear it. There's more where that came from, too. But if you're finished, then put on warm clothes—you should find new ones beside your bed—and come outside with me. It is snowing, and the green will soon be gone for another year!"

"But what about Väinämöinen?" asked Ulla. "Where is he?"

Turi laughed and pointed to a round yellow door. "He's in there, still asleep! You don't want to wait for him or you'll grow quite bored. Come with me!"

For the next three days, the girls spent most of their time with Turi and other new friends they'd made among the Erilaiset of Väinölä. They did not meet with Mielikki again; Turi would only tell them that she was in her garden and they would see her soon enough. When Väinämöinen emerged from his bedroom, groggy and pulling on his tangled beard, he was in good spirits—rare good spirits, as Ulla now knew well—and played with the girls in the newly fallen snow. He took down the curious instrument, which he called a *kantele*, and plucked its strings, playing strange and beautiful music at night under the stars while many folk of Väinölä gathered to listen. The kantele was made of fine birch wood, bleached white and hollowed out by the old magician, and strung with ten golden hairs from a legendary horse of old. It was not the first kantele Väinämöinen had made, but only a beautiful copy of the original, which was lost forever. Though a copy, its bell-like sound was perhaps clearer to mortal ears.

After only a few days, he told the girls that he and Turi were leaving.

"We won't be gone long," said Väinämöinen. "And you needn't worry. There are plenty of friends here to take care of you. You can explore all you want, but don't stray too far from Väinölä. The Valley can be a dangerous place for mortals. Remember the Näkki!"

Kirsikka was untroubled by Väinämöinen's departure, but the comings and goings of the past year, the tragedies, farewells, and goodbyes had left their mark on Ulla. Her one constant had been Väinämöinen, and though he had gone away before and always returned, she feared that, this time, he wouldn't come back. The little girl with dark hair, now alone in the world, desperately held on to the thought that at least Väinämöinen would not leave her. But Kirsikka would stay with her; her friend's infectious, good-natured cheerfulness and refusal to despair would keep Ulla's hope alive.

Väinämöinen spoke truly; there was no lack of friends to care for the girls. Ulla and Kirsikka spent most of their time getting to know the inhabitants of Väinölä, which was perhaps a little larger than Ulla's home village of Grankulta, and was home to people from several *väki* of the Erilaiset: their different races and folk. Sylphs lived nearby and often watched the girls from the trees, though they said little. Of those who dwelled in the little village or in the woods nearby, many looked like mortal men and women, even as Väinämöinen did, save for their spiraled, fluted eyes, which shone at times with a certain light and held a color far too clear and bright for mortals. Others appeared similar, except that they were smaller in stature, perhaps half the size of full-grown mortals: they were *Menninkäiset*, sturdy, stocky folk, with thick arms and legs, chests like barrels, and round, red faces. Most of the Menninkäiset lived in cabins, like those of the Reindeer Folk, among the trees behind the Great Oak, and the few children in Väinölä came from these families. One Menninkäinen, Lempi, took a great liking to the girls, and the jolly little gnome soon became their regular companion and best friend.

The two little girls slept in their bedroom in Väinämöinen's house every night, and every morning found cold milk and fresh food waiting for them on the table. During the day, they played with Lempi or with the children who lived nearby. The folk of Väinölä delighted in walking with them through the woods, singing songs for them, and telling them stories. Their favorite game was hide-and-go-seek, and the girls raced about the snowy woods in their warm cloaks and fur-lined boots, chasing Lempi. They found it easy enough to hide among the trees, but, whether seeking or hiding, Lempi always appeared out of nowhere to surprise them. At last, when they once cornered him near the Great Oak in the midst of the clearing, the Menninkäinen turned to face them, wiggled his arms, and quite literally disappeared. Many of the Erilaiset had worked magic for them, sending glimmers and colored lights to dance here and there among the trees, but they had never seen anything like Lempi's disappearance into thin air. They were astonished.

Lempi's voice called out to them from different spots around the clearing before he suddenly appeared right in front of them.

"Where were you? How did you do that?" cried Ulla. The strange little man laughed and slapped his knee.

"Ah," he said. "Now that's my secret! But I thought I'd show you just how strong Lempi's magic is!"

"I've seen you make lights," said Ulla. "And I've seen Väinämöinen make fire, but how can you make yourself invisible?"

"It takes strong magic," said Lempi with a wink. "But I learned the song long ago. You can't wear it for very long if you don't take the time to sing it right, but, after all, you two were chasing me."

"Wear *what*?" asked Kirsikka.

"Tulikki's Cloak," said Lempi. "That's how I disappear; it hides me!"

"But you're not wearing a cloak," said Ulla.

"Of course not! I took it off, silly girl."

"But what does it look like?" asked Kirsikka.

"Now how can I describe something that can't be seen?" he laughed. "Really! But there it is. When I sing up Tulikki's Cloak, it covers me all over as if I'm not even there; not even Väinämöinen's eyes can see me. Not just anyone can put on the cloak or make it last long, but Tulikki herself taught it to me. I was young and strong back then!"

"Who is Tulikki?" pleaded Ulla. "Where is she?"

"Don't you know? I suppose mortals don't remember much any more. Tulikki is Mielikki's daughter. She made that *loitsu*, that spell, long ago. But where she is now in the Far Northern Land, I wouldn't know; she's been gone a long, long time. Maybe Mielikki knows, but not old Lempi!"

"Can you teach us how to make Tulikki's Cloak?" asked Ulla. "Please, Lempi?"

The red-faced gnome laughed and shook his head. "I can teach you the words alright; that's no secret. But little mortal maids don't have the power of the Erilaiset!"

Lempi drew himself up to his full height—which wasn't very high—and began to chant in a singsong voice.

> *"Weave a cloak around my body,*
>
> *shroud to cover arms and shoulders.*

> *Legs be hid from eyes unfriendly,*
> *spin for me the hidden mantle."*

The stocky little man repeated the verse several times, and to the girls' amazement, vanished in the blink of an eye.

"Lempi!" they yelled together. "Where are you?!"

"Boo!" he cried. They turned around to find that he had slipped behind them and was visible once again. "You'll have to be quicker than that to catch me! But you've tired me out. It's no easy work wearing Tulikki's Cloak, and you have to keep up the spell to stay hidden. Come on; let's take a break from games and see what's left to eat in Väinämöinen's house. Little girls can at least make bread and berries disappear, and so can Lempi!"

From that moment on, a new thought came into Ulla's mind, one that she hadn't considered before—the thought that she, too, might weave the spells of the Erilaiset and become a singer like Väinämöinen and Turi. She then remembered the strange feeling that had come over her when she touched the reindeer totem inside the forest's Green Gate; she had felt the totem's power as surely as a man feels the bite of winter's wind upon his face, or the hot summer sun upon his bent back as he plows the rocky fields. Had not Väinämöinen chosen her to come with him across all the long miles from High Länsimaa to the Enchanted Valley? Was there not a mark upon her shoulder that set her apart from all others? Väinämöinen had told her many stories about mortal wizards in the days of old, wizards as strong as the heroes, who had fought against Löhi just like Lemminkäinen did.

Thinking about this as she lay under warm covers inside the Great Oak, she pressed Lempi to teach her magic words and spells, to show her how to tap into the power that might be inside her. But the little man just laughed and told her that the Erilaiset did not teach magic to children.

One night, however, when Kirsikka was fast asleep and the snow fell gently upon the Valley, Ulla again begged Lempi to teach her a trick, and he finally relented. He taught her special words, then made her close her eyes and think of colors: red, blue, and golden yellow. All at once she felt a tingling, as if her hair was standing on end, and when she opened her eyes in surprise, little dancing lights flickered about her. They slowly blinked out, and the gnome chuckled.

"I knew it!" he cried. "I can tell when a mortal has power, even a little girl like you. Look at what you've done now! Very nice trick, little one."

"That was me?" exclaimed Ulla. "Oh, Lempi, was that really me?"

"Well, it wasn't the sleepyhead in bed over yonder," he answered.

"Can you teach me something else? Anything!"

"Oh no," said Lempi. "That's more than enough. Väinämöinen would be very angry, and I don't need to be on his bad side. He's very serious about magic, you know—he and Turi both. Children don't know right from wrong yet, and magic's all about such things. Little lights may be all in fun, but there's much more to it than that. Ask Väinämöinen if you want to know more, but listen here, Ulla. We'll keep this a secret between us, like good friends do. And maybe someday, when you're older, I'll teach you even more."

True to his word, Väinämöinen returned with Turi within a fortnight. It was almost Midwinter's Day, the shortest day of the year. Outside the Enchanted Valley, a hard winter with deep snow had descended upon the Far Northern Land. Within the Valley, however, all was mild, for the ancient heroes could order things as they wished. The power of Väinämöinen ran strong around Väinölä, and in Mielikki's garden, everything grew green despite the cold and dark.

When Ulla asked Väinämöinen where he had been, he would only say that he had been up and down the Valley, speaking with many Erilaiset and gathering what news he could. The news was bad, for Löhi was stirring and had declared herself openly to the Erilaiset, setting in motion many things long prepared. Väinämöinen said that the Erilaiset would hold a great council to decide what should be done. But first would come the winter celebration, when, for what might be the last time, the Erilaiset could forget their cares.

The Erilaiset called the winter feast *Tulen Yö*, or *the Night of Fire*. Across the Valley, and everywhere they still dwelt in the Far Northern Land, the Erilaiset gathered together and lit bonfires just as they did on Midsummer's Day. The folk of Väinölä were joined by many others who lived in the nearby woods, and they built a great fire of felled logs in the snowy clearing. Ulla and Kirsikka joined them, dressed in fine new clothes of rich colors—chiefly red and green—and their warm Karelian boots.

Väinämöinen played the kantele and the people sang ancient songs, including the lay of the Sampo, which told of how Ilmarinen, the great smith of the Erilaiset, had forged the magical Sampo long ago to bring peace and prosperity to all who dwelt in the Far Northern Land. The Sampo was a great pole fashioned of many precious things, its making foretold by an ancient prophecy only half-remembered. All the totems of the Seven Clans were upon it, and it was set upon a hill in the midst of the first homeland of the Kaamoslaiset, the fair white city of Tapiola. Weddings were celebrated there, and festivals, and the High Kings of the Far Northern Land, of whom Lemminkäinen was the last, were crowned in its shadow.

But Löhi coveted the magic totem, and wished to take it to Sariola to increase her own folk and ruin the clans. Secretly, she came to Tapiola in the depths of winter, when her power was greatest, and stole the Sampo and spirited it back to Pohjola. Thus began the Witch's War between Löhi and the Seven Clans. Eventually, the three heroes—Väinämöinen, Ilmarinen and Lemminkäinen—went even to Pohjola and stole it back. Löhi found them in the Wastes as they fled, and the Sampo was broken and lost in the swift-running waters of the north. Legends told that the various shards were carried south by the rivers and lakes, and where the shards came to rest, the land became rich and fertile; north of the Wall of the Giants, where good land was scarce, and wherever the earth was fertile, the people called it Sampo-land.

The blaze burned low as the long night passed, and most of the Erilaiset went to their homes to sleep. But Väinämöinen and Turi sat long by the fire with the two little girls, bundled in warm furs, huddled at their feet. The old men gazed at the glowing embers as men have done since the world began and talked about what was to come. Ulla was awake and heard all they said, but Väinämöinen no longer seemed to care that she listened.

"It's a pity you left Etelamaa so quickly," said Turi. "I think now that the lord of the Swan Folk is our only hope. It would have been wise to open your heart to him and seek his confidence. You no doubt caused quite a stir by your untimely flight."

"Aye, no doubt," said Väinämöinen. "I should have sought out Nigan ere I fled. But I was in great fear after what I saw, and more than a little shaken by whatever assailed me on the Verimäki. I thought only of riding to Keskimaa and doing what I could to help. And if I had stayed in the city longer? What then, Turi? I might have been—no, I *would* have been too late to save these little ones." The old singer reached out and touched Ulla's braided hair.

"Yes, that's true enough," said Turi. "And though the choice was yours, who can say how the thought came to you? In any case, what's done is done. But what do you hope to do now that Löhi has sent her message? It would seem that most of our folk aren't ready to forsake the Valley, at least not to help any mortals besides the Karelialaiset. I don't know if many will listen to you."

"Then maybe they'll listen to Mielikki," replied Väinämöinen. "Let them reject the call of Tapio himself if they will, and doom their souls! The Erilaiset are the children of the gods and should know better. What promise has Löhi ever kept? But you're right, my friend." The old man sighed. "Our own folk may reject our warning and counsel. Among the Seven Clans, what mortals will heed our call? It will be a cold winter without end if Löhi prevails, and the snows will be stained red with blood. The Witch's star is in the sky, even as the prophecies of old foretold. Still, there is the girl. And she gives me hope."

Turi fell silent, poking the burning logs with his copper-shod staff. After a while, he spoke again—softly, as if musing to himself. "The Reindeer Clan are a small, scattered folk and the forest protects them, but the Bear Folk are a great people now and numerous; the Elk Folk, too, have increased. They are not warlike folk, however. Löhi will strike again, and harder. They will be hard-pressed to resist without help from the other clans. There is no hope in Akkala, where the old songs are forbidden, and little in Tavastia unless something unlooked-for happens. No—it is in Etelamaa, where the White Swan flies, that hope lies, if anywhere. It has become a mighty kingdom, and has much strength of war. The Folk of the Swan must bear the burden. Väinämöinen, what is your measure of Nigan?"

"Well," said Väinämöinen, "I only saw him once. He was fair-spoken, as befits one from the Houses of the Vales, and patient. But I can say no more than that, except that there was honor in his eyes. If any is to wield that which I still keep safe, perhaps he is indeed the one." The old singer tossed a chip into the fire. "I met his son, too: Egan, a likely lad with a bright light in him. Reminded me of this little one here. There may be a role in this for him, too, before it's over. Hard to say."

"Löhi will strike hard," sighed Turi. "Where the clans will find swords enough to withstand her is beyond me, even if the Erilaiset put forth our strength."

"You put your hope, such as it is, in the swords of Etelamaa," said Väinämöinen. "They will indeed be needed. But Löhi will not win all she seeks with a single battle, nor lose all. The swords of the clans and the Erilaiset can only delay her victory, not stop it. You can feel the world changing even as I do, Turi. The Witch surely feels this, too, or else she would have waited while her power grew, until she was so strong that no one could stop her, and then unleashed a blizzard upon us all. She hurries. Her time is short and, if she does not win through, she will fade.

"The clans are sundered, and the songs silent, and therein lies her hope. The folk of the Far Northern Land must put aside their quarrels and come together again. They must return to the Old Ways and honor that which should be honored. The songs must be sung again in mortal lands. That will give them the strength to resist her—the strength of the land itself, of the forest. Your hope fails when you think of their lack of spears, but mine fails upon their lack of faith. They have forgotten almost everything, Turi. How they will relearn it, I cannot say."

"You've made a great journey, Väinämöinen," replied Turi. "But you never left the forest for a generation of mortals before. The songs are not all forgotten, not everywhere. Beyond Karelia, there are still those that live by the Old Ways and sing the songs as best they can: humble folk of hamlets and villages, poor in goods but rich in spirit. In the Green Vales of Etelamaa there are some, and in the southlands of High and Deep Länsimaa. And even among the Tavastialaiset they can be found, near to Kyöpelinvuori, where the Seer dwells. Perhaps a seed remains, my friend; perhaps that is where hope may still be found."

Väinämöinen sighed again. "Maybe you're right, Turi. We shall see. But again you mention the Seer, and not by chance, I think. So you still believe that she may be of use to us?"

"I'm not sure," answered Turi. "It has been many a year since I've seen her. A strange woman then, and now she is old, very old. But she has the ears of the Hare Folk in Tavastia, that much is certain. And even the lords of Akkala consult her. What influence she has—or what real power—who can say? It might be worth the attempt, though."

At this point, Ulla had grown quite expert at piecing together the strange places and names that Väinämöinen let drop. Only a few short months earlier, she had been an ignorant child who had scarce left her own small village, and then only to hunt in the woods with her father, but no longer. She now knew the names of all the Seven Lands and Seven Clans, and of many towns, lakes and rivers all across the Far Northern Land. Moreover, she could guess about where they lay and what manner of folk dwelt there. She had never heard Väinämöinen mention a seer or Kyöpelinvuori, however, and it piqued her interest. She roused herself from the edge of sleep.

"Who is the Seer?" she asked suddenly, looking up at Väinämöinen's face in the fire's glow. "Is she another Erilainen?"

"Would that she were," Väinämöinen said without a trace of surprise at her sudden inquiry. "The old crone of Kyöpelinvuori is a mortal, a witch—or at least she fancies herself one. But she practices a strange magic, if tales be true."

"She has a glass into which she peers," said Turi. "That much at least is true. I saw it once, long, long ago—a beautiful crystal ball like the old stories tell of, only this one is real. She can see things far away, and perhaps glimpse the future. And she reads fortunes. Of all her powers, they say this is the greatest. The rich and powerful, the ambitious and ruthless: they all go to her for counsel and to divine their fate. She tells many useful things to the Hare Folk in Tavastia, where she lives, and even to the king of Akkala at Langvika. So they tolerate her, and all the land around Kyöpelinvuori, the Witch's Hill, is reckoned hers. She has never been a particular friend of the Erilaiset, although at times she seeks us out when she wants something. But she will fear Löhi, and her help might be useful."

Ulla hesitated before asking what she really wished to know. "And will we go to her, Väinämöinen?"

The old man looked at Ulla with a face both sad and thoughtful.

"You'd like to stay here, wouldn't you, little one?" he asked. The little girl with dark hair was silent. Väinämöinen sighed again. "Put it from your mind, child. Who knows what tomorrow may bring? And first must come the council of the Erilaiset. Much will be decided there."

The low fire popped and crackled. Väinämöinen suddenly added, "But don't you worry! I'm not leaving you, child. You won't ever be alone again."

***

A few days after the Night of Fire, Väinämöinen bundled up the girls and struck out deeper into the heart of the Enchanted Valley. Leaving the Great Oak of Väinölä behind them, they passed cleared fields where barley and rye grew in the summer, and stretches of heather where animals—chiefly sheep and goats but also reindeer—were kept. Many Erilaiset of Väinölä also journeyed to the great meeting, but Väinämöinen preferred to travel with the girls alone—to think, or so he told them. Indeed, he said little as they tramped through the snowy woods and across frozen lakes and pools. Once, they passed a well-marked path bordered with grey stones. Väinämöinen said the path led to Turi's home, Kivipolku.

They camped that night under the stars, wrapped in warm furs and blankets. Ulla and Kirsikka were very tired, and soon fell asleep beside the small campfire. The old man stayed awake late into the night, however, listening to the forest's sounds and watching the bright lights move across the sky in their appointed course.

They hadn't walked more than a few hours the next day before their path joined a larger way that soon opened out onto a broad, round lake. Light snow fell about them. Ulla could see cabins here and there beside the frozen water, sending smoky trails toward the sky. Distant figures moved about the tranquil landscape.

"Well, here we are," said Väinämöinen. "This is Loulajärvi, the gathering place of the Valley. I lived here for a while a long time ago. The summer water is very blue."

They moved out onto the lake, crunching the frozen snow, and Ulla could see that it was nearly ringed with cabins. Loulajärvi was the chief village in the Valley, and at least a few members of each *väki* of the Erilaiset lived there. As they walked across the lake and neared its farther shore, many folk recognized Väinämöinen and called out to him. The old wizard raised his new staff—made from yellow yew wood and still unshod—but said nothing as he tramped along toward a narrow jetty of stone that led up to the icy bank. The girls trudged behind him as best they could.

As they gained the shore, Ulla looked up and found a strange sight looming ahead in the falling snow. A great drumlin marched down almost to the frozen bank. Trees grew on its heights, but its flat face was covered with a sheet of ice like a frozen waterfall, but with a few visible patches of grey stone breaking through. She could not tell if the face was solid rock or earth mingled with boulders, as was so common throughout the Far Northern Land, but warm light spilled from a wide opening at its base, and Ulla saw several people walk inside.

Väinämöinen motioned to the girls to wait for him, so they sat on a snow-covered stump, playing with the braided hair sticking out from their caps and looking around. Turi emerged from the opening with another old man and winked at them. It seemed that most of the Erilaiset were already gathered within and waiting for Väinämöinen to arrive. The old singer spoke awhile with Turi and several others, then finally came to fetch them.

Ulla suddenly noticed how richly he was dressed. His long, thick, red tunic was hemmed all about with bright yellow stitching in clever designs of sun, moon and stars, all entwined with symbols of the clans: reindeer, bear, swan, elk, hare, eagle and wolf. He put his hands on his hips and looked down at the girls.

"The time has come," he said somewhat solemnly. "Let us go inside. Many folk are within, but don't be worried. All will be as it should be."

He led the girls through the opening into the ice hill. Broad steps led straight downward, unlike the spiral staircase within the Great Oak. Ulla counted thirty steps before they reached a great chamber filled with the buzz of many voices.

Now, the little girl with dark hair had seen some incredible things during the past year, but the strange scene there still astonished her. The chamber was round with a smooth wall curving outward near its base, but inward as it climbed, as if they stood inside a giant egg; but Ulla thought not so much of an egg, but of how the inside of a beehive must appear, at least to the bees gathered within. Two great yellow lamps hung from the roof high above, suffusing the whole chamber with a warm, golden glow. Some folk sat on wooden stools or stood about the chamber's stony floor, but others sat upon shelves and ledges that protruded from the curved wall at regular intervals. There must have been hundreds all told, men and women alike. Ulla turned round in a circle, gazing up at them as they talked and laughed all at once, some pointing at her when she caught their eyes.

Off to one side, Ulla saw a tall, thin man clad in black mail, his long, braided hair banded with gold. She didn't know all the *väki* yet by sight, but remembered her father's stories well enough. She knew the strange man and several others besides him were *Haltiatar*, or those that the folk of the clans called elves. Their faces were long, with thin mouths and leaf-shaped ears—cruel, perhaps, to mortal eyes, like the masks of clever demons. The mail-clad elf had a long sword at his side, and others were seated with swords laid across their knees. They stared intently at Ulla with narrowed eyes.

She turned away and suddenly saw Mielikki, dressed in yellow and brown like autumn leaves, with many Sylphs around her. The tall woman smiled, but Ulla looked away and grabbed Kirsikka's hand. The din overwhelmed her; Ulla's head swam and she felt faint. She saw that Kirsikka's face had turned bright red and that she was blinking quickly. Mielikki appeared beside them then and laid her hands upon their braided heads. The panic was gone in an instant.

"Don't be afraid, little daughters!" said Mielikki. "The steps lead back out again into the waking world. This will all pass and we will return to Väinölä, you and I. Be at peace."

Väinämöinen sat them down on little stools. An old man clad in rusty brown, who was shorter than Väinämöinen, but had a beard that was just as long the old magician's, strode to the middle of the great chamber and brought his staff down hard on the stone floor. The Erilaiset paid little heed.

"Folk of the First Clan!" the man cried. "People of the Erilaiset! Hear me now, oh my people! Listen to me!" He brought his staff down several more times, and the noise gradually subsided. "Hear me now, folk of the Valley! From all corners of the land have you gathered! A great storm will soon break upon us, and upon all of the Far Northern Land. What are we to do, good folk? How are we to face the threat of a new age of snow and ice? Hearken now to the words of Väinämöinen, the immortal singer and the eldest still among us!"

Väinämöinen took the floor amidst great uproar and raised his arms until the crowd grew quiet again. Even in the yellow light, Ulla could see a certain radiance about him, and she remembered him standing in the flickering light of her home in Grankulta, bargaining with her aunt and uncle.

"So here we are," the old man began. "Aye, from all the *väki*, here we are, gathered in conclave, such as has not happened in many a year. And the words Satatieto just spoke are all too true; there is indeed a storm upon us, and soon even the Erilaiset will feel its full force." He raised his staff and a thunderous boom shook the chamber, causing several to cry out in surprise.

"I bring no comfort, but a warning! Beware, Folk of the Erilaiset! When I left the Valley, I felt the world was changing; now it *has* changed! Löhi has returned! She has unleashed war upon the Seven Clans, and has been among us in Taikalaakso. The walls of Sariola are manned again, and evil things creep back to the south. A choice is before us, and nothing will ever be the same. Hearken to my tale!"

Then Väinämöinen told the Erilaiset the tale of his journey and how, over a year ago, he had gone north into the Wastes beyond the lands of the clans. He had seen riders of the Itäläiset on the old road that led to Pohjola, and he had seen bands of Hiissia, the Dark Erilaiset who worshipped Löhi of old, hasten south on missions of mischief. The further north he had gone, the more he had felt a great enchantment about him, and the more difficult it had grown to hide himself; he had tired quickly. Then he knew that his fears were realized. Löhi was indeed awake and plotting ruin for mortal kind. It was magic—her magic—that oppressed him.

The old man next told how he had fled to High Länsimaa and sought out Pekka the Fat, though he did not mention Ulla and what befell them in Grankulta. Finally, he spoke of the journey south to Etelamaa, of the dark phantom in the woods, and of his frantic ride from the Stone City all the way to Karelia to save what could be saved from the wreck of the Karhulaiset. He paused then, leaning heavily on his staff as if telling the tale made his body weary as he relived it. As murmurs ran through the crowded hall, a fair-haired woman sitting high on the wall raised her voice.

"But how can you be sure these things are signs of Löhi's return?" she asked. "Have not the Itäläiset raided the Far Northern Land innumerable times since we first met mortals on the shore? And do not the Hiissia yet haunt many places in the world? Surely these things could be, and yet not be, proofs that the Witch walks again among us, or that her dreary halls in Sariola again are occupied."

"Did you not hear my words?" asked Väinämöinen. "It is clear that the traffic in the Wastes was from the north, and the Hiissia wore the old livery of Pohjola. And I have known Löhi, as both friend and enemy, for many ages of this world. I know her power and magic like no other. Surely, I tell you that she has returned! But you need not take only my word for it, for, as some of you here know, Löhi has been among us. Even to Taikalaakso she has come and delivered her message!"

Väinämöinen looked at Turi, and the green-clad wizard came and stood beside him. Ulla was struck again by just how alike they were, save perhaps their voices. If Väinämöinen's voice was strong, it could sometimes be harsh, but Turi's voice was evermore gentle and temperate.

"Löhi has indeed returned," said Turi. "For I have seen her." A commotion rose throughout the hall, and it was some time before Turi could continue. "Long I sought to find Väinämöinen after he left. I reached out my mind to the North Marches and beyond, but all was dark there and I could not find him; my *sight* was blind. Then came news of the raid of the Itäläiset and war on the borders of Karelia. One day, I walked through the woods, thinking of these things. I came upon a woman standing silently by a still pool shrouded in mist. Her back was to me, but when she turned around, I knew her. It was Löhi!

"Indeed, I saw her own *etiäinen*, robed in white and shining palely in the gloom. Her hair was long and her skin fair—very young and beautiful she seemed, save for a strangeness that made her face almost seem like a mask. And her lips did not move when she spoke.

"And this is what she said. 'I bring a message for my people, Turi, and I charge you to deliver it to them. For I have returned, and will soon reclaim all that once was mine. And I forgive the injury done to me of old, when I was betrayed, for the Erilaiset were fooled by the lies of mortal men, and so betrayed in turn. What have you ever gained from them but scorn as they drove you from your lands and shut you in the deep woods of Karelia? But I shall take back those lands, and my power shall flow across the face of the world, for I am its queen. Those who would serve me shall have great reward. And, as long as the Erilaiset never again resist me, Taikalaakso will be yours forever, to order as you will, and other places besides. This is my message to my people.'"

Turi sighed and looked down. "That was all she said. There was no more. She raised her hand as if in invocation and I thought she meant to cast a spell on me, but she turned and disappeared into the mists. There was no more."

"Others among us have also heard such words," said Väinämöinen. "In dreams and visions she has spoken. This, then, is Löhi's message, and the choice before us. We can serve her or, at least stand aside while she destroys the clans and covers the Far Northern Land with winter everlasting; in exchange, she will not destroy us. Or we can oppose her, even if we risk failing and sharing the fate she has in store for mortal kind."

Even as Väinämöinen spoke, the mail-clad elf rose from his seat and strode to the center of the hall.

"Others among us have heard such words," said the elf. "And I am one of them. The day after the Night of Fire, I stood atop Birchbark Hill with my folk, watching the sky. There was a glimmer on the lake below, and the snow suddenly shifted. It seemed to us that we could see a face within the shifting pattern and a cold voice rang out, a voice I knew from long ago. The words she spoke were much as Turi reports, save that she also added a sterner warning—unless Turi chooses to forget it. 'And do not listen to Väinämöinen and his conjurors,' she said. 'For whosoever follows them will feel my wrath. You shall be destroyed utterly, so that not even your spirit will remain to seek Tuone's dark halls; but the nothingness of oblivion shall be yours forever!'

"So spoke Löhi," said the elf. "And I need not recall her deeds of old to know that she is evil. Did I not fight against the foes from Pohjola for long, bitter years? Did I not take the field at the Great Battle to challenge her champions? But evil may still speak the truth. Why should we risk ourselves again for the likes of mortal men? What indeed have we ever received from them but scorn? None are our friends save the Reindeer Clan, and none still hold to the Old Ways or honor the Vanhalaiset. Why, Väinämöinen, should we follow you to oblivion when we may yet remain in the forest until chance again turns our way?"

The elf spoke with great passion, and many lifted up their voices in agreement, but Väinämöinen raised his arms and faced the Haltia.

"Chance, you say, Lúven? Chance may turn for you or against you. But it is not chance, but choice that lies before us now. We can choose to do what is right, that which we know in our hearts. Or, we can do nothing in the face of evil, which is an evil unto itself. We are the Erilaiset! We are the children of the gods, servants of the Vanhalaiset, put here by Ukko—who made this world and yet exists outside its bounds—to order things for good. We are to shepherd living things and teach those that came after the mortal clans of this Far Northern Land.

"Löhi is mad; she will not rest until all are her slaves, mortal and Erilaiset, and the very earth is turned to ice. Such is her lust for power and dominion. And I say to you that Löhi will lead you into oblivion, not me! Nothingness awaits all those who know good, but choose evil, even the evil of standing idly by when the time for deeds is at hand."

Great authority rang in Väinämöinen's voice and it seemed to Ulla that he grew in stature as he spoke. Regal and majestic he looked, his beard white as a summer cloud and his eyes shining with a piercing light. The power within him was scarcely veiled, for he knew that the fate of many things, perhaps the entire Far Northern Land, hung in the balance.

But the elf, Lúven, was undeterred.

"Well and good," said Lúven. "Or it would be, had we any real hope of defeating Löhi. But I deem such hope is false. The power in Pohjola is great. We have dwindled to a small folk, and even if all the Erilaiset gathered from the four corners of the Far Northern Land, we could not hope to stop the Witch.

"And what of the clans? Lemminkäinen is dead, and his like no longer exists among mortal kind. The Kaamoslaiset are divided, warring at times among themselves, or else so blinded by greed so that the rich among them grow ever richer, heedless of the poor who work the fields and mines and are ever uncertain of their next meal. And in mighty Akkala, the Kotkalaiset cut the tongues from their slaves, and hunt the Erilaiset and those who befriend us! What hope is there in the Seven Clans? Why do you think they would even listen to you before the storm overtakes them? It is not evil to preserve our folk until such a day when they may rise again! And the seed that is saved thereby may yet do many things to heal the world of its hurts in days to come."

The Erilaiset again murmured their approval of Lúven's words, but looked to Väinämöinen for his response. Yet Mielikki came forward, her white feet moving silently across the stone floor, and at once the crowd fell silent. Even the mail-clad Haltia moved aside and bent his head, for Mielikki, Mistress of the Woods, Lady of the Forest, was the greatest of the Erilaiset save for Löhi herself.

She was the daughter of Tapio, and so a child of the Vanhalaiset. Her power, wisdom and knowledge ran as strong and deep as the roots of the greatest of trees. Her beauty dazzled like diamonds, and her green eyes shone with a clear light, like the cold waters of a swift-running mountain stream as it reflected the forest hues. Her magic was strong and her bright song melodious, but hers was the power of growth, renewal and prophecy, not of conquest. The Reindeer Folk loved her and worshipped her as the goddess of the trees.

The great lamp dimmed so that she shone, luminous, in the darkened hall. And when she spoke, her words made pictures in the minds of those who listened.

"Of Löhi's return, there is no doubt," she began. "Even Lúven admits as much. The Witch's star, red and baleful, has been seen in the northern sky for many years now, as the ancient songs foretold. Three seasons of the Witch there are, say the songs. The first we lived through, an age of ice and snow; the second we endured as a time of war and strife. The third season of the Witch has come now, and while it is the shortest season, it is also the most deadly. If the people of the Far Northern Land stand together, if they honor and obey that which should be revered, we shall win through. Löhi will fade away into the nothingness, the same with which she threatens us. Her hope lies in our disunion. If she can conquer us all in turn, then her dominion may truly come to be and last even unto the ending of the world.

"Hear me now, Folk of the Erilaiset, for I am my father's daughter! Listen to the words of Tapio, Lord of the Forests, which he spoke to me long, long ago, for I am now his vessel here on this earth! This he spoke and this I heard, though I did not then understand. But now all is clear and at last revealed!"

Then Mielikki closed her eyes and began to sing in a voice both melodious and rich.

"When the cold hand reaches southward,
reaches with its frozen fingers,
comes a child into the Northland,
all the clans to bring together.

Mortals and immortals listen,
listen to these words of wisdom.
By the Clan Mark shall you know them,
favored child of northern fathers.

Listen to my words of warning!
Shield against the Witch's terror.
Comes a child into the Northland,
all the clans to bring together.

Let the songs be sung in summer,
winter's dark gives voice to power.
To the songs return your children,
listen to my words of wisdom."

She stopped then and opened her eyes. The great lamp spilled out its yellow light. The people breathed again, as if her words had held them enchanted and still. Mielikki threw back her long hair and cried, "Heed these words, my people! The time of the prophecy is at hand. Löhi has returned, but in our darkest hour, hope reappears. For we have been sent the one whom the words foretold. And it is not a male child, such as the wise among us looked for, but a simple girl of this Far Northern Land. Look now upon hope, Lúven! This is the child who now stands before you!"

Väinämöinen held out his hand to Ulla and, with a quick glance at Kirsikka, she took it and rose. The old man walked her to the center of the chamber's round hall. If Mielikki's touch had calmed her before, its power was now spent. The little girl, painfully aware of the hundreds of eyes on her, blushed deep red. She could feel the magic of dozens of Erilaiset reaching out to her. She felt faint.

But the elf was undeterred. Lúven circled Ulla, his black armour ringing faintly, and for the third time he raised his challenge.

"The hope of the Far Northern Land!" he mocked. "'By the Clan Mark shall you know them!' I, too, know these words, Mielikki, from long, long ago. And I do not blaspheme or doubt the words of Tapio, but words may have many meanings. You may be his vessel, but you are not Tapio himself, and are still Erilainen, even as I am. Who can say if the prophecy of old belongs to this time? Or, if so, that this gangrel child belongs to it? And if the wise would look for a male child, the reincarnation of Lemminkäinen, perhaps it is because the prophecy itself does. This is no Lemminkäinen!"

"Nevertheless, this child is the one," said Mielikki. "And in the old tongue, the words may point to man or woman; there is no distinction. I do not know what part she is to play, and I can give no certainty that we will prevail, but she is a sign unto mortals and Erilaiset alike—a sign sent to guide our choice."

"No certainty!" he said. "No part to play, no proof! Väinämöinen brings home an orphan from the wreck of the Karhulaiset and says, 'Here! Here is your hope against Löhi!' And armed only with this, we are to stand alone against Pohjola or sway the closed hearts of mortal men? Most assuredly you jest, Väinämöinen. But I will not lose the last remnant of my folk to counsel such as this!"

Many voices rose in protest, but Väinämöinen brought his staff down hard and cried out above the din.

"There is no proof but in doing! Behold! This child is Ulla Karhulainen, and she bears the Mark of the Clan!"

Väinämöinen suddenly grabbed the neck of Ulla's warm shirt and pulled it down, ripping it almost to her belt. Ulla clutched at the rent cloth to keep it from falling off altogether, but the little girl, trembling with fear, was bare from the waist up. Even in the yellow light, her skin was pale and fair, but the black scar on her shoulder shone with a dark gleam. The Erilaiset gasped with astonishment. It could only be the mark of a mighty claw, the oldest sign of the Seven Clans and the mark of the Karhulaiset.

"Look well!" cried Väinämöinen. "For when I first came upon the girl in the scattered woods near the North Marches, it seemed mere chance. She was attacked by a bear and would have died had I not stayed the blood and healed her wounds. When she ran back from Tuonela's river and her flesh mended, this very mark appeared, and it was not my doing! I would have kept her with me, but her folk would not part with her. And yet, against all odds, I found her again amidst the ruin of the Karhulaiset, on the very borders of Karelia.

"Look well! The choice is upon you, Folk of the Erilaiset! But as for me, I am free. And as a free man, I make my choice! Never will I be Löhi's slave, or stand aside while she makes war upon the clans!"

Lúven, no less astonished than the others, stared for a long while at the mark on Ulla's back. Several other elves rose from their seats to join him. He turned the frightened girl around and traced the scar's outline beneath his hand. Ulla felt a shock at his touch; the elf stiffened and drew back. Ulla knew that he, too, felt the power that coursed within her. A hush fell on the hall. Finally, Lúven sighed and bowed his head. When he looked up again, he turned first to Väinämöinen, then to Mielikki, and nodded.

"So be it," said the elf. With a swift motion, he drew the long sword from his belt. "So be it. I choose. I accept your counsel. For better or worse, though all my *väki* may meet their end in this war, I shall not hide from or bow to Löhi. The child bears the Mark of the Clan. This can only be Ukko's sign to his people. So be it. I make my choice."

Slowly, one by one, the other elves drew their swords and stood beside him. All around the hive-shaped hall, people began to cry out—some calling Ulla's name and some Väinämöinen's, and others cursing or challenging Löhi, and still others shouting out strange words in a tongue the girls could not understand.

If the noisy hall was overwhelming before, now the very chamber itself seemed to shake. Kirsikka screamed and ran to Ulla, who still stood half-naked and seemingly in shock in the middle of the hall. Mielikki was there before her and, taking both girls into her arms, sprang up the stairs and out beneath the open sky.

Outside, the cold night air hit them like a gale as the cacophony faded behind them. Mielikki drew Ulla close and wrapped a robe around her.

"You did well, little daughter," said Mielikki. "Very well. Do not think that you were ill-treated. Väinämöinen did only what he had to do; nothing else would have sufficed."

But Ulla burst into tears and buried herself in the woman's warm embrace, sobbing inconsolably, as if all the pain of her brief life had in that moment, at last, broken her heart.

Chapter Ten

Lights in the Dark

Ulla stood knee-deep in snow, peering through the blowing flurries at the old man. Near a stand of fir trees, Väinämöinen talked with two Karelians in shapeless green hats, his foot resting on the runner of a sled. Ulla knew he was haggling with the men. Finally, she watched him hand them several silver coins. The Karelians stomped off through the trees, smiling and slapping each other on the back, so Ulla knew that Väinämöinen would be in a foul mood.

The old man came up to the girls with a frown and clapped his hands. "Alright, let's go. What's done is done, and I didn't have any other choice. But your father's kin are a race of thieves."

The sled was a *reki*, a sturdy Karelian work sled made for hauling goods rather than people, similar to those Ulla's father built for the folk around Grankulta. Heavy and long, it had well-crafted runners on each side that slid easily over snow and ice in winter, or sedge and grasses in summer. Väinämöinen settled the girls in a sort of basket near the front, where the runners curved upward in a graceful arc. Then he checked the harnesses on the two reindeer that would pull them. The reindeer stood in single file, one behind the other. They were both female, with medium-sized antlers they would not shed until summer, and shaggy winter coats. The reindeer closest to the sled was clearly pregnant, but her calf would not be born for three months, when spring thawed the Far Northern Land and opened the waters. It was not an ideal situation for Väinämöinen and the girls, but most of the reindeer in the nearby herds were half-wild. The Karelialaiset were loath to part with any of the few draught beasts they had broken to harness.

Väinämöinen sat on a small box fixed to the sled, and, with a glance at the girls in their basket, lashed the coursers. They were off, sliding quietly into the falling snow while the old man picked his way through the trees and lakes. They travelled close to the forest's southern eaves, where the land was more open and the wood less dense. Chains of lakes, large and small, were everywhere, however, and although it was impossible to chart a straight course in the summer when the water was open, at least winter's ice and snow made for speedier, if colder, travel. That was why Väinämöinen chose to set out for Etelamaa before the thaw.

News of many things had reached the Enchanted Valley, most of it bad. Speed was of the essence if there was any hope of stopping Löhi. Ordinary folk might have feared travelling any distance in the northern winter, when the night air bit like knives and a man could be lost amidst the snowy fields or freeze to death in an unexpected storm. But not old Väinämöinen! His songs were the strongest, his *sight* the most powerful, and he feared no snowstorm or blizzard, not even if it blew out of Pohjola itself.

After the great conclave of the Erilaiset, the girls had stayed at Loulajärvi for several days while Väinämöinen, Turi and Mielikki took counsel with many others. Ulla found herself quite popular, even among the tree maidens. It seemed that almost all of the Valley's inhabitants wished to speak with her, the mortal child whom Tapio had foreseen long ago. Of course, they all wanted to see the Mark of the Clan on her shoulder, too. Väinämöinen frowned at this and tried to keep Ulla as close as possible. He said nothing to her, but she knew he feared that Löhi would soon learn of the girl's existence, if she hadn't already. Unlikely though it seemed, he knew the Witch might come herself or as an *etiänen* to Loulajärvi. For her part, Ulla came to like the attention, though she often felt shy among strangers.

She had never told Väinämöinen about the *loitsu* that Lempi had taught her. She knew without asking that the singer would not approve, just as the little man had suggested. From time to time, she snuck off into the woods, away from everyone else, and practiced making the colored lights and speaking words of power. Some of the Metsänaiset taught her new words, delighting in showing her tricks for forming and shaping the power she now knew was within her. Though always eager to make mischief for sport, they were careful not to be caught by the old wizard or any of the other Great Ones among the heroes of the Valley.

At last, the Erilaiset made their plans. Mielikki put forth all her power and, with her *sight*, discovered all she could about what was happening in the wide world outside the forest. There was great movement among the Itäläiset north of Karelia, where they would not normally winter. Evil things crept about the North Marches. A shadow of fear hung over the City of Etelamaa, and the sickness of Lovêatar had returned to the Far Northern Land. Löhi's power stirred again everywhere, but Mielikki deemed the heaviest blow would fall on the Bear and Elk Folk in Länsimaa. Löhi knew now that, despite their numbers, the March clans were weak and had little power to resist her attacks. When she had destroyed the strength of High and Deep Länsimaa, the way would be open for an assault on the kingdoms of the south.

Then came the difficult decisions. It was one thing to guess at Löhi's designs, but quite another to counter them. The Reindeer Folk still revered the Erilaiset, and even if they—wisely—did not trust all of the *väki*, they still honored the great among them, and lived at peace in the forest. The Reindeer Folk might defend their own borders for a time or help repel a raid, but their small numbers could do little against a determined assault out of Pohjola.

Only Etelamaa had the strength to aid the Bear and Elk Clans, so Väinämöinen was chosen to return and speak to Nigan, to urge him to make common cause with their northern cousins. The Erilaiset hoped that Ulla's presence would sway the Swan Folk, although, besides being a sign unto the Seven Clans foretold in prophecy, not even Mielikki could guess her destiny.

But Väinämöinen had another journey in mind as well.

The Erilaiset had at last accepted that the only real hope against the Witch's power lay in the strength of the Far Northern Land itself, in the Seven Clans uniting and returning to the Old Ways—unlikely though this seemed. So Väinämöinen also planned to journey to Kyöpelinvuori and seek the Seer, in the hopes that the mortal witch would help him convince the clans to come together.

Other Erilaiset had also been sent out on different missions. Many went throughout the forest to succor the Karelialaiset, especially to help them prepare safe places for themselves or refugees from other clans, should disaster strike. Some prepared to go among the villages in Etelamaa and High Länsimaa, where singers and men of power might still be found. Still others—Lúven among them—prepared for journeys to distant places to seek out Erilaiset who yet dwelt apart in their homes of old, or to scout the Marches for signs of the Witch's plans. Turi departed for Keskimaa and Pekka to do what he could for the Bear Folk. But Mielikki, daughter of the living forest and child of the gods, remained in her garden in the Enchanted Valley, for there her power was greatest and her *sight* reached the farthest.

The old man and the little girls had left Väinölä in the misty dawn. Väinämöinen told them he didn't have the heart for long goodbyes, so they slipped away while their friends still slept. Väinämöinen carried a great pack on his back, a sword on his belt, and a strange bundle wrapped in colored cloth. Ulla and Kirsikka also bore small packs outside their hooded woolen cloaks, but they had made good time as they walked due south, crossing the icy Mustajouki in a small boat and leaving the Enchanted Valley without seeing another living soul. They had taken narrow paths through the forest for many days, sometimes passing near settlements of the Reindeer Folk, but never stopping. At last, they reached the southern eaves of the forest, where Väinämöinen bought the reindeer and sled.

As they left Karelia, Ulla and Kirsikka sat in the sled, huddled close beneath warm reindeer pelts, while Väinämöinen drove the coursers swiftly through the snow. The little girl from Grankulta had plenty of time to think as she watched the reindeers' strong legs endlessly pump up and down.

Mielikki had taken Ulla to her garden ere they departed, a garden filled with flowers that bloomed all year round, and spoke to her for a long time about the words of the prophecy. She, Ulla of the Karhulaiset, was the child foretold long ago, the one who would bring the sundered clans together once again. None of them—not Mielikki, not Väinämöinen, not anyone—could tell her what this meant, beyond the fact that she bore the strange scar on her shoulder where the bear's claw had torn her flesh.

She was a symbol, according to Väinämöinen; Turi said she was a sign. Ulla wished to be neither. She wanted to stay in the Valley and live in a village again, to forget about Löhi and what happened outside the deep woods. She wanted to learn the magic and songs of the heroes, and to live in peace with Kirsikka and her newfound friends. Wild thoughts crossed her mind, such as feigning sickness so that Väinämöinen might return to Karelia, or even seizing a flaming brand from their fire at night and burning her own flesh so that the Clan Mark would disappear and she could again be herself, a simple girl from the north. She said nothing of these things to Väinämöinen, and if the old singer guessed her mood, he gave no sign.

Väinämöinen knew the lands well where the borders of Karelia and Etelamaa came together, close to the shores of Lake Etelajärvi. There were mingled settlements of the Reindeer and Swan Folk along the lakeshore, fisherfolk who built boats and swept the open waters with their nets during the summer. Others lived on little islands, crossing the lake in rowboats as others might ride horses to a neighboring village. The Wall of the Giants did not extend all the way to Etelajärvi, and from the crossing of the Jouksi west and southwest round the lake's great bend, was a narrow gap, a land of little lakes, pools and kames where few people lived. The old man drove the sled across a frozen ford some miles north of the Jouksi's mouth and made his way through the rocky, tumbled moraine.

The kames rose from the mists and dotted the plain like so many eggs in a basket, some of them as tall as hillocks, covered with mossy turf or scattered trees. Väinämöinen told the girls that a few of the little hills still bore the ruins of old towers built long ago, when the Swan Folk had defended the gap against raids of the Itäläiset during the war with the Witch of Pohjola.

The towers were gone now, crumbled away by winter's freeze and summer's thaw, and the lakes and pools had risen and spread so that it was unlikely any large force could come that way again and so threaten the Green Vales of Etelamaa. Cold wind whistled through the barren lands, and were it not for Väinämöinen, the girls would have been very afraid. He, too, was uneasy; he feared no ghostly voices on the wind, but rather Löhi's *sight*. Despite the trees and hills, he felt exposed in the white, lonely wastes.

After several days, they came out onto a high shelf and saw a large lake below them, and away northwestward. It was frozen and covered in snow, but boulders and rocks stood out here and there, marking little islands in the mists. The days were noticeably longer as winter passed and early spring approached, but it was near dusk when they reached the shelf, and the sky was overcast and gloomy. The reindeer dug at the snow with their thick hooves to get at the moss buried beneath. As Väinämöinen and the girls stood looking out at the lake, several lights suddenly appeared in the distance, pale yellow and blue-green, flickering in the murk far below.

"Väinämöinen, look! What are they?!" cried Ulla excitedly, pointing at the lights.

"Well, well," said Väinämöinen. "There are many of them tonight! Perhaps they are welcoming us."

The tiny lights seemed to move about the misty rocks, sometimes flaring bright, then almost going out. Ulla thought of the flickering light in the woods near the Marches with her father and shivered.

Kirsikka tugged on Väinämöinen's sleeve. "What are the lights, Väinämöinen? Are there people down there?"

"No people, at least none that I can see. There's no good land out that way, just marshes. You're looking at the Devil's Lights, and the lake below is Kurppajärvi. We've come further west than I thought."

They watched the dancing lights for a while until Kirsikka broke the silence.

"Devils are evil. Are those evil lights?"

"The Devil's Lights are what mortals called them long ago; you can call them anything you like. They've been there as long as I can remember. You should see them during summer nights, when the wind is on the water! I don't know *what* they are, if you want to know the truth."

"*You* don't know what they are?" said Kirsikka. "Then it must be a real mystery, since you *usually* know everything."

"As opposed to you, who *usually* knows nothing," said Väinämöinen irritably. "But some things are meant to be a mystery, I suppose. Only mortals need answers and explanations, whether right or wrong, for everything under the sun. Not every question has an answer, or at least, not one based on mortal conceit and reason. Some things need to be felt in the heart to be truly understood.

"But the lights...I don't know. There are others elsewhere in the Far Northern Land. Sometimes they mark graves or places where treasure may be found. Some folk say that they are spirits, good or ill, and may lead unwary travelers astray, to their ruin. The Devil's Lights of Kurppajärvi—they just are and always have been. If they do have meaning, it is hidden from me."

Ulla watched a pale, wavering light disappear behind a tree-topped kame far below. She threw back her hood and narrowed her eyes.

"I think they are evil," she suddenly said with passion. "They were sent by Löhi to trick people. I don't wish to look on them any longer! Let's go from this place."

Väinämöinen turned to Ulla in surprise and opened his mouth, but checked himself. He looked hard at her. Her hair was tied back from her face in a single long braid. Even in the murky gloom, he could see her shining hazel eyes and the freckles that dotted her white face.

"Perhaps you are right, little one. Perhaps you know more about it all than old Väinämöinen." The old man looked down at the lights. "Look, Ulla, we're going to go down this slope, but we'll pass to the south of Kurppäjarvi. The lights may be on our right, but we don't need to cross the lake. We'll turn due south now, and in a day or so, we'll be in the Green Vales of Etelamaa. There are villages scattered about that place, and it's rather fair in spring and summer when the sun is shining. We'll soon strike a road that leads straight to the sea. A good thing, too—it's been a long, cold winter, even in the south, but the snows will be melting soon and the water opening up. We won't need our sled much longer."

They descended to the lake lands, which were all but impassable during the summer, save by boat. After two days, they came out into a more solid region with fewer lake and pools, but many thick stands of birches, pines and spruce, with solitary oaks and maples here and there. It was known as the Green Vales both because of the trees and because the land was divided into many small, flat-bottomed dales, where rivers and streams escaping from the lakes to the north emptied themselves. The land was fertile, but often flooded, and the Swan Folk who dwelled there had learned to live with the seasonal rhythms of thaw and rain.

The villages of the Vales were poor compared to the rest of Etelamaa, though not so poor as those of the Bear Folk, where Ulla and Kirsikka had lived. The people grew rye, but also kept many animals, chiefly cattle and sheep, but also reindeer. They hunted like the Karelialaiset and were good archers, but had few craftsmen and little of value to trade for the things they needed.

Alone among the Swan Folk, the folk of the Vales still held somewhat to the Old Ways and honored the Vanhalaiset. There were shamans and singers among the villages, men of power and women of magic who helped the sick and performed the rituals of land and bow. For that reason, many in the south looked down on them as backward and rude, little different from the wild Karelians in the forest. Yet there was strength in the simple villages and uncomplicated folk, a strength that had been lost in the towns and walled cities, and a strength that Väinämöinen hoped might yet save the clans.

The old man would have liked to rest in the Vales and seek out the villages' singers, but he was in a hurry to reach the Stone City and see the king. He also wished to travel as secretly as possible, causing no commotion. Löhi had surely learned by now that the Erilaiset had united to oppose her, and that the child foretold by Mielikki's Prophecy had been revealed. They skirted the villages and settlements, stopping only a few times for bread and milk or to shelter for the night in a barn or empty *pirtti*. As Väinämöinen had told the girls, the spring thaw was coming and, while their sled might also speed across grasslands and sedge when the snows melted, it was of little use on the hard-packed roads or cobbled streets of the south.

Near to the place where the river valleys failed and the broad Plain of Etelamaa began, Väinämöinen found a farmer who was willing to part with a horse. Unlike the Karelialaiset, the Etelalaisen farmer and his household were in awe of the singer and would have given him the horse for free. But the old man made a fair deal and gave the farmer two gold crowns struck in Etelamaa; moreover, Väinämöinen gave him the reindeer and sled, asking only that, should he ever come that way again and be in need of it, they would return it to him.

So Väinämöinen set Ulla and Kirsikka before him, tied their packs and his strange bundle behind him, and rode off to the south. The brown mare, sturdy and fat, had been well cared for during the winter. She was too small for the tall wizard, however. The girls perched uncertainly in front of him, and his arms could barely reach around them to handle the reins. It was a slow, difficult ride, even after they struck the road. They stopped frequently for the mare to rest and for Väinämöinen, stiff and saddlesore, to stretch his legs.

When they rode, Ulla clutched the mare's shaggy mane and nuzzled her neck, frequently dozing as the steady crunch of hooves in the snow and Väinämöinen's toneless humming lulled her to sleep. She felt safe atop the horse, as if it could carry her away from the sadness of her past or anything bad that might ever happen to her again.

Finally, a day came when the sun rose early, then shone clear and bright in a cloudless blue sky. The snow began to melt, and rivulets of icy water trickled down to form pools where the snow had already been thin. Ulla woke up inside a tumbledown sauna house not far from the road, where they had sheltered for the night. Kirsikka, buried under furs, still slept.

The little girl peered out the broken doorway and saw Väinämöinen by the road, speaking with two men, their black horses standing nearby. The men wore livery like the guards Ulla had seen in Keskimaa, but their colors were blue and white. One of them also wore a tattered, weather-stained cloak, and his boots were wrapped in cloth. They pointed south, down the road, and Väinämöinen nodded. After a few more words, they mounted their horses and left with a wave. Väinämöinen watched them for a while, then tramped back to the cabin, his staff making holes in the thin, patchy snow along the way. Ulla could see the worry on his face.

"Who were those men?" she asked. "They had bad news, didn't they?"

"Aye, little one. That they did. The worst I've heard in a long, long while." He went inside the old sauna house and sat down on the makeshift bed. "There is a spirit of great evil in Etelamaa," he said. "Mielikki perceived it from afar—a spirit of sickness and disease loosed from Tuonela by Löhi's dark magic. Many Etelalaiset have died of Plague this winter, and there is fear throughout the kingdom. The men you saw are messengers from the Stone City. One of them was sent north after the Night of Fire and has journeyed all the way to the eaves of Karelia, and in deep winter, too. He was sent to bring tidings of these things to me and ask for counsel, but he missed us as we left the woods and turned south. The Karelialaiset told him our plans and he followed us, but only now caught up with us. He lost two mounts along the way."

The old man began to wake Kirsikka, pulling back the furs and stroking her loosely braided red hair.

"Who was the other man?" asked Ulla.

"He, too, is a messenger," said Vaianmoinen. "But he set out only one week ago. And his news is very ill." He sighed heavily. "The king of Etelamaa is dead. Nigan, Lord of the Swan Folk, has perished from the plague. We have come too late."

It was quiet for a while as Kirsikka slowly stirred and the sun shone more and more through gaps in the broken walls.

"What will we do now?" Ulla finally asked.

"What we must," said Väinämöinen. "The new king is just a boy, not much older than you. He will be hard-pressed to meet the coming storm. They say he is at Nummela now, so on we go."

The red-haired girl arose, they packed their few things, and, mounting the brown mare, continued down the road as the snow turned to slush, and the slush to mud.

***

Egan stood outside the large tent, blinking in the sunlight. Blue and white pennants snapped in the breeze. Wagons rumbled in and out of the camp, and horsemen galloped here and there. More soldiers came into the camp every day as the regular companies of the Swan Folk were marshaled and armed. Egan had been at Nummela for several weeks now. Word had arrived that Väinämöinen had finally been found—not in Karelia, but in Etelamaa, on his way to the Stone City. Egan waited for him, against his counselors' advice, before he made the urgent decisions that only he could make, decisions that might well deteremine his fate.

They had made camp just outside of Nummela, a small, well-ordered town of perhaps five hundred with cobbled streets and a stone fountain in its single square. It lay north of the Stone City, on a crossroads. One way led north to the villages and farms on Etelamaa's rich plain, but the other led west and ran to the Itämeri coast.

Long ago, more than three centuries before, the queen of the Swan Folk had given birth to a son here. The baby had come early and was weak, so, rather than risk the journey to the city, the king stayed in Nummela for some months, and the lords of the noble houses of the Swan Folk came there to pay homage. The baby lived, and in time became a great king of his people. From then on, though the kings of Etelamaa were crowned in the Stone City's Great Square, they afterward removed to Nummela to receive greetings and pledges of fealty from the noble lords of the Folk of the Swan in remembrance of the child who became king.

So Egan had come to Nummela, too, leaving behind the sadness that lingered in the city after the terrible winter. He had not wished to leave at first. He took a strange comfort in the Keep's cold passages and winding stairs. Though he would not admit it to himself, the young king doubted his own ability to rule and make wise decisions. This was a strange thing for Egan, for he had never lacked confidence before. But when his counselors had urged him to go to Nummela and so establish his legitimacy, he had known they were right and followed their advice.

Egan would not only receive the fealty of the lords at Nummela, but had called for a muster of Etelamaa's arms. His father, Nigan, had sent a company of soldiers north for the winter in the event that the Easterners attacked, and ordered another company to remain along the coast. The kingdom only maintained five regular companies in times of peace, each with one hundred men, although the city's company was somewhat larger. During winter, most of these men lived with their families and gathered together again only in spring. But Egan ordered Juvari to marshal as many men as possible at Nummela, including the mounted Knights of the Swan. He rode forth to meet them with his own guard.

Messengers from the Stone City went to all the districts of Etelamaa, carrying the ill news of Nigan's death and summoning the noble houses to pay respect to the new young king. And they had come. From the lands near the Stone City, from the Green Vales, the shores of Lake Etelajärvi, and the fertile croplands of the Plain of Etelamaa, they had come. They acknowledged Egan as king of Etelamaa and chief of the clan, and some nobles had remained in the camp. But from the coastlands, only Lord Meripäivä had yet appeared. Kallas, Lord of Harmaaniemi, and the other lords of the Great Houses of the south remained in their keeps and did not answer the summons.

The lords of the coast had not acknowledged Egan, but neither had they yet openly defied him. They feared more assaults on their ships, for they were great traders, and raids on their towns. They complained bitterly that their defenses had not been strengthened. And, while they knew the Plague had killed many in the city, they dismissed rumors that Lovêatar had appeared, signaling the return of the Witch. Moreover, they doubted Väinämöinen and deemed it no coincidence that, even as he reappeared in Etelamaa after many years, an evil time settled over the kingdom. They knew that both Nigan and Egan had sought his counsel, and some whispered that the boy-king—for so they called him—was enamored of the Erilaiset, and had been bewitched by the old wizard they considered their enemy.

With the greater part of the army mustered, Juvari reported that, within a fortnight, they would be fully armed and ready to move. The question before Egan was where they should go. Sinio urged that they march to the coast in a show of force, for that would discourage any thoughts of rebellion and perhaps force the lords of the coast to acknowledge Egan's rule. But if they did not assent, and if Kallas or another rose in challenge, then they might crush him before he could gather strength. Not all of the king's counselors shared this view, though. They were still concerned about the northern borders and the possibility of another raid by the Easterners. If it came, there was but one company of men in all the north that was fit to meet the threat.

Egan pondered all this as he stood in the bright sun waiting for the old man to arrive. Apart from such questions, the boy—and he was still a boy, though he had turned fifteen after the new year and come into his manhood, as it was reckoned in those times—felt terribly and completely alone. His mother remained in the Stone City, still distraught over her husband's death and the coming of the shadow. His uncle had ridden with him to Nummela, but had then gone to the coastlands to reason with the uncertain nobles.

Egan was accustomed to feeling different from those around him; his quick wit and sharp mind, of which he was well aware, set him apart. He had never been so lonely, however, and the emptiness threatened to swallow him whole. He relied more and more on the one presence always with him: his father. Egan felt Nigan watching him, urging him on, and he desperately hoped he would not disappoint him or fail his trust.

The young king had known his counselors, men like Toiva and Sinio, all his life. Though he knew they judged his every move, he felt no trepidation and spoke openly to them. But it was not so with the soldiers. The men-at-arms mustered at Nummela were respectful of the new king, but Egan was painfully aware of how he must appear to them: a short, slight boy, little more than a child, who had never commanded a detachment of Guards, let alone the whole of the Army of Etelamaa. His entire life he had dreamed of glory in battle, of becoming a leader of men and a hero like the clan chiefs of old. Reality was turning out to be much different than fantasy.

Egan tried to look the part of a king, even if he didn't feel like one. He always wore the burnished armour and traps of the Royal House among his men. And though Tervo and his other masters had stayed behind—for Egan's formal education was now over—he still trained with his fencing and horse masters. He decided to do so where the soldiers might see him, hoping to win their trust by proving his skill with arms.

A group of horsemen, the Knights of the Swan, were parading near the royal tent, clad in heavy mail and mounted on huge black horses wrapped in barding, when a galloping rider on a smaller horse raced up to Egan and bowed his head with his hand across his breast.

"He is here, my lord," said the rider. "Väinämöinen just rode through the town and will be here very soon. The two children that we have heard of ride before him."

Even as Egan shielded his eyes from the sun and peered down the muddy lane that ran the length of the camp, he saw Väinämöinen riding toward him, flanked by two Etelaisen horsemen. As they neared, he looked curiously at the two little girls bouncing up and down on the brown mare. He wondered who they were and why the mage brought them with him. One of them had red hair, thick and curling about her shoulders, but the foremost had loose, dark brown locks that gleamed in the sun. Her white face, with freckles sprinkled about her nose, seemed serious for one so young; he instantly thought her strange and unlovely. Then she smiled, laughing at some word from Väinämöinen, and Egan perceived her to be not so much strange as singular and unique.

"Perhaps they are Erilaiset, too," said Sinio, coming up behind him. "But who knows what to expect with one such as Väinämöinen."

The old man reined in the mare and climbed down gingerly, for he was *very* stiff, then lifted the girls down as well. He was dirty and sore, and his travel-stained clothes were caked in mud, but he tried to maintain his dignity as he bowed low to Egan.

"Hail, Egan, King of the Etelalaiset," he said solemnly. "It is with sorrow that I return to the south. I grieve for the loss of your father, and for all your folk who perished in winter. There are no words to lessen your pain, so I will not try, but my thoughts are with you. And know that Nigan has passed through Tuonela's darkness and his spirit is at home with his fathers of old."

"Hail, Lord Väinämöinen," Egan replied. "It has indeed been a sad winter in Etelamaa. I wish that you had stayed longer when you visited us before."

Väinämöinen considered the boy for a moment. There was a sadness about him, to be sure, but the light within him was only veiled, not diminished.

"I am very sorry, my king," he said at last. "And you are right; perhaps I erred. But you know what happened in High Länsimaa and why I fled as I did, outlandish though it might have seemed at the time. Many Bear Folk were killed or taken captive despite my haste. Still, I beg your forgiveness."

"Could you have saved him?" asked Egan suddenly. "My father, I mean. Could you have stopped the plague from coming?"

The old man's face turned sorrowful.

"I don't know, Egan. I truly don't know. I can heal many ills, for that power is Akka's and is in the earth itself, yet I am but its servant. I cannot heal all things. Lovêatar's evil is strong. To be sure, I might have helped, but I really don't know."

Egan looked at the ground while the blustery south wind whipped the flags and rustled his pale blue cloak.

"Well, I am glad that you're here," he said at last. Then he smiled, something he had not done in many days. "And who are your companions? Are they, too, Erilaiset?"

"They are friends," said Väinämöinen. "Karhulaiset from the distant north. The Easterners sacked their homes and scattered their folk. May I present Ulla and Kirsikka? They have come a very long way and survived great peril."

"Then welcome, Ulla and Kirsikka of the Bear Clan. I am pleased that you have come to Etelamaa. But forgive me—I am sure that you are tired and would like to rest and be refreshed."

"Tired, to be sure," said Väinämöinen. "And my young charges especially so. But I would speak with you now, my king, if we may. The winds of the world are blowing strong, and for this reason and no other have I come to Etelamaa."

"I thought as much, and this is what I, too, wish. I am tired of waiting! Let's go inside; Sinio and the others will join us." Egan touched the two little girls on the head and smiled. "My sister, Marjatta, is about your age, although her hair is yellow. She could play with you if she were here, but she's in the Stone City with our mother. Perhaps one day you will meet her."

He signaled to a servant, a young woman, who came forward to meet the girls and then, with Väinämöinen and Sinio, went into the great tent. The old man looked back and winked at Ulla as he disappeared inside.

In a smaller tent close by, the girls were offered copper basins to bathe in, which was new to them. They traded their travel-worn Karelian clothes for light and finely woven attire that had simple yet elegant embroidery done in the fashion of Etelamaa. Food was brought to them, and Kirsikka began eating while Ulla was still braiding her wet hair. Egan fascinated the red-haired girl; she couldn't stop talking about having met a "real king."

"And can you believe how young he is?" Kirsikka said. "He looks no older than my poor brother. But he is so handsome, and Väinämöinen said he lives in a real castle far away by the sea."

"He is only a boy," said Ulla, no longer so easily impressed. "No bigger than several who lived in my village. And he wouldn't be king if his father hadn't died."

"I'm surprised Väinämöinen didn't take you with him," said Kirsikka. "To show them your mark so that they'll do as he wishes."

Ulla started at the mention of the mark on her shoulder. She seldom spoke about it herself, even with Kirsikka, and had come to wish it weren't there, although she knew it was her only claim on Väinämöinen.

"They all want to see it," she said slowly. "That is why we're here."

"Oh, I know," said Kirsikka, tossing a sweet, green fruit to Ulla. "It's not about me! You're the important one, with the mark and prophecy and all. I don't seem to come into it anywhere. Maybe they'll make you their queen when you grow up, and you'll marry King Egan and go live in his castle. You can take me with you!"

"I'd rather go back to the forest," said Ulla. "My father is Karelian. That's where I belong."

The girls rested for the remainder of the day, and in the evening they were taken to watch horsemen parading through the camp, but they did not see Väinämöinen again until they awoke the next day. The old man was washed and in new clothes, with his white beard brushed and forked. His staff, kantele, and other things rested in a corner. He sat at a little table eating—and drinking. He winked at them as they popped up, rubbing the sleep from their eyes. The noise of voices and the camp's bustle was loud outside the tent.

"'*Bread and beer make the best breakfast,*'" said Väinämöinen, wiping his mouth on his sleeve. "Especially when it's good southern brew. I've had my fill of *sahti*, that's for sure."

He motioned to the girls, who sat next to him while he poured cold milk into wooden cups.

"Where were you last night?" asked Ulla.

"Talking," answered Väinämöinen. "With the new king and his men—where else? And there will be more talking today, too. Egan is sharp, as I knew already. But he is very young and should not have come to the throne so soon. He is unsure, which is no fault of his. Even the wisest are often unsure, though they've learned to hide it."

"But what should he do?" said Ulla.

"That, you should know well enough. He should do as I counsel, at least in this matter. He should go to the north and lend aid to the Karhulaiset, and maybe the Hirvilaiset, too, if they need it. Messengers will come soon from High Länsimaa begging for help. Etelamaa may stand for a season, but if the northern clans are overrun, it will stand alone. And fall alone."

Ulla considered his words while Kirsikka dug into the honey-covered loaves. Finally, she asked, "Does he not wish to go north?"

"Yes and no," said Väinämöinen. "I believe the boy understands the peril of Löhi better than any other. He has seen the shadow of Lovêatar himself, and lost his father, too. But he has many problems with his own folk; there has often been rebellion among the Clan of the Swan. It would seem wise to settle his own house first, if he can." The old man sighed.

"But I also spoke to him of the return of the Erilaiset to Etelamaa, and the singing of the songs again among the Seven Clans. I know in my heart that our only hope against Löhi lies therein, but it is difficult for these mortal men to consider when they are faced with plague from Tuonela. They have forgotten so much, and snicker in their sleeves when the names of the Vanhalaiset are invoked. And it is true, my name and counsel are unwelcome in the coastlands of Etelamaa, where Egan's trouble lies. Perhaps—yes, perhaps I should have waited. As Turi said, swords will be needed more than songs this summer. So be it! I am a free man and I made my choice as best I could. None can ask more of another, no matter what may come afterward."

They stayed in the camp of the Swan Folk at Nummela for another week while the last snows melted and the roads became a muddy mess.

Throughout the Far Northern Land, the thaw meant rising rivers and lakes, and treacherous travel. In the east, the Jouksi became a great flood as the river rushed down to Lake Etelajärvi. In the west, in Akkala and in Tavastia and in Etelamaa, along the coasts of the Itämeri Sea, great fleets of ships and boats, large and small, made ready to put to sea again. The Mariners of the Shipwrights Guild, who hailed from all the clans and owed allegiance only to their Master, prepared their galleys and clinker-built crafts.

Spring had at last returned to the north, and the folk of the Seven Clans kept busy with the hectic rush that the warm sun and longer days brought with them. Spring and summer were green, blue and beautiful in the Far Northern Land, but they were also very short. Those who failed to make use of them might not live through another winter.

Ulla saw Egan only twice in all this time—once when some jugglers and acrobats performed for the king's retinue, and again when a great meal was set out for many people under a billowing white canopy. At the feast, the girls were seated in places of honor beside Väinämöinen. For the most part, the girls saw Väinämöinen only in the mornings, then spent their days with women and children who had followed their husbands and fathers to the camp.

The women took them into the surrounding countryside and to Nummela when they bought things in the market. Clothed like village girls of the Swan Folk in embroidered dresses of white and blue, with long aprons decorated with elaborate designs, Ulla and Kirsikki went unremarked. Many women wore blue veils over their hair, and had spirals of bronze sewn onto their hems and cuffs, with chains and clasps of bronze and silver. Girls nearer their own age braided their hair after the fashion of maidens in Etelamaa. This pleased Kirsikka greatly, but Ulla preferred her Karelian attire.

One morning, Väinämöinen was waiting for them at the little table inside their tent with a somber expression. He told them they would be leaving soon, probably the very next day. The old man had tried, with his wizardly power, to reach out to Turi in the north and to others of the Erilaiset, but without luck. Now he had heard the voice of Mielikki in his dreams.

The Itäläiset were indeed poised to attack High Länsimaa with a great force, and other evil things out of Pohjola were with them. Löhi had determined that the clans were weak; she planned to strike while Etelamaa bickered. Väinämöinen had done all he could to convince Egan to march north; now he resolved to go straight to the Seer at Kyöpelinvuori, then back to the Marches to help there as he could. He was still uncertain as to what the Swan Folk would do.

That night, Kirsikka fell asleep early. Väinämöinen, as usual, was nowhere to be seen, and Ulla felt lonely. The tent was dark save for a single oil lamp burning on the table that cast strange, wavering shadows. The camp was never silent, and even at night, Ulla could hear the sounds of people and horses all about them. Restless, she crept to the entryway to see what was happening outside. She had half a mind to sneak out and wander around by herself for a while until she was finally missed, and the hue and cry was raised to search for her. Just as she was about to pop out into the cool night, a shadow loomed in the entryway and a cloaked figure slipped inside. It wasn't Väinämöinen, however—it was Egan.

Ulla hopped back, startled by the young king, but Egan was just as surprised to find the little girl hovering inside the dark tent. He hesitated for a moment, then bowed low and stood before her with an uncertain expression.

"I beg your pardon," he said. "I didn't mean to disturb you."

If Ulla had been a maiden of Etelamaa, or perhaps Tavastia, she might have done a courtesy and replied with generous words. However, she was only a little girl from the poor north. If she was no longer easily impressed after all she had seen, she could still be very shy. She said nothing, but simply stared at the sandy-haired boy with her large hazel eyes.

"Um, I was looking for Väinämöinen," said Egan. "I wished to speak with him again. My uncle has returned and we would see him this very night if we could."

"He's not here," said Ulla. "He's usually gone at night. But in the morning, he has always come back again."

Egan glanced at Kirsikka, asleep in a corner with her long red hair glowing orange in the unsteady light. "I'm pleased to see you again, Ulla. Truth be told, I had hoped to speak with you, too. I think Väinämöinen will be leaving soon, and you, of course, will go with him."

"We're leaving tomorrow," said Ulla. "That is what Väinämöinen told us."

"I thought as much," said Egan. "All the more reason to see him tonight." Egan looked around the little tent, noticing the old wizard's kantele sitting on the table. "You know Väinämöinen very well, don't you?"

"I don't know. I have been with him a long time now. He saved my life last year in the woods near Grankulta."

"Yes, he told us. He told us about the bear in the woods and the mark on your shoulder. He told us about the words of Mielikki, the Lady of the Forest, whom men deem only a legend. I do not know if all my lords believed him. Many strange things have happened to us."

"Do you believe him?" asked Ulla. "Do you not wish to see the mark? You may, if you like. Then you must believe him and do as he tells you. You must go north with your army and fight the Witch!"

Ulla jerked down the neck of her dress, exposing her right shoulder. The bear claw was bright against her pale skin. Taken aback, Egan reached out his hand to touch her and traced the mark with his fingers, even as others had done, but quickly pulled back.

"'*By the Clan Mark shall you know them,*'" he mumbled. Ulla pulled up her shirt.

"That is what the bear did," said Ulla firmly. "That is what appeared after Väinämöinen healed me. Now that you have seen it, you know that Mielikki's words are true. You must help the other clans, and the Erilaiset, too."

Egan, son of kings and Lord of the Etelalaiset, student of sages and lore masters, stood speechless before the child. He looked into her eyes and felt a chill run through his spine. Words finally came to his halting lips.

"Your parents are dead, aren't they? I mean your family, in the north—"

"I don't know what happened to them. They are all gone."

"My father is dead. He died of the Winter Plague after Lovêatar came to the city."

"I know," said Ulla. And then, after a moment, she added, "I'm sorry."

A rush of emotion suddenly flooded the boy and tears welled in his eyes.

"Well," he said hurriedly, "please tell Lord Väinämöinen, if he returns, that my uncle is here and would like to see him." Egan moved to leave the tent, but looked back at the little girl from the entryway. "Perhaps you will indeed come to the Stone City one day and play with my sister."

Without another word, he walked out.

Ulla stood stock still for a long while, listening to Kirsikka's slow, rhythmic breathing. She briefly considered going out into the camp to look for Väinämöinen, or even to look for Egan, though she didn't know why and had no idea what to say to him if she found him again. Finally, she lay down next to Kirsikka and waited for morning.

She must have fallen asleep at some point, because she opened her eyes to find Kirsikka already awake and eating while Väinämöinen packed their things. The old man said he'd been awake all night, walking outside the camp at first to clear his mind and think, and then, after Egan's servants had finally found him, speaking with Alder, the Grand Duke of Etelamaa.

Alder brought word that the coastal lords would not yet relent and acknowledge Egan, but still equivocated, claiming various excuses. The captain of the company that now guarded the southern shore was close to Kallas; many men in that company were from the coastlands as well. Alder feared they might form the core of a rebellion and tried to convince Väinämöinen to stay with them and throw his lot in with Egan, even as he had aided the Royal House of old. But Väinämöinen would not stay, nor openly give aid to one faction in the Swan Folk's affairs ever again. He could only repeat to Alder that the threat to Etelamaa would come not from rebellious lords in their coastal fiefs, but from the north.

Egan and his retinue said their farewells to the girls under a shining sun in a bright blue sky. In addition to their new clothes, the young king gave them fine silver chains to be worn on their dresses with tiny figures of swans attached, and soft leather pouches stitched with golden thread. Egan also ordered that a cart be prepared—not a lumbering wagon or country cart such as Ulla's father had made in Grankulta, but an Etelaisen cart with seats for its riders, pulled by a strong, swift horse. The brown mare would stay with the king.

Väinämöinen asked to speak with Egan alone before they set off. Ulla watched as he fetched the odd bundle he had carried all the way from Väinölä, still covered with its colored cloth, and took it with him into the king's tent. They soon came out again, and the old man lifted Ulla and Kirsikka into the cart. He hopped into the driver's seat—his staff and kantele beside him—and, taking the reins, turned the cart around and checked the big, black horse next to where Egan, Alder and Juvari stood. The young king's blue eyes shone in the sunlight.

"Farewell, my king," said the wizard. "Choose your path well, for much depends on it. But my thoughts and the blessings of Ukko go with you wherever you go!"

Väinämöinen shook the reins violently and the cart took off, two tall knights riding escort beside them. But Egan watched them drive through the camp toward Nummela, until the cart dwindled in the distance and finally disappeared from view.

Chapter Eleven

The Eagle
and the Arrow

Of old, Turi had been a great traveler. From the snowy heights of the mountains in Talvimaa, where the dwarves mined for gold, to the far shores of the Itämeri Sea, where mortals of strange races dwelled, he had explored Ukko's creation with the eyes and mind of a curious child, always thinking to learn more and never in want of wonderment or amazement. A mighty singer and wizard, and a clever shape-shifter, he crossed the Far Northern Land in forms diverse and magical, running through the woods as a swift deer and even swimming in Ahti's waters like a slippery, silver fish. He had run with Löhi in days gone by, for she was also a shape-shifter and could assume many forms. Always a friend to mortal men, even in later times, when the Crilaiset withdrew into narrow places and were estranged from the world of men, he travelled still among the Seven Clans and spoke with the singers that yet remained.

So Turi was chosen to go to Keskimaa and attempt to do what Väinämöinen had failed to do the year before; he would try and convince Pekka Verikiven to marshal the strength of the Bear Folk and to return all his folk to the Old Ways, uniting with the other clans so that Löhi might be frustrated, and her plans come to naught.

Long he spoke with Väinämöinen and Mielikki as they sat together by the fire in the frozen woods while the *Linnunrata*—the starry bird's path set in the nighttime sky by Ilmatar—shone above. Mielikki turned her *sight* to the north, even to Pohjola, to descry from afar Löhi's intentions. The Witch's power was great, however, and she had shrouded her plans in mist, clouding Mielikki's mind so that even the daughter of Tapio saw little. The winter had passed slowly, and the unease of the heroes had grown.

Turi left Väinölä a week before Väinämöinen set out. He said farewell to the girls on a frosty night beside the Great Oak, for he delighted to walk through the woods at night, even in the cold and snow. Mielikki went with him since her garden lay in that direction, and they parted near his home at Kivipolku. She gave a gift to him ere he left: a bright emerald on a gold chain.

"It has no power," she said. "It is only a beautiful thing. But think of me when you look at it, and remember that you have friends. Perhaps it will bring you hope when all seems lost."

Turi smiled. "Maybe so. I don't despair easily! But keep those eyes and ears of yours open and let me know what you see and hear with them."

He stayed the night at Kivipolku to sleep in his own bed one last time, then started out the next morning. The old mage wore a heavy winter cloak of russet brown and tall russet boots to match, but his woolen clothes underneath were a deep Karelian green, as was his tall, peaked hat. The heavy pack on his back was filled with thin, round crisps of rye bread and he leaned hard on his staff as he tramped through the snow. Two other Erilaiset waited for him at the Ankkaportti, friends also travelling to mortal lands and journeying in the same direction. They passed over the Mustajouki on the white bridge and set out down the narrow path, until they came at last to the forest road and turned west.

Snow lay thick in some spots along the road, and their going was slow. But they soon met some Karelialaiset travelling west on sleds, and Turi and his friends hopped aboard where there was room. They went more swiftly then, and after some days of sledding down the dark forest road came to the great totem of the Karelialaiset, looming ever vigilant, like a silent, snow-covered sentinel. One of Turi's companions went his own way then; his task was to warn the Reindeer Folk who lived in the nearby villages and scattered homesteads, and to help them prepare against the gathering storm. But Turi continued until they drove out of the forest and, as the days slowly lengthened, came at last to Metsäposti.

Turi stayed some few days in Metsäposti, speaking with Osmo and other lords of the Reindeer Clan, telling them to heed Väinämöinen's words of the previous year. He especially urged them to add to their stores of food and fodder, and to move these deeper within the woods, for he believed many Bear Folk might come that way in need of shelter from marauding Easterners. They also bought horses, for they had need of greater speed now, and the snow would soon melt. There were few horses in Metsäposti, and most of these were draught beasts, but Turi paid a heavy price in gold for two sturdy animals that were broken in well and used to long journeys.

His companion then rode south, for he was sent to warn the people who lived in that direction, between the Jouksi and the forest, and then finally follow the river to the Green Vales far away. But Turi went west, and, from Metsäposti, crossed the icy Jouksi and left Karelia behind. He took the very path, though he did not know it, that Ulla and Kirsikka had come down as they fled from the Easterners. There were few people in that region, and the men who worked the peat marshes for bog iron and mined bloodrock had not yet returned for the spring and summer. The wizard saw scattered signs, however, of the past year's tragedy: broken carts along the road and scraps of abandoned things partially buried in the snow. He sensed rather than saw the restless spirits of the dead that haunted that sad place where so much evil befell them, though the bones and bodies would wait for the snows to melt before they revealed themselves.

At length, he came to the lakes and pools south of Suurijärvi. Many folk lived in that district—fishermen and herders for the most part—and others from the north had joined to them since the great raid. There had been little time to prepare dwellings for the newcomers, and so they built log cabins that looked more like the houses of the Karelialaiset than most *pirttis* in High Länsimaa. People came to the road when Turi passed by, for they could see he was a wizardly man with his staff and tall hat—indeed, most thought he was Väinämöinen. They begged for news and some asked if it was safe to return to their villages in the north. Turi admonished them to stay where they were, and, if war came to them again, told the villagers to go east, not west, and seek safety across the river in Karelia.

So the wizard rode his horse across High Länsimaa until he came to more settled lands, and on a bright day with the sun high in the sky, he finally reached Keskimaa, the chief town of the Clan of the Bear. The town was much changed since Väinämöinen had been there. Many dwellings had been built for the refugees on the broad, empty plain outside the walls, and others now lived in the town itself, swelling its numbers. The gate stood open, although it was manned by more guards than before, and the streets within buzzed with activity, for spring was come and there was much to be done.

Turi passed a long line of wagons, their great wheels spiked for traction on the last of the ice. All of them were loaded with bloodrock: the first wagon train of the year headed south to the smiths in Etelamaa and Tavastia. Although the wagons were full, the trade in bloodrock had been disrupted by the Easterners' attack, and the Bear Folk had little set by to sell. Nor was all the rock to go south, for their own smiths were busy forging swords and iron-tipped spears. Pekka had at last raised an army; in Keskimaa and near Suurijärvi, hundreds of men gathered, many of them from the north, where villages and homes had been despoiled by the Easterners.

Turi rode through the crowded, bustling city and past the tall wooden buildings until he came to the open place before the Hall of the Karhulaiset. It was filled with people, chiefly traders and hawkers, but also a company of men-at-arms being drilled by a mounted captain. The wizard watched the scene for a while and smiled. He had a soft heart for the Kaamoslaiset and their noisy, selfish, innocent and childlike ways. Mortals, always unpredictable, could be cruel to one another one moment, but then surprise each other with love and kindness the next. They were weak and short-lived, and Turi understood better than most Erilaiset how little time they had to learn wisdom. But they refused to despair, even in the face of the Far Northern Land's bitter clime, or sickness and misfortune, or any of the other perils that followed them all their lives. And so Turi had come to love them.

He tied his horse on the wooden palisade and walked through the muddy courtyard, past the alder trees, and into the hall. Pekka Verikiven was not there, but guards went at once to fetch him while Turi waited. When Pekka heard there was a wizard in the hall, and that some of the guard thought him to be Väinämöinen, he hurried back. All the people in Keskimaa knew of Väinämöinen's warning, and there had been hard words spoken against Pekka in many quarters for not heeding it. But when he reached the hall, accompanied by Ilkka, who was now the Captain of the Wardens of High Länsimaa, the lord of the Bear Folk saw that he did not know the visitor.

When Pekka bustled in, red-faced and puffing, Turi swept off his hat and bowed low. The wizard was disheveled after his long journey, his boots caked with mud and his thick brown cloak stained and worn, but he looked every bit the great Erilainen from Karelia.

"Hail, Pekka Verikiven, Lord of the Karhulaiset! I bring you the greetings of all the Erilaiset of Taikalaakso! I am Turi, sometimes called the Changer in your tales and legends. I have not been to Keskimaa in many long years, not since your grandfather's time. But I have often been among your folk in in Itäranta, and they know me there."

Pekka looked sideways at Turi, then bowed as best he could, given his girth. "Hail and welcome," he said. "Truly, I've not heard your name, but I can see you are...you are a singer and wizard, are you not? And a friend of Väinämöinen?"

"All those things I am," answered Turi. "And the last not the least!"

"I have heard of you," said Ilkka. "My folk, the Clan of the Elk, tell many tales about Turi the Changer. My name is Ilkka, the Chief Warden of High Länsimaa, and for my part I, too, welcome you to Keskimaa."

Turi smiled.

"You are no doubt tired if you have come all the way from Karelia," said Pekka. "Let us have food and drink for our guest! But, if I may ask, what can we do for you? What brings you to us on the edge of spring?"

"Alas, I do not come for a pleasant visit to the lands of the Bear Clan. I come with the same warning that brought Väinämöinen here last year: a warning of battle and war."

Pekka frowned. "Guests from Karelia seem to come with nothing else, but with few specifics. Had Väinämöinen told us more, we might have been better prepared, and avoided much grief and pain. Do you have counsel that will be to our benefit? Or if not, what then do you want of us?"

"Peace!" cried Turi and again he bowed low. "I cast no blame, far from it. Neither you nor Väinämöinen could have known what was to come or when. The raid came very late in the summer, so as to leave little time to prepare for winter. But, if I may be so bold, you have done well, Lord Pekka. You have succored your folk and saved many from death in the cold. And you have raised an army, which I little thought to find. Your smiths are busy. Yes, you have done well for your folk.

"No, my lord, there is nothing I want of you. Rather, I come to offer my service. I know your enemy well. I have fought many times against the Itäläiset, and Löhi will send other servants, too—the Hiisia of Pohjola, among others. With your leave, I would help train your men. And it may be that news is more important to you now than my sword or my staff. I can go to the North Marches and beyond, where no mortals, not even the Wardens, can go now. It may be that I will see things of great use to you, perhaps even the designs of your enemies."

Pekka considered his words for a moment and then said, "Miko Verikiven is the Captain of the Karhulaiset, but the March Wardens are gathering our men and teaching them what they can."

"Yet there are not enough of us," said Ilkka. "Any aid you could give would be welcome. We have sent scouts to the Marches, but they have seen little, or else have not returned."

"Let us hope that they will," said Turi. "It is a perilous venture now that Löhi is stirring. But I will go, if I may, and in other form, too, so perhaps I will not be caught! What say you, my lord? Will you accept my service?"

Pekka hooked his fat hands in his golden belt and nodded his head.

"I will," he said at last. "If Ilkka agrees. Your words are fair, if grim. But I fear for my folk and will take the hand that is offered. I hope your staff is as strong as those in the tales of old."

"It is strong," said Turi. "We shall see if it is strong enough."

Turi went then with Ilkka to the Warden House, and for the next two weeks, he helped to marshal the men-at-arms of the Bear Folk and make them into an army. Some were armed with axes or swords, but most were given long spears tipped with iron and made with wooden hafts hardened by fire. The Karhulaiset were strong men, but mainly farmers and fishermen who had no experience of battle. Turi taught them as best he could how to stand against horsemen, and, though it pained him, how to strike at the horse rather than the rider, for in this way the fight might be made more equal, and their enemies would suffer loss even in victory. The Bear Folk had few horsemen themselves, however. There were several companies of Wardens in High Länsimaa, but each had no more than thirty men, and this worried Turi greatly.

The wizard was more worried still by Pekka's plans to march his army north, as he had last year, to chase the Easterners away. Miko Verikiven, Pekka's cousin, had ordered many wagons prepared with great stores of supplies, and sent word to the villages of Suurijärvi to make ready as well. The men would move as soon as the spring floodwaters went down.

Turi opposed this. He feared that Löhi would send such large numbers against them that they would be overwhelmed in the north. He urged the Bear Folk to send messengers to Etelamaa to beg their help and told them that Väinämöinen had gone to the great southern kingdom for that very same purpose. But Turi told only Ilkka that Ulla travelled with the old singer, and shared with the Warden the full tale of Mielikki's words and their meaning.

So Turi made ready to leave for the North Marches as a scout for the Bear Folk, but first went to Pekka and told him of his fear. "It is well for you to send your men to the White Road and wait there for news, but go no further. For, if Löhi's force is not so great, you may quickly march north and defeat it. But do not send them blindly to the north of High Länsimaa! This will be no mere raid, and your enemies will not flee your approach. If they are numerous, as I fear, they will have many horsemen, and there is no good field for your army in the north. The Easterners will go around them in the woods and entrap them. There will be sorcerors from Pohjola to ensnare them in webs of wizardry. There are no forts or strong places from which to defend to your advantage.

"It is better to tell the folk of Suurijärvi to hide in the forest and flee east, even to Karelia. But, for your army, there is a good field for battle here before the city, and even if you are defeated, your men may retreat within the walls. Your enemies will try to set fire to Keskimaa, but fire is always a threat and you know how to meet it. And if the Swan Folk come, they will come swiftly to Keskimaa and rescue you!"

Turi found a new horse, a swift brown charger, and set out for the Marches on a day that the rain poured from the sky. He rode quickly to the White Road, despite the mud, then turned north, stopping only when his horse needed rest. The people he passed in their villages and homesteads called out to him, but he said little until he reached the lands near Suurijärvi. Then he told the people to be wary and to prepare hiding places stocked with food, where they might flee if the Easterners came that way. Few took him seriously, though, for they could not believe any enemies would come so far south.

In a small town called Gamla near the junction of the White and North roads was a large company of men, perhaps two hundred, as well as a company of mounted Wardens: the northern force of the Karhulaiset. Several of the Wardens had just returned from the Marches. They had seen little, but reported a strange, brooding silence and a feeling of unease all about the land. Two of their number still had not returned. Turi rested several days in

Gamla, but, when he left, he rode faster, putting his power into the horse to give it strength and endurance.

He found a sad sight as he neared the Marches. He passed empty villages and burned farms, and wet, melted fields with the previous season's uncut rye. He slowed down then, a lonely rider among abandoned lands where much evil had befallen. He came across a few people here and there—folk who had returned to their homes after the raid and endured the harsh winter with little food or comfort. They were despondent and hungry. Instead of welcoming the spring, they felt the same disquiet the Wardens reported. Turi told them to leave the north and flee toward Gamla. Like them, he could feel a heaviness in the air, and a strange tiredness—even lethargy—came over him. All was quiet and still; even spring's bright birdsong and the sound of life stirring anew were faint and muted. He knew that the power of Löhi or one of her servants was over the land, and that the Bear Folk were in great danger.

Just within the borders of High Länsimaa, the wizard let his brown horse run free. He had left the road some miles before it dwindled to an uncertain path because he felt exposed, as if unseen eyes watched him. Instead, he picked his way through the trees and pools. The horse lingered nearby, reluctant to go its own way on unfamiliar ground, but Turi spoke gently to it, and at length, it wandered away.

The old singer stood very still for a long time amidst the trees and blooming green. He could feel the power of Akka beneath his feet, running through the very earth itself, and above, in the wind, the strength of Ilmatar, Mistress of the Skies. It was her strength he called on now.

Casting away everything except his staff and Mielikki's jewel, he chanted the ancient words that worked the change. Had there been mortal eyes to see, they might have beheld a strange thing, as if a sudden shaft of sunlight fell upon him—blinding, like a star from the heavens. And when the light faded, the old man was gone, disappeared, as if the verdant forest had swallowed him up. But where he had stood, perched on a lichen-covered grey stone, was an eagle.

The great bird had dark feathers, deep brown on its broad shoulders and black underneath, but its crest and nape were like rusty copper and a spot of green shone on its breast. The sharp beak curved downward; the bird's eyes were clear and bright. The golden eagle of the north spread its wings, which stretched beyond the measure of other birds', and gave a loud, harsh cry that broke the unnatural stillness and echoed throughout the woods.

The eagle took flight, rising above the forest's canopy and climbing into the sky toward the clouds. It soared ever higher, describing circles in the air, then turned north and sped away from that place. With its sharp sight, it could see for many miles and spy even the smallest beasts upon the ground. The eagle's strong wings carried it swiftly over the land, but it didn't have far to go ere it found what it sought. Beyond the Marches and only a little way into the Wastes, in that region that was once known as Suonpää, many things were afoot.

Thin trails of smoke rose from scattered fires; horses and tiny figures moved among the woods. The eagle dropped lower, until it skimmed the treetops. There, just below, were hundreds of Easterners, their red and black banners clashing with the forest's green. Groups of horses were gathered in clearings, near many carts and sleds.

The eagle flew on, skipping across a shallow lake of clear water and chasing away the ducks and geese. On the lake's far side were more horsemen, and still more smoke trails were visible in the distance. Some of the Easterners looked up at the great bird as it passed overhead. There were hundreds, possibly thousands, all told—this would indeed be no mere raid for slaves and plunder.

The dark-plumed eagle flew on, for it could descry movement ahead in an even greater clearing across a little stream that wound its way through the woods. The bird alit in the upper branches of a spruce tree at the clearing's edge, startling the cuckoos into flight. There were many figures within the clearing, but they were not mortal men. The eagle's bright eyes gazed upon Hiisia, in the hundreds.

Now the Hiisia were a *väki* of that folk called the Dark Erilaiset because they served Löhi and worshipped her as one of the Vanhalaiset. Small in stature like the Menninkäiset, they were unlovely to the eyes of mortal men. Their faces were cruel, with dark green or black skin and hooked noses like the fearful masks that some folk wore at *Kekri*, the time of autumn festival and ritual. But their eyes were white as the snow of Pohjola, with no pupil or color to be found therein.

Alone among the Erilaiset, they were short-lived, for they failed even sooner than the mortals of the Seven Clans. It was said that long, long ago, when they first came into the world, they had done some great evil, and so were cursed by Tapio and Akka to have their lives cut short. But not even Väinämöinen knew the truth of this.

Löhi gathered them to her, for they were useful servants. She promised them life everlasting when she came into her own, and so they worshipped her and hated the mortal clans. And yet it was still their choice to follow Löhi's crooked path. The goblins died in droves during the Witch's War, and when it ended, they were reduced to a little folk, a memory of menace that haunted lonely woods and distant cots, or dwelled far to the north of mortal lands, for they could withstand the bitter cold. And when the Witch returned, they answered her call and came again to Pohjola. Löhi put her power into them so that their numbers swiftly increased and filled her dreary halls in Sariola, the Witch's Keep upon Mount Kipuvuori.

The golden eagle watched the Hiisia now, observing that their great camp held many tents and small, rude cabins of rough-hewn logs. A larger tent stood alone to one side of the clearing. The banners hung from its canopy and the standards pitched before it were deep blue or black with a single token upon them: Löhi's Sign, the shining North Star set amidst the dark sky. A few black horses stood nearby. The eagle took wing and flew closer to the large tent, alighting upon the low, bare branch of a dead pine. Up close, it could see inside, where noisome tallow candles burned and tall figures moved about. The great bird had senses other than sight or smell, and recognized the presence of sorcery and powerful magic. Suddenly the tent flap was thrown back, revealing a tall elf in a white cloak that was clasped at the neck with a black-jeweled brooch. He turned his dark gaze this way and that, as if he, too, sensed an elusive and powerful presence.

The eagle tensed, ready to flee back into the deeper woods, but, as it turned its head, it spied two goblins clad in black leather in the trees behind. One crouching goblin pointed at the bird with one hand, its other hand resting on his companion's shoulder. The second Hiisi held a bow, the arrow already notched and aimed. The eagle leapt into the air, but too late. The bow twanged and the arrow found its mark, missing the wing and piercing the great bird just below the breast. It took flight despite the pain and shock, breaking through the canopy as voices cried out below.

Due south it flew, the arrow still in its side, no longer caring about spying out secrets on the ground. Its powerful wings cut through the heavy, hot air as the red sun lingered in the early evening sky. Drops of blood fell to the earth as it passed, and the pain became terrible. When it was finally too much to bear, the eagle weakened and dove to the ground, landing in some bracken beside a little northern pool, short of the Marches and still in the Wastes beyond.

Had there been anyone to see, they might have beheld a bird in the brush, its beak open wide, before a dark shadow not unlike a storm cloud obscured it. When the watcher's blurry eyes cleared, the eagle would have been gone. In its place, lying in the brake, was an old man with a bloodstained shirt.

Turi rolled over and lay flat on his back for some time, staring at the yellow twilight sky above. He laughed at himself, though it hurt. What an end—struck down by a Hiisi's arrow, of all things, in the Wastes of Suonpää! After a while he stirred and looked at his wound. The arrow had not gone in too deep. It broke a rib, but the bone had stopped the shaft from piercing his vitals. The wizard sat up and carefully plucked the arrow from his side. Blood spurted out, but Turi immediately chanted the ancient song that closed flesh. No less a healer than Väinämöinen, Turi knew where the iron came from and where the arrow's wooden shaft once grew; he knew the bird that gave its feathers for the fletching, and he knew the cold hands of the Hiisia who bound them all together.

Turi knew the origin of all these things, and so he could sing the song and close the flesh and be whole again. He lay back after the blood had stopped, the arrow still in his hand, and closed his eyes. The sun finally sank, and the old man went to sleep; he slept throughout the short night and most of the following day.

He awoke the next evening and drank some water from the little pool. The Changer felt terrible. He was sick, his head hurt, and his ribs ached, especially the one still broken within the closed wound. The old man finally arose, leaning on his staff, and, with a heavy sigh, shuffled through the sparse woods to the southeast, toward the Marches and the road. He had no food, no horse, and little strength—only his staff and Mielikki's jewel, still around his neck. Turi knew he had to get back to High Länsimaa, however. Erilaiset though he was, he might die in the Wastes without help, and the Bear Folk had to be warned.

Toward the end of the second day, the wizard came to the straggling path that fed into the North Road. He hadn't gone far when he heard the distant rumor of horses behind: likely a company of Easterners riding out of the north, the vanguard of Löhi's army. They had not been idle while the singer slept. Turi hid himself as they passed, but grew fearful. He knew the main army could not be far away; the people and soldiers in Gamla were in danger.

Now Turi felt very weak; his strength was less than it should have been. He began to suspect an evil thing; the goblin's arrow might have been poisoned. That was an ill chance, because there were many poisons in the world, and without knowing which it was, wizardry was of little use. In this area, it might be hard to find herbs or plants to help. Turi needed to reach the Marches quickly, so he worked another change and took on another form. He was too weak to take the form of an eagle or any other winged creature, so he took a form that he knew well, one he had worn countless times since the world was young. Where Turi had stood on the path, there appeared a great red deer, its coat shiny and brown, its proud head crowned with antlers. The deer sped off to the south and soon struck the road, running swiftly, though halt of one foot.

All through that night, and the day and night that followed, the great deer ran, stopping only to drink or rest for a few brief moments. The road turned this way and that as it sought a true course, but the sure-footed deer ran due south, finding a way through the trees, lakes, and empty fields. It passed the forward company of the Itäläiset and went before them on the road. Of all the deeds ever done by the great Changer of the Erilaiset, this was perhaps the greatest. Every step became more tortuous, every breath more ragged; sweat lathered the deer's coat and its heart pounded within its mighty breast. No thought or flash of animal instinct entered its mind, save one thing alone: to keep running, keep moving, and not give up its lonely chase.

At last came a time when sight and sound faded. The wizard stuck out his staff to keep from falling. He stumbled nonetheless, dropping to his hands and knees onto the muddy lane, and realized he had shifted back to his native form, too weak to maintain the change. Never in all his years had that happened to him. He slumped to the ground in the middle of the road.

Turi lay there for some time with the morning sun shining down upon him, clutching the emerald jewel—a filthy, famished old man in tattered clothes, looking like a starving beggar out of the wild. Exhausted and sick, he knew well he might be dying. Now, Turi did not fear death; he was one of the great among the Erilaiset, and had crossed the dark river into Tuonela many times, daring its dim woods and dreary fields. He knew he would find his way through Tuone's realm and come to whatever home Ukko had prepared, but he despaired now at the thought that Löhi might conquer all the Far Northern Land, that the living folk of the Seven Clans and unborn generations to come would fall beneath her yoke.

Hoofbeats suddenly sounded from the north. Turi rolled on his side, expecting to see Itäläisen riders galloping down the road; he tried to get up, but could not. Only one horse appeared, however, and, as it drew near, Turi saw its rider was not an Easterner, but a March Warden on a small brown mount. The Warden pulled up, looking at him askance, but when he recognized Turi as a living man, got down and helped the old man sit up.

"Take this, father," said the Warden, handing him a full waterskin. "What happened to you? There is blood on your clothes and you look like you've been attacked."

Turi took a long drink of water, then looked him in the eye. "Thank you, friend—for your kindness as much as the water. I needed both. But yes, I am hurt, shot by a goblin's arrow in the Wastes, though I deem it is poison and not the wound that has laid me low."

The Warden started. "Wait a minute—aren't you the wizard who passed through Gamla? I didn't recognize you!"

Turi laughed weakly. "No doubt! I am Turi, though I don't look it or feel it at the moment."

"My name is Laso," said the Warden. "I saw you there some eight—no, nine days ago. I set out myself several days ago to scout the Marches, but I turned back. There is a strange, oppressive air all about; the lands seem empty and desolate. A terror came over me like I have never felt before. At night, there are voices on the wind."

The Warden took some black bread from his pouch and gave it to Turi.

"The Witch's thought lies heavy on these lands," the old man said as he slowly munched on the bread. "Löhi's army will soon pass through here. I have seen it just north of the Marches: at least a thousand riders of the Itäläiset, and hundreds of Hiisia from Pohjola, Löhi's goblins armed for war. One of them shot me, but not before I saw Löhi's captain—a Haltia, or an elf as you'd say. A powerful sorcerer whom I knew of old."

"Hiisia!" exclaimed Laso. "Then the rumors are true, and there really is a Witch in the north!"

"They are true," said Turi, struggling to his feet and leaning on his staff. "You must ride to Gamla and tell the people there to flee! Löhi's army is much too great. And Pekka must be warned in Keskimaa. The main force of the Bear Folk should stay south and draw itself up before the city. Therein lies your only hope—at least, if the Swan Folk come to your rescue."

"But the army of High Länsimaa is not at Keskimaa," said Laso. "Messengers reached Gamla just before I left. Miko Verikiven is their captain, and they were already on the White Road some days ago. They should almost be in Gamla by now. I do not know for certain, but I think they mean to meet the raiders north of Suurijärvi, if not on the North Road itself."

Turi ran his hand through his dirty grey hair and sighed. "So I feared. Pekka will not cede the north or Suurijärvi without battle, for there are many folk there, and much bloodrock, too. But it is no raid this time; it is an invasion.

"Listen to me, Laso! You must be even swifter if this is true. Tell Miko, tell your Captain Ilkka, tell whomever will listen to you—they must turn around at once and flee to Keskimaa! Leave the wagons and stores behind. Some men must form a rearguard and slow the enemy's advance. That will be a hard task with little hope, but so it must be. If the Karhulaiset come north, they will be destroyed!"

The March Warden sprang on his steed as if he would ride off at once, but checked himself and held out his hand to the wizard.

"Come, Turi, let's go! If what you say is true, we should go at once. My horse will bear us both."

But the wizard stood in the road and shook his head. "Your steed is small. It may bear us both, but not swiftly. Speed is of the essence, for Löhi's vanguard is not far away."

"But I cannot leave you here," said the Warden. "You are hurt and tired, and you should bear these tidings, not I. Take the horse!"

"Are you not a scout?" asked Turi. "Then fly from here and give your report! Remember my words and repeat them exactly. Before you came, I thought I lay dying, but there's life in me still; I feel it coursing through my veins, poison or no. For that I owe you great thanks, and not only for your bread and water. But I will make my own way now. I won't be caught on the road, that's for sure! And I will go to the Karhulaiset as quickly I can." Laso tossed his waterskin and pack onto the road next to Turi, and the wizard smiled before he cried, "Go!"

Without another word, the Warden shook the reins and galloped off to the south.

The old man sighed as he watched the horse dwindle into the distance, its image fading into wavy heat lines as the warm sun shone down on High Länsimaa. He picked up the waterskin and pack. Wearily leaning on his staff, Turi took one step, and then another, beginning the long journey down the North Road toward Suurijärvi.

Chapter Twelve

The Seer of Kyöpelinvuori

A shallow, babbling stream that men called the Rajavesi marked the border between the northwest parts of Etelamaa and Tavastia. Though the Rajavesi was narrow and easily forded at most points, wooden bridges had been built here and there to speed along traffic and commerce. Tax collectors went there at times to ensure the tolls were paid, but the border was open. There was much coming and going, and much trade between the Folk of the Swan and of the Hare. Although there had been wars between them in the past, the disputes had been over ships and sea trade, and the fighting had been mostly in the south along the coasts. Now the two great kingdoms had known peace for many years, so the farmers and peasants in the north went about their lives with little thought to old battles. In fact, they differed little from one another, regardless of which side of the border they lived on.

Väinämöinen drove the cart over a small, sturdy bridge built of unpainted birch while the two girls bounced up and down. He looked back over his shoulder and said, "There you go! We are in the kingdom of Tavastia and have left Etelamaa behind! You can both stop badgering me now and go back to sleep, if you like. There'll be little enough to see for a while, until we've put some miles between us and the Rajavesi."

After leaving Egan at Nummela, Väinämöinen had driven northwest, straight across the kingdom of Etelamaa. The roads were good and the warm sun quickly dried the dampness of spring's showers. All about them, the Far

Northern Land came into bloom. Even with good roads and weather, it was still almost two weeks before they struck the border where the lands of the Elk, Hare and Swan Folk came together, and where the tumbled rocky slopes of the Wall of the Giants could be descried away to the northeast.

They stopped often among the country villages, where they sometimes found singers who still knew many old songs and tales. They had also met an Erilainen from Karelia, a slight, flaxen-haired woman who had set out from the Enchanted Valley about the same time as Turi did. She had tarried among the villages, teaching them songs, warning them of the Witch's return and the troubled times ahead. The two Erilaiset stayed up late into the night in the little wood with a small fire before them. In the dark, Ulla watched them chant, rocking back and forth, as Väinämöinen reached out with his mind to Mielikki and others of the Erilaiset for news of the north. But all was dark, even to the great singer, for Löhi had put forth her power to cloud the *sight* of her enemies and confuse their counsels.

After they left Etelamaa, they pushed the horse hard as the cart rattled along the well-worn country roads of the Hare Folk. The girls eagerly watched as the countryside rolled by. Kirsikka, proud of the clothes she was given in Nummela, looked the part of an Etelalaisen maiden, but Ulla had put her stained and faded Karelian things back on.

They were making for Kyöpelinvuori, the home of the Seer, which lay some ways off in northwest Tavastia. Now they drove across a part of the kingdom called the Neck, for it was narrow and lay south of the drunken hills that stretched from the Wall of the Giants to the sea. That part of Tavastia was rich and fertile, if not as densely settled as the golden plain of Tapiola further south. The people of the Neck lived for the most part in small villages and scattered, but regular homesteads and farms. They grew many things: grains, greens, and fruits and berries in full summer, and they kept some orchards and vines. Even in poor years, they did not starve. They raised cattle, and many swine and sheep. Nowhere in the Far Northern Land was the country as prosperous, except, perhaps, in neighboring Etelamaa. Indeed, the Tavastialaiset and the Etelalaiset were similar save in one thing only; the Etelalaiset, like the clans of the north and east, were a free folk, but among the Tavastialaiset lived villeins and serfs.

Of old, all the folk of the Far Northern Land had been free, and serfdom was not native to the people of the clans, but rather to the Itäläiset and the tribes that lived on the opposite side of the Itämeri Sea. The noble lords in Tavastia became more powerful even than the Etelalaisen nobles, and their king had not the authority of the kings of Etelamaa. The most powerful Tavastian lords gathered much land to themselves, along with many rich fields. Copying the practice of foreign enemies, they bound landless peasants to their estates so that, in exchange for their sweat and toil, the poor folk might also work the land for some benefit of their own.

It was true that the *maaorjat*, the serfs of Tavastia, lived better, on the whole, than Ulla's folk and the people of the hardscrabble villages of the north, but the Bear Folk were free and the *maaorjat* could not leave their homes and villages without their lord's permission. The Erilaiset held this to be an unnatural thing, and it was one reason for the estrangement between the heroes and mortal men, and part of the tensions of old between Tavastia and Etelamaa.

They saw few serfs in the Neck, though, since most worked the wide fields in the south. The villages and farms that Väinämöinen drove past belonged to freemen. The Hare Folk marveled at the old wizard, with his sweeping beard and staff, and at the strange little girls who rode with him. They had heard of Väinämöinen, of course, but the tales wound about him were the stuff of legends, and few heroes ever visited their lands.

Amidst their plenty, the Hare Folk were troubled. The winter had been a bad one, and spring had come late; now they had much to do. From the south came news of attacks on their ships and unrest along the coast; from the north came word of the Eastern raiders. Some people shunned the old man and stayed inside until he passed, but others offered him beer, and sour milk and bread for the little girls. Then they pressed Väinämöinen for whatever news and tales he could tell them. Wary, the old man said little, except that the ill news from both north and south was true and that all folk should prepare against a difficult time to come.

Väinämöinen often left the girls at night to roam about alone, and Ulla began to sneak off from their little camps as well, sometimes dragging a sleepy Kirsikka with her. She had practiced the magic the Erilaiset taught her until she was quite adept at making lights and illusions, as well as calling birds and other animals to her in the dark. As she realized how naturally she came to the craft, Ulla changed the words, discovering that she could do tricks all her own, tricks that none had shown her. She made Kirsikka promise to say nothing to Väinämöinen, and the red-haired girl reluctantly agreed, but one night, when Ulla had just sparked a fire for the first time with the word she had heard the old man use so often before, Kirsikka grew afraid.

"You can't keep doing this!" she cried. "He's going to find out and he's going to be angry. Do you want him to send us back to High Länsimaa?"

"Why in the world would he do that?" answered Ulla. "He's not going to find out, anyway. If I have the power to make magic, why shouldn't I? I'm not doing anything wrong, and it's so much fun. I don't understand why it even matters."

"Clearly you don't," said the wizard.

Both girls scrambled to their feet. Väinämöinen looked down at them, his eyes glinting in the moonlight.

"You do not understand if you think I'm so blind and deaf that I do not know what you're doing out here, or what you were doing in the Valley, for that matter."

"I wasn't doing anything!" Ulla blurted out.

"Do not lie to me!" said Väinämöinen sharply. "You're not very good at it. But look about you! Your fire's catching on and the bracken here is dry."

The spark from Ulla's spell had spread to the nearby turf; the old man stamped it out with his great yellow boots. Ulla suddenly burst into tears, shaking like a lonely leaf in the north wind. The old man considered her for a moment, then knelt down beside her and gathered the little girl into his arms.

"Alright, little one, alright. But do not speak falsely to me again. '*Better a bitter truth than a lie sweet as honey.*' And you answered your own question just now when you said you don't understand why it even matters. Listen to me, both of you! Magic and wizardry may make beautiful things and seem harmless enough, but it's a serious matter. It's not a gift given to everyone, and not everyone has the wisdom to use it correctly. You don't put a staff in a child's hand, just as you don't put a child at the tiller of a boat in rough seas. You may know right from wrong within your heart, but to choose wisely, you need the experience and teaching that only comes with time. Without it, this power may cause you to stray down strange paths to your peril.

"Be patient, little one. Do not play with such things any longer. I don't know what the future holds for you, Child of the Prophecy; not even Mielikki can see that far. If the trail for singers is the path you must take, then we'll teach you the right way and at the right time. But that trail may be for others, and your own way still hidden from us."

"You won't send us back, will you?" Ulla asked between sobs. "Kirsikka told me you'd be angry, and it's not her fault."

Väinämöinen drew Kirsikka next to him and hugged them both. "You know I'm not leaving you, so get that notion out of your heads. But see here, Ulla. You have the Mark of the Clan upon your shoulder. You were chosen by Tapio. That ties you to Löhi, and she'll know it soon enough, if she doesn't already. I could feel your little spell a mile away and guessed what you were up to. The Witch's sense is even keener. If she's searching for you, there's no surer way to catch her attention than to play around with magic. Remember that!"

The weather soured the next day and the skies turned dark. Rain came down in sheets, gray and cold, and the hard-packed road grew muddy and slick. As they journeyed west across Tavastia, Väinämöinen's mood turned again. He brooded behind the reins as the horse plodded on through the muck. But as they drew closer to Kyöpelinvuori, Ulla grew more curious about the Seer and, as she sometimes did, peppered him with questions.

"You'll see for yourself what she's like soon enough," he answered. "And as I've told you before, I've never met this one. I haven't come this way in a very long time—maybe a hundred years, child. We'll see. I'm almost beginning to regret this journey. A cloud has been over me this past year, and all my choices have gone ill. There is battle in the north now, I can sense it, and here I am, hundreds of miles away, on a fool's errand to a mortal witch. And for what?"

"You said she might help the Seven Clans," said Ulla. "And convince the Tavastians to fight Löhi."

"I know that!" Väinämöinen snapped. "Spare me your insight and we'll both be the wiser! But so it is, the Seer has much influence in Tavastia and Akkala. They say she can see many things with that glass of hers, that crystal ball. Maybe she's seen Löhi and grown afraid. She should be! Löhi has little use for a mortal witch who serves the interests of the Seven Clans, twisted and entwined about her own strange desires."

It took several days to cross the Neck of Tavastia, but at length they came to a little town called Piikkimaki, north of Tavanlinna, the old castle and fortress that stood close to the field where the Great Battle had been fought, when Löhi was thrown down so many years before. Väinämöinen stopped in the town's cobbled square to let the horse drink and to stretch his legs.

Ulla and Kirsikka drew water from a round stone well and were soon surrounded by a group of girls, some shy, some less so, who were all dressed in white, not unlike the maidens of Etelamaa, except their clothes were trimmed in red and had red sleeves. Their hair was curiously and intricately braided, interlaced with fine silver and gold thread, or held back by shiny red bands. The Tavastian girls laughed—not ungenerously—at the strangers with their odd clothes and foreign accents. Ulla and Kirsikka could scarcely understand them in turn, for the accent of the Hare Folk was very different from that of Länsimaa.

When Väinämöinen told the gathered townsfolk of their journey to Kyöpelinvuori, they drew back and looked at him askance. The folk of

Piikkimaki lived in the shadow of the Seer's dwelling, but had little love for her. Kyöpelinvuori was a fearful name among the Hare Folk.

Four paths ran from the square in Piikkimaki. Hard-packed roads ran to the south and east, with a narrow road for carts and horses to the north. But to the west, a lesser track gently bent somewhat southward, seldom travelled and overgrown by grass in the summer, leading through a little wood of white birch and pine. That road led to Kyöpelinvuori, the haunted mountain, where the Seers had dwelled for many centuries, and that was the road Väinämöinen took, leaving the little town behind.

Kyöpelinvuori was a tall hill rising up from a tumbled plain, a hill that had long excited the fears of mortal men. Old tales told that the spirits of maidens who died unmarried before reaching full womanhood, especially those killed violently and in anger, would gather at the hill and haunt all the surrounding lands, seeking to bewitch any they could. Legend held that, at times, these dark spirits could be seen flying about like ghosts on the wind. During the Witch's War, a small fortress and tower were built there to defend against the might of Pohjola. The keep had largely crumbled away, but the tower still stood, and there the Seers of Kyöpelinvuori had dwelled for nearly five hundred years.

Not even Väinämöinen knew for certain how the first Seer came to be. But when the Erilaiset were expelled from Akkala and the Tavastian lords turned their backs on the Old Ways, an old woman of the Eagle Clan, a magic-user and prophet, came forward and spoke to the chiefs of the Seven Clans. She abjured the Erilaiset and joined in their abuse, speaking of a magic and power native to mortals, unlike the unnatural wizardries of the Erilaiset, which were akin to the power of Löhi and the domain of evil things such as trolls and demon spirits.

And the old woman had a secret; she had a looking glass with a strong magic trapped within it. Shaped like a crystal ball, it was made by a great smith in ages past. The beautiful glass allowed one with power to see many things distant and near, to uncover what lay hidden, and to read the fortunes of those who sought counsel and advice. The old woman told many useful things to the lords of the clans, and with her help, the last mortal wizards who had followed Löhi were found and slain in Akkala. Then she was given Kyöpelinvuori to dwell in, and was acknowledged as the Seer, growing very old before she finally died.

But before that day, she took an apprentice, a young girl chosen from among the villages, and trained her in those arts she knew—including the use of the glass. And when the old woman died, the apprentice became Seer in her turn. From then on, in a line unbroken, there was a Seer in Kyöpelinvuori, and as each woman aged, she chose her own successor and passed down to her all the lore of the tower. The kings of Akkala, Tavastia and Etelamaa asked many questions of the Seers, the Masters of the Shipwrights sought their advice, and the Lord Captains of the Wardens followed their counsels. They sent many rich gifts to Kyöpelinvuori, and the Seers gathered to them the lands and fields nearby to rule as their own. At times, the Seers had traffic with the Erilaiset, if it suited their purposes. And some Erilaiset, such as Turi, had known several of the strange women on lonely Kyöpelinvuori. They were loved by none, and feared by many, but they were very useful and some grew very strong.

Väinämöinen told the girls somewhat of this story as they drove along. At last, they began to climb a dusty way, a raised road with a sheer drop on one side, spiraling three times round a rocky height like an ancient fluted shell. They saw freshly sown fields below wherein scattered *pirttis* lay—homes of the serfs who worked the land—but above, on the great hill's cap, loomed the tower. The broken remains of the wall and keep were a tumbled mass of black and gray stone, save for a few intact chambers where such servants as the Seer had yet lived. But the tower stood tall, its grey stone mottled and streaked with white, where moss and other growths had colored it. A few irregular windows stood out here and there, but a parapet rose on its crown about a round, open court—the roof of the main chamber just below.

"Now both of you listen to me!" said Väinämöinen as he checked the horse near the foot of the tower, where the path ended. "You don't need to be afraid; remember that I'm with you, and that should be enough for you. The crone inside may be a witch, and then again, she may not. She's certainly not Löhi and won't hurt you, at least not while you're with me. Mind yourself and keep quiet; do what I tell you, and swiftly! We may find ourselves wishing to leave this place in a hurry!"

"But Väinämöinen, what about—" began Ulla, but the old man stomped his foot and cut her off.

"Enough! Now come with me and keep quiet!"

The wizard paused for a moment and nuzzled their horse, speaking a few soft words into its ear. After several seconds, he made a slow, sweeping gesture with his staff and wove a spell of protection to safeguard their beast and keep it from harm—or theft—as best he could.

But even as he turned toward the tower, a woman appeared, clad in the peasant garb of the Tavastialaiset with her head covered by a long red veil so that only her wrinkled, ruddy face was visible. She came toward them and motioned to an open archway in the tower wall.

"My mistress awaits you above, Lord Erilainen," she said in a thickly accented voice. "You are expected. Follow me; your animal will be cared for."

"I daresay," replied Väinämöinen with a bow. "Lead on!"

Ulla and Kirsikka at once became very nervous. The woman's tone and manner unsettled them, and the girls clasped hands as they walked through the tower's shadow and under the archway.

"I think *she's* the Seer," whispered Kirsikka, but her voice echoed in the cold, grey hall. Väinämöinen immediately shot them a withering glance that was much more unsettling than the old woman.

There were several closed doors in the tower's lowest hall, and to one side, a stone stair climbed up to the top. They followed the servant woman up the stair, the girls in front and Väinämöinen behind. The cut steps were broad and dry, but the space itself was narrow and very dark, the only illumination coming from occasional windows. Child of open fields and wide meadows, Ulla felt closed in. Breathing quickly, she fought back panic. Just when she felt she couldn't take another step without dissolving into tears and rushing back to the bottom, they stepped into a large, level space that was lit by an open window and had several small chambers besides. The servant said nothing, but rested for a moment until she caught her breath, then began to climb again.

Two more times they came to open levels and paused, but, at last, as Ulla's legs began to ache and tremble, the stair ended at a great door of polished black wood flanked by guttering torches. The servant rapped lightly, and the black door opened; Väinämöinen came up quickly and pushed the girls through.

At first, they stood blinking in the sudden bright light after the passage up the dark stair, but as their eyes slowly adjusted, they saw that they were in a large, round room: the tower's topmost chamber. In the curved wall, four long windows with open wooden shutters faced the compass points. Tapestries covered the walls and the chamber held many objects of gold, silver and bronze, as well as many things made of glass. The rest of the tower and its environs might have seemed crumbled and dilapidated, but the turret was like a treasury, filled with centuries of gifts from the lords of the Far Northern Land to the Seers. And, in the middle of the room, standing four feet tall, was a golden copy, four feet tall, of the ancient Sampo, the world pole of the north, which Väinämöinen himself had stolen from Pohjola long, long ago. Ulla and Kirsikka marveled at the many rich things, as rich as a king's court in Etelamaa or Tavastia, but they were startled by thin, dry laughter and turned to find a figure, neither tall nor short, standing beside a wooden stair that led to the courtyard above—the Seer of Kyöpelinvuori.

The Seer was clad in long black robes with the hood thrown back. Old, but not aged or decrepit, she wore her grey hair in strange, intricate braids. Her long nose was sharp, her face gaunt and angular. Though her eyes were very clear and grey like Väinämöinen's, when she smiled they saw that her teeth were black and rotten. She leaned heavily on a short, black crutch, its head carven with the likeness of a wolf with jaws agape, but walked steadily enough as she came forward to greet them.

"You are welcome in Kyöpelinvuori," she said, her voice high-pitched yet even, and her accent scarcely less thick than her servant's. "I have been waiting for you. I have seen you from afar and watched your journey. So at last you choose to return to mortal lands, Väinämöinen. Already much evil has befallen. I wonder that you did not come to me sooner for my counsel."

Väinämöinen bowed.

"I have come as I could," he replied. "I have many cares, and not only among the clans. The fate of the Erilaiset, too, is at stake, though that has never concerned the Seers of Kyöpelinvuori."

"My mothers did as was needed," answered the Seer. "And so fulfilled the prophecies of old. But that was long ago. It may be that new counsels are called for in a time of new peril."

"I knew many of your mothers," said Väinämöinen. "And those days are not so long ago to one such as me, who was born with the world itself and walked through the Far Northern Land when it was yet silent and empty. But as you say, new peril may bring new counsels."

The Seer smiled and then, for the first time, turned her attention to the girls. She looked straight into Ulla's eyes.

"So this is the girl," she said. "Her eyes are green. That is a sign of power... or of madness. Has she power, do you think, Väinämöinen?" The old man said nothing, and the Seer motioned to Ulla. "Come here, child."

But there was no compulsion in her words, as there was with Mielikki. Ulla didn't move, but looked at Väinämöinen for direction.

"Show her the Mark, Ulla," he said. Moved by his voice, she lowered her stained green shirt and turned her bare shoulder to the old woman.

"Ah!" the Seer said softly. Then, in a strange tone, she began to chant.

When the cold hand reaches southward,
reaches with its frozen fingers,

> *comes a child into the Northland,*
> *all the clans to bring together.*

"I, too, know the words well, Väinämöinen," she said. "The Vanhalaiset speak not only to the immortal heroes. My mothers foresaw this child and looked for her, but it seems the words may be fulfilled in my time."

"Many know these words," said the wizard. "If you wish to consider them more fully, I can take you to Mielikki. But this is the child and the sign of our hope: Ulla of the Karhulaiset."

"And the other?" asked the Seer, looking at Kirsikka.

"Her friend, another scatterling of High Länsimaa."

"Very well," said the Seer, still smiling. "And what have you come to ask me, Väinämöinen, greatest of singers? What questions would you put to the Seer of Kyöpelinvuori?"

"I have no questions," said Väinämöinen, "For I already know the answers. Perhaps you do, too. But I come with a warning, Mechtil. Löhi has indeed returned and put forth her strength. Her *etiänen* has come to Taikalaakso. She has unleashed the Easterners against the clans, and even now, I deem the Bear Folk are assailed. The curse of Lovêatar has returned from Tuonela and brought death to Nigan the king. The Witch of Pohjola will not stop until the Seven Clans are destroyed and the Far Northern Land is within her grip. And you are in danger, too, Mechtil. Löhi surely knows who you are and will come for you."

The old woman frowned at the use of her right name—Mechtil—for she had not used it since she was a child and was displeased that Väinämöinen remembered it. She strode to the golden Sampo and touched its star-shaped crown.

"Löhi cannot enter here," she said, smiling again swiftly. "The power of Kyöpelinvuori cannot be so easily overthrown."

Väinämöinen laughed.

"Perhaps you'll have a chance to put it to the test," he said. "But you would be a fool to do so. Don't start! There is no power in the Far Northern Land that can resist Löhi by itself. Certainly not me, nor my folk! But if the Seven Clans can be joined, as this child portends, and if the songs are sung again throughout the lands as they once were, there is hope. Thus was Löhi defeated before."

"'Twas the sword of Lemminkäinen that felled Löhi," said the Seer.

"So it was," said Väinämöinen, his eyes flashing. "I know it well, for I stood beside him."

There was a pause, and Ulla, child though she was, felt as though she watched a contest that might go either way, and that even as Väinämöinen had said, they might soon be flying back down the stair. But when the Seer spoke again, her voice was steady and even as always.

"I already know these things of which you speak. And you are right. The great Witch of the North will put forth all her strength, and she is very strong. There is no land, not even mighty Tavastia, that can long stand alone against her. I see many things, Väinämöinen. I watched you journey across Etelamaa. I've watched the young king at Nummela; unsure, he hesitates while his enemies gather. I have seen the might of Pohjola with my own eyes, and I have seen the Bear Folk wither before the curved swords of the east. And I know the name of your enemy, he who leads Löhi's army and sees your every move. He, too, has a jewel like unto the looking glass and so cannot hide from me."

The Seer moved her hand across the Sampo's crown and Väinämöinen and the girls saw a crystalline glint, for the tines of the golden star held the looking glass.

How the first Seer came by the glass in ages past was lost in the mists of time. There had once lived a smith called Seppo, whose father was a mortal man and a chief among the Hare Folk, and whose mother was Erilaisen. Seppo, a powerful singer and wizard, put his magic into his craft. And, he made pieces of glass in diverse shapes and colors, like jewels resembling the sun, moon and stars. One who mastered their secrets could look within and see many things, piercing the world's darkness or the nets woven by wizards to defeat their enemies' *sight*. But the greatest of Seppo's works was the crystal ball the Seers now held; the others had been lost in the wave of destruction that swept across the Far Northern Land during the Witch's War, and were now forgotten by all save by the wise.

"Yes," said the Seer. "This is the looking glass of Kyöpelinvuori, the glass that sees furthest in the Far Northern Land and that may read the fortune of any who dare ask. The other is of small account, I deem, though useful, perhaps, in battle. One of the gems made by Seppo long ago, it gives *sight* and nothing more." The Seer fell silent for a long moment, then smiled tightly. "And the one who leads your foes and has this gem is called Työ."

"Työ!" exclaimed Väinämöinen. "He is a powerful wizard among the Haltiatar and served Löhi long ago, but most of his folk were destroyed in the Great Battle. So he still lives! This is ill news. He is a skilled captain and led Löhi's servants into battle many times; this jewel will only give him a greater advantage."

"There is worse news still," said the Seer, though she seemed strangely pleased. "For, by your words, I judge you do not know what has happened in High Länsimaa."

"I know there is battle and death, and the Bear Folk are hard-pressed."

"Indeed," she replied. "And more than that. Their army is routed and the Easterners have taken Keskimaa. The Witch has won her first great victory."

The old man looked hard at the Seer and shook his head, but the girls stared at her with wild eyes. At last, he asked, "How do you know this? It is yet early summer. Our enemies could not have come so far, so fast. The Karhulaiset are a great folk."

"And yet it is so, Väinämöinen," she said, her smile once more drawn and thin over her black teeth. "There was a great cloud over High Länsimaa for many days, for Löhi's thought was upon it. But at last, perhaps a week ago, I pierced the gloom. I saw the Itäläiset raping and sacking the city; there was a great burning. Already, Työ and a large part of his army move west toward Deep Länsimaa. The weather has been good for marching, and the people of the Elk Clan are not a warlike folk."

The Seer walked to the north window, her black crutch tapping the stone floor; the old man stood beside her, and together they gazed out at the green fields and tumbled hills. Light spilled in. It was hot outside, and thunder rolled under dark clouds in the northern sky, which was strange for that time of year.

"Ukko's Hammer," muttered Väinämöinen as the thunder boomed again. "If you knew these things, Mechtil," he said louder and more sternly, "then why have you done nothing? Why did you not warn King Asikkas in Tapiola so that the strength of the Hare Folk could move north and join to that of Etelamaa?"

"I have done as I could," she answered. "And I have not known these things long. It is no easy thing to pierce Löhi's clouds. Warnings were sent to Asikkas and the lords of Tavastia, and to Teemu as well in Deep Länsimaa. But I am Mistress of Kyöpelinvuori, not Tapiola. I can only counsel, not command. The Hare Folk fear for their ships; they fear attacks on their coasts, and indeed, more ships have been assailed. They may march north after this, but not soon enough to save the Karhulaiset or Keskimaa."

Väinämöinen strode back to where Ulla and Kirsikka stood and laid his hands on their heads. "Not by swords alone will Löhi be stopped. If you know that much, then you know why I came to you, spending precious days that might have brought me to Keskimaa before the Itäläiset. Strong arms and bent bows may stem the tide for a season, but unless the Seven Clans return to the teachings of the Vanhalaiset and take up the songs and rituals that made them strong, there will be no victory over Löhi.

"What say you to that, O Seer of Kyöpelinvuori? For the very foundation of this place, and of your power, was the rejection of the Old Ways and betrayal of the Erilaiset. The Child of the Prophecy, sent as a sign by Tapio, stands before you now, as do I, Väinämöinen Erilainen! You must make your choice! Will you help me and use your counsel to sway the Seven Clans? Will you do what must be done? Or will you gaze into your looking glass until the Witch comes to take you, taking comfort that at least you shall know the hour of your death beforehand, unlike those with less wisdom?"

Now Väinämöinen spoke in heat, for he was distraught over Keskimaa and feared for Turi and all the Bear Folk. He had little hope that the Seer would help the Erilaiset against Löhi. He thought her like an old spider in a ramshackle barn that was seldom used or visited, weaving webs and designs that none would see, catching just enough to feed on and unaware that the barn would soon be set on fire.

Yet old spiders were clever, and did not grow old by chance alone. The Seer of Kyöpelinvuori was no exception. She did not become indignant at the wizard's words, but approached the golden Sampo. When she spoke, her voice was calm and measured.

"My mothers did what needed to be done, but the world is changing. New peril may call for new counsels. Do we not both serve the Vanhalaiset, Väinämöinen, each in our own way, as is right and proper? Maybe the day has come when those ways should be joined again, for the good of all. What say you to that, Lord of the Erilaiset? Should Kyöpelinvuori and Taikalaakso together deliver the clans from the threat of Pohjola?"

She surprised the old mage, though he tried not to show it. He had not expected to hear such words, nor such an offer. He did not trust the Seer, but badly needed her help, so he chose his next words very carefully.

"The Erilaiset of the Valley have already decided. We will do whatever we can, though we are dwindled to a small folk now compared to days of old. But your aid would be welcome if the price is not too steep."

"There is no price," said the old woman. "For I belong to all the Seven Clans, and they are my people. There is no price save this; if the counsel of Kyöpelinvuori is to sway the clans, then Kyöpelinvuori must play a part in the return of the Erilaiset as well. If the songs from the forgotten world are sung again, they must first be sung in Kyöpelinvuori. You must go to Deep Länsimaa, Väinämöinen, and do whatever you can to stop Tyë and blunt this invasion from the north. But leave the child with me for safety's sake; I will go to Tapiola and take her with me, for so I will be able to convince Asikkas that what we have agreed to must surely be done."

In a flash, Väinämöinen perceived the Seer's game, and he thought her very shrewd, though her magic might prove weak. And she was bold, willing to gamble the lives of thousands for her own purposes. The old woman would bind the Erilaiset to her, making them dependent on her influence, and at the same time, she would make Ulla her apprentice. Using the little girl, she might achieve the union of the clans and resist Löhi; then all roads would run through Kyöpelinvuori, and the Seer would be the power behind every throne. It was a daring plan, but it reckoned without the Witch of Pohjola—and without Väinämöinen.

"Indeed, I will seek out Teemu in Deep Länsimaa," said Väinämöinen. "And I will send word at once to Egan, too. If Keskimaa is lost and the battle moves west, it is there that the Swan Folk must turn. But Ulla—and Kirsikka, too—will go with me. I almost lost the girl once, and Mielikki has charged me with her care. If I live, though, I will return here as quickly as I can. I will come with you to Tapiola and other places besides. We may decide what must needs be done to further our cause and concerns."

The Seer's face remained impassive, but she hesitated before she spoke. Väinämöinen knew she considered her words as carefully as he had.

"Is it not dangerous to take the girl in harm's way?" she finally said. "If things go ill, as they may, what then? Perhaps much depends upon the mark upon her shoulder; it may be that Löhi knows this and is already searching for her."

"If the Witch is looking for her, it won't be on a battlefield in the north, but rather where things seem safest. I have given thought to this. Ulla will be safe, no matter what befalls us."

"Very well," said the Seer. "I hope you choose wisely in this. But you cannot tarry here longer, Väinämöinen. Indeed, my counsel is that you should set out tomorrow, for it may already be too late for the Elk Folk. There are chambers here prepared for you and your charges tonight."

"I appreciate your hospitality," said the old man. "But I will not tarry even that long. We will go north at once to seek Teemu."

The Seer came very close to Ulla then and reached out a long, thin hand to touch her hair. Ulla looked into the old woman's grey eyes—clear like Väinämöinen's, despite her age, but with a strange sheen, as if the long years of peering at the crystal ball had turned them to glass as well, leaving the smith's imprint upon them. Her touch was just as cold.

"Take the road north through the hills and strike the line of the Clearwater," the Seer said as she straightened up. "Pass into Deep Länsimaa west of Siinesaare. That is where Teemu was last, and where most of the Elk Folk now dwell. If need be, you can make for Valkeakosk from there after you learn more. I will wait for you here, Väinämöinen. And if the Vanhalaiset reward our efforts, we may yet save the folk of the Far Northern Land from Tuone's darkness."

"We may save the land from Löhi," replied Väinämöinen. "But every man and woman, mortal or Erilaiset, must save their own soul from Tuonela. Whether the songs be sung or no, still they know within themselves what is good and what is evil."

The wizard bowed low, then they left the Seer high in the tower and descended the long, dark stair back to where their horse and cart waited amidst the crumbling stones. The old serving woman waited there, along with several others, but Väinämöinen declined their offers of food and shelter. After loading up the girls, he began the drive back down Kyöpelinvuori's winding path. When they reached the foot, he struck a cart path that ran northeast and drove the horse quickly over the bumpy, uneven ground. The girls pressed him with questions about the Seer, but he told them to hold their tongues.

"I need to think now," he said. "We will not go far this evening. There should be a village up ahead, just beyond the Seer's domain. We will stop there for the night and rest; maybe, if I feel like it, I'll answer your questions then."

"But why didn't we just stay in the tower?" asked Kirsikka. "You told the old woman that we were leaving at once."

"I am not spending the night on Kyöpelinvuori. It is a spider's web and I don't want to be a fly. I do not trust her, to be sure, nor does she understand Löhi if she fancies herself the Witch's equal in cunning or power. *He who digs a pit for another may fall into it himself.*' The crone plays a dangerous game.

"Still, I did not foresee any of this. I am surprised, very surprised. We will see. But calm yourself, child, and rest while you can! We will fly tomorrow and race the storm you see in the north sky! Keskimaa may be lost, but I was not there; it must go differently with the Hirvilaiset!"

He shook the reins hard and the horse shot off while the girls bounced about in the cart. Thunder rolled in the distance, however, and as the low, dark clouds sped toward them on the north wind's wings, the warm air of early summer carried the scent of rain and the promise of showers ahead.

Chapter Thirteen

Sword of Legend

The muster at Nummela was completed as the bright spring sun grew warmer, bathing the grey coast of the Itämeri Sea in its nurturing glow.

Blue waves, blown by winds from the south, crashed ashore, flinging foam onto rocky beaches and into the green beyond. The men of the Far Northern Land, accustomed to the sea spray and wind, launched their fishing boats from sheltered bays and island coves, while trade galleys sailed from the harbors. The coastlands of Etelamaa came alive with long days and gentle clime, just as the fertile fields and blooming meadows of the plain did. But spring's promise, the hope of the men and women of the Seven Clans since their forefathers first came to the harsh lands of the north, was less generous this year. Ill news of threats within and without spread everywhere. And still, the young king was in doubt.

Five full companies of men-at-arms were now marshaled in the camp. Over five hundred men, well-armed and trained for battle, stood ready to march speedily to wherever Egan commanded. But that was not all. A company of Swan Knights—heavily armoured in chainmail, with long lances and steel swords, mounted on swift, strong horses protected by ornate headstalls and barding—had joined their camp. It was a strong force reckoned by the measures of the Seven Clans in those days, and could prevail over larger armies less prepared or determined.

But other armies mustered that spring in Etelamaa. Word had reached the camp at Nummela that Kallas, Lord of Harmaaniemi and grandson of the old Duke Verro, was coming north at last in response to the summons. Another southern noblemen, Tyssi of Etelarannta, rode with him, leading a force of four hundred men. Verro had been a rival to Egan's grandfather years before, and Kallas remembered well that if things had gone differently, he might now be heir to the throne.

The lords of the coast did not come to pay fealty to Egan. Their messages to the "boy-king" said that they wished to make known their grievances about how and why their counsels had been ignored. They proposed to meet him, not at Nummela, but at a place some miles to the southwest. They came with men-at-arms, so they said, only because they feared rumored threats against them. As Sinio had predicted, they spread rumors of their own, claiming that Alder used Egan for his own purposes and intended to rule himself, in deed if not in name.

It was a bold move by Kallas, for he and his men had left the safety of their strongholds, and might well have been overwhelmed on the open plain. But Kallas was clever, and his gamble calculated. If Egan struck first and failed to achieve complete victory, the folk of the coastlands would rally to Kallas, seeing his cause as just. Moreover, some of the lords on the central plain, disquieted by Väinämöinen's "meddling," might also rally to Kallas in shock after any open assault. Yet if Egan did nothing, he would be seen as weak and vacillating, a boy unfit to rule in times of trouble. This, too, Kallas hoped to turn to his advantage.

Sinio was pleased when they learned that Kallas and Tyssi were marching north. He urged Egan to strike swiftly, for Kallas's actions amounted to rebellion in deed, if not yet in open word. He counseled Egan to march afterward to Harmaaniemi and establish his rule by strength and force. Not all of the king's counselors agreed, however. Some feared the very thing that Kallas hoped for—that folk would rally to him after any assault—and others were loath to shed Etelalaisen blood and risk civil war, a peril Etelamaa knew all too well.

In the midst of all this turmoil, messengers arrived from High Länsimaa. Three riders rode into the camp from the north, two on an errand from Pekka and the third a March Warden sent by Ilkka to warn the new king, for news of Nigan's death by the Winter Plague had at last reached Keskimaa. The three men carried ill news and earnest pleas.

"The Easterners are massing on the North Marches to invade High Länsimaa," the messengers said. "They are bringing evil creatures from Löhi's realm with them. All fear the worst, and Pekka begs the king of the Swan Folk to send men north to help stem the tide from Pohjola and save our land. In return, he offers trains of bloodrock and other precious things that the Swan Folk might desire. But you must hurry, or it will be too late."

The March Warden asked for news of Väinämöinen, since Ilkka hoped to ask for the wizard's help before the Bear Folk were overwhemed. But if Väinämöinen had not already reached Keskimaa, then neither Egan nor any of the Swan Folk knew where he might be.

So Egan remained in doubt. To make matters worse, his uncle became very sick—not with Plague, as was first feared, but sick nonetheless. He lay abed, feverish and weak. Around his counselors and servants, Egan tried to act confidently; he told them he was considering all options and would soon make a decision. He ordered camp to be broken in three days and told Juvari to prepare the men to move, and their stores to be carted and ready. He did not say where they were going, however, because he did not know himself.

At night, the boy withdrew to his tent, behind the fine curtain that made a bedroom for him. Men filled the camp, but he was utterly alone, both afraid of and angry at the change that had come over him. He almost cried while he lay in his low bed and thought of his mother the queen, her fair hair and pale skin. He wanted nothing more than to be with her back in the Stone City—not a king, but a child in his mother's arms, where everything was safe, where there was no war or strife. He wanted his father, brother, sister, and the entire household around him, as they had been all the days of his life. Then, ashamed of these thoughts, he imagined what Kallas would think, or

Sinio, or his own captains and soldiers. What if they knew he hid in bed like a frightened child rather than acting like a king and the chief of the Clan of the Swan? What of his dreams of becoming a hero and warrior?

Egan remembered Väinämöinen's counsel. In his heart, he believed all the old man had told him, not only about the threat to the Bear Folk, but also about the Vanhalaiset, the Old Ways and the songs, and the Mark of the Clan, which he himself had seen on Ulla's shoulder. He remembered the wizard's whispered words at their parting. He wanted to do as the old man counseled and march his men straight north to High Länsimaa, but he could not discount the advice of Sinio and others. He put Etelamaa and his throne at real risk if he ignored the threat of Kallas; all the coastlands might be aflame with rebellion by the time he returned—*if* he returned—especially if there were more attacks in the Itämeri Sea or along its shores. Some of his counselors championed a third way, advising that he split the arms of the Etelalaiset, sending some north and some south.

So the three days passed, and still Egan had no clear notion of what he should do.

The sun rose early on the third day, for summer would soon come to the Far Northern Land. It was a bright morning, full of promise, the type of morning Egan once might have spent atop the Keep, watching the yellow sun play upon the glassy water below, an infusion of gold spreading across the bay from east to west. Here was no bay or play of light on water; the day promised only battle and bloodshed.

The Army of Etelamaa waited at the edge of the camp when Egan left his tent. He mounted his horse, a strong white charger flecked all about with grey. The young king wore a full set of battle armour, the ancient arms of the king of the Swan Folk, forged, so men said, by the great smith Ilmarinen of the Erilaiset, who had forged the Sampo. Though Egan was small of stature, the shining breastplate fit well, displaying a golden swan in the midst of spotless white enamel. Silver swan wings swept back on each side of his high helm, studded with clear gems of garnet, amber, and ruby from the nosepiece back.

The armour was heavy, but not as heavy as it looked due to the craft of its maker. Egan bore it well, sitting erect and unbowed upon his horse.

Juvari waited for him at the head of the Swan Knights, with Sinio beside him. Alder waited there, too, despite his fever, for he would not abandon his nephew in his hour of need.

"You are ill, Uncle," said Egan as he rode up to the men. "You should not be here. You need rest and care. I could not stand to lose you, too, after all that has happened."

Alder smiled, though his wan face betrayed his weakness. "I am not much use with a spear, perhaps," he said. "But that is not why I am here. I will not leave your side. Let us speak no more of it."

"So be it," said Egan. "Is everything ready?"

"The men are ready to march," said Juvari. "And the train is ready to follow, but they do not yet know where to go."

"The men await your orders now," Alder said clearly. Then he lowered his voice, his gaze holding Egan's. "The men are loyal to the Royal House, but rumors fly among them. Some say we will march north, others west; some even say we will return to the Stone City. You have had many counsels, my king; you know where I stand, and the minds of all your other counselors, divided as they are. Only you can make the choice, hard as it is. Tell us now your decision!"

Egan looked to the west where only a few high clouds marred a clear blue sky. "What news of Kallas?" he asked.

"The scouts say he marches for Päivämäki, maybe two days from here," answered Juvari. "If we leave now, he will still reach it before us. It is good ground to defend."

"And the men with him?"

"The report is still the same—some four hundred. Few on horse, mainly on foot."

The young king looked at his captains and counselors, and then at his uncle who sat shivering on his horse despite the warm breeze from the south.

"Very well," said Egan. "Let the herald sound the horns and carry my orders to the men. We march to Päivämäki to meet Kallas, and whomsoever is with him!"

Juvari bowed his head and saluted the king, then rode off to carry out Egan's instructions. The messengers from High Länsimaa, who sat nearby on their horses, were crestfallen.

"I beg your leave, my lord," said one. "For we must return swiftly with this news to Keskimaa. And, if I may be so bold, it will not be received well by Lord Pekka and all the Karhulaiset, who placed great hope in the strength and good faith of the Swan Folk."

"Nonetheless, we will go first to Päivämäki," said Egan. "But you have my leave and the goodwill of the Clan of the Swan. Tell your lord that we may yet lend our swords to his cause this summer; do not despair!"

The messengers bowed and rode off.

Sinio, though greatly pleased, spoke in a stern and grave voice. "It is a hard choice, my king, but I judge that you choose wisely in this. One way or another, the challenge from Harmaaniemi must be stopped before it grows too great. There will be no succor for the other clans if there is civil war and strife in Etelamaa."

They moved out then, marching slowly through Nummela to the crossroads, then on to the westward road while the townsfolk, mostly women and children, crowded about to catch a glimpse of the young king in his lofty helm and sky blue cloak. Egan rode in front with his uncle, Lord Meripäiva, and a few other noblemen, all of them escorted by a small company of mounted knights. But most of the mounted men followed the long line of men-at-arms. Soon they left Nummela behind, passing through a land of gentle rises and folds covered in green grass and wildflowers, with only the occasional boulder here and there to remind them that they were still in the north.

The army stopped in the late afternoon and made camp after a march of perhaps fifteen miles, for many scouts had been sent out to spy on Kallas's force and its disposition. In the early evening, a rider came to their camp from

Kallas and Tyssi with messages for the "prince." The lords of Harmaaniemi and Etelarannta awaited him at Päivämäki. They came in peace, to present their grievances, but, if attacked, they would defend themselves. When the messenger departed, the king's counselors wished to discuss the strategy he should employ the next day, what words he should say to the rebellious lords, and when to give the order to attack.

Egan remained alone, however, and saw only his uncle, who was exhausted after even so light a journey, and Juvari, who discussed matters of battle with him, should it come to blows. The young king had no desire for more counsels. In fact, he was sick of them. Though he still had little idea of what he meant to do, a certain calm came over him, as if his course might indeed already be charted and he need only discover where it waited for him. Egan slept that night, though he had not expected to, and had vivid dreams in which a voice whispered many things to him. The voice was not Väinämöinen's, but a woman's.

The king's men broke camp early, as birdsong filled the air in the growing light, but there were dark clouds to the south and the smell of rain on the wind. They left their wagons and stores behind and moved swiftly. It was only six miles as the crow flies to Päivämäki, and it did not take long to get there.

Now Päivämäki was a grassy hill set apart from the rises and hillocks of that region. It was named as such—the Day Hill—because folk would come, at times, to stand upon its pleasant crown and watch the rising or setting sun. No fort had been built upon Päivämäki, but its steep slopes commanded a wide view of the lands around. A river ran by its southwestern foot, shielding it from approach save by a narrow ford. Juvari led his men toward the hill from the northeast, where they formed a line three deep with the horsemen split on the flanks. But Kallas and Tyssi were there before them, and their men looked down from Päivämäki as storm clouds darkened the sky.

With some four hundred men in his army, Kallas was outnumbered almost two to one. Moreover, he had few horsemen and none to compare to the Knights of the Swan. The core of his force were soldiers from the regular company sent south to guard the coast, most of whom hailed from the coastland in any case. Amrod, their commander, came from a great family of Harmaaniemi, and was closely allied to Kallas's house. The bulk of the men were mariners and dockmen, but though these men were not trained for war, they were strong and disciplined. The entire force was heavily armed with swords and long spears, and many wore coats of fine ring mail, for the cities of the coast were rich beyond the measure of the rest of Etelamaa, and Harmaaniemi boasted many smiths trained by the great Guild in Seppälä. It would be no easy thing to defeat them in battle.

They had little hope of winning the field, and some might have thought that Kallas had marched from safety to certain doom, to be either besieged on the hillside or cut down and scattered. But Kallas, cunning and bold, did not aim to win the field outright. His skill lay in words, so he sought to parley with Egan and turn the situation to his advantage as opportunity arose. He hoped to outwit or embarrass Egan, or expose Alder as the real power, as he believed him to be. Indeed, he hoped he might even win over Egan's men.

If it did come to blows, Amrod had instructed his spearmen to hold fast against the horsemen's charge, spitting the horses as they came up the hill at disadvantage. Perhaps Egan's men would draw back, unwilling to shed so much blood. But Kallas had considered all possibilities; even if his men were worsted, they might still retreat across the ford, holding back the king's men while Kallas and Tyssi escaped to publish the news of Egan's "betrayal" and cruelty. A small company with fresh horses waited at the river to speed his flight.

"What is your counsel now, Juvari?" asked Egan as they looked up at the hilltop where their enemies stood, grey spears pointing skyward like a thicket of sharp thorns.

"If we must fight, it should be soon," said his captain. "The sky threatens rain and that will make the footing even more difficult for the horses as they charge uphill. I will send all the men forward at once, from all sides, for so we may break them swiftly and limit our losses. Several men have been charged to ride within bowshot and especially look for Kallas. If he is slain, his followers may lose heart and surrender. But if they do not break, or if this storm blows strong, it will be a bloody day. I await your word, my king."

"Do not hesitate, my lord," said Sinio, who hovered nearby. "Do not waste words or precious time with this traitor. That is what he wishes. Do as your captain advises and strike now, swiftly!"

Egan looked at Sinio, then at the other men on their horses beside him—Juvari, Meripäiva, and Satou, the chief of his knights, as well as his uncle and several others. Thunder rumbled low from the south and the wind picked up, snapping the banners and pennants as the rare morning storm blew in. Suddenly Egan signaled to his herald, a man clad in the regalia of the royal guard and mounted on a black horse with a checkered caparison, bearing the blue and white banner of the Swan Folk.

"Come with me!" he ordered. To the surprise of all, the young king spurred his horse and started up the hill, the herald trailing close behind.

Atop Päivämäki, Kallas watched the boy break from the ranks of his soldiers and come toward them. He looked regal indeed in the ancient mail and helm of his forefathers, with his blue cloak streaming behind him. But Kallas smiled, for it seemed to him that all went as he wished it, and even the wind and clouds were in his favor.

"Stay here," he said, turning to Tyssi. "I will take care of this boy."

Motioning to his own herald, he rode down a ways to meet Egan. They came together on a level spot, like a small grassy step, not far from the hilltop and within earshot of the men above. Kallas inclined his head and his companion did likewise, but Egan sat erect in his saddle, saying nothing.

"Hail, Prince Egan," said Kallas, in a loud, clear voice. "It is long since last I saw you. You were only a little child then, still bouncing on your father's lap. But you have grown! You will be a bearded man after a few more summers, though now that I see you, I think that you resemble your mother the queen more than your father, whose unhappy loss is a grief to all the Swan Folk."

Still, Egan said nothing.

Kallas pursed his lips and a tight, thin smile came upon his face. "It is sad that we must meet in this fashion, Prince Egan. It is not as I wished it. Indeed, I would that you had come to Harmaaniemi rather than your uncle, whom I see among the men below. The folk of the coast are rightly worried by the troubles that beset us: strange news from the City of Etelamaa, bloody raids on our shores, and our ships assailed at sea. Even now, two more ships have been attacked and one is feared lost—or did you not know?"

Egan felt his pulse quicken. Finally he spoke, fighting to keep his voice steady and even all the while. "You have taken up arms against your rightful king, Kallas; you would lead all these men into rebellion. Do *you* not know what has happened in the kingdom, and throughout the Far Northern Land?"

Kallas laughed. "The crown does not pass to children—or to anyone, for that matter—without the consent of the Great Houses and the will of all our folk. Do not flaunt a title that is not yet yours. Do you forget our history and what evil has come of such a thing before? As for what you ask, I know of the rumors of Plague and troubles in the north, but it is here, in the south, that the Swan Folk are threatened!"

"Etelamaa and all the Seven Clans are threatened from all sides," said Egan. "The Witch of the North stirs; the shadow of Lovêatar spreads sickness and death. The Easterners assail the Bear Clan and will next turn against us. Väinämöinen of the Erilaiset has seen all these things and brought a dire warning."

"The Witch! Lovêatar!" mocked Kallas. "Väinämöinen! So it is true; he has returned to Etelamaa and become your counselor. Is he with you?"

"He returned to the north to fight the Witch," said Egan.

"As well he might!" said Kallas. "So while our folk waste from disease or suffer the assault of a new foe from the sea, you welcome Väinämöinen the Conjuror to our land and base your policies on his tales—he, who has long stirred mischief in Etelamaa. Are the times not evil enough without foreigners meddling in our affairs, bearing stories of magic and myths? Go back to your masters, Egan! You speak still as a child—or as one bewitched by that old wizard. I mean you no harm and bear no ill will, but tell Alder to come himself and not hide behind his nephew or the tales of the Erilaiset!"

Now, many men on the hilltop heard these words. Some smiled to one another, for it seemed to them that Kallas spoke to Egan as a man speaks to a boy, and had dismissed him. Indeed, Egan pulled his horse about as if he meant to go.

Just at that moment, the wind blew the low, ragged clouds over Päivämäki. In the sudden dark, a shaft of golden sunlight fell straight upon the young king, its brilliance almost blinding. The strange radiance clung to him, as if his burnished armour were alight. The laughter died on their lips as they watched in wonder.

Egan drew his long sword from its aged leather scabbard as the wind gusted from the south, lifting his cloak behind him. The sword burned like a flame of ice.

"Enough, Kallas!" he cried. "I came here not to parley with a petty troublemaker, but to speak to my people. Behold, ye Etelalaiset! The Sword of Lemminkäinen shines before you! This sword, carried of old by the hero who led the Seven Clans against the Witch and threw down our enemy long ago. It returns to us as a sign that great deeds are at hand. I, Egan of Etelamaa, will wield it against the enemies of our time!"

For, ere he left for Kyöpelinvuori, Väinämöinen had given Egan the sword, the bane of Löhi, which Lemminkäinen had borne in ages past: the mightiest of blades known to mortal kind. The singer had plucked it from the battlefield where Lemminkäinen's broken body lay and saved it from the wreck of war. For many years, he kept it for the next High King of the Far Northern Land, but never had such a one arisen, and the Erilaiset became estranged from the Seven Clans. Through the long years, it lay at Väinölä, lost in the mists of time if not wholly forgotten in legend and song. But when Väinämöinen left the Enchanted Valley with Ulla and Kirsikka, he took it for Nigan to wield in war against the danger from Pohjola; when he found that Nigan was dead, he gave it to Egan, his chosen heir. And all the clans knew well the words that went with it.

> *Sword of heroes from the Northland,*
> *blade of Mighty Lemminkäinen:*
> *all shall kneel to him that wields it,*
> *Sword of Legend, Sign of Power.*

Egan raised the legendary sword over his head, where it shone against the darkling sky above. The long, sharp-edged blade, forged from bloodrock and made winterfast by the smiths of old, was cunningly damascened with red and white traceries of some unknown metal, long since lost to mortal kind.

Lightning flashed in the sky and thunder rolled. To the gathered men, the young king seemed to grow in stature, a mighty figure like a hero of old returned to life. And when he spoke, it seemed to Egan that another voice spoke through him; he felt a power move within him. The gathered Etelalaiset, even those most distant, heard Egan's voice as if he stood beside them. Its strength and power awed them, holding them as men enchanted.

"Will you follow me, Folk of the Swan?" he cried. "For the Witch of old, Löhi of Pohjola, is verily come again, plotting ruin for the people of the clans, seeking an end to mortal kind in the Far Northern Land. The world changes; nothing will ever be as it was before!"

And with one voice, both the king's men and those from the coasts cried, "We will follow you!"

"Will you follow me, Folk of the Swan?!" cried Egan. "For your kinfolk, the Karhulaiset, and all the other clans are in danger. Only if we unite in arms can we preserve our fields and homes. We were one great folk once, and so we must be again! Let us march north and strike the evil foe, ere the hordes of Pohjola threaten even the fair fields of the south!"

And with one voice the men cried, "We will follow you!"

"Will you follow me, Folk of the Swan?!" cried Egan. "For I have seen the child prophesied by Mielikki in ancient days. She is a sign unto all the clans that the time is at hand. The Erilaiset have come forth to join us, and the Old Ways will be our ways once more. The songs will be sung again throughout the Far Northern Land, and all Ukko's creation!"

And with one voice, the men cried, "We will follow you!"

Three times Egan called upon the gathered men to follow him; three times they cried out in answer, feeling a purpose and power that they did not understand working within them. They knew his words to be true in their hearts and souls, no matter what they had believed as they marched to Päivämäki.

But Kallas stood amazed, for he felt Egan's power like all the rest and could not understand this strange turn of events. His horse jumped at a roll of thunder, throwing him to the ground. Even as he scrambled to his feet, Egan stood before him, his blue cloak snapping in the sudden wind. Rain pelted down as Egan pointed the Sword of Lemminkäinen straight at Kallas's heart. The noble shrank back, for though Kallas was no coward, he thought Egan meant to run him through there on the hilltop before the gathered Swan Folk. But Egan called out to him in a clear voice that all could hear.

"What will it be, Lord Kallas? Greater things are at hand than your intrigues and mischief. Will you bend your knee and give me your fealty, then lead your men beneath our ancient banner against our foes? If not, you will be the first victim of Lemminkäinen's Sword in this war, though surely not the last!"

Kallas looked about him, seeing that his herald sat with bowed head and his own men watched Egan with shining eyes; and, to his wonder, Kallas found himself kneeling before Egan's horse, Egan's sword point at his head, and giving his fealty to the young king with the ancient words used among the Swan Folk.

"I give you my love and loyalty, king of the Etelalaiset and chief of the clan; my honor and my spear are yours, and may I be struck down if I fail of my oath!"

Then the king's men gathered below, the men-at-arms, and the mounted knights gave a great cheer. The men on the hilltop, soldiers of Etelamaa and mariners of the coast, marched down to meet them as brothers-in-arms and kinfolk, rather than as enemies. The rain poured down on Kallas, who stood alone in disbelief. Juvari, Alder, Sinio, and the other captains of the Swan Folk were no less amazed, for they, too, had seen and felt the power manifest in Egan.

Sinio turned to the others and said, "Never have I seen such a thing in all my days. The world is changing, and we must change with it. No more will I doubt Väinämöinen and the wisdom of his counsels, or the judgment of the king. For at least I am wise enough to see a power at work here beyond mortal measure, a power greater than the sum of the world and its parts, and which transcends it; and the doubt of mortal men cannot grasp or comprehend it."

The men marched past Egan, presenting their arms and pledging fealty. Then Juvari and his officers marshaled them into lines, a great force ready to leave Päivämäki and march north. Egan, moving as if in a dream and scarcely comprehending the power that he still felt coursing within him, rode to the head of the line.

And he led them forth while the black skies emptied and soaked the southern shores with the cool rain of spring.

***

The rain continued for days, choking swollen rivers and streams and slowing the army as it marched north. Egan led a large force, for many men from the coastlands had joined them, swelling their numbers—some eight hundred men-at-arms marched beneath the blue and white banners, with another hundred on horseback. Not all the men from the coast marched with them; Egan left some at Nummela with orders to return to their homes, both to strengthen the defenses of Etelamaa's southern shores and to spread word of the majesty and might of the young king who held in his hand the Sword of Legend. Following Sinio's advice, however, he commanded Kallas to come with him. So the lord of Harmaaniemi, rich beyond measure and head of the greatest house of the coastal fiefs, rode along sullenly toward High Länsimaa through the rain, all hope for the crown and greater glory forgotten.

The army had been on the move for days, marching straight north from Nummela until they neared Kotanrannta and turned northwest. They passed through the heart of Etelamaa's rich farmlands, where fields of barley, rye and oats were sown. From there, carts filled with yellow turnips and green cabbages rumbled off after every harvest, going to towns all over the kingdom, even to Keskimaa in the north. As they journeyed across the Plain of Etelamaa, the villagers and farmers were amazed, for the people in those parts knew little of the troubles north and south, and had heard only vague rumors of the Plague in the Stone City and of Nigan's death. They marveled to see the king and his men dressed for battle, marching and riding through their lands.

Although Keskimaa lay almost due north, there was no easy way for an army to pass through the Wall of the Giants, so they turned somewhat west to skirt a thick wood and finally came to a tumbled region where the Wall, less high and steep, was broken in many places. There lay a pass called the *lansikita*, the westernmost gap in the true Wall, through which much traffic went. The *lansikita* actually passed into Deep Länsimaa, but the Old Trade Road turned east again, crossed the river Clearwater at a great toll bridge, turned round the lakes, and came to Keskimaa from the south.

In all that time, they heard no news from the rest of the Far Northern Land. No messages came from High Länsimaa or the Wardens, no word from Väinämöinen, and no troubled dreams or visions. Egan held to his purpose to go to Keskimaa and lend the strength of Etelamaa to Pekka's men. Then, as they left the wood behind no more than two marches from the *lansikita*, a flurry of messengers came to them from different directions.

Late in the afternoon, a rider overtook them from the south. The Karhulainen had been sent with terrible tidings from Pekka the Fat; the army of the Bear Folk had been overwhelmed near the North Marches, and then destroyed or scattered. A great force of Itäläiset was swiftly riding south. Pekka begged for help, lest Keskimaa be attacked. The messenger had crossed the Wall at a point further east, making for the Stone City, so he had wasted several days on the road south before he learned of the king's whereabouts and finally caught up with them. But there was worse news yet to come.

Only hours later, an Etelalainen rider from the north arrived and reported that Karhulaisen refugees were fleeing south into Etelamaa, telling of war and fire near their homes. Shortly thereafter, several messengers came flying down the road from the *lansikita*, among them one who had reported to Egan before, at Nummela. Ragged, their horses spent, they brought tidings just as grim, for Keskimaa had been taken by the Easterners. None knew if Pekka was slain, alive or captured, but the Bear Folk were scattered and put to flight, or else under the yoke of their enemies.

The tidings of woe shocked the Swan Folk. Egan called a council of war to consider their next move. Some believed they should remain in Etelamaa to guard the pass against any incursion. Others said that they should move east and join with the company near the Green Vales. The king was unmoved, however. Despite Keskimaa's fall and the prospect of many foes ahead, he purposed to go forward, and, gathering what strength of the Bear Folk he could, retake the city and offer succor to the folk in those lands. They still had no news of Väinämöinen, though, and this worried Egan greatly, for he desired his counsel above all others.

When the nobles and captains had retired, Egan sat alone in his tent, as was his wont. He laid Lemminkäinen's sword across his knees and ran his fingers along its sharp edge and fine traceries.

The great doubt he had felt before Päivämäki was gone, yet another, different one remained. Before, it had been self-doubt, doubt about his own worth. That he felt no longer. Egan believed in his heart that he was meant to be king and play some role, large or small, in the great things that were in motion. The magnificent gift of the sword bestowed strength and power, but it could not make him Lemminkäinen. Egan he remained, and he still needed wisdom and counsel to choose the right course. This caused his doubt, and he sorely missed the old wizard's guidance.

Even as Egan sat with the sword across his lap, thinking these things, his servant rang the small silver bell outside the fine curtain.

"My lord, another messenger has arrived," he said.

Egan sighed; he felt for the Karhulaiset, but he was weary in body and soul, and could not face the prospect of yet more grim news from the north.

"Very well," answered Egan. "I will come to him presently."

"Yes, my lord. This one is not a man, but a woman, and—wait!"

The curtain parted and a woman walked in as Egan sprang to his feet, the sword still in his hand.

"I beg your pardon, King Egan," the woman said. "But I have a message that is best heard without delay, ere things are set in motion that cannot be undone."

The servant put his hand on her shoulder, but Egan shook his head. "It is alright, Arijoutsi; let her be. And have Neito bring food and drink. So, from where have you come and from whom? And what is the message that cannot wait?"

The strange woman looked around with a drawn smile on her face, as if curious to see what a king's tent contained.

"I am Taika of the Erilaiset," she finally said. At once, Egan could see that it was true. She resembled a mortal woman in her stature and features, with flaxen hair tied back in a long braid and intertwined with string, but her blue eyes shone like Väinämöinen's, the irises spangled and spun like a fluted shell. She dressed in the fashion of the Karelialaiset, in hues of forest green and red, with soft leather boots wrapped around her tiny feet. She slowly walked around as she said, "I come from Karelia, from the Enchanted Valley, and Mielikki sent me, though that was now many weeks ago. But the message I bear is from Väinämöinen."

"Väinämöinen!" exclaimed Egan. "Where is he? Does he know what has happened to the Bear Folk?"

Taika looked at the long sword. "Is that it? The old hero's sword? I have only seen it once in Väinämöinen's house, and that was long ago. But I am not old enough to have seen it wielded, or to have known the hand that swung it."

"Yes, this is Lemminkäinen's Sword," said Egan. "Väinämöinen gave it to me when he left our camp in the south, but that was more than a month ago. Tell me, Taika, where is he? Have you seen him?"

"I saw him many days ago, making for Kyöpelinvuori in Tavastia on an errand to the mortal Seer, but he gave me no message then. It was two nights ago that he reached out to me with his mind and asked me to find you. All has been dark for the Erilaiset of late, so it is hard to reach others with *sight* or along the twisted paths of dreams. Löhi has put forth her power."

"And what is his message?" asked Egan. In the dark tent and flickering candlelight, Taika's eyes seemed especially strange and unworldly, and held a hypnotic quality.

"Go not to Keskimaa," she said, "for the battle there is over, for a time. But Väinämöinen is in Deep Länsimaa, west of here and south of Siinisaare. There, in a strong place called Linnavuori, you will find Teemu, High Lord of the Elk Folk, and many of his people. The Witch has split her forces. Many Easteners and goblins out of Pohjola have left Keskimaa and invaded Deep Länsimaa. There will be battle. And if it goes ill with the men of the clans, the Hirvilaiset will be scattered just like the Karhulaiset, and all of Länsimaa will be lost. The line must be drawn at Linnavuori. So spoke Väinämöinen to my mind."

Egan felt his heart sink. Of all the counsel he might have expected to receive from the mage, he could not have imagined this. The Bear Folk were fleeing to Etelamaa, begging for the spears of Etelamaa to deliver them, but Väinämöinen would have them go to Deep Länsimaa instead.

"How can I do this?" said Egan, shaking his head. "The Bear Folk are in need, and we are poised to move north. Fifty more riders await us on the road tomorrow. I do not even know where this place is, or how long it would take to get there."

"It is not so far," said Taika. "I can show you gaps in the hills, west of the *lansikita* and where you may be hidden to the enemy scouts who already watch the pass. They do not know the land in these parts and sit only on the main road. But several paths lead to Linnavuori, paths that are dark to the

Easterners. A hard ride may bring you there in only three days, faster even than it would take for you to reach Keskimaa."

"But our army is not horsed—only some hundred are, not counting the riders who await us."

"Men on foot will come too late. Perhaps not too late for battle, for the Army of Pohjola may still be there, but too late to help those now gathered at Linnavuori. Speed matters over numbers now."

"Speed over numbers! But how large is the army of our foes? How can seven or eight score of horsemen hope to stop the might of Pohjola?" Egan shook his head again and looked down at the sword, which suddenly felt heavy in his hand.

"Who can say with any certainty what you may or may not do?" said Taika. "They say your mortal Seer can tell fortunes, but I do not know if I believe them. I know few mortals. But such were the words of old Väinämöinen to Taika the Young! Choose as your wisdom allows.

"There is one last thing. The mortal girls are with him: Ulla and her companion. He will send them away ere the battle begins. I will meet them and take them with me. If things go ill and Väinämöinen does not return, they will come back with me to the Enchanted Valley and to Mielikki. If you will not go to Linnavuori, then lend me three men, brave and strong, on swift horses to be my companions. They can help speed us across Etelamaa, however things may go with you beyond the Fence."

Egan looked at her then, but she said no more. Without even a bow of her head, she walked out of the king's tent to find the food and drink they'd prepared for her. The young king sat alone for some time, with only the sword and his confused thoughts for companions. At last, he sent for Juvari and Satou.

The short night was already giving way to light in the east when the two captains came into the tent, shaking sleep from their stinging eyes. They bowed with their hands on their breasts, but Egan looked at them hard.

"Do you believe what you saw at Päivämäki?" he asked. "Do you trust my judgment, even if it differs from your own?"

"Of course!" answered Satou. "You have our loyalty and trust, my king."

"And will the men still follow me, no matter how strange my commands seem, as they swore to me at Päivämäki?"

"My king," Juvari said, "the men are loyal and do not doubt you. You are the rightful heir and chief of the clan. All saw and heard your majesty and power revealed that day. They will follow you anywhere, Egan, no matter what betide—as will I."

Egan nodded, resting his hand on his tall captain's shoulder.

"That is well, Juvari," he said. "Very well indeed. For there is going to be a change in our plans."

Chapter Fourteen

Tulikki's Cloak

Linnavuori lay in the southeast of Deep Länsimaa, south of the island of Siinisaare in the great Blue Lake. There, in a region of gentle clime and watered by many streams and brooks, was a rise of land with a green, open field before it. Set amidst scattered stands of thin birch, pine and fir trees, it backed onto a steep slope. The back slope fell sharply to a narrow channel through which a shallow river ran, babbling over rocks and stones until it joined the Clearwater some miles beyond.

A hill fort had been built upon the rise long ago: a strong place made of earth and felled trees. Though it had been many lives of men since war passed over this land, or any foe assailed it, the fort had always been repaired and never wholly fallen into disuse; now it was used as a pen for animals or a place for markets and fairs. Its main wall, made of tall logs, had been constantly replaced over the years, faced north, and had a large, open space where once a gate had been. The west wall was also built of wood, though it was not as strong in some places. To the east, however, the wooden wall had crumbled and was gone. There, a high berm of packed earth ran from the north face to the drop down to the waterway; a low wall of logs and stone ran the length of its southern march, at the top of a nearly sheer slope.

Such was the fashion of Linnavuori, and Teemu, High Lord of the Hirvilaiset, the Elk Folk, had withdrawn to the hill fort to defend his people against the wrath of Pohjola. The capital of the Elk Folk, Valkeakosk, lay far to the north, and was the only town of any size in Deep Länsimaa. The Hirvilaiset of Valkeakosk were husbandmen and herders, raising horses—a rare livelihood in the Far Northern Land. Miners lived there, too, lifting ore and bloodrock from the marshes and bogs. But the Elk Folk lived mostly scattered across the south of the land, as hunters and fisherfolk on the shores of the Blue Lake or on the countless isles therein: some with small villages, and others no more than slips of earth and stone where a single *pirtti* stood.

Teemu had been staying in the region when word came from High Länsimaa that a great force from Pohjola had passed south of the Marches, so he gathered to him what men he could and sent messages to the lords in Valkeakosk to do the same. The threat seemed far-off then, but worse news had come—much worse. An army of foes had taken Keskimaa, and even now marched toward his own lands in Deep Länsimaa.

The Elk Folk were not warlike, and kept little strength of arms. A few of the Guards of Valkeakosk travelled with Teemu, acting as much as servants as they were soldiers. The young lord of Deep Länsimaa had marshaled men from the regions south of Blue Lake, near the isle of Siinisaare, and from the fields to the southwest. The woodmen and farmers were, for the most part, armed with axes, clubs, and hunting bows instead of swords and spears. All told, there were no more than four hundred, a token force to challenge the Easterners and goblins. So Teemu retreated to Linnavuori, where at least they had walls to defend, and many people went with him. Others fled their homes in panic, joining the Bear Folk who passed through to escape the devastation in High Länsimaa. In addition to the armed men, hundreds more, chiefly women and children, had crowded into the hill fort seeking safety and shelter.

Thus did Väinämöinen find Linnavuori as he rode out of Tavastia with Ulla and Kirsikka before him. The cart had lost a wheel three days out from Kyöpelinvuori, and though the wizard might have fixed it with a spell, he had neither the time nor patience. In any case, they made greater speed on the horse. The old man shook his head as he rode through the open gateway and looked about.

A mass of frightened people milled around, all arguing over whether their animals should remain within or without. Here and there, a few Guards and March Wardens tried to drill the husbandmen of the Hirvilaiset into a fighting force. Ulla and Kirsikka marveled at the sight, for the Elk Folk, in manner and dress, if not in speech, were very similar to their own clan. Nowhere in all their travels with Väinämöinen had they met people who reminded them so much of their homeland. Indeed, the Elk and Bear Clans were close kin, and the Hirvilaiset were a people of small villages and homesteads—poor for the most part, as was reckoned in the Far Northern Land.

If Teemu had been nervous the previous year during the old man's strange visit to Siinisaare, he now felt otherwise. He was joyous at Väinämöinen's unexpected arrival. He welcomed him and begged for his help, and his young wife, a thin girl with hair so fair it was almost white and blue eyes like a summer sky, seemed to believe the legendary wizard could sing up an army of thousands to rescue them, or grow stone walls that reached a mile high and shut out any evil. These things Väinämöinen could not do, but there was still much he could do.

After speaking with Teemu, he set about managing things within the fort and bringing order to the chaos. He began by instructing the Hirvilaiset to drive most of their animals out, even if it meant mingling their herds and flocks, and losing many in the neighboring woodlands.

"There are folk enough within the walls without adding the filth and confusion your herds will bring with them. The choice may well be between your beasts and your lives. But keep any horses that can be ridden or that can pull carts, and perhaps some cows and goats so that at least the smallest children may have milk; if we must, we can slaughter the beasts and have meat for several days when all other stores are gone."

Their first night at Linnavuori, Väinämöinen left the girls with Teemu's wife and the other ladies of the Hirvilaiset. He went out into the woods by himself and, when he came back the next morning, his tired eyes were red and his face was troubled. Only a few hours later, a group of men, perhaps a hundred, came along the road from the northeast, some on horseback and others in ramshackle wagons or carts. They were Karhulaiset, survivors of the disaster in High Länsimaa with a score of Wardens. Väinämöinen and Teemu rode out to greet them, and Ulla and Kirsikka ran across the green grass behind them, eager to see the newcomers. Gaunt and ragged, their clothes tattered and torn, the refugees hobbled toward them, mostly wounded from battle or hurts along the road. But at their head, scarcely recognizable in a rent, dirty cloak and with a wild, tangled beard, was Ilkka, Chief Warden of High Länsimaa.

"Hoi, Ilkka!" said Väinämöinen. "Little did I think to see you here. I can see you've had an evil time of it, you and all these men, and I daresay the chase is not far behind."

"Not far," said Ilkka. "Had I not been born in these lands and known where Linnavuori lay, we might already have been trapped against the lake. But it is good fortune to find you here, for I was only guessing the old fort was manned. Some folk we met, Lord Teemu, said you had gone north, others west. There is much confusion all around."

"What is the news from High Länsimaa?" Väinämöinen asked grimly. "How is it you came here?"

"The news is ill," answered Ilkka. "But for all that, it must wait until these men are within the walls, for they are near exhausted and starving. Let me say that you were looked for in Keskimaa, Väinämöinen, and sorely missed in the end."

Väinämöinen frowned. "That I know. All I have done the past year has been too late, with Löhi one step before me."

Just then Ulla and Kirsikka caught up to them, and Ilkka, upon seeing them, smiled for the first time in many days. Painfully stiff and saddlesore, he got down gingerly from his tired mount and put his hand on Ulla's shining dark hair.

"So you are still with him, Ulla!" he cried. "You've made quite a journey through the Far Northern Land, and now you are here, of all places! How are you?"

"I'm fine," she said with a smile, happy to see her friend again. "But what happened, Ilkka? You saw the Itäläiset again, didn't you?"

His smile faded. "Yes, Ulla. Many more than when they raided your home in the north. But don't worry, you are safe with Väinämöinen."

The refugees and March Wardens moved toward the fort, but Ilkka motioned to Väinämöinen and the wizard dismounted. They went to a rickety cart pulled by a small brown pony. Within lay several wounded men; one in particular looked old and haggard, his tattered beard a dirty grey and his clothes torn and faded save for a gem around his neck. His sallow skin looked unhealthy, and his eyes remained closed.

"He came to us in the evening four days ago," said Ilkka. "He has journeyed far across the length of High Länsimaa, even as we have, but he has not spoken for the past two days."

"Turi!" Väinämöinen cried as soon as he recognized his oldest friend. "What happened to you?"

For indeed it was Turi, wizard of the Erilaiset. He had journeyed on down the North Road to hide from the Easterners, but the Bear Folk in Gamla were routed ere he came to them. So he turned west, picking his way through woods and lakes, making for Keskimaa. Again, he came too late. The town fell before he reached it. The spies and servants of Pohjola were everywhere, so he turned southwest and made for Deep Länsimaa. All the while, the poison from the Hiisi's arrow coursed through his veins and sickened him. Though he worked no spell or change, he grew ever weaker. At last, very ill, he came upon Ilkka and his men near Siinisaare.

"Turi!" Väinämöinen said again. Such was the power of his voice that the sick man opened his eyes and the shadow of a smile crossed his lips.

"I thought I'd find you here!" he whispered weakly. "The Swan Folk did not come."

"No," said Väinämöinen, "but the young king is not far away now. I have sent him tidings to hasten here—to Linnavuori."

Suddenly Turi rallied and reached out to touch his old friend's shoulder. "It is Työ," he said with great effort. "I saw him in the north. Työ leads Löhi's army—Työ of the Haltiatar—and his *sight* is strong."

"I know," answered Väinämöinen. "So the Seer said, for I went to her in Kyöpelinvuori. But what happened to you, my friend? Tell me so I can help you!"

Turi did not speak again, however. As if his effort had exhausted him, he closed his eyes and seemed to sleep. Väinämöinen sighed and shook his head.

"He said it was a poisoned arrow," said Ilkka, "Shot by a Hiisi of Pohjola when he was changed into the shape of an eagle. I had heard of wizards in old tales taking other shapes, but in truth, I did not believe them, even after everything I have seen this terrible year. Alas, none of us have the skill to treat such a poison, even had we been there when it happened."

"Nor have I," said Väinämöinen. "Many are the poisons of the world, and evil are those of Pohjola, where the Witch of the North rules. If I do not know what kind it is or whence it came from, there may be little that I can do." To the men, he said, "Take them within, and put them to rest in the *kotas* by the south wall! I will do what I can. But give food and drink to the newcomers, and have them rest, Ilkka. They will have to fight again soon enough."

Ilkka put the girls on his horse, for, despite his weariness, he was glad to see them. Seeing Ulla again somehow stirred hope in his heart. Despite the grim news and faces, the little girls laughed as they bounced on his steed. Väinämöinen had never failed them, and they trusted him completely; neither Ulla nor Kirsikka could imagine anything bad happening that the old man could not remedy.

Linnavuori held many structures, some old and some newer: makeshift *majas* and *kotas* for shelter, and pens and sheds for animals and stores of goods. They took Turi and the other wounded men inside the fort, where women skilled in healing cared for them. Väinämöinen came to them and helped the men who were most stricken. He sat for a long time by Turi, chanting with his rich voice and weaving spells of protection and healing. But Turi already walked among the eaves of the colorless wood that led to the dark river, and then to Tuonela. Though he tarried as one lost and did not go forward, Väinämöinen could not call him back.

Wizards used powerful spells and incantations to heal sickness or banish evil, locking it away in stones or deep holes, but they had to first name the evil to know its nature and from whence it came. Väinämöinen could not guess what evil this goblin's arrow had carried.

Men labored the rest of that day to repair the hill fort and strengthen it, as well as build a barrier across the open gateway. Evening fell and the red sun hung low for hours in the western sky. Suddenly, cries arose from the people who had ventured outside the fort, and they swiftly ran back inside.

To the north, all along the tree line that hid the road beyond, appeared a line of riders, all clad in black and red and sitting atop brown horses: scouts of the Itäläiset, or else the vanguard of Löhi's army. They had captured several men and now dragged them forward with bound hands and ropes around their necks. In pain and afraid, the captives cried out to their friends and families within Linnavuori. The frightened people shouted back, while women began to wail, lamenting the doom that seemed at hand. After a while, though, the horsemen left, taking their prisoners with them—save for one man whom they cruelly choked and left dead in the green grass. The Easterners knew then that Linnavuori was held against them, and that Teemu, Väinämöinen, and all the enemies they most wished to destroy were within those walls.

For the next two days, all the Elk Folk, save for a few left in the woods to the east and west, stayed inside the fort. They sent out scouts, mounted and on foot, to gain what knowledge they could, and to watch for Egan's coming. No more folk came to Linnavuori, however. All who lived nearby were within or had fled the region altogether.

Across the grassy field and in the woods all about, the Army of Pohjola arrived. Soon they surrounded Linnavuori, except to the south, where the water channel lay. Hundreds of men moved among the trees, and the sounds of a great herd of horses reached the fort. Red and black banners appeared here and there, bearing the strange devices of various clans of the Itäläiset.

They saw other banners, too: black, but with the token of the North Star upon them. These were clustered along the western tree line. The frightened people saw dark shapes there, smaller than mortal men, swarming about the woods like ants. The Hiisia terrified the Elk Folk, and if they had not fully believed that their foes came from Pohjola—or that such a land existed save in old tales—they did then. Most felt as if they were in a nightmare, a surreal dreamscape where their worst fears lived, breathed, and walked among them.

Watch fires burned during the short night, their smoke rising high above the trees, but the servants of Löhi made no sign and did not move to assault the fort.

So it was that on the third day after Ilkka's arrival that the defenders held a council of war. The next day would be Midsummer's Day, and throughout the Far Northern Land, from the Karelian Forest to the Thousand Isles of the Akkalan archipelago, folk would celebrate the shortest night of the year. There was little mirth in Linnavuori, however.

Teemu had quarters in one of several small stone buildings within the walls, and the captains gathered in his round chamber. Two other Hirvilaisen nobles attended the high lord of the Elk Folk, as well as Hannu, Teemu's chief counselor. Ilkka was there with two Wardens, who also acted as scouts, and, of course, Väinämöinen. Turi, who lingered between life and death, had not risen from his bed.

Ulla and Kirsikka crept into the dark, smoky chamber and sat unnoticed against the wall. They had enjoyed having the run of the crowded, noisy fort as Väinämöinen went about his business. The Elk Folk marveled at them: Kirsikka with her red hair and fine, if dirty, Etelalaisen dress, and dark-haired Ulla in her tattered Karelian garb. Now the girls listened to Väinämöinen speak, his staff laid across his knees as he sat cross-legged on the ground.

"There are no easy choices before us," said Väinämöinen. "And perhaps no good ones, either. Would that Turi were well, or that others of my kin were here, but, alas, not many remain of the Great Ones among the

Erilaiset! For a great sorcerer leads Löhi's army, one whose magic matches even mine. I can feel his power in the woods, focused on us."

"But how great a force is set against us?" asked Teemu. "What do the scouts say?"

"We cannot say for sure, my lord," answered one of the Wardens, even the same Laso who met Turi on the North Road in flight from the Easterners. "There are hundreds of riders all about the roads and fields nearby. And this morning, perhaps two hundred or more others rode away to the southeast."

"They ride to cover the approaches that the Swan Folk might use," said Väinämöinen. "Our enemy is aware of King Egan and his men."

"That is not all," said Laso. "There are other things, too; evil goblins, I deem them to be, dark shapes like the bogeys of old tales come to life. There are many scattered among the woods, and some have crept close to Linnavuori, where they watch us. Only south, across the river, is there any chance of escape."

"They are Hiisia," said Väinämöinen. "Dark Erilaiset of Pohjola. The Witch has increased their numbers and sends them as a plague to mortal men. Their magic is weak, but they are fierce fighters, and they hate the folk of the clans."

"That I know," said Ilkka. "For the Hiisia attacked us first in High Länsimaa, and they came on in a frenzy of hatred."

"Tell us your full tale, Ilkka," said Väinämöinen. "For we have been busy and you have only mentioned in brief all that happened to you."

Ilkka sighed and hung his head. "It is an evil tale," he said, "and I don't wish to recall it, now or ever. But I will say this much, in case there is something of use in the report."

Then Ilkka told them how he had marched north with Miko Verikiven and the Bear Folk, despite his misgivings. They had finally pushed past Gamla and moved up the North Road itself. Ilkka had been sent with some three hundred men, chiefly on horseback, to hold a westerly side road and ambush their enemies from the rear when they passed. Despite their precautions, they had been discovered by the Easterners, and were ambushed themselves.

As Turi had foreseen, the main host of the Bear Folk had been surrounded by the Easterners and routed, with great loss life. Ilkka's men had been swept away, but he had gathered those he could, fleeing west through the woods and lakes. They moved slowly through lands where few men dwelled, until at last they came down upon Keskimaa from the north, even as Turi had. But it was too late. The Easterners and goblins were there before them.

The villagers and farmers Pekka had marshaled to defend the town had been no match for the Army of Pohjola, and were swiftly defeated. Ilkka and his companions arrived only in time to watch Keskimaa burn. The Easterners did not destroy the town entirely, for they wished to make it their winter camp, but enslaved all the Karhulaiset who had not fled. So the Wardens again fled west, pursued by many riders in red and black. A score of Karhulaiset—men who had been in Keskimaa until the last—joined them on the way, telling how Pekka Verikiven had finally been taken by the goblins in the very Hall of the Bear Clan, then dragged through the streets of Keskimaa behind the Easterners' horses for sport. But Ilkka led the men to Deep Länsimaa, his homeland, where he found Teemu at Linnavuori.

"And it was strange," said Ilkka. "From the Marches to Keskimaa, it seemed our enemies knew our plans and were always a step ahead. Löhi must indeed be strong if her *sight* is so powerful."

"She is strong," said Väinämöinen. "Perhaps not as strong as of old, or else she would come herself and make a swift end of us. And her power wanes at midsummer. But if your enemies saw your every move, it was not due to Löhi alone. The captain of her army has a piece of glass like a jewel with great magic inside it. A man of power can use it to see things near and far, spying on what he will. That is why all your plans went amiss.

"His name is Työ, and his folk are the Haltiatar, those whom mortal men call elves. He served Löhi long ago and he, too, has returned to plot our ruin. You may not feel it and you may not see it, but I have cast spells and woven webs of darkness around us to hide Linnavuori and all within it from unfriendly eyes. But I fear he may still see all that we do. This jewel can pierce spells and help a wizard see things that are hidden. My magic may not avail against one such as Työ."

"But how do you know these things, Lord Väinämöinen?" asked Hannu. "Have you seen this elf—this Työ?"

"No, but I do not doubt that it is he. Turi told me ere he slipped into his fever."

"He told me, too," said Ilkka. "He saw him north of the Marches in the camp of our foes."

"And, as you know, I have also been to Kyöpelinvuori," said Väinämöinen. "The Seer has the greatest of these glasses, a crystal ball like an orb of clear water from the stillest northern pool. She saw him and named him, and she saw his jewel."

Teemu stood up, glancing out the open doorway. Light still spilled in, but it was growing darker outside as a summer storm approached. "What, then, are we to do? We do not know how great our enemy's host is, but it is great enough. Few of our own men are warriors or trained to fight. We do not know where the king of Etelamaa is. Even if he comes, we do not know if his numbers will suffice. We have some store of food, but many mouths to feed, so we cannot withstand a lengthy siege. And all the lands about, the farms and villages, will be spoiled and laid waste. What, then, are we to do?"

Teemu spoke as if to himself, and the others made no answer, but they were all thinking the same thing. They looked to Väinämöinen, the eternal singer who had walked through the woods of the Far Northern Land since time immemorial, to save them again. If he could not, what hope did they have against the army that had already sacked High Länsimaa and wrecked havoc among the Clan of the Bear?

The old man sighed and ran his hand along the staff. Thunder rumbled in the distance and a sudden cool wind blew into the round chamber. All else was quiet, and to her surprise, Ulla realized she was holding her breath.

"If I thought I could get away with it, I'd sneak into our enemy's camp," said Väinämöinen. "Perhaps I could steal his jewel and challenge him to a duel of spells. I'm not so bad a thief. I might make an *etiänen*, but Työ is already aware of me—that I know. I cannot hide my presence from him so easily now—nor he from me, for that matter. And I am tired. Very tired. I cannot keep up the spells that shroud us from their sight, tend to Turi and the others who are hurt, and raid our enemy's camp to boot. Would that there were more of my kinfolk with us!"

"Then what hope have we in battle?" Ilkka asked. "I have already seen the Army of Pohjola defeat men of the Seven Clans—twice. Would it not be best to leave this place, under cover of the short night, and flee into the wild? Perhaps many might be saved that way. If Löhi can be stopped by the sword, it must fall to the Swan and Hare Folk."

"That might be best," said Väinämöinen. "I believe we should send some out—women and children, in any case. But we cannot abandon Linnavuori without Työ seeing it, not if he has the jewel that gives him *sight*. He would fall on us as we fled and destroy us. It is too great a risk to abandon these walls."

"Then we are back where we started!" cried Teemu. "We have no hope of victory, yet cannot flee the trap. Is there nothing to be done, Lord Väinämöinen?"

"No hope?" said the old man. "Perhaps not. But do not forget the Swan Folk. And at least we may make the Pohjolaiset pay dearly for Linnavuori, and so help King Egan. I know some tricks; aye, I do indeed. Were it not for this jewel, I might still come up with a thing or two. But now? I just don't know." Väinämöinen rubbed his red eyes and shook his head.

"Väinämöinen," said Ilkka, "since I met you more than a year ago, all your counsel has been wise. If men had listened to you then, perhaps things would not be so ill. For my part, I will do as you say."

"As will I," said Teemu. "It is still hard to understand how this Witch, whom we believed but a child's tale from ancient days, assails us. I beg you to do all you can to save my folk, my lord. My men are yours to command."

Thunder boomed again in the south. At last, the old man rose and stood tall before them.

"So be it," he said. "We will not flee. We will defend these walls and do what we can. And if we fall here, let us do so with honor, taking as many of Löhi's servants with us to Tuonela as we can. I will try once more, when I have rested some, to reach out with my mind to Egan and see where the Swan Folk might be. But let carts be readied so that groups of women and children, no more than thirty at a time, can flee. I don't think Työ will pursue them—not yet. If they cross the river, perhaps some can be saved."

The men left the round chamber and walked back out under the open sky. The two little girls slipped out afterward, wondering what these things might mean. Väinämöinen appeared behind them, putting a hand on each girl's shoulder. Startled, they wheeled round. The wizard and Ilkka stood behind them, frowning.

"Interesting council?" said the wizard.

Neither girl replied.

"Hmm, well. Be that as it may, you heard my words. There will be a battle here—very soon, I should think. It will be even worse than what you saw in High Länsimaa." He looked at Ilkka, then knelt before them. "Listen to me, little one, and you, too, Cherry. You will have to go away now, just for a while. You cannot stay here; it is much too dangerous. If the first group is left alone and escapes, you will go out with the next."

"No!" they cried together.

"I will not go," said Ulla angrily. She had heard Väinämöinen say as much to the Seer, but hadn't believed he would really send them away. Tears welled in her eyes as she wailed, "How can you do that?! You promised us! You promised!"

"I promised not to leave you, and I'm not. I'll catch up to you soon. But look at me! You cannot be caught here, Ulla. You know that. You bear the Clan Mark, the sign that gives us hope in the end. I found you once before, and I'll find you again. But you cannot stay in Linnavuori." Ulla looked at Ilkka, then back at Väinämöinen, her white face flushed a deep red. Väinämöinen continued, "The Erilainen woman we met in Etelamaa, Taika, is waiting nearby.

The scouts will take you to her. Maybe Egan will be there, too. You can wait for me there. But if not—Ulla, listen! If I can't come, she will take you to Mielikki in the Enchanted Valley. You will be safe there."

"Don't worry," said Ilkka. "You both are strong. We shall meet again!"

Ulla tore away from them and ran through the mingled crowd as the midsummer's wind picked up, blowing in black clouds from the south. The scent of rain filled the air like a fragrance of something fresh and wild.

***

"I will *not* go away!" shouted Ulla, narrowing her eyes and grimacing at Kirsikka as if she might hit her. The red-haired girl was hastily packing the bundle of goods she had accumulated on their journeys. Ulla carried nothing but the two wooden figures of her brother and herself that her aunt had put into her pouch on that fateful morning, which now seemed so far away and long ago.

Kirsikka snorted testily. "As if we have any choice. You know Väinämöinen isn't going to change his mind. I don't want to go, either, but there's no point in arguing about it. And if we do have to go, I want to go now, not after those things—those goblins—come here. Bad things are going to happen, Ulla."

"Well, if they are, it's because of that elf. He can see everything with his jewel, just like the Seer." She hesitated while Kirsikka, pink-faced and sweating, tied a piece of rope around the top of her badgerskin pouch. Slowly, thoughtfully, she said, "In fact, if we had the jewel, maybe the Elk Folk would win the battle and Väinämöinen wouldn't send us away."

"Oh, yes! We'll just use magic to run and steal it!" Kirsikka's mockingly cheerful expression and tone fell flat. "Even Väinämöinen said he couldn't do that."

"Because the elf would know he's there. The elf knew him long ago and can feel when he's nearby because of his magic, but he doesn't know us, does he?"

Kirsikka glared at her. "You're not serious. How in the world could we steal that jewel?!"

"*I* can do it," said Ulla. "I have the Clan Mark. I can—I can put on Tulikki's Cloak, just like Lempi, and sneak into the enemy's camp!"

"You can't do that, and neither can I!" said Kirsikka hotly. "You may have a Clan Mark on your shoulders, but you don't have much of a head on them! Making lights and calling birds is one thing, but you'd need real magic, *serious* magic for that. Väinämöinen told you not to even try. Besides, even if you could weave such a spell, you'd never find the stone."

Ulla took her by the arms. "Yes, I can; *we* can. And we *must* do it, Kirsikka. Do you want to be sent away from Väinämöinen, away from Ilkka, and go who knows where to a place full of strangers? What if the Easterners capture us again? They'll take us north, back to their homes as slaves, or even worse, to the Witch. Look, we can sneak out of—"

A tall March Warden, one of Ilkka's company, came up to their little *kota*.

"There you are," he said. "Are you not the Karhulaisen girls who ride with Väinämöinen? He bids you come now, for the first group is away and passed unhindered to the river below. The next group must leave swiftly and follow close behind."

The girls followed him through the noise, crowd and smoke to a place along the western wall where there was a gap, just wide enough for a cart or horses to pass through. The gap was left open for the moment, although a stout barrier of felled logs had been lashed together, ready to drop in place and close the fort to their enemies. Several old carts waited there, pulled by skinny ponies, while a crowd of women and children milled about.

The first group had passed unmolested and disappeared into the mists; it seemed Väinämöinen was right, and Työ had no desire to chase after small groups of stragglers. Two more carts were ready to leave Linnavuori. The carts could not cross the river, but one would carry many children down the old, rutted path that ran from the hill fort to the reed beds at the river's edge. The other held several injured men, including Turi. Väinämöinen had done all he could for his friend, and wished to send him to safety. Ulla stared at Kirsikka as if her eyes might bore holes in her, but the freckled-face girl shook her head and mouthed, "No."

It was still late afternoon, and should have been sunny and bright, but the storm darkened the sky and a fine, misty rain fell in fits and starts. Väinämöinen came to them then and spoke gentle words, mixed with spells of ward and protection. Though Ulla felt the old man's wizardly power, as she always did when he worked magic, she said nothing in return and stared off at the foggy tree line across the way. Finally, he told the girls to obey Taika and to take his greetings to Mielikki, should he be delayed and fail to meet them as planned. When all was ready, one of the Wardens moved to lift them into the cart with the other Hirvilaisen children, but Ulla stopped him.

"Let us ride with Turi," she pleaded. "We can help take care of him."

So they put the girls in the second cart, and set off a moment later through the gap and down the cart path. The wizard stood just within the walls and watched them go with a sad look on his face. The two little girls stared back over the lip of the cart while he grew smaller and smaller.

Two Wardens rode near the driver, on either side of the wet cart filled with frightened children. They would escort the little group to the river, where other men waited to help them cross. After that, the riders would take Ulla and Kirsikka to where Taika awaited at a standing stone beneath a silver fall.

The cart path ran south, right beneath Linnavuori's western walls, then veered away from the fort and dipped down toward the water channel and the river. They drove in plain sight of their foes and could see the Witch's banners across the misty fields, but were unmolested by any arrows or galloping horsemen, which they had feared most. Where the cart path turned southwest and left the walls stood an outcrop of grey stone: tumbled boulders and one larger rock like a small shelf, wet and slick. There, they would be hidden momentarily from the fort's view.

Ulla looked at Turi. The wizard, cleaned and dressed in fresh clothes, looked peaceful as he slept, if far older and frailer than when they met him in Taikalaakso. There were several other men in the cart, wounded or ill, but only one nurse: an older woman with stringy grey hair. She looked up at the girls, a tired smile briefly playing across her careworn face. Then one of her charges moaned in pain and she turned away to help him. Ulla dug her elbow into Kirsikka's side as they passed under the stone.

"Now!" she whispered urgently. "Now's our chance! Hop out!"

"No!" hissed Kirsikka. "Leave me alone!"

Ulla pulled one last time on her friend's sleeve, then made up her mind. She bent down, quickly kissed Turi on the cheek, and, with a fluid motion, grabbed the back of the cart, jumped, and dropped to the ground. Kirsikka peered over the edge of the cart, her face a mixture of anger, panic and astonishment. Ulla frantically motioned to her and she, too, leapt out, sprawling face-first on the wet, muddy path. Ulla helped her scramble up and then they ran under the large rock's curling lip. The cart rambled on; neither the old nurse, nor the Wardens, nor anyone else looked back and saw that the girls were missing.

Water dripped from the rock onto the kerchiefs atop their heads. Only half a mile away, across the wet field, there was a stand of woods, and within, shrouded in mist, was the Army of Pohjola. Kirsikka started to cry.

"My pack, all my things," she sobbed. "They're gone now. Ulla, what are you *doing*?"

"Kirsikka, listen to me. We can sneak across and hide in the trees; it's darker now. No one can see us. Maybe we can find the jewel and steal it!"

Kirsikka began to sob even harder and, as if in sympathy, rain began to fall again. Ulla looked around. She had no clear idea of what she was doing or what she wished to do, but her excitement carried her along, as well as the vague notion of finding the glass and bringing it to Väinämöinen. Ulla suddenly thought of Tulikki's Cloak and the words Lempi used to make himself invisible while they played in the deep forest. She had only been half-serious before when she told Kirsikka that she could weave the spell, but now the thought formed in her mind.

Why not?

At times, when she lay near their dying campfire and looked up at the stars, she had repeated the incantation, even sung it to herself to see what would happen. She had felt the power stir within her then, the same power that she had learned to draw upon, though Väinämöinen forbade her to use it. And Kirsikka was right. Ulla knew that the spells she had worked were only the toys of the Erilaiset. The true *loitsu* of the Erilaiset, the spells that called upon the power of the Vanhalaiset, were very different. Did she have the power to work those, child though she was? The Seer had asked Väinämöinen if Ulla had true power within her, and he had said nothing. Did he not wish to speak to the old woman about her, or did he doubt what lay within her? Yet she was the child who bore the Mark of the Clan!

Ulla suddenly grabbed Kirsikka and held her firmly.

"It's okay, *sisku*; stop crying! You don't need to come with me. I want you to stay here and tell them I'm alright when they come looking for us. I'm going to go over there, but I'll call if I need you!"

"No!" cried Kirsikka, "Ulla, let's run back to the fort now, before someone sees us!"

"No," said Ulla. "No one's going to see me."

The little girl with dark hair stood up and backed away from the rocky shelf while the rain kept coming down. She turned, looked at the tree line across the way, and then closed her eyes. She began to chant in a singsong voice that was almost lost in the wind, slowly at first, but then quicker. As she said the words, she felt the world begin to spin around her.

> *"Weave a cloak around my body,*
> *shroud to cover arms and shoulders.*
> *Legs be hid from eyes unfriendly,*
> *spin for me the hidden mantle."*

An extraordinary sensation came over her, like when she was bewitched by the Näkki, but this time she was in control. Most incredible of all, as surely as a man can close his eyes to shut out rain or light and open them again when he wishes, Ulla knew that she could break the spell at will.

Kirsikka's cry brought her back into the moment. "Lumikki! What happened? Where are you?"

A thrill coursed down Ulla's spine. Kirsikka was staring straight at her, but couldn't see her. She had woven Tulikki's Cloak and was enmeshed in its shadow, like the moon wrapped in cloud.

"I'm right here in front of you," said Ulla, as a flash of lightning lit the southern sky, followed by a distant rumble. "I did it, Kirsikka! I did it!" She held her hand out in front of her and looked down at her boots. She could still see her own limbs, but dimly, as if she was covered by something dark and opaque. "Can you see me?"

The freckled-faced girl shook her head, her eyes wide and wild with fear and amazement. Ulla turned to gaze at the silent trees.

"Listen, Kirsikka, I'm going now to see what I can find over there. I'll be alright, and so will you. I'm sorry about your things. They'll come looking for us any moment, and if they find you, tell them that I'm fine."

Without waiting for a reply, the dark-haired little girl took off across the grassy field, leaving the shelter of the rocks and the wooden walls of Linnavuori behind her. The rain fell in big drops, and a bank of fog hugged the woods like a low wall where dimly guessed shapes flitted here and there in the gloom.

Ulla didn't quite understand what she was doing, but felt compelled to keep going, driven by some instinct that was not hers alone. She had the vague notion that, unless she kept Väinämöinen from sending her away, she would lose him and never see him again. As she crossed the field and neared the woods, the trees came into sharper focus. She could see them clearly—birch and fir, woods like she was used to seeing near Grankulta, where she had grown up and lived all her short life. She watched her feet tramp through the wet grass: quick-moving shadows that only her eyes could see. Finally, she reached the tree line.

The wood seemed silent and empty. A banner, deep blue with a rayed star upon it, was pitched into the ground some ways to her right, but the girl could see nothing among the trees save patches of creeping mist. Ulla glanced back; she could just make out the rocky outcrop beneath Linnavuori's distant walls. For a brief moment, she imagined she saw the red of Kirsikka's fiery hair. Then she stepped forward into the sparse forest and began to pick her way through the trees as she had done hundreds of times before. Despite the damp and darkness, she could see a break ahead, perhaps a path or clearing where the woods thinned. The spongy green turf sank beneath her boots and she stepped carefully; then, as she hopped over a fallen birch, rotten and crumbling, she came up short. Her heart skipped a beat, then thumped hard against her tiny chest. No more than five feet in front of her, crouched behind an old, broken stump, was a goblin out of her worst nightmares: a Hiisi from Pohjola.

The little girl froze. At once, unbidden thoughts of the bear cub in the woods near Grankulta flooded her mind. She fought back the urge to turn and run. This was different. The cub had met her gaze, stared back; the goblin looked straight at her, but clearly saw nothing. Ulla felt the power of the spell coursing through her limbs and willed the enchantment to continue.

The Hiisi's face was ghastly, a dark, sickly green with leathery skin and a hooked, beak-like nose. Its thin, black lips did not cover the sharp fang-like eyeteeth protruding from its mouth. But it was the goblin's eyes which both fascinated and repelled her, as they did all mortals: white, with no iris or pupil to be seen, blinking open and shut like pale windows into nothingness. The goblin licked its thin lips and turned to its right. Ulla, shaking off the morbid fascination, realized with a shock that there were others nearby; indeed, the wood was full of goblins, stretched out in a line to either side of her, hidden from sight from those still at Linnavuori, but watching all that transpired, waiting for a command from their captain.

Ulla took a deep breath and steadied herself. Stepping some few feet aside, she slowly passed the goblin to the right, making as little noise as she could. A trailing branch caught her sleeve and snapped, a faint but sharp sound amidst the wet mould. The goblin jerked its head toward her, narrowing its white eyes and grimacing as if sniffing for a strange scent. But it relaxed just as quickly, turning back to its vigil. The girl moved on, looking back only once at the line of goblins behind her.

She discovered that the clearing was actually a road, running south in one direction toward the river and disappearing behind a bend in the other. Slightly raised, it sloped down into thicker woods on the other side. She didn't know it, but the hard-packed road circled Linnavuori, looped through the woods and joined several other ways leading to and from the ancient hill fort. The rain had stopped again, but grey fog lingered in hollows along the roadside.

With no idea where to go, Ulla began to walk north, away from where she guessed the river lay. She saw no one else on the road, neither goblins nor men, nor any other creature, and she could see nothing in the trees on either side. The road bent this way and that, following some natural line or ridge, but always pushing northward. Ulla plodded on, repeating the *loitsu* a few times to reassure herself and to bolster her courage.

Then she came to a sharper turn to the east and heard the whinny of horses, followed by hoofbeats splashing in thin mud and coming around the bend right in front of her. Before she could react, two riders appeared: men on swift brown horses, clad in black and red, and whose long brown hair flowed behind them. If the Hiisia had reminded her of the encounter with the bear, the Itäläiset evoked even worse memories, and Ulla panicked.

She sprang aside, trying to leap the road into the bracken, but slipped in the mud and fell flat on her face. The horsemen were upon her. Ulla closed her eyes and clenched her fists, expecting to feel the horses' hooves trample her at any moment. But whether the horses were unaffected by the spell, or by some chance of the world—if chance it was—they leapt over her, leaving her unharmed. As she lay there, two more swiftly ran by.

After a long while, Ulla picked herself up. She was filthy, but the spell's magic power still coursed throughout her body like electric energy. She walked faster now, keeping to the side of the road in case more riders appeared.

As the lane turned east, she began to see, and hear, things in the forest on her right—goblins perhaps, but she wasn't sure. A lone rider galloped by, but she saw him coming and crouched beside a tall fir tree as he passed, instinctively hiding from the horseman even though his eyes were blind to her. Finally, about a mile from where she had first emerged from the wood, the path straightened for a ways before plunging down in the distance. Several figures stood about the head of the trail: goblins with spears and two Easterners on horseback. Ulla scrambled into the brake on the southern side and crept slowly forward until she drew level with the horsemen. Looking down, she stared in wonder.

The path descended into a wide dell, which was mostly cleared of trees. Small *majas* and makeshift shelters filled the bowl of the dell. She saw black-garbed goblins everywhere—goblins cooking over firepits and emptying wagons, and goblins hammering away at spearheads, shields, or other bits of iron or gear of war as they prepared for their great assault. Across the dell, she spied a camp of men, where tall Easterners moved to and fro. Further still, she made out horses, picketed away from the men's tents. A stream trickled down a rocky fall and neatly bisected the bowl; figures, big and small, were busy drawing water and hauling it away. Ulla was looking at the main camp of the Army of Pohjola.

Not far from where she stood on the lip of the bowl, set in a sheltered spot where a few trees still stood, were several tents larger than any others. In the center stood a black tent, the largest, which reminded Ulla of Egan's tent at Nummela. Her heart sped up.

Surely this is the elf's tent—Tyë's tent—and whatever treasures he has must be inside!

She had to find a way in, and quickly. Ulla climbed down, slipping a bit on the steep, muddy slope, and finally, panting, drew near to the black tent.

Ulla approached it from behind, pausing for a moment to catch her breath. Whispering the incantation to herself over and over again, she carefully crept along one side until she came to the front and slunk into the shadow of a tall banner pitched into the soft, mossy ground. Level with the dell's floor now, she could see the bustle of the camp spread out before her. Just around the corner was the opening, curtains thrown wide, with two goblins who were taller than most, standing guard and holding long, black spears.

She heard voices and movement within, and almost turned away in fear and panic. But the strong will that had carried her through the snowy woods when her father disappeared, through all the days of her life as an orphan in Grankulta, and along the bitter road of the flight of the Karhulaiset—that same steadfast will carried her now.

She set her jaw and closed her eyes; when she opened them again, her mind was made up. Child though she was, she did what she had come to do.

The little girl with dark hair took a deep breath and darted past the loathsome sentinels into the tent. It was very bright inside, with a dozen tall candles illuminating the tent and casting long shadows all about. She felt naked, exposed; she glanced about frantically for her own shadow, but saw none. The opaque web still covered her, even in the light, and she stood unseen amidst her enemies.

Two men sat to one side on stools: Easterners, their black boots wet and muddy. The older one's dark hair was streaked with grey, and he wore bands of gold around his wrists and arms, and golden rings in his ears. Their faces seemed weary.

In the very middle of the tent was a round table of rough-hewn wood, set with various objects, and about it stood several tall elves—the Haltiatar of Löhi. They looked little different than the elves Ulla had met in the Enchanted Valley. They had long, narrow faces, dark locks hanging to their shoulders, and the multifaceted eyes of the Erilaiset. She moved around them, watching carefully, and listened as they spoke in their strange tongue that she could not understand. They pointed and gestured at something—perhaps a map—that lay upon the table.

As she circled them, she thought that one in particular resembled Lúven: a dark-eyed elf with a deep blue cloak. She wondered if it was Tyë; she wished that Väinämöinen was with her or that she was a strong warrior like Ilkka and could strike him down. The elf suddenly straightened, turned, and looked directly at her, a strange expression on his face. The little girl almost cried out, but checked herself and dashed through one of the gauzy screens that divided the tent into chambers.

She found herself in a large, central chamber partitioned off by heavy drapes. She immediately thought of Väinämöinen's home at Väinölä. A large alder tree rose up from the ground and straight out of the tent's canopy, with cunning lamps hanging from its lower branches. Fair tapestries adorned the drapes, and precious objects of gold or carven wood were displayed on small wooden tables. Beside a low bed, a suit of black mail was arrayed upon a stand. Next to it was a strange thing: an instrument shaped like Väinämöinen's kantele, yet somewhat different and with fewer strings. But, of all the oddities, a small white box on a round table by the bed drew in the little girl the most.

Ulla reached out and touched it; the box was cold, its hard, alabaster face unblemished as if it were chiseled out of a single piece of pure white stone. No line or mark marred its beauty, no design or device could be seen upon its flawless surfaces. She touched it, sliding her hand back and forth over the cool stone. A tingling came over her arm and a chill spread straight through to her fingertips. To her surprise, a faint line appeared. A lid popped up, revealing a hidden space within. Ulla gasped, for the alabaster box was not empty. She gazed in wonder at the shining piece of glass inside. Against all odds, she had found Tyë's jewel!

Ulla picked it up. At once, she felt a great weariness come over her, as if the jewel had drained her strength and will. Though not large, it felt very heavy in her little hand. But it was beautiful. Star-shaped, with seven identical rays, its face was smooth and clear like untroubled water, and it reflected the light cast upon it in the palest hue of pink. The rays were sharp and skillfully wrought, yet its nether side was rough, even jagged—for though Ulla had no way of knowing it, the glass had once been set in gold and worn as a talisman of power. But that was long ago.

She clutched the jewel like a greedy child, then quickly buried it in a pocket inside her Karelian shirt. She was relieved when she saw it disappear under the shadowy weave; the Cloak hid the jewel as well. Replacing the lid on the alabaster box, Ulla hesitated, just for a moment. Then, with a deep breath, she ran from the curtained chamber straight through the tent without so much as a glance at the elves, raced past the goblins with their long spears, rounded the next corner, and scrambled up the slope that led back to the road. Ulla half-expected to hear an alarm raised as she struggled up the steep rise, using her knees and hands as much as her feet, but there was nothing—nothing except the buzz of the great camp behind her, still oblivious to the little stranger within its midst.

When she reached the road, Ulla rested a while in the moss and bracken, hiding among some fallen trees. The mists had cleared, though the sky was still dark. It seemed a very long time since she had left Linnavuori, though it had actually been less than two hours. The little girl's head hurt and she could feel the electric charge of the spell she had cast wearing off. She realized with a start that she could clearly see the green of her shirt, the red of her now torn boots, and her long, muddy hair; her kerchief was long gone. The Cloak was unraveling.

A sinking feeling swept over her, fear mingled with despair, and she clenched her fists. She sang the *loitsu*, louder this time despite the danger of unfriendly ears.

> *"Weave a cloak around my body,*
> *shroud to cover arms and shoulders.*
> *Legs be hid from eyes unfriendly,*
> *spin for me the hidden mantle."*

The same chill surged up her spine and her hair stood on end, but it did not feel as strong as before, not as sharp. Ulla moved through the trees a ways until the horsemen and goblins, still on the path, had dwindled in the distance. Climbing back onto the road, she plowed forward, temples throbbing and head cast down, in a desperate race back to the hill fort before her strength—and the spell—gave out.

Ulla thought about plunging into the woods on the left, though she guessed there were enemies within, so she could come out onto the open field near Linnavuori's northern approach. But she would have to cross a mile or more of open field between the tree line and the fort in that direction; she knew she would never make it without being spotted if the spell wore off. So she retraced her steps, hoping to come closer to the place on Linnavuori's western wall where Kirsikka waited, but all the while she grew more tired, weaker. Her eyes began to flutter.

As the Army of Pojhola moved into place and tightened its grip on the beleaguered folk inside Linnavuori, traffic on the road increased. Small groups of horsemen rode past, but none seemed to see Ulla. Out of sight, where the ground sloped away from the road, Ulla flattened herself against the ground as they rode by. Then she heard a commotion behind her, a large troop of Hiisia hurrying to some predetermined position. She peeked out when they drew near: row after row, their wicked faces unique, but all with an expression of hate or of mischief. Short, curved scimitars hung from the goblins' belts, and some carried spears tipped with black iron. An officer walked down the line, barking orders in a foul tongue that Ulla could not understand, passing only a few feet from her hiding place. The goblin's face was like a frightful mask, an evil visage from some terrible nightmare fantasy. When it came close to her, she almost cried out despite herself.

Finally they were gone, and she climbed back onto the road. But Ulla didn't go far before weariness and pain overwhelmed her. Beyond the bend, where she had nearly been run down by the Easterners before, she stopped. There were enemies all about, but looking south and east, she thought that she could see the tree line and wisps of smoke rising from inside the distant fort. Ulla realized it was now or never; she closed her eyes and breathed deeply.

The little girl left the raised highway and moved down into the woods, her muddy boots slipping on the wet turf and slick, mossy stones. Goblins were everywhere. The line of watchers that she had slipped through earlier was still there, but many others had joined them to stand about the forest in small groups. They held their spears pointed up to the sky, and some had quivers slung on their shoulders and small bows made of horn or bone, like those used by hunters among the Bear Folk. A few were busy felling trees and chopping logs.

Not a one seemed to notice her as she tripped and stumbled over branches and stumps, like a feverish child with a swimming head, bumping about her *pirtti* at night looking for her mother. More by instinct than design, Ulla headed for a gap in the Hiisia's line. Shaking free of a pile of brushy fir that tore at her clothes and hair, she ran, putting all her strength into one last effort to get past the goblin soldiers and out of the woods.

A shrill voice cried out like an alarm bell, and Ulla knew that she had been spotted. She felt no power running through her limbs, no uncanny vigor propelling her forward or shielding her from unfriendly eyes. Tulikki's Cloak was gone; she was Ulla, the little girl from the north, and she was alone.

The goblin that had spotted her running pell-mell through the trees called to its companions. At least a dozen more immediately saw her, and started shrieking and shouting in turn. But the Hiissia were surprised; they had been on the lookout for spies or scouts creeping out from the hill fort—or even old Väinämöinen himself—not a mortal child running *toward* Linnavuori. They stood dumbfounded for several moments while Ulla ran on. She was almost out of the woods before one group finally gave chase.

Ulla crashed out of the trees and onto the grassy field just as the red sun of Midsummer's Eve finally dipped below the dark canopy of cloud that had shrouded Linnavuori all day long. Its light bathed the field in an eerie amber glow. Her breathing was ragged as she pumped her little legs as hard as she could, running toward the refuge and its safety.

She had come out of the woods somewhat east of the point where she'd entered. She was closest to the hill fort's northwest corner—where the wooden walls came together in a great V—but still more than half a mile away. The little girl lowered her head and aimed for the walls.

The goblins followed close behind her. When they reached the tree line, she was no more than fifty paces away. At a word from their captain, they stopped; two archers drew their bows and aimed for the mortal girl with wild, flying hair. The bows twanged and arrows loosed. Though Ulla never saw them, she felt the barbed shafts pass just above her shoulder and heard them vanish into the soggy grass ahead. She was a small target and the westering sun was in their white eyes; the next two arrows also missed their mark. The captain cried out again and three goblins took off in a sprint, chasing the little girl across the sodden field.

The soldiers wore black leather armour with heavy boots, and carried wooden bucklers at their backs: gear for fighting, not running. Ulla had a lead. It was a long way to Linnavuori, though, and she was, after all, just a little girl. They gained steadily.

Before she had come a third of the way, the foremost goblin was upon her, reaching out to grab her from behind. Ulla felt rather than saw the goblin, but was too far gone to care. Just then, as she came up over a sudden rise near a great, grey stone, she tumbled and fell, sending the Hiisi tumbling over, too. Recovering, it came at her with its knife, spittle flying from its gaping mouth. Ulla jerked her head violently to the left, then to the right. Twice, the goblin's knife just missed her and drove into the muddy ground. She screamed in terror as it raised the knife again, both hands wrapped around the hilt. Then, for the second time in her life, she heard a booming voice above her and saw a flash of white light from the corner of her eyes: Väinämöinen!

The old man stood over her, eyes blazing and a long, shining sword in his hand: *Jääpuikko*, the icicle of the Erilaiset. With one swift stroke, he cut down the goblin as it tried to scramble away. With another, he ran a second goblin through as it came running up close behind her. The third goblin, trailing its companions, had spotted him and drew a long knife from its leather belt. The Hiisi stopped short, shouted what sounded like a curse at the wizard in its own tongue, and then threw the knife like a dagger, aiming straight at his heart.

Väinämöinen swung his sword, knocking the knife away, then strode toward his foe. Whether it recognized its own death in the wizard's eyes or not, the black-garbed goblin didn't flinch. Ducking below Väinämöinen's first sweeping stroke, it reached for another blade at its belt, but the old man's next stroke didn't miss. The goblin fell dead, its dark blood staining the green grass as the white light faded.

Ulla had lain motionless throughout the short affray. When she tried to rise, the old man swept her up in his arms. She saw his horse standing beside the grey stone; Ilkka and two Wardens rode up bearing long spears. Väinämöinen hopped on his steed and set her before him. With a shout, they set off, galloping full speed back to Linnavuori while the cries of the Hiisia came to them from the trees.

The riders quickly reached Linnavuori's main gateway, where a makeshift barrier of old carts and hewn logs had been fashioned in place of a gate. Teemu and his wife waited there with Kirsikka and many others besides. Väinämöinen pulled his horse up and stopped just within the gateway. Dismounting, he pulled Ulla down and threw her to the ground with a violence that shocked the girl, exhausted as she was. Kirsikka cried out and rushed forward, but the old man held her back.

"What do you think you're doing, you foolish little scamp?" he cried. "Do you know how many people are looking for you? Risking their lives for you? Do you think this is all a game in the woods by your muddy village near the Marches? Have you not, child, in all these months, learned what you mean to us all? You are Tapio's chosen, the Child of the Prophecy, the child who bears the Mark of the Clan!"

His red, angry face twisted with anger. Ulla, already trembling, began to cry. No words came to her faltering lips, but she reached into her filthy, rent garment. From its pocket, she drew out a small bundle and something that glinted in the twilight. She let the bundle, along with the figures of her brother and herself, drop to the ground. In her shaking hand, she held up the jewel, and the faded daylight suddenly sparked it to life like a prism of a thousand colors.

The old man looked at her, then fell to his knees and took the star-shaped jewel from her tiny hand. He shook his head and sighed, but the angry color left his cheeks and the lines on his careworn face smoothed out. And then, still shaking his head, he broke into a smile.

Chapter Fifteen

The Army of Pohjola

In peaceful times, the longest day of the year called for celebration throughout the Far Northern Land. Feasts were held, and merry weddings celebrated with bright flowers and gay songs; bonfires burned throughout the short night. In the furthest north, in old Talvimaa—the land that became Pohjola in the time of the Witch—there was no night at all. For days on end, the summer sun never set. Its red orb hung over Sariola, the Witch's Keep, like a baleful talisman from Tuonela.

South, in the lands of the Seven Clans, there were a few hours of deep twilight before the new day dawned. The clans saw Midsummer's Day as a symbol of life and renewal, a sign of the earth's bounty, of the green forest's promise, and the blue water's riches, all of which gave hope to the folk of the north. To the Erilaiset, though, the children of the gods, midsummer was no mere symbol. Bound as they were to Ukko's creation, midsummer was life made manifest by the Vanhalaiset, whom they served long ago, and whom some served still.

Työ of the Haltiatar, Löhi's great captain, sat on his horse atop a rocky hillock and gazed across the wet fields at Linnavuori. Dusk deepened as the sun finally sank. Two elves on horseback sat upon his right, and two Itäläiset upon his left. Työ's long white cloak, clasped at the neck with a black garnet mined from beneath the Kääpiövuori Mountain far to the north, spread out behind him and faintly glimmered in the dusk. Tiny fires burned within Linnavuori. The great elf narrowed his dark eyes and reached out with his mind toward the hill fort. His will was strong, but Linnavuori was enmeshed in wizardly shadow, protected by a web of spells that defeated him, powerful sorcerer though he was. But Työ could sense a presence within that he knew well. Mind of steel, hand of iron, spirit of fire: the presence of Väinämöinen.

Työ knew Väinämöinen of old; they had walked together through the Far Northern Land when the world was young, and they were young, too. When Ilmatar soared in the blue skies with her white wings spread wide, and Tapio tramped through the woods shaking his shaggy beard, Työ was there as chief of a great *väki* of the Erilaiset and a lord among the Haltiatar. Long were the years and happy the hours for the Haltiatar then, as the grass grew green and the waters ran silver and blue.

But all things must end at their appointed time, and the world changed for Työ and the Erilaiset. The Vanhalaiset came less and less among them until, at last, the ancient ones' power merged with the elements themselves. Then came mortals into the world, and finally, the ancestors of the Seven Clans were cast upon the shores of the Itämeri Sea, where Työ and his *väki* dwelt beside the whitecaps of the ceaseless tide.

At first, even as Väinämöinen did, Työ took pity upon the mortals whom the heroes named the Kaamoslaiset, the People of the Dark—lost in a strange, harsh land without purpose or direction. The elf's magic was strong and his knowledge deep and subtle. He taught them many things, and for a time lived among the Kotkalaiset, showing them how to thrive in the western woods of the land that became known as Akkala.

As time passed, the Seven Clans increased, but the Erilaiset did not. The Seven Clans built towns and great cities, and ships to sail the seas. They felled trees, cutting down the southern woods, and always pushed north with their fields and farms. When the Haltiatar of the coasts were displaced, strife arose between them and mortal men. Työ and his folk fled their homes and dwelled in the deep woods in the north of Akkala.

Then there was Tulikki. For Työ greatly loved Mielikki's daughter: she of the long brown hair, clad in sewn leaves of the forest that never faded. They walked together beneath the forest's verdant canopy and skied the white trails of the Far Northern Land, and glad was the time that passed between them; in his smithy, Työ made a necklace for her, fashioned of gold and silver, and of such wondrous design that it was held the most beautiful thing in all the world.

But Tulikki, ever a friend to the mortals of the Seven Clans, would not turn her back on them. She quarreled with Työ, and, at last, left the western lands, returning to Karelia where her mother dwelt, and saw him no more. Then his heart hardened and became as cold as ice, and it was perilous for mortals to walk in the woods of Työ of the Haltiatar.

So it was that when Löhi first arose in flesh incarnate, he joined her, and throughout the Witch's War, he commanded her western armies. By then, he hated the clans and hoped the Witch would drive them into the sea. He won many victories for her, and instructed certain mortals among the Eagle Folk in the ways and arts of the dark sorcery of Pohjola. And Työ defeated Valtakkä, the great wizard of the Erilaiset, and threw him down, destroying all his folk. The elf commanded one wing of Löhi's army in the Great Battle, but on that day, the power of Pohjola was overthrown. Mighty Lemminkäinen defeated Löhi, and victory went to the Seven Clans.

Työ escaped with the last of his *väki* and fled far to the north. In a remote valley filled with snow-covered spruce trees, far west of Sariola, he made his dwelling. There, in lonely Kamala, he and his people lived for hundreds of years, abandoned and forgotten by the world, seldom dealing with other folk save for the dwarves in their inaccessible stony homes in the darkling mountains.

But Löhi only slept. When she awoke and whispered again like a voice on the wind, he reentered her service. Lamps were rekindled in dismal Sariola, and the Hiisia multiplied; trolls gathered from the lonely fells and evil spirits from Tuonela walked the earth. The Itäläiset were roused and marshaled. Now Tyë again led an army, crowned with victory, and this time there would be no Lemminkäinen.

Tyë had no illusions about Löhi; she was no goddess. She was mad, but her very madness gave her great strength. And if she styled herself as one of the Vanhalaiset, what did Tyë care? The old gods were faded and gone, and Ukko removed from the waking world; Tyë feared no divine retribution. Through Löhi, he would gain his vengeance and see the clans destroyed. Then he would dwell again by the shores of the sea, and the summer grass would grow amidst the mortals' ruins. The Easterners, cheated of their reward, could still rule the remnant of the Seven Clans—a helot folk and meanest race of the Far Northern Land.

That was yet to be. Now, he gazed across the wet field to Linnavuori. For the first time since High Länsimaa was broken and Keskimaa taken, he felt unsure. The great Haltia turned to the nearest Itäläinen, the chieftain Rusku, and spoke to him in the Easterner's own tongue.

"Have you heard from your companies that rode away at dawn?"

"Only this," said Rusku. "Messengers came back down the road before the rain stopped. The companies have ridden far and reached the first river; there is a ford. There was nothing on the road before them. But it is still a long way to the gap, and they may not reach it until midday tomorrow."

"And the others?" asked Tyë, referring to the riders who had gone north toward Valkeakosk days earlier, and were being summoned back.

"You would know best," the grey-haired chieftain said with a curious glint in his eyes. "But none from the Snake Clan have returned. They are still north, among the lakes, and we have no word of them."

With a last glance at Linnavuori across the way, Tyë turned his horse and descended a natural stair on the hillock's blind side; his companions trailed behind him, silent. At the bottom, they rode along the ridge of a long esker until their trail fell sharply down into the dell, where the camp lay hidden. Though the Army of Pohjola was scattered about the dell, the riders kept themselves apart from the Witch's goblins. The hardened

Easterners didn't fear the Hiisia as much as loathe them, but their horses became shy and restless around the goblin soldiers. When the signal came, however, they would march together wherever Työ led; their hatred for the Seven Clans gave them common cause.

Löhi's captain looked about as he rode through the camp, but he was deep in thought and vaguely troubled. His great army was splintered into several parts, spread out across wide lands. When he had taken Keskimaa, his mistress instructed him to remain there. The Bear Clan would be enslaved and subdued, and if any army from Etelamaa came north, Löhi's servants would meet them in High Länsimaa. But the summer was yet young, and Työ was bold. They were very near to Deep Länsimaa, and his scouts reported that the Elk Folk who lived there were scattered and weak. So Työ pressed on, unwilling to wait until next spring. Leaving half his force in Keskimaa, he drove west and invaded the land of the Hirvilaiset. He had sent some three hundred riders toward Valkeakosk, burning and pillaging whatever villages they found along the way, but soon learned that Teemu was in the south. So Työ had trapped him in Linnavuori. When that was taken and Teemu slain, all the land north of the Wall would be under his sway.

But still there was Väinämöinen, and a new king in Etelamaa besides. Väinämöinen was crafty and devious. Löhi had reached out to Työ and warned him of the approach of the Swan Folk. Egan had, indeed, made for Keskimaa at first, marching toward the *lansikita*. With the old wizard at Linnavuori leading the defense, the Witch guessed that Egan might come to his rescue instead. The great Haltia was in doubt. He planned to starve Teemu and his people while waiting for his northern force to return before assaulting the hill fort. Yet if the Swan Folk arrived in force, they might raise the siege and take shelter within, or Työ himself might become caught between two foes on open ground.

Just that morning, he had sent some two hundred Easterners toward the gap to contest any force out of Etelamaa so that he would not be taken unawares. But his *sight* had failed him and all had grown dark; the Witch's power waned at midsummer. Väinämöinen had cast spells all about Linnavuori and Egan's whereabouts were strangely shrouded.

Työ was not afraid, however. He was a great lord and powerful sorcerer, and his mistress had given him a precious gift: a piece of glass, cut and fashioned as if it were a jewel, with the pale light of the setting sun captured within. Made in ancient days by the great smith Seppo, it gave a wondrous *sight* to those in whom the old magic ran strong. Looking within, one might see things far away; it pierced night's darkness and the murky webs of wizards, for it was made in the far north when winter's gloom held sway. The jewel could not see everything; its reach faded and failed the further away one gazed. It required great strength, and the watcher might become spent and exhausted. It was very useful, however, and gave clarity that no wizardly *sight* could match.

All thought that Seppo's works had perished or been lost. Yet somehow the Witch had obtained this thing to give to her great captain when he rode south from Sariola. Työ had used it on the North Marches, and had seen the array of the Karhulaisen army; he had seen Pekka the Fat in his halls in Keskimaa as he ordered the last, futile defense of his city. He had seen the mortal Seer and had read her mind; only two days ago, Työ had peered within Linnavuori's walls. He knew the number of his foes and their weaknesses, and he had seen the old singer with his long white beard and bleary eyes.

All these things he had seen, but not the Etelalaiset, and it was Egan and his men that caused Työ's discontent. He resolved to take up the looking glass again, weary or no, and to find his enemies if they were near. Then he would determine his plan of attack.

Työ rode through the dell and across the stream. Many goblins had already left camp to fan out in the woods and await the signal to attack, but those that remained watched him with their white eyes. When Työ approached the black tent, several folk came forward, including a taller goblin clad in a hauberk of metal rings and with a long, curved scimitar at his side: Kauther, the captain of Työ's Hiisia. He would lead the goblins in the assault.

"All is ready, my lord," said Kauther in the harsh tongue of Pohjola as he took the horse's reins while Työ dismounted. "The legion can attack as soon as you give the signal. They have their weapons; only arrows are in short supply." The goblin licked his black lips and added, "They are eager, my lord."

"Are they?" asked Työ. "Then counsel them this; none are to move until I give the order! And I shall slay any without the wit to obey me. What have you seen before the hill fort?"

"No more have left since nightfall," answered Kauther. "The rest are still inside. We caught a man away yonder, but he had nothing new to say. There was yet another—a spy of some sort in the woods southeast. It fled back to the fort. It is hard to see across the way, my lord. The night is not dark, but this place is enmeshed in shadows."

"*Loitsu* of Väinämöinen," said Työ. "The old man is in there weaving his webs." The elf spat on the ground. "So be it. Bring this mortal to me; I will break him and read his mind, and then we shall see what he knows or doesn't know. But I must be alone now for some time."

Työ walked into the tent, but, as he crossed the threshold, he turned to a tall elf with a blue cloak draped across his shoulders.

"I can feel the spells and they are still strong," said Työ. "Keep them up, Vepsa! I do not trust the old fool of Taikalaakso."

"I will keep them up," said Vepsa. "But hasten to use the glass, if you would, and decide our course. There is something strange in the air and I do not like it. The winds have shifted, and other things besides."

"I feel this, too," said Työ. With a last glance back at his captains and chieftains, the Haltia strode into his private chamber.

The great elf was tired and weary. It was three months since he had ridden south from Sariola, leading the goblins out of the iron gate of the Witch's Keep while Löhi watched from the battlements. The Army of Pohjola had come hundreds of miles and fought two great battles. Now, poised for the third, Työ was wary. Despite his fatigue, he purposed to use the jewel, the magical glass that would pierce his enemies' spells and show him where the

Swan Folk were. He paused for a moment, considering his own dim reflection in the polished black mail by his bedstead, forged by the dwarves in their fiery smithies beneath the mountains of the north. Then he sighed and reached for the alabaster casket that held Löhi's precious gift.

The smooth white box had been made by Löhi herself. Wrapped about with magic spells so that only one who knew its secret might open it, its lock especially targeted the Great Ones of the Erilaiset. Työ moved his hand across its seamless face and opened it, revealing the hidden space within, but his eyes grew wide with astonishment. There was nothing inside, no star-shaped jewel set within the red velvet lining. The casket was empty.

Stupefied, he gazed at it like a stunned, slack-jawed child whose mother has just slapped his face for sins unknown. Then his eyes narrowed and his wrath blazed high. He threw the box to the ground with such force that it shattered.

How could this have happened? How could Väinämöinen the thief—for surely it was Väinämöinen—have come there, into his very chamber, and stolen his glass? The camp of the Pohjolaiset was set about with spells of ward and warning. No Erilainen, especially Väinämöinen, could come near without Työ and his chief servants knowing, no matter what shape they assumed. But Seppo's jewel was gone, even as the old man had stolen the Sampo of old from the very halls of Sariola!

Työ raged through the chamber, tearing down its curtains and upsetting the tables as if his fury alone might reveal the jewel and its thief. Then he stormed out of the tent to where his chieftains waited and clutched an elf who stood in wonder of his captain's distress.

"It is gone!" cried Työ. "The glass is gone! Stolen by the old fool of Taikalaakso! How came he here?!"

"But, my lord, no one has come here," stammered the elf. "We have neither seen nor felt a thing."

"Then where is it? What could have happened if it were not Väinämöinen or one of his friends?"

"He did not come here," said Vepsa, incredulous. "Neither flesh nor *etiänen* of Väinämöinen has been here. I would swear to it. But that does not mean all is right. A strange sense is all about."

"*Ka,*" cursed Työ. "A strange sense, and yet you stand about and do nothing? And now he can see our every move!"

Työ screamed at his servants, questioning and cursing them until the Hiisia cowered and covered their faces, the Itäläiset turned away, and the Haltiatar stood as one amazed. But still they did not find either the jewel or the thief.

The short night passed quickly, and a red dawn spread slowly in the eastern sky as the clouds broke up. At last, Työ mastered his wrath; his mood cooled and he grew cold and grim. Kauther brought to him the mortal man they caught earlier, a Warden from the Marches sent out as a scout—Laso, who had rescued Turi north of Gamla. But he could tell them nothing they did not already know, and Työ took him by the throat and strangled him.

Työ then gathered his captains and spoke to them as the morning light spread throughout the woods. "I will wait no longer. Let the attack begin at once. So what if the old man can see our strength? He can do nothing about it, and this time he will not escape the trap. Destroy all you find inside, even the women and children; take no captives or slaves. Every mortal within Linnavuori must die, and I want the Hirvilaisen lord's head brought to me as proof!"

Word went out and preparations were made. The Easterners formed to the southeast, where there was a broad opening in the forest; the goblins gathered in the woods to the west. And Työ summoned two great trolls, who came dragging the Hirvilaisen captives behind them. The trolls were not there for the battle, but the aftermath. Löhi had sent them, along with other evil things, to haunt the mortal lands and afflict the remnants of the clans who would dwell there as slaves or serfs. Tall and thin, with big noses and tiny eyes, the trolls had horny grey skin knotted with muscle, and their unkempt hair hung long behind them. The trolls walked some way out into the wet field, in plain view of Linnavuori, then cruelly slew their captives. At that signal, the Army of Pohjola began its assault.

The goblins, more than five hundred strong, moved out of the woods and marched toward Linnavuori's western wall. Their iron-tipped spears were as black as their banners; they cried out in the foul tongue of Pohjola as they went, cursing the mortal clans and seeking their doom. A line of archers went before them, ready to shoot anyone who appeared on the walls. As they marched, one group, perhaps a hundred all told, veered east to the fort's northern face and gate. Some fifty riders joined them there, and both men and goblins kindled arrows soaked in oil and shot them at the barrier across the gateway and at the carts and wagons piled before it. A sorcerer of Pohjola waited to help set the wet wood alight if he could. Työ deemed that most of Linnavuori's defenders would gather behind this gateway, so he wished to contest it fiercely, keeping them there as a ruse; but his main attack would fall upon the walls on either side.

Even without the riders sent to find the Swan Folk, Työ still commanded some four hundred Easterners. He kept a strong company in reserve to sweep the field and ride down any who might escape from the fort. Afterward, they would pursue and destroy those who had already fled across the river. But the remaining horsemen rode toward Linnavuori's eastern side and gathered beneath the earthen berm. They bore black and red banners marked with the symbols of their clans or the tokens of Pohjola, and their horses bore two men apiece, for they would fight this battle mostly on foot. While some grouped the horses together, the greater part dismounted and scaled the berm, ready to join battle with the defenders.

So the assault on Linnavuori raged and the fort was beset on all sides. Fires sprang up at the north gate and where the goblins attacked the western wall. But, although Löhi's army made a terrible din, all was uncannily quiet inside. The Elk and Bear Folk made no sign, save for a few arrows shot from atop the earthen wall, which felled the first Easterner to reach its height.

Along the western wall, the Hiisia shot flaming arrows, then gathered at the makeshift barrier that blocked the gap through which the carts had departed. They tore the barrier apart, and used iron chains to pull down a part of the adjacent wall, the rotten timber crashing in ruin. With the wall breached, the goblins poured inside, shrieking in dreadful cacophony like demons from Tuonela. They ran throughout the fort, seeking to slay and rend all they came across, even as they had done at Keskimaa.

Slowly, they realized that, although fires burned here and there among the *kotas* and rude buildings, and animals bellowed and bleated, there were no mortals to be found. The spears they had seen from outside had been set against the walls, but no hand held them, no foe was there to challenge them. The goblins' howls and laughter faltered amidst the emptiness and eerie silence. Behind them, fire quickly spread along the walls despite the dampness, and the gap they had come through was soon choked with flame and thick black smoke.

The Easterners came over the berm and saw three men fleeing. Two they stopped with black-feathered arrows shot into their backs; the third disappeared round a makeshift wooden *maja*. The Easterners gathered into bands, and with their swords drawn, ran through the hill fort just as the goblins had. To their wonder, they found no one else. Linnavuori seemed deserted.

At the northern gateway, where horsemen and goblins had forced their way into the hill fort, great flames, blue and yellow, suddenly shot high into the sky, while red fire spread across the wall. Acrid smoke boiled and fumed, rolling back within the walls. Both men and goblins were scalded and overcome by the fumes. The Army of Pohjola looked about and saw that it was trapped within a burning fort. The Witch's soldiers, so confident when they left the cover of the woods to begin their attack, began to panic, running this way and that, seeking a way out of the flaming fortress.

Löhi's captain sat atop the hillock and gazed at Linnavuori across the green field. The darkness that had shrouded it, even after sunrise, had lifted. He watched the fires burn high and smoke climb into the sky. His soldiers, now inside, should be killing their mortal enemies, striking down the men and butchering their families in retribution for the thief's great affront. With his sorcerer's ear, Työ could hear the crackling flames, but not his enemies' cries of despair.

Strange, very strange. Strange, too, were the colored flames, clearly of wizardly design. It seemed they might consume the place and doom all within, Pohjolaiset and Kaamoslaiset alike.

Several riders had left the blazing gateway and were madly galloping back, doubtless with messages from his chieftains. But at that moment, even as Työ rose in his stirrups to train his magical gaze upon Linnavuori, there came shrill horn blasts from the southwest; others soon answered from the southeast. A mass of men came into view before the western wall, and, as Työ stared on in amazement, another company approached the earthworks from the east. Väinämöinen had sprung his trap at last.

For when Ulla had returned with the jewel, Väinämöinen knew his enemy was blind. He recalled a trick he had played long ago, when beset by his enemies in a similar situation. First he turned the looking glass upon his foes, learning their strength and guessing their plans. Then he wove his strongest spells to make a gloom all about them; when darkness fell, he led the gathered folk, Hirvilaiset and Karhulaiset, to a place in the southern wall that was made of stone, where water spilled out of a culvert and splashed down a rocky stair to the water channel below. The opening was large enough for men to pass through. The stair sloped outward, so Väinämöinen and Ilkka helped the people pass through and half-slide, half-climb down to the river's edge. In this way, they emptied Linnavuori, save for some few brave men who stayed behind to help the old wizard and keep up the appearance that the hill fort was still manned.

The sheds within Linnavuori held many barrels of tar and pitch, for the people of the area burned pine tar and traded it with the Hare and Swan Folk to the south. The old wizard instructed the defenders to pour pitch on the barriers at the gateway and western wall, and then wove a spell to ignite it all like a great, flaming candle. Then, while the women and children crossed the shallow water, the men hid in the reed beds along the river's edge to pass what remained of the cold, miserable night and uncertain dawn. When Löhi's army finally attacked, the men listened to the wailing cries above and shivered in the muddy reeds. Then Väinämöinen appeared to lead them out again. With

Teemu, he took half their number up the steep slope to the western gap where the goblins had gone, while Ilkka led the others round to the east.

So they gathered, and Ilkkas's men shot arrows into the horse herd at the foot of the berm to startle them. They slew or drove off the guards, scattering the horses. But, within the burning walls of Linnavuori, the frightened Itäläiset and Hiisia saw the gateway blocked by fire; without order, they spilled out any way they could.

The Easterners gained the berm's height and came tumbling down its outer face, where Ilkka's archers rained arrows down on them. Those who reached the foot unscathed were cut down with axes and clubs. On the western side, the goblins forced their way through the flames and charged at the gathered men, mad with anger and blinded by smoke, fire and fury. The goblins were hideous in their frenzy and, if not for the old wizard, the defenders would have broken and run away.

But Väinämöinen steadied them, crying out in a great voice that rang across the field, "Stand, men of the clans! Stand and fight! No foe from dismal Northland can defeat us on Midsummer's Day! Stand and fight, and do not be afraid!"

Bows twanged as the goblins advanced. Väinämöinen's long sword *Jääpuikko* rose and fell until it was black with the blood of his enemies. Teemu stood beside him, along with other lords of the Elk Folk, and they rallied their men as they cut down the goblins emerging from the blazing gap. The goblins panicked, caught between fire and foes, and ran right into the waiting lines of their enemies.

With whatever weapons they had, the Elk Folk slew them. Goblin bodies lay all about, some smoldering from the blaze, but the Hiisia still outnumbered the Hirvilaiset. At length, the goblins made a space before their enemies and gathered beneath the flaming wall. The glow of the fire reflected in their empty eyes, and they drove against the mortal men with iron-tipped spears and swords. The fighting was fierce, but men began to fall and slowly give way before the goblins' assault.

To the east, the Itäläiset came together. Although many had been killed, they were a warlike folk and fought with great courage. Those who remained attacked the clans, striking them down with their cruel, curved swords and cutting a path away from the berm toward a half-ruined dike. They rallied there, and some managed to catch and master a few loose horses. The Easterners, too, had escaped from the trap.

The battle now turned against the clan folk, the hunters and farmers who had never held a sword before, but were now locked in deadly strife with the might of Pohjola. Väinämöinen found Teemu in the midst of the carnage and shouted to him above the uproar.

"Gather your folk, Teemu; let us draw off to the north or else we shall be destroyed. Sound your horns and call on Ilkka so that we may join together before the gateway. Whatever hope we have lies that way. The flames should have trapped our enemies within, but now all is uncertain."

The horns blew, and answering calls came from across the way. The men of the clans withdrew from their foes and, from east and west, gathered in one mass before the smoldering gateway. The ruined fort offered some measure of protection against attacks from behind, but it could also act as the anvil to the hammer of Työ's army. Väinämöinen knew they might only be gathering to their doom. If so, he still hoped to make a last stand and kill as many enemies as possible. The longer they fought, the better chance the women and children had to escape, and even in death, they could aid the Swan Folk who might come afterward.

The goblins and Easterners used the respite to reform their own ranks. Soon they came against the men of the clans with renewed fury.

Työ watched the battle from his hillock. Väinämöinen's trickery inflamed his hatred for the Kaamoslaiset; it grew to madness as he watched his army grievously reduced. How could this have happened? Only short hours before, he had been poised for a victory so complete that all of Deep Länsimaa would have been his, and half of the Far Northern Land under the Witch's yoke. Now it would not be—not yet!

He might defeat the Hirvilaiset and slay their lord, but his own loss was great, and he still had to consider the Swan Folk; there was no choice but to withdraw to Keskimaa. And as for Väinämöinen, he had no doubt the old man would flee, saving his skin at the last moment. But if he fell into Työ's hands, the elf would not kill him. He would stop his mouth with spells, bind him with unseen chains, and return with him to Pohjola. Löhi could have him and punish him slowly and terribly, as only she, the cruelest and most powerful of Ukko's children, could.

The elf saw his chance as the battle moved to the middle of the field. He turned to Rusku.

"Take your company onto the field," he commanded. "It is time to finish this. And when you have broken them, chase down those who flee until none are left alive. I will come myself to deal with Väinämöinen if he stays to fight."

The Itäläinen bowed his head, then called to his men: more than a hundred riders who stood nearby. The last of Työ's reserves were a picked guard from a great clan of the east, their brown horses swift and sure-footed, and their red and black banners snapping in the brisk summer breeze. With a shout, the Easterners moved out of the woods. They formed two parallel lines as they rode toward Linnavuori, passing wounded kinsmen making their painful way back to the camp.

As they neared the fight, at a word from Rusku, they reformed and fanned out into a solid front ready to charge. Looking up and down the line, the Easterner drew his sword. As one, his men did the same. Rusku nodded to the rider next to him. The man raised a great horn to his mouth and let loose a blast—a rich, rising note to warn the men and goblins before them to make way for their assault. The note faded, the riders tensed for their command—and suddenly answering calls rang out from the southeastern woods.

Everyone on that field—Itäläinen and Hiisi, Hirvilainen of Länsimaa and Karhulainen from afar, and Wardens from all the Seven Clans—turned his head. In the distance, horsemen spilled onto the grass. Riders came pouring from the road that led from the *lansikita* and galloped hard toward the hill fort.

Many Easterners cheered, for they deemed their comrades had returned to lend their weight to the attack. And they were glad; it would be no battle now, but a slaughter of their remaining enemies on the open field. But sharp-sighted Ilkka sat on a horse near some other riders: all they had with which to contest the Itäläiset. The Warden gazed at the onrushing horsemen and saw no banners from the east. These riders bore white and blue pennants, and carried long lances. At their head rode a warrior with a lofty helm and the image of a swan on his breastplate.

Ilkka raised his clear voice above the fray and cried, "The Folk of the Swan are come! Men of the clans, lift your heads! The Etelalaiset are come!"

So came Egan and the Swan Knights to the Battle of Linnavuori. They had ridden hard for several days with Taika of the Erilaiset guiding them through the hills and around the rivers and lakes. The Easterners on the road never saw them. As the morning came on, the Etelalaiset had spied smoke from afar and raced toward it as swiftly as possible.

When Rusku saw enemies instead of kinsmen, he barked an order and his riders wheeled round to meet them. Had their numbers been greater, the Easterners might have made a running ring around their foes, for their horses were light and swift. By wearing out the great horses of the Etelalaiset, burdened with armoured men, they might have attacked them in quick sorties until they were overcome—but they had not the numbers.

Egan drew his sword and signaled the charge. Without slackening their pace, they crashed into the Easterners' line. Sword rang on sword; lances and bitter spears found their marks. The Swan Folk drove straight through the Itäläiset, and as the ghastly sound of screaming men and horses filled the air, the Etelalaiset turned, staying together, and drove through their foes yet again. The Easterners were fierce warriors, but lightly armed and armoured, they were no match for Egan's cavalry. Dozens were slain and the remnant fled, riding wildly toward the safety of the forest.

Then a great shout went up over the battlefield and the men of the clans drove against Löhi's servants. The Swan Knights reformed and joined the attack, and the Easterners and goblins were beset on all sides.

Away on the hillock, atop the empty camp, Vepsa turned to Tyë, his voice grim. "Let us leave this place. The field is lost. We should gather what riders we can from the wreck and send word to those guarding the pass. Let us withdraw to the Blue Lake, and there await the sundered companies. There we may also seek Löhi and learn what to make of the Etelalaiset and this new king who leads them."

But Tyë's eyes betrayed his wrath and unbridled hatred; his great pride overwhelmed him, clouding his keen mind. He said no word to Vepsa, but, with a sudden start, spurred his horse straight down the hillock, jumping over stones and fallen trees. He crashed out of the woods and onto the field. The elves of his guard shouted warnings, but to no avail; and so they followed him, chasing after his black horse as he rode madly toward the battle.

His magic was great and his will strong. Wrapped in spells, he rode straight at Väinämöinen with his white cloak flying behind him; he knew without a doubt where the old wizard was, despite the press. Riders of Etelamaa tried to bar his way, but he cut them down. When Satou, Chief of the Knights of the Swan, came before him, Tyë dealt him a deadly blow. Trampling friend and foe alike, at last he spotted Väinämöinen and launched his attack with words of doom on his lips.

Väinämöinen saw his enemy riding hard at him. Victory or no, he knew his own death might be near. He had no time to sing a proper spell or incantation, and, in any case, the fires of his wizardry burned low. He was exhausted after all his efforts. Even were he fresh and strong, Tyë was great among the Erilaiset and might prove mightier.

The elf charged. The old man felt a terrible power wrapping itself around him, but Löhi's captain had made one mistake. Blinded by rage, he had woven spells of protection around himself, but not his mount. While Väinämöinen could not bind Tyë, he could bespell the unprotected horse. Weak though he was, he uttered one word ere his voice was stopped, tying the animal's legs with unseen cords. The beast stumbled and screamed, crashing to the ground. Tyë pitched onto the bloodstained earth with violent force.

A mortal's body would have been broken by such a fall, his life extinguished in an instant, but the great among the Erilaiset were not so easily dispatched to Tuonela. His shoulder crushed, his face bloodied and marred, Tyë rose from the ground like a black ghost from Hell. He raised his sword, and, with a cry of hatred, sprang at Väinämöinen, beating him back until the old man stumbled beneath the assault.

Flames flickered about the elf's blade, *Pohjanpiiki*, which had slain many heroes of old. He shouted words of power and destruction in the old tongue, piercing his enemy's wizardry to bind him, render him defenseless. No longer did the lord of the Haltiatar seek to take the old man to Löhi. In his terrible wrath, he wished only to kill him. With all his evil will bent on his ancient foe, Tyë prepared the final stroke.

Väinämöinen, now in his enemy's power, could do nothing. He looked up; Tyë's flaming sword hung above his head.

But Tyë stopped midstroke, a look of sudden wonder spreadacross his face. Crimson blood poured from his lips. The elf sagged to his knees and collapsed in ruin at Väinämöinen's feet.

For Egan, King of the Folk of the Swan, stood where the Haltia had been. Having run up behind him, brandishing the blade of mighty Lemminkäinen that cut through magic and iron alike, Egan had pierced Tyë's heart.

Egan had spotted the mail-clad sorcerer across the field and raced to Väinämöinen's aid. When his own horse shied and would not come near the dark warlock, the young king had slid from the saddle. Running to his friend, he silently slipped behind them. With the elf's madness fixed upon the wizard, he thrust the Sword of Legend, Lemminkäinen's *Tarunmiekka*, forged by Ilmarinen the Smith himself in days of old, straight through him.

Egan tore off his helm and helped the old man up. Together they stood over Tyë's ruined body while the battle yet raged around them.

"I said there was a light in you," Väinämöinen said weakly, leaning on the boy. "I was right. But what a light! You have saved us all, my king—for a king you are, and were always meant to be. You have saved my life, too, Egan. I will ever be your friend in need."

Egan smiled, a wide, gleaming smile, and clasped the old singer by the arm. "No, Lord Väinämöinen. Your counsel brought me here and helped me choose wisely; your strength brought all this to pass. But let us win the field ere we speak more of this. There are yet foes to fight!"

Then Egan mounted his horse and returned to the battle, but Tyë's guard were slain or scattered, and all the Pohjolaiset routed. When the goblins saw Tyë's ruin, they fled in terror, casting aside their swords and running for the woods. The Swan Folk hunted them down, chasing them wherever they fled, and the field before Linnavuori was strewn with their dead.

But it was still high summer, and the day was long ere the sun finally set on the smoldering ruins of Linnavuori.

Chapter Sixteen

The Harvest of the Erilaiset

There was much to be done in the days following the battle. The women, children, and wounded men returned, and when the burning embers at last died out, they went back inside Linnavuori's ruins and began its repair.

Ulla and Kirsikka had hidden on a small islet in the midst of the river during the fight. Taika, ready to spirit them away if things went ill, had found them there. Ulla soon fell sick; drained after her great feat of stealing Työ's jewel, she lay in a fever, her pale skin flushed and pink. Yet the little girl was strong. Taika tended her, and so did Väinämöinen. As she had after the bear attack, she swiftly recovered. Kirsikka never once left her side.

Turi also recovered, though he was very weak. When they brought him back to Linnavuori, the mage still wandered in a delirium and would not awaken. Väinämöinen came to him, and despite his own hurts and exhaustion, stayed with him. He used what healing magic he still possessed, which grew as the Witch's dark thought faded from the lands about Linnavuori. A great burden lifted from all of their hearts. At last, Turi heard Väinämöinen calling him and shook off his fugue. Leaving the pale woods behind, he turned his back on the dark river that marked Tuonela's border and returned to living lands. He opened his eyes to see friends beside him, and all hearts were glad.

Turi had dreamed many strange things as he wandered those woods, however, and urged Väinämöinen to go to Kyöpelinvuori and seek the Seer again as quickly as possible.

The danger had not all passed, and there were yet many plans to consider. The goblins were mostly destroyed, save for some that escaped the field to haunt the woods and roam the barren places of Deep Länsimaa. A great fire was made and their corpses burned within it, the charred bones and ashes thrown into a pit with a mound raised above it. Men called it the *hiidenkiuas*, and ever after feared to linger there. The bodies of the dead Itäläiset were buried in a deep pit along Linnavuori's eastern side, however, along with those who had fled on foot into the wild and perished. Those who survived became outlaws in the forest, troubling the Elk Folk that winter.

Only a handful ever returned to Keskimaa to rejoin their kinsmen. The men of the Seven Clans spared the wounded Easterners and those who had thrown down their arms—only a score at most—but old Väinämöinen kept the Hirvilaiset from slaying them afterward in their anger.

So it was with the Army of Pohjola; but no few had fallen among the clans, either. Satou of the Etelalaiset was slain, and Amrod, who had marched with Kallas, and many knights and horsemen besides. Laso the Warden was dead, and Teemu's counselor, Hannu, was cut down by the Hiisia. Teemu himself had been wounded in the shoulder and arm. Many who fought on that field were slain or wounded; when the women of the Elk Folk returned, they sang laments and wept tears of grief and sorrow, for the cost of victory is always high, and there is little thought of rejoicing among the mangled bodies and broken dreams attendant on battle and war. It is only later, when time has passed and songs are made, that it may seem glorious to recall; yet it is chiefly those who have not shared the pain and terror who would revel in the telling.

There was little time to mourn, however. A large force of Easterners remained on the road between Linnavuori and the *lansikita*, and others were posted northeast near the Blue Lake. Egan and Ilkka worried that these riders might unite and possibly outnumber them. But scouts soon returned with good news.

The horsemen who had ridden toward Valkeakosk were gone. When their kinsmen who fled the disaster at Linnavuori reached them, they turned east and made their way back to Keskimaa.

The riders Työ sent to meet the Swan Folk near the gap were less fortunate. Lost and leaderless in unfamiliar land, they fled when the main force of the Etelalaiset appeared. They split into many bands, as was their wont, and tried to pick their way through the lakes and trees back to High Länsimaa. Some found their way in the end, but many were never seen again, having died alone, famished and exhausted in the deep forest, or slain by wrathful Hirvilaiset and Karhulaiset.

A week after the battle, on a day with blue skies, Juvari reached Linnavuori with the main army of the Swan Folk: a thousand men-at-arms, for even more soldiers had joined them from Etelamaa's northern parts. They made a great camp on the bloodstained field before the hill fort, and Egan was reunited with his uncle and counselors.

More Hirvilaiset from the surrounding lands joined them, too, and Linnavuori swelled with people and animals. When Ulla was well, she and Kirsikka ran about with the many children who had arrived. The girls were happy now that they knew that Väinämöinen would not leave them.

They all remained in the camp for several weeks, while the wounded healed and Teemu saw to the ordering of the nearby lands, for the invasion had disrupted the growing season. It would soon be time for harvest, or the people would starve. Men and women needed to cut the rye, tie it into sheaves, dry it in the fields, then carry it to the threshing barns. At last, they made a great council of war, gathering all the chief leaders together: King Egan and Juvari, Teemu and his nobles, Ilkka, and, of course, the Erilaiset, Väinämöinen, Turi, and Taika.

Väinämöinen spoke to the lords first, sharing his counsel. "It is now high summer, and we have recovered from Löhi's first onslaught. But do not think that she can be defeated so easily. This was only her first move; she did not intend to destroy the clans all in one season. We have indeed won a victory, and the king has slain the Witch's champion, who would have enslaved these lands and ruined its folk. That was a great deed, and someday many songs shall rightly be sung about it. But this struggle is only beginning.

"There are Seven Lands and Seven Clans, and I fear we shall have seven years of war before us. We may see many defeats, even if somehow we gain victory in the end, for Löhi will not be brought down by the swords of men or Erilaiset alone. But let us have hope! The Child of the Prophecy is with us, a sign unto all the clans. And all here know what she has done for us, she who bears the Mark of the Clan, Ulla of the Karhulaiset. Truly, she is the chosen of the Vanhalaiset, and a child of the gods."

"But what should we do now, Lord Väinämöinen?" asked Teemu. "Forge weapons, gather food, and await the Witch's next assault?"

"That might be wise," answered Väinämöinen. "The world is changing. Ukko will bring a new age to this ancient earth, and the great among the Erilaiset can feel it. The Vanhalaiset will always be here, for theirs is the strength of the earth itself and all natural things therein. But long have the Erilaiset dwindled, and perhaps our time runs toward its end. So, too, it is with Löhi. She can surely feel this, and knows her time runs as swiftly as the sand slips through the hourglass. If her magic and will are to triumph and order the world as she would, she must not wait too long or tarry overmuch. If the clans can unite and weather the assault, she will fail and fade, even as winter gives way to spring, and to summer afterward. But we must prepare and not be idle!

"And, as for now, Teemu, Työ is dead and many of Löhi's servants have been destroyed, but she has others. She has accomplished much and done great harm to the clans, even without winning the Battle of Linnavuori. High Länsimaa is laid waste, and Keskimaa yet occupied by enemies; the Bear Folk suffer under the Easterners' yoke. The Itäläiset cannot be allowed to fortify Keskimaa and make it their dwelling. My counsel is that the army camped on this field should move on Keskimaa while the summer lasts, and take it from the enemy."

"That will be a great battle," said Ilkka. "There are still many Easterners in the city. Would it not be best to wait and gather our strength while winter takes its toll, then retake Keskimaa after the thaw?"

"More enemies will have come by then," said Väinämöinen. "And winter will take its toll on the Bear Folk, too. We cannot stand by idly while they suffer and perish, not if we have any strength ourselves. In such counsel lies the Witch's hope."

So they agreed to do as Väinämöinen advised; they made preparations for the army to march on Keskimaa. Messages went out to all the clans, telling them what had transpired. Scouts were sent to High Länsimaa to spy on the Easterners and give hope to the Bear Folk. Teemu gathered what men he could, chiefly archers and horsemen, and the army made ready to leave: some thousand men on foot and perhaps ten score of horsemen, as great a force to challenge Löhi's minions as they could muster.

Try as he might, though, Väinämöinen's *sight* failed him. He could not reach Keskimaa with his mind; even after many weeks, his wizardry had not recovered from his mighty efforts in the battle. Turi struggled in the same way, and Taika's sight was not so long, nor could the jewel see so far as Keskimaa with any clarity.

They had not yet left Linnavuori when they received tidings from High Länsimaa—tidings as welcome as they were unexpected. The Easterners had quit Keskimaa and ridden to the White Road, presumably making for the Marches and the Wastes beyond, from whence they came.

Spies reported that the Easterners had learned of the Battle of Linnavuori and Työ's downfall, the deaths of their kinsmen, and of Egan and his army from Etelamaa. They guessed—rightly—that they would soon be assailed. The Easterners were still strong despite their losses, but loath to fight again at Keskimaa. Even if they prevailed, their own loss would be great. They would be alone in the midst of their enemies with winter coming on. So they abandoned Keskimaa, burning much of the town ere they left and taking many slaves with them.

Some of the slaves later returned home and told how Löhi's servants met the Easterners on the North Road, bearing news of the Witch's wrath at their flight, for she had instructed them to remain in Länsimaa and fight. She cared nothing for spoils and plunder, only the destruction of her enemies, and she had planned for Keskimaa to become the base from which even more attacks were launched, until all the Seven Clans were ruined.

Väinämöinen made new plans then. Juvari and Alder continued to Keskimaa with many men to succor the folk there and help them prepare for the long winter soon to come. But Väinämöinen felt the need to go to Kyöpelinvuori, as if he had been summoned. Turi and Taika felt the same. Egan, too, resolved to go with them; the young king wished to hear the Seer for himself. If Egan could not feel the strange, urgent compulsion that troubled the minds of the Erilaiset, his curiosity was stoked, and he did not wish to part so soon from his friends.

The Elk Folk cheered when they finally set out for Kyöpelinvuori. King Egan rode with six Knights of the Swan, and Teemu with six Guards of Deep Länsimaa, and Ilkka with three green-clad Wardens. The Erilaiset rode with the two little girls at their head. Never in all the long years had so many great lords gone together to Tavastia. Speedy riders went on before them to herald their coming.

The little group rode across the Clearwater and south through the tumbled hills into the Neck of Tavastia. Folk marveled at their company, at Väinämöinen's long, snowy beard, and Turi's wise, piercing eyes, and the young king's proud face and bright armour.

They also marveled at Ulla. The story of the child with the Mark of the Clan had spread like wildfire across the land. Some said she was a witch herself, and had flown like a bird into the enemy's camp to spy on them. Others said she had slipped into the enemy's camp at night and smitten their captain to death with his own black sword. Still others came nearer the mark and told how she had stolen a magic jewel and brought it to Väinämöinen, who used it to destroy a host of foes. But all eyes watched her as she bounced along on the old wizard's horse, holding onto a birch strap, her long hair flying freely behind her.

On a golden afternoon with a bright sun and a warm breeze, they came round a bend and saw Kyöpelinvuori before them. The old mottled tower rose up from its rocky height, streaked with white and beckoning all from miles around; on such a day in the Far Northern Land, even that haunted hill seemed fair and welcoming.

They passed the *pirttis* and tilled fields and climbed up the hillside, three times round. As they neared the top, a strange sight awaited them. Väinämöinen had expected to find only a few people—the Seer's servants or perhaps some peasants and serfs with carts full of goods to deliver. As they came round the final bend, however, they heard a commotion of voices. Many folk waited among the crumbled stone and ruined walls, and the Seer herself, robed in black, leaned on her wolf-headed crutch in their midst. She smiled at them, her thin lips tight and pursed, but made a slow, sweeping gesture of invocation.

"Welcome, my lords," she said. "And to you, Lord Väinämöinen, welcome back. Look round you and see the fruits of your labor! Three days ere midsummer, the first arrived, and the last only yesterday. They are here to learn the songs."

Then Väinämöinen did indeed look around. He saw that the people were not the Seer's servants, nor villagers of the Hare Folk from the lands nearby, but a diverse lot: young and old, rich and poor, men and women alike.

While war had raged throughout Länsimaa, Mielikki sat in her garden, putting forth her strength and calling on her father. Strange dreams and a burning compulsion came to chosen folk across the Far Northern Land. They left their cottages and houses, families and kin, and, as surely as birds knew where to fly when the air turned chill, they made for Kyöpelinvuori—though they knew not why. Woodman of Karelia, farmer of the Elk Folk, daughter of Akkala, and trader from the coasts of Etelamaa: in them, Mielikki sowed the seed that would make the Old Ways again the ways of the Seven Clans.

Väinämöinen dismounted, marveling as he wandered about and mixed with the unfamiliar folk from different lands; Egan and all the others did the same. The little girl with dark hair walked among them, too, examining their strange garb and clothes, all so different one from another, and listening to their funny accents and curious speech. At last, Ulla approached a tall young woman, as tall as Mielikki, with flowing hair so fair and golden that it seemed blessed by the sun's own fire. She reached out her hand to touch the young woman's beautiful face, and the woman smiled and gently touched Ulla in return.

The warm, late summer sun shone down on the green trees and blue waters. The south wind blew in measured, gentle gusts as the flickering aspen leaves shimmered and seemed to change color with each breath. The lands glowed with summer's blush of life, for everything was in a hurry: to live, to grow, to bloom and thrive before the seasons turned again. For such is summer in the far north of our world.

FINIS

What does an author stand to gain by asking for reader feedback? A lot. In fact, what we can gain is so important in the publishing world, that they've coined a catchy name for it. It's called "social proof." And in this age of social media sharing, without social proof, an author may as well be invisible.

So if you've enjoyed *The Mark of the Bear Clan*, please consider giving it some visibility by reviewing it on Amazon or Goodreads. A review doesn't have to be a long critical essay, just a few words expressing your thoughts, which could help potential readers decide whether they would enjoy it, too.